SISTERSONG

Lucy Holland works for Waterstones and has a BA in English and Creative Writing from Royal Holloway. She went on to complete an MA in Creative Writing under Andrew Motion in 2010. Lucy lives in Devon and co-hosts *Breaking the Glass Slipper*, an award-winning feminist podcast.

Sistersong
LUCY HOLLAND

PAN BOOKS

First published 2021 by Macmillan

First published in paperback 2021 by Macmillan

This edition first published 2022 by Pan Books
an imprint of Pan Macmillan
The Smithson, 6 Briset Street, London EC1M 5NR
EU representative: Macmillan Publishers Ireland Ltd, 1st Floor,
The Liffey Trust Centre, 117–126 Sheriff Street Upper,
Dublin 1, D01 YC43
Associated companies throughout the world
www.panmacmillan.com

ISBN 978-1-5290-3905-4

1 3 5 7 9 8 6 4 2

A CIP catalogue record for this book is available from the British Library.

Typeset in Minion Pro by Jouve (UK), Milton Keynes
Printed and bound by CPI Group (UK) Ltd, Croydon, CR0 4YY

MIX
Paper from
responsible sources
FSC® C116313

Visit **www.panmacmillan.com** to read more about all our books
and to buy them. You will also find features, author interviews and
news of any author events, and you can sign up for e-newsletters
so that you're always first to hear about our new releases.

For my sister

Oh sister, oh sister, lend me your hand,
I'll make you heir of my house and land.
I'll neither lend you my hand nor my glove,
Unless you grant me your true-love.

'The Twa Sisters', *The Child Ballads*

There is no agony like bearing an untold story inside you.

Zora Neale Hurston, *Dust Tracks on a Road*

1

KEYNE

Imbolc – a festival celebrating the end of winter

I will tell you a story.

Seven years ago, when I was a child of ten, I became lost in the woods. My sisters and I had been travelling the road that skims the coast like a stone from Dintagel. I loved our summer home – a spume-silvered rock of houses and workshops, its docks piled high with amphorae. But there is a place, many leagues to the east, where the road slows, turning inland. It loses itself amongst the trees, straying into giant country. Branches interlace here; it is easy to slip away into the green space between a giant's fingers. Easy for a careless child to disappear.

Looking back, I wonder whether it truly was carelessness. Perhaps it was *her* doing. Given everything which came after, that would make sense.

Between one scout's holler and the next, I am lost, a prisoner of the wood. I feel no fear, more an irritation that I've let the trees trick me. I can hear my father, the king, calling me and the irreverent footfalls of men rending foliage.

I wander so long, it feels as though I've crossed some hidden boundary. I've left our world for *theirs* – the nameless land where goddesses sing to the stars, where lost spirits linger in the twilight.

Dark quills scratch me; I am surrounded by yews, the terrible grave-trees which grow from death. I shiver, as irritation turns to fear. Deep voices seem to call my name, anthems to lost children. And now I *am* lost, hopelessly so.

The sky darkens and with the light goes hope. Hunger claws at my stomach; I am old enough to know I cannot survive long without food and water. Tears well. What if I die here and the yew grows stronger, roots curling through my bones?

Despair is a sharp scent and I suppose *she* smells it upon the air, for suddenly a woman stands before me. She is old, but not so old as Locinna, our nurse. Eyes peer beneath a heavy brow, blue, and piercing as a gull's. She wears rags, tattered and rent, but after a blink, these become a cloak of moths, their wings a-flit in the evening. Another blink and it's just an ordinary cloak, albeit a strange one made of patches and ribbons fluttering free.

She extends a hand and I realize I've collapsed to the leaf mulch, the seat of my skirt now damp through. My legs wobble as I stand. Her fingers are rough, calloused like a smith's. I wonder what strange trade might have marked them.

'Are you a witch?' The dangerous question is out in the open before I can stop it.

She smiles. 'Perhaps.' Looks me up and down. 'Would you like me to be?'

'No.'

'And why not?'

'Because witches are to be feared.'

She pauses. 'A good answer, if not entirely true.'

'I want to go home.'

The witch tilts her head, her gull's eyes narrowing on my face as if it were a fine fat fish. 'I wonder if you do.'

'Of course I do.' But I glimpse her meaning. I have never felt at ease in my home.

'You are wet through. Come and get warm.'

2

They are such inviting words. And I'm freezing, it's true. But she's a witch. 'My father must be worried.'

She steps back and something jingles – her stick-wrists gleam with silver bracelets. My eyes widen; only Mother has silver like this. Where hers is solid and silent, however, the witch's bracelets sing. I feel a desperate urge to touch them, to capture those chimes between my palms, as if I could draw the melody inside me.

She notices my gaze, smiles again. 'Would you like one?'

Throat dry with want, I shake my head.

'Here.' She slides off a single band, passing it over gnarled brown knuckles. Before I know it, my fingers have closed about its shining curve.

'I can't . . .'

'But you already have.'

My cheeks flush. Shaped like a horseshoe, the band is too big, hanging on my wrist like the crescent moon above us. But it shrinks to a perfect size even as I watch, and I catch my breath at the tingle of magic. When I look up, she's half turned her back. 'Wear it when you are ready to find me again.' And she is gone, returned to the forest that birthed her.

The forest I am no longer within, for I now stand upon a wide road, and voices – human voices – are shouting my name. One laughing, one crying, my sisters rush towards me.

I remember burying that silver bracelet, sweating and fearful. I hadn't planned to hide it, but inside Dunbriga, our capital, I began to question my gift. It felt nothing like the spells spoken over hearth and home. Not even akin to Father's ability to spark a flame or ask the skies for rain. It was otherworldly. It had come from the dangerous heart of the forest, warmed by a witch's skin.

And yet for all that, the bracelet was mine now. My parents would surely take it away if they found it. So in the shadows cast by Dunbriga's oldest yew, I gouged a hole in the raw earth and dropped the silver in, weeping to see my shining crescent amidst the dirt.

I've ventured into the forest many times since then and have never once glimpsed the witch. As the years pass and the magic fades, she seems more and more a figment of a fevered mind. 'Just a fancy,' I tell the wheat doll taking shape between my hands. She is nearly finished – a shoulder shy of complete.

'Keyne!'

I twitch. I should have seen Mother coming, sitting as I am at our hill fort's highest point. A waft of rosewater precedes her and then she's towering over me – her shadow blotting out what little sun struggles through the clouds. 'What are you doing?' she demands.

My blasphemous fingers are busy weaving a brideog. We make the goddess's dolls every year for the festival of Imbolc. Gildas, the Christian priest, doesn't like it, but I find the work soothing; it takes my mind off other things. And from my perch on the steps of the great hall, I can watch the hold tumbling out below me down the hill. Cattle on the lowest level are tiny as a child's toys.

'I told you to put this practice aside,' Mother says sternly, and I hear the priest in her words. Beneath the queen's skin runs the blood of old Rome, the jewel of the empire that abandoned us to our fate. Father took her for her blood; he thought it might give him strong sons to guard his lands and legacy. Instead he has two daughters . . . and me. Rome's last laugh, I suppose, before the legions left our shores for good.

'We are not prepared for Candlemas on the morrow,' she adds, and the word forces my head up. Bright fox fur frames my mother's shoulders, her curls tamed into an elegant braid. Her skin is a shade browner than my own, though we share the same dark hair. 'And do try to sit graciously. This –' she waves a hand at my trouser-clad legs – 'open sprawling is improper.'

My hands clench around the wheat woman. 'We've always made brideogs, Mother. I don't see the harm in it.'

'Brigid is no longer our concern. We need candles for the ceremony, enough for every woman who—'

'Why is it only the women who must be "purified" at Candlemas?' I snap, imagining what my sisters might say. Wild Sinne would scoff at the thought, eyes sparkling with some planned mischief. Riva would probably grit her teeth and bear it while murmuring prayers to the old gods under her breath. I almost smile, but it dies when I think about Rome's god and the way his priests seem to delight in punishing women. Gildas believes all Britons sinners, despite being a Briton himself. He condemns our festivals, our traditions, even our little wheat dolls. But every tale he spins, of revelation and ruin, pushes his Christ further away from me. Gildas's Saviour is a stranger who died long ago in a hot land I have never seen.

Mother's gaze briefly strays from my own: part of her agrees with me. But when she says, 'Make candles, Keyne,' it is Queen Enica who speaks.

'Let Riva do the candles. You know she cannot weave the—'

'Riva is making them already. And when I find Sinne, she will join you.'

She won't find Sinne. My younger sister has a talent for making herself scarce whenever there is work to be done. And to Sinne, everything looks like work.

Our home, Dunbriga, is a smudge of smoke on the edge of the world. I know it's not really – Armorica is just across the water, and ships come from further still, bringing us oil and olives, the taste of sun-drenched lands to the south. I like to imagine cargoes of silks and spices cocooned in ships' holds, waiting to be abused by our rough hands and palates. But when storms keep the ships away, the walls of Dunbriga close in and the fort seems to shrink.

We need travellers to remind us that there's a world beyond our borders.

I make my way to the workshop, feeling the holdsfolk's customary stares as I pass. The brideog is coming apart in my hands. I don't know why I care, except that she's an antidote to Christ and his earnest suffering. I am tired of being called sinful. Half my father's hold already thinks me so. I need no help from Gildas and his followers.

At the creak of the door, Riva looks up, her good hand coated in tallow. She's wearing a bandage around the other, hiding the scarred flesh she cried over every night for years after the fire. No one knows how it started, except Riva herself perhaps, and she claims she doesn't remember.

'So,' Riva says, as I take the stool beside her in the dim room. 'Mother found you.' She's as tidy as Sinne is tangled, her chestnut hair braided neatly, sober dress crease-free. Riva has a stillness in her that soothes me. She listens where my younger sister would speak.

I nod. 'Now she's after Sinne.'

'She won't catch her.' We share a fond smile before my sister's eyes stray to the tattered figure in my arms. '. . . Brigid.'

I let her fall. 'Mother forbade me. I'm to help you with the candles instead.'

Riva scoops the brideog from the rush-strewn floor. The doll is a sorry sight, broken wheat sticking out of her like pins. 'Finish her, Keyne,' my sister says. 'It's important the goddess feels welcome here. I'll see to the candles.'

I force myself to protest. 'There are dozens. And you don't like fire.'

'I am coping.' A tremor in her face. 'You can help when you're done.'

'Thank you.' The words hiss from my lips and I sound ungrateful. I can't seem to sound any other way these days. Riva, however, just nods and returns to her shaping and dipping.

I know she's watching as my fingers flash in and out of the brideog, perhaps mocking the dexterity she no longer has. But I don't move, because it's warm beside the stinking tallow and the fire that keeps it soft. And that stillness I love in my older sister is here in the room between us. I can feel my earlier anger slowly seeping away.

An hour passes in companionable silence. I stare at Brigid's blank face. She could be anyone. She doesn't even resemble a woman, just a figure with arms and legs, trunk and head: human. That's something we all share. That's what really matters.

Isn't it?

Raised voices pull me from my thoughts. Riva and I exchange a glance before we creep to the workshop door. We don't want to be seen. People clam up around us, the king's children, as if we're his spies. I grimace to myself. It might look that way, but Father doesn't listen to us as he used to do. These days only Mother, his lords – and Gildas – are welcome to speak.

'Hush, Siaun. If someone hears and tells the priest—'

'Then we'll know who's a traitor.'

I put my eye to a crack. Three men lurk outside, one checking the yard is empty. I guess they'd never dream of finding the royal children with their hands in a tallow vat.

'Do you *want* to be caught? The king will lock you up . . . or worse.'

Siaun snorts. He's a slight but rangy man in a farmer's overall and his cheeks are lean with hunger. Last summer's harvest was the poorest in years and the winter has been hard. 'Lock me up for speaking truth?' he demands.

The other man shakes his head. 'For speaking against the priest.'

'Whose side are you on?'

'It's not about sides, Siaun,' the third man hisses from where he's keeping watch. 'Plenty of folk are beginning to listen to the priest. The king listens, so they do too.'

'The king is *wrong*,' Siaun says, and I hear Riva draw a startled breath beside me. Her eyes are wide in the dim space.

Siaun's friend clamps a hand over his mouth. 'Holy Brigid, Siaun. Say that any louder and you'd be lucky to escape with a whipping.'

I swallow tightly. Siaun's expression doesn't change, but his fists are clenched and trembling.

'Will you die for this, Siaun?'

The farmer turns so I can't see his face. 'Our women don't need purifying for the festival of Imbolc, so why is this Candlemas different? Would you let the priest shame them?'

'Of course not, but what can we do when 'tis the queen's will for us to follow new ways? Besides, Gildas is not all bad. I hear he's building proper houses for Brys and his family. Times have hit them hard. And not just them.'

Riva mutters something under her breath and I think, *Candlemas is only the beginning.*

Once Siaun's friends have bundled him away, I meet my sister's eyes. 'Is it true what they said? That there are already people who follow the priest?'

Bandaged hand held close to her chest, Riva says, 'Gildas doesn't care a wit for them, so why build them houses? It must be part of his plan to convert us all.' Her face firms. 'We should talk to Father. Not to tell tales,' she adds hastily when I open my mouth to protest. 'About Gildas. Father allows Mother to honour the priest's festivals, but perhaps he doesn't know how far it's gone. That people are prepared to give up the old ways altogether, that Gildas is essentially bribing them to do so . . .'

'What if Father does know?' The stink of candles clogs my nose. *And what if he doesn't care?*

8

2

RIVA

My numb fingers feel as if they've shaped a thousand candles before Mother allows me to return to the women's quarters. When I open the door, a swell of heat and small talk escapes into the afternoon. I exchange a few nods, impatient. Keyne, Sinne and I share quarters with the other unmarried women from noble families and a few of the higher maidservants. It's a big hall but feels cramped on winter days when the herb and flower gardens are too cold for women to gather there. Heart already skipping with nerves, I duck behind my wooden screen, pull it across for privacy. It's painted with willow trees and the healing herbs I favour most.

My hand shakes as I unwrap the bandage, which hides the old scars of the fire that changed my life. Beneath the reek of tallow, I can smell the honey and myrtle packed into the poultice. The words of the song come back to me, the healing song I whispered to Brigid for fear of being overheard by Gildas. 'It will work this time,' I murmur under my breath, willing it so. Imbolc is Brigid's festival, when the goddess is at her most powerful. Goddess of fertility, of spring, of rebirth.

Then why is my hand shaking? *It will work*, I tell myself again. *My healing always works.* The last coil of cloth slips free.

Feverishly, I scrape away the paste to see familiar red, the fused lump that used to be a hand, individual fingers. A sob wells, chokes me, and I fling the dirty bandage at the screen. I've done everything right, more than right. Although they'd never tell Father to his face, the people of Dunbriga can attest to my skills; over the last year, I've probably treated every family at least once. It is an open secret that I can break a fever, set a bone so that it heals in days, not weeks. That I can sew a gash and whisper a word to guard it from infection. That I can stop women in childbirth from bleeding out and ease the suffering of the old so that they pass in peace.

But why can't I heal myself? Why, though I've tried a dozen times or more, can't I heal the marks of the fire? Disappointment drags my skipping heart to a crawl. I'd thought the festival would make a difference. Perhaps I shouldn't have whispered the song, but thrown it to the heavens. Perhaps seven years is too long and my wound is now too old for magic. I have to blink to keep the tears from spilling.

'What *is* that smell?'

Hastily, I wipe the rest of the paste onto a fold of my skirt and look up in time to see Sinne, barrelling into the women's quarters. She weaves past the screens that divide the welcoming room, its walls hung with detailed loom-work. The central fire pit smokes with a fragrance of sweet cedar. I watch as it curls up into the rafters, where wind from the tiny windows catches and carries it away.

Before she can spot the bandage in the corner, I clamp a blunt knife between my knees and scrape at the tallow that's set on my good hand after my work with the candles. Sinne wrinkles her nose.

'You could have helped,' I say.

'I'm glad I didn't. You stink of dead animal.'

I ignore that. Sinne scampers about the room, watched idly by Mother's ladies. My heart lifts a bit to see her pulling cloth out of chests in her wild way, tutting impatiently. After a few moments, she appears before me, holding up a white dress. I roll my eyes when I see that it's little more than a nightgown. 'Do you think this will do for tonight?' she asks. Before I can tell her she probably won't be allowed to take part, she bursts into one of the traditional songs.

'Bright mother, dark father
Goddess of hearth
Sing, winter-born king
Hanged One, untamed.'

She has a skylark's voice, sweet and high and sad, one I can't hope to match. But still I find myself singing with her, sisters together:

'Stag and fox
Forest beast
Sailor of the last sea
Brother and lover
Seed sower, grain giver
Come, Horned One
Drink of the land its blood.'

'I've always thought that a silly last line,' Sinne concludes and I realize my eyes are closed. 'The land doesn't have any blood.'

'How do *you* know?' I ask with a smile, opening them. The tune has calmed me, its cadence warm in my throat. All the old songs have power.

'Because it's ridiculous.' Sinne's cheeks are flushed. She barely looks her fifteen years as she fiddles with a lock of her fair hair.

'What about the battles fought here?' I say, reaching over to tug the lock free before she starts chewing on it. 'The great warrior

Aurelianus slew thrice a thousand men. What happened to *their* blood?'

'It dried up in the sun.'

'Some of it. But if you stick a man, he bleeds half a dozen pail-fuls. Think how much blood you could get from three thousand men. Where do you think it all went?'

'What do you know about "sticking men"? Nothing.' She gives me an impish grin and scoops up the lock again, twisting it around her finger.

I poke her in the ribs. 'I know more than you, *little* sister,' I say and swiftly turn the poke into a tickle.

'*Riva*.' Sinne's squeal has covered the sound of the door opening. 'If you must talk, recite the Lord's Prayer.' Mother stares down at me. 'I will be ashamed if you misspeak it at Imbo— Candlemas.'

'Our gods have served us well enough so far.' *Except for with-holding their powers of healing from you, Riva.* I shake off the snide, silent voice and look up at her as defiantly as I dare. 'I don't see why we should forsake them for another. Especially Gildas's Roman one. The Romans *left*.'

'He is everyone's God, Gildas says.' Mother's lips thin. 'And the priest is our honoured guest.'

'I thought guests left too,' Sinne mutters. 'The old coot's been here for months.'

That earns her a slap. Sinne claps a hand to her reddening cheek, her eyes filling. They are big blue eyes, like our father's, and I've been jealous of them since childhood. Sinne's tears usually buy her instant forgiveness.

But not today. 'Get you on, both of you.' Mother stabs a finger at a pile of cloth. 'There's stitching to be done before night.'

As soon as she leaves, in a rustle of linen, Sinne throws herself down to lie on the skins that warm the floorboards. 'I wish we still lived at Isca.'

'You don't remember Isca,' I say, retrieving my needle and thread. I've become quite adept at stitching one-handed. 'You were a baby when Father abandoned it. Besides, Isca's the Roman name. It's Caer Uisc.'

'*You* don't remember it either. You were five.'

'Five years is old enough for memories. Thread this for me, please.'

Sinne huffs, but does as I ask. In truth, I remember little of the civitas except stone and an impression of size. When the Romans left, they took their secrets with them. We're a proud people and Father didn't like the idea of living in Rome's shadow – except for the slim dark one cast by my mother. He didn't like the idea of picking through the ruins of all their clever broken contraptions. So fifteen years ago, he moved the heart of Dumnonia to this chill cliff instead.

Thinking of the scene we'd overheard with Siaun, I wonder whether Father would have made that same decision now.

The door opens a second time. I finish a stitch and glance up as Keyne comes around my screen. She's in her usual attire: a boy's tunic and trousers, her lower legs wrapped snugly with leather. Sinne rolls her eyes. 'I hope you don't intend to wear *that* at Candlemas.' She gives Keyne her impish smile. 'Gildas won't like it.'

Keyne's hands clench. The priest doesn't care for any of us royal children, but he reserves a special vitriol for my sister. I think she angers him, striding around in male garb, her face as distant as the stars. And I think she unnerves him too, much as she unnerves the rest of us when she looks a certain way. Her eyes, dark and flecked blackbird-beak's yellow, seem to see more than she lets on. Occasionally I glimpse someone else peering out of them, curious, bitter and knowing. Even with those eyes, Keyne had once smiled freely. Now, at seventeen, grimness clings to her like winter mist that rarely cedes to sunshine.

'I don't think Gildas likes anything,' I say, trying to thaw the ice in Keyne's face. 'Except Jesus.'

'And he's dead,' puts in Sinne helpfully.

Keyne shrugs, as if she doesn't care. I know she does.

It's hard to deny the effect Gildas has on our household. He is like one of the dark beeswax candles reserved for my parents: tall, slim and burning with zeal. No one knows how old he is, but he sweeps about Dunbriga as if *he* were king, his quiet steps easy to miss until he's upon you.

'Why does Father put up with him?' I ask in a voice pitched just for the two of them. 'It can't only be because Mother invited him here.'

Keyne grimaces. 'Gildas has powerful friends, or so he claims. Perhaps Father is worried we may need to call on them against the Saxons.'

'What friends?' Sinne says loudly and winces. 'Other kings?' she adds in a lower voice, dashing a glance over her shoulder at the women by the fire.

'God?' Keyne softens the word with a raised brow. 'But probably other kings. Lots are embracing Christianity.'

'And Gildas is an educated man,' I remind them. 'Fluent in Latin, Greek and history. Perhaps Father thinks the priest's learning will rub off on him. Like charcoal.'

'Even so,' Keyne says darkly, 'I don't see what harm our traditions do. Which reminds me –' she nods at my blankets – 'give me the clothes for Imbolc. I'll go and hang them outside. *We* remember the old ways.'

I reach under the bolster for the tunics hidden there. All over the hold, other women will be doing the same, furtively so the priest doesn't see. I smile at my sisters and they smile back. Gildas hates anything to do with magic and our traditions, but he can't stop us all. 'We'll make sure Brigid feels welcome here,' I whisper, stroking my thumb over the cloth.

14

Sinne's smile fades and she collapses back on her heels. 'I know it's tradition, but I'm not sure why you bother with this part.' I don't miss the disparaging glance she gives the tunics. 'We do it every year and every year is the same. No special blessings.' She mutters the next bit under her breath. 'No wishes coming true.'

'You don't think our continued prosperity a blessing?' I ask, a bit nettled. 'While the rest of Britain falls to the Saxons, our culture lost, our men slain—'

'*Our men?*' Sinne scoffs. 'You don't have a man, Riva.'

My skin prickles, a hot flush of embarrassment. 'This isn't about me. The point is—'

'We should be grateful for what we have,' Keyne finishes, but she doesn't sound as if she means it. And, after hearing Siaun's rebellious words, I find I'm not in the mood for doomsaying either.

'I'll take these myself.' I grab the bundle of tunics, and rise unsteadily. Pain spikes in my damaged foot, as soon as I put weight on it. My hand isn't the only part of me the fire touched. I grit my teeth.

'Don't forget to leave your own clothes out for Brigid,' Sinne calls after me. 'She might make you less of a sourpuss.'

She doesn't mean it, but even a small jibe stings. Keyne motions as if to comfort me. I push past her, Brigid's tunics clutched tight to my breast.

Sinne's teasing words stay with me as I search for a place to hang the clothes. I can't put them by the entrance – Gildas or Mother will see and I'll be ordered to take them down again. I clench my good hand around the cloth, angry at them for disdaining the old ways, irritated at Sinne's needling when we three only have each other as friends, as confidantes.

Maybe I can hang the tunics from the eaves behind the women's quarters, hidden in the shadows. The wooden building that houses us isn't tall, but neither am I and, no matter how I stretch, I can't reach. *Curses.* I look about for a crate or barrel to stand upon. Nothing. Annoyed, I jump and my foot gives way with a spiteful flare, sending me sprawling, burned hand twisted beneath me.

I cradle it, grazed from the rough landing, and hot tears threaten; Brigid's tunics have landed in a puddle. I gaze at my boot, as if I can see through the leather to the foot it encases. I stare and I wish that I'd never argued with my sister the day of the fire, that I'd never gone to the old smokehouse. I can almost hear my own screams again, echoing between the walls as the fire ate at my skin. A child sobs in the background: Sinne? Her face is one of the only things I remember before darkness took me.

'Riva, *stop.*'

The voice filters down from a distance and I realize I've been crying, trying to tear the tunics, my throat raw with the awful memory. Someone catches my arm and holds it still. When I squirm to get free, the grip tightens, and I suddenly know to whom it belongs. 'Let go, Arlyn.'

When the smith's apprentice ignores my command, affront knocks the memory away. *I am the king's daughter.* 'Let me go, I said.'

Arlyn looks at me with serious eyes. 'Are you sure you won't start up again?'

'I'm sure,' I grate. 'Now let go.'

As if I am a bucking horse in need of calming, Arlyn slowly releases his hold. I snatch my arm back, and bury my grazed hand in the folds of my dress.

'What were you doing?' he asks, helping me to my feet.

I know Arlyn won't run to tell Gildas. 'Trying to hang up Brigid's tunics.'

He clicks his tongue. 'You know what I mean. Why were you sitting here, crying?'

I don't answer. It's none of his business, after all.

'Riva.' His wide, placid eyes are on my face and I cannot meet them. 'Why?'

'I hate feeling so helpless,' I hear myself whisper, looking at my hand. 'None of the healing I try on myself works.'

Arlyn doesn't reply. Instead he takes the clothes, brushes the mud off, and – stretching – just manages to hook them over a protruding spar of wood. We watch them billow for a few moments, the wind filling out the bellies of the tunics.

'We ought to clean that,' he nods at my hand. 'Wash the dirt off.'

The wind or his words have hollowed me out. I suddenly feel weary. 'All right,' I say and let him steer me through the hold.

At the forge, I have to stop myself shying from the open flames like the nervous mare he thinks me. I choose a stool furthest from the furnace and the banked fire in the corner. Although it's taken years of effort, I can usually hold myself together around fire. But the memories crowd close today.

Swords hang suspended from hooks; weapon-racks of spears and daggers line the walls. A few pieces of leather armour are scattered here and there, and the iron framework of an unfinished helm waits on a workbench. Pots and cauldrons take up the other side of the room, eating knives and the like: the tools required by a busy household.

'Farrar keeps you working hard.' My voice shakes a little.

'Aye, he does.' Arlyn pokes the fire awake and hooks a pail over the flames. Though I long for warmth, I cannot bear to pull my stool closer. While the water heats, I watch as he sweeps the packed earth floor, retrieves stray tools and replaces them in their holders. Farrar is famous for punishing sloppiness. Arlyn's arms, I notice, are tanned, corded with muscle from working the forge.

My eyes return to the swords. 'More weapons than usual,' I note, studying their hilts.

'King Cador's request.' He shoots me a sidelong look. 'There are rumours that Saxon scouts have been seen as far west as Durnovaria.'

I remember what I said to Sinne. The hold needs Brigid's protection more than ever. *She's like as not been keeping the Saxons from us, not Gildas . . . or his Christ.* I draw a breath – does Arlyn share Siaun's concern? 'What do you make of the priest?' I ask him. 'You can speak freely,' I add when he hesitates.

'I don't much care for him, if truth be told.'

'Why?'

The smith turns, big arms folded. 'I think I live a good life. Might not be saintly, but whose is? I charge fair prices for our work, help others who need it.' He half smiles at me. 'But Gildas caught me folding a blessing to Brigid into the metal and called me heathen and wicked and everything in between. I've never given cause for complaint before. Everyone knows that, without Brigid's blessing, swords are just lumps of iron.'

Maybe it's only the extra wood he's tossed on the fire, but Arlyn's words warm me. Still, I'm beginning to worry that the hold doesn't care whether our gods are forgotten. 'Mother forbade Keyne to make her brideog earlier. And Gildas is why I was hanging tunics in the eaves instead of by the door.'

Arlyn's scowl deepens. 'Then he's not going to like what the women have planned for this evening.'

'So they're going ahead,' I say, my pleasure dampened only by the fact I can't take part. Although Keyne hasn't attended for years, Sinne and I always process at Imbolc. We wear white like the other maidens, our hair loose, carrying a huge brideog from house to house and speaking the ancient words. Perhaps some wishes are small: a girl child for a house of boys, a healthy marriage, strong calves in spring, but – despite what Sinne thinks – they've always been granted. The thought of missing out raises the hairs on my arms and, all of a sudden, foreboding wraps me like a damp cloak. I shiver.

'Here,' Arlyn says, clearly mistaking it for a chill. He lifts the pail from the fire, dips a rag into the water and kneels before me. When he reaches for my hand, I pull away.

'I'll do it.' Before he can argue, I swipe the rag and glare at him until he moves off. I only start dabbing at my grazed skin once his back is turned. But I can feel his eyes on me from time to time. Probably trying to hide his disgust.

'Riva . . .' He lets it hang.

I rinse the rag in the water, say nothing.

'Promise me I won't find you like that again.'

A knot tightens in my chest as the face of Gildas swims before me, his mouth twisted in contempt at my bag of herbs. I remember the last woman who came to me for healing, stealthily in case he saw. I remember the smell of my own failed poultice. Angry again, I drop the rag and lurch to my feet. 'I am the King of Dumnonia's firstborn. I won't *promise* you anything.'

Grinding my teeth, I leave him with his tainted concern. In his grey eyes, I'd seen no anger at my retort – only pity. And pity was the last thing I wanted. From him, or anyone.

3

SINNE

Boring. I love Riva – she's looked out for me more than Mother has – but I hate it when she moans about Gildas and his religion. Who cares which gods we worship? They're all the same: follow their rules or there's a beating. I only obey to make people happy. But I'm *smothered* by rules: Father's rules, Mother's rules, the rules of my older sisters. I don't need a priest's rules too.

I lick my lips, imagining milk – the best thing about Imbolc. It's been so long since I tasted it. Otherwise it's a quiet festival, nothing like Ēostre or Beltane when we have singing and dancing, colourful dresses, breads and crumbling cheeses.

I hear distant chanting and scramble to one of the tiny windows in our quarters, hooking the covering aside. It's twilight; I can barely see, but the dusk is bright with torches. As part of the royal residence, the women's hall rises above the rest of the hold and from this height I spot the maidens, their hair unbound, going from house to house. They're hoisting a much bigger brideog than Keyne's, straw and bits of fraying reed on their clothes. I'm too far away to hear properly, but I know what they're saying as they knock thrice at each door. I mouth the words to myself.

'Brigid, Brigid, come to my home tonight.
Open the door, let Brigid come in.
Her bed is ready, her supper prepared.'

Brigid receives a gift from each family, until she sparkles with
tiny trinkets that flash in the torchlight. I look at my white nightdress, remembering Mother's harsh refusal when we asked to join
in. I've always loved the processing part, the wind's brisk fingers
in my hair. A tugging in my belly tells me her decision is wrong.
I'm unmarried, all of us are. We should be *down there*. Even
Keyne, though I can't imagine her wearing white and swirling her
skirts through the streets.

The chanting makes me restless and I want to dance. Want to
wear my best dress and fling myself into the music that follows
later. Or should follow . . . The planting tune is one of my favour-
ites, and this time I want to dance with someone other than
Bradan – though I know he worships me. But no one ever visits
our hold except traders, and they're gone again in days.

Brigid is supposed to grant wishes. 'I want the *magic* to come
back,' I whisper to her. 'Real magic like Father used to do.'

I want something to *happen*.

Perhaps Brigid finally hears my wish.

I wake suddenly at dawn, skin prickling. It's Imbolc morning
and Gildas is ringing his cursed bell again. I turn over, desperate
to slip back into the warmth of a world where everything is tinged
with golden light. In my dream a man, more beautiful than any
I've seen, lifts my chin with careful fingers. My heart races. I can
still feel his hand on my waist. In a way, I feel we've met before,
or we will meet . . . somehow.

But the noise of the hold is starting to intrude – normal
sounds, stupid sounds, sounds I've heard all my life. Who am I
fooling? Father will pick out a husband for me. I'm a piece on his

game board, the best he has. Riva might be beautiful, with her high cheekbones and heavy chestnut hair, but people whisper about her scars. And Keyne . . . well, she's far too strange. Yes, I will become a wife and be just as dissatisfied as Mother.

What if I were *his* wife? I imagine it, seeing him again with his glittering gaze and slender hands. Being his wife would be different . . . We'd leave this place and visit the hot countries where sweet fruits grow, living each day as it came. And the nights we'd have—

'Lady Sinne! Are you up?'

I growl into my pillow.

'You lazy child,' Locinna exclaims when she pulls the screen aside, sees me abed. 'It's well past cock's crow.'

Smiling, I stretch languidly in answer. Locinna tuts and starts laying out clothes suitable for a festival day: a creamy underdress, an overdress of blue that will go well with my hair. Not that there's anyone I want to impress. Well, maybe Bradan, the fisher boy, upon whom I like to practise my glamour.

'I'll wear my knotted belt,' I say, remembering how his eyes are always drawn to it. Locinna frowns briefly, but she can't very well ignore a request from the king's daughter. I smile again, a secret smile just for me. Maybe today won't be all bad.

There's an odd atmosphere outside, though. Nearly all the women are dressed in sober colours, even the unmarried ones. I think of last night; the gleam of bright white garments, the chanting, the unbound hair. Now most heads are covered with modest scarves. My own exposed and plaited locks are attracting a fair number of raised eyebrows.

'. . . cannot believe it. The gall of the man.'

'What did he do?'

I edge closer. Ganieda, one of my mother's seamstresses, is talking quietly to another whose name I've forgotten. Mother *does* have a lot of seamstresses.

'. . . stood before the royal door and denied them entry.'

'What? But he has no rights over the *king*'s household.'

'That's what my girl says too. He was all in black, showed them the cross. Told them they shamed "Saint Brigid" by carrying around a "heathen effigy".'

'*Saint* Brigid?'

'Aye, that's what he called her. Says she weren't never a goddess, but some holy woman from Éire who gave all her things to the poor.'

The other woman sucks in a breath. 'Bad will come of this.'

'You haven't heard the worst. Cador's lady queen comes out and stands beside the priest. Tells us to burn our brideog and go home. Wouldn't let her daughters take part either.'

My mouth falls open. Mother said to *burn* Brigid?

'It will bring nothing but bad,' the other woman murmurs and then she spots me. 'Lady Sinne.'

I ignore her, pushing through the crowd to Riva. I squeeze her arm in greeting. 'Did you hear what happened last night at Father's door?'

Riva nods. She's dressed sombrely in a colour I think of as forest black. She makes the drab shade elegant, though; it brings out the green in her hazel eyes. A glove, I notice, hides her burned hand. For a moment I feel garish in my blue, a child's colour. But the feeling passes when I spot Bradan, staring open-mouthed at me from across the way. I smile, straighten, turn back to Riva. 'They tried to give Brigid's blessing to Father, but Mother and Gildas stopped them.'

She frowns. 'Nothing good will come of mocking the old ways.'

'You sound like those old women.' I study the crowd. 'Where's Keyne?'

'Not here,' Riva says tightly. 'Locinna claims she saw her early this morning, but then she disappeared.'

I wince at the thought of Keyne being punished. If she misses the Candlemas service, she'll be in for a whipping. Mother's always talking about our duty to set an example.

Riva is silent, clearly worried too. 'You're quiet this morning,' I tell her and it's true – my oldest sister is usually much livelier. I'd have thought to find her loudly reminding people that Candlemas is Gildas's religion, not ours.

'I didn't sleep well.'

'Bad night?' I ask, thinking of my own, which had been far from bad.

Riva's expression darkens because Gildas has appeared and Mother is stuck to his side. 'Something like that.'

We can't talk further. Mother gestures for us to fall in behind her as she and the priest lead the way towards the wooden church, the crowd parting like the sea before Moses. That's one Bible story I like. Forget all the business with healing the blind and washing the feet of the poor. Imagine having the power to command the ocean. It makes my fingers itch to possess it.

The church feels oppressive. It wasn't always a church, just a big storehouse Gildas blessed and called a church. Passing into its shadow, I realize all our old festivals take place out of doors. When we look up from our dancing or feasting, it's to see the sun or stars above us. Now when I look up, all I see is the suffering, benevolent face of Christ hanging over us like a thunderhead.

Before we sit, we take a beeswax candle from a small basket set aside for us alone, and hold its wick to a brazier. All the candles are supposed to be beeswax, but wax is expensive and hard to come by. Gildas wasn't happy when Mother told him the majority of the congregation had to have tallow candles. I wrinkle my nose at the bigger basket where they lie like knobbly fingers – poor Riva stank of them when she came in yesterday.

We sit on long benches, clutching our sputtering candles. There are a few faces absent, besides Keyne's – stubborn holds-women who believe the priest is nothing more than a storm to be weathered until a calmer season comes. I wonder if Mother's noticed. Then, with a chopping motion, Gildas orders the doors shut.

I jump when they boom together, killing the daylight. I'm struck by a feeling that I've lost something, like a ribbon torn free in a gust. Even Mother looks pale. Maybe she's regretting giving Gildas free rein.

"*Et postquam impleti sunt dies purgationis eius secundum legem Mosi tulerunt illum in Hierusalem ut sisterent eum Domino . . .*"

My Latin is terrible, but I gather it's something about purification according to Christ's law – whatever that means. Gildas is clearly enjoying himself, rattling off his incomprehensible streams. Judging from the blank faces around me, I'm not the only one who doesn't understand it all. Or at all. Keyne's the best at languages. I let the words wash over me, envying Keyne her absence.

My thoughts return to the dream. Dream . . . the word doesn't fit. Dreams are messy things, like churned-up surf. This one's still as clear as the best kind of sky and I find myself wondering about the man's name. Something handsome, something daring. And of course he would have a horse, a majestic beast as black as midnight. Such a fine mount needs a name too. Like Hanternos or Kastell, the magnificent steeds of legendary warriors.

Maybe I'm a seer. I've heard tell of them: rare people granted visions of the future. I've always had vivid dreams. Perhaps I can do more than spin silly glamours to enchant fisher boys. My heart begins to thump. He could be real. He could be out there, waiting for me.

Suddenly, I hear shouting beneath the Latin drone and Gildas trails off mid-phrase. The shouts are louder now he's silent. Then light floods over us as the church doors are flung wide. A dozen men block the entrance, common folk. I recognize most of them:

Bradan's father; Deroch, son of our chief huntsman; several of the older farmers – all men my Father has listened to in the past. It's hard to make out expressions against the glare, but their leader's eyes are narrowed in anger.

'It's Siaun,' Riva whispers beside me and I frown. Isn't he the one she and Keyne overheard yesterday?

'What is the meaning of this intrusion?' Gildas's voice echoes oddly, as though there are more priests lurking amongst the crucifixes.

Siaun points. 'We want our women back.'

Silence. Riva and I share a tense glance. 'They will rejoin you in due course,' Gildas says. 'Once they have been cleansed.'

'Cleansed?' one of the other men asks. It's Arlyn, the smith's apprentice, and I can't help being impressed at his daring. 'Cleansed of *what*?'

'Their sins,' the priest says coldly.

'What have they done?' Arlyn demands, his eyes flicking in our direction. I swear he's looking at Riva.

'My lady,' Gildas entreats Mother. 'I insist this intrusion ceases. These men disgrace themselves and dishonour a house of God.'

Mother rises gracefully, every inch a queen – but she's still as pale as earlier. 'Do as he commands. You will leave this place or the king will hear of it.'

Yet something gives him courage, for Siaun steps beneath the church's heavy lintel. *Don't be foolish*, I think at him, but he opens his mouth regardless. 'With respect, my lady queen, this is wrong. It dishonours *our* gods, our people. The old magic is weaker every day since the priest came.'

In the shocked hush, I hear Mother's sharply indrawn breath. When she speaks again, her tone is hard, as wintry as Gildas's. 'Aedan, Rinus.' The queen's bondsmen; I hadn't noticed them in the shadows. Neither had Gildas, I guess. He frowns slightly as they come forward. 'Take this man and place him under guard. The king will decide what to do with him.'

'Siaun!' A woman near the back of the church is all elbows and knees, trying to reach him. But the other women hold her back. And though their hands are firm, their expressions are flinty as they stare at the bondsmen dragging Siaun away.

'Our women have done nothing wrong,' Siaun cries hoarsely, struggling with his guards. 'No one here sins but *him*.' He tears a hand free and jabs a finger at Gildas.

'The king's justice awaits the rest of you – unless you leave at once,' Mother snaps at the remaining men, raising her voice over Siaun's protests. 'This is a holy place.'

The other men seem to reach an agreement. Their faces are as hard as the women's, but they leave. The doors crash shut, plunging us into gloom once more. And with it comes a terrible silence. Again I feel that sense of loss, as the world is shut out. Riva's good hand is curled into a fist on her lap and I take it in mine, squeezing solace. My sister's lips are white with fury as she looks at our mother.

The queen's nod to Gildas is stiff and short. Another might think her angry, but I know her better. It isn't anger Mother is feeling. It's guilt.

'Let me be clear,' Gildas says. He's pacing slowly, up and down, in front of the wooden crucifix. 'You have been led to worship *lies*. False deities that glorify man's baser urges.' His voice softens. 'This is not your fault. Last night's *activities* –' in his mouth, it's a dirty word – 'shamed those maidens that took part, at a time when they should be preparing themselves for the sanctity of marriage. But Our Lord will still look kindly on those who come to Him, to renounce their barbaric practices.' He glances briefly at Mother. 'He will take them to His bosom and, for them, there will be no more suffering.'

I realize my heart is thumping a warning against my ribs. His threat is as clear as the sentry bell. What will he do to those who don't obey? I look at the blur of women's faces. Some are angry, more are uncertain. The seamstress's words echo in my head. *Bad will come of this.*

I have no doubt she is right. But how bad will it become?

4

KEYNE

On Imbolc morning, I wake, sweating, before dawn. In the early darkness I can't see the room. I could be anywhere, could still be dreaming. But I know I'm not because I can smell wool, baking bread and a hint of the dried flowers Riva sewed inside my pillow. I breathe out, clinging to wakefulness; I don't want to slip under again. Only a nightmare, I tell myself, but it lingers behind each eye-blink: a world of black skies and sunless seas. And a rumble in the east.

My outflung hand finds Brigid and I clutch the wheat doll to me like a talisman. Maybe she really does protect us; maybe she woke me before I felt the worst of it, before the dark nothing consumed us all. It's like a scene from Gildas's Bible: the punishment that awaits a sinner. I know what Gildas would say too. He'd tell me the dream is a warning, that if I don't change my ways, *I* will feed that waiting maw.

Slowly, I calm. The high window begins to let in light. The smells of the fort are joined by sounds: the shouts of servants, the errant whinny of a horse, the ruckus that heralds a new day. Imbolc. Or Candlemas, as Gildas insists we call it now.

When Locinna appears, I am already up and warming my hands over the central fire pit. 'Ah, Lady Keyne.' She sounds pleased. 'You always rise earliest.' She moves behind my screen, opening chests, rustling cloth. 'I've laid out your clothes,' she says, her voice faltering at my silence. 'I must go to your sisters. Excuse me.' I nod, but she is gone, disappearing into the ember-lit gloom of our shared quarters.

On my blanket is a dress, brown with pale stiches. It swims in my vision. All at once the dream returns and my nose fills with the stench of carrion. My legs wobble, but I force them still. It's just a dream. It's just a dress.

I can't do it.

My stomach heaves at the thought of going to church, candle in one hand, bunched skirts in the other. It's a betrayal of everything I am. I reach for the pail, but nothing comes up; we're not allowed to break our fasts this morning. My skin is clammy and I want desperately to shed it, like snakes do. I want to run free. I want out of this dim room with its dresses and prospects and Gildas's censure. I want to be *me*.

My heart is racing again, gooseflesh creeping along my arms. I could say I'm ill, but Locinna has already seen me up. And anyway, illness won't stop Mother dragging me to church today. When people look at me, they see the king's *daughter* – no matter what I say or do – and I well know that Gildas wants to cleanse me alongside my sisters.

But I can't do it. I *won't* do it.

It's early. Mother might still be dressing. Riva rises later than I and Sinne will have to be poked out of bed with a spear. My mouth twitches briefly, despite my sombre thoughts. If I'm quick and quiet . . .

I seize the linen I use to bind my chest flat, wrapping it round and pulling it tight. I cough out a breath and hope I won't have to run. Shirt next, fumbling the laces, then green tunic over it, followed by trousers and shoon. I don't bother with the leather wraps that secure them to my feet; time is short. Still struggling to take a full breath, I peep around the edge of my wooden screen. There's no one visible beyond, though I can hear the sounds of dressing. A guttering torch throws my shadow across the floor. With my hair tied back, it's a man's shadow, anonymous.

Once outside, I spot only royal servants and townsfolk as I weave through the upper terraces, slipping between buildings, flipping up the hood of my cloak as I go. No one recognizes me. The cold finds its way between the layers of my clothes and I wish I'd brought mittens. There's a scent on the wind, sharp and green as the wilderness outside the walls.

The church squats on the second terrace, lower than our great hall. And not as large or imposing as Gildas would like, I wager. I don't want to look at it, or imagine my sisters inside it. Somehow it ruins the pattern, as if Dunbriga is a tapestry and the church a rogue tear.

When I reach the lowest terrace, I see guards lining the wall – ever watchful for Saxon scouts. But I don't intend to go that way. There's a hidden place, a landslip on the eastern side. Here dirt has fallen from the high earthen banks that guard the hold, leaving a gorse-filled hole just large enough for a person to crawl through. Muddy and cold, it's the only unguarded way out of Dunbriga.

The gorse pricks me as I push it aside and I wonder whether Father ought to know about this breach in his defences. It's a question I've asked myself ever since I discovered the landslip – is my freedom worth risking our safety? Were an enemy to find this place, my selfishness would endanger more lives than just my own. Still I say nothing. This taste of freedom is the sole reason I survive – living in a world that does not see me for who I am.

The morning is thick with mist, a poor herald of spring. It's fit for my purpose, though. Keeping low to the ground, I scurry fieldmouse-fleet through the long grass and into the shadows of a copse known as Cêd Hen. It encloses one of the nemetons, those old sacred spaces where our people can talk to the gods. My feet weave between brittle branches, trying to remember the way. But the path to the glade is lost now – lost, or closed to me.

I used to go there with my family at least six times a year, to dance and sing, worshipping the gods as our ancestors had done. We made offerings to Andraste of the Moon, to Epona and to Cernunnos, the horned god: blood, gold and our hunters' best pelts. I remember my father in his true crown; it could only be seen during rituals, or when he called up magic in defence of our home. It was woven from light, the symbol of the bond between leader and land. My sisters and I laid offerings on the altar, then linked hands so our family formed a circle around it. And even though I stood between Riva and Sinne, I could feel my father through them, as if some invisible cord joined us all together. It was as if the king's blood flowed into the land we stood upon, and his power infused us in turn. That was, until Mother put a stop to it.

'No, Cador,' she said one midwinter day, before we set out for the nemeton. 'I have shamed my ancestors enough with these barbarous rituals. The priests that pass through here say they are wicked and base.'

'Christian priests, who know nothing of our gods or our way of life. These ceremonies are our heritage,' Father replied, frowning. 'The Dumnonii people have always drawn power from the earth and we guard it in turn. What are we without the very land beneath our feet?'

'Stronger,' Mother snapped back. 'While you waste time in dance, we could be receiving emissaries, striking trade deals, drawing up plans to deal with the Saxons, should they decide to push west. We are already vulnerable here. What allies we have will abandon us if we continue to worship heathen gods. The world is changing and it is leaving us behind.'

I think that was the day the doubt began to eat at Father, and the old ways suffered for it. We still went to the glade, but the gold we brought with us was tarnished, the pelts rougher. Bandits killed on the fringes of our land were food for the crows, their skulls abandoned – instead of being added to the eerie ghost fence that kept our boundaries strong. We would linger at the altar for minutes rather than hours. And then the visits ceased altogether. I haven't seen the king in his true crown for years. Now he wears an ordinary metal band, just like the Christian kings of other tribes.

Maybe the poor harvests are simple bad luck. Or maybe the gods have grown tired of us.

I come to a stop in front of Dunbriga's oldest yew, and I shudder. The great tree stands alone in one of Cēd Hen's clearings; a silent sentinel. It seems larger every time I see it, with its split trunk and mass of dark branches. My breathing is harsh in the quiet, the last note of the dawn chorus long since faded. I stare at the tree, catching my breath. Then I reach out and place a hand on its trunk.

Silver around my wrist. In the dirt. The earth is cold beneath my knees. I blink. What am I doing here, kneeling amongst the tree's roots? I feel the urge to dig, but my hands are no match for the frozen ground. Before I know it, I've seized a stick and begun gouging the dirt. My gift was only a fancy, wasn't it? The fevered imagining of a lonely child, lost and terrified – that's all. But still I stab at the earth. Clouds stifle the sun. They must be looking for me, my mother cursing my name. I will be punished, probably whipped, but I cannot go back. Not yet.

Time passes. The ceremony will have begun. I imagine my sisters in church, one dark head, one light, my mother severe beside them, and Gildas looming over all three. Something about the image makes me work faster and the earth finally begins to loosen.

I drop the stick and plunge my hands into the hole I've made. Dark soil collects beneath my nails. I hit a rock and cut myself, a little blood mixing with the dirt. Muttering a prayer to Cernunnos, I keep going. *This is madness*, a part of me says. *You won't find anything.* I ignore it. I can't help wondering what really lies beneath the world. A land of stone and silence guarded by towers of unhewn jewels? Or Gildas's Hell, where the flesh of sinners blackens in the flames?

This hole is surely deeper than the one I made with my child's fingers. But finally I see something. I scrape away the dirt, my heart throwing itself against my ribs. Tarnished by seasons, the silver bracelet is still the same. I lift it with trembling fingers, hardly daring to believe it's real. But my child's fancy now glimmers in the daylight . . . and I can almost feel the rough pads of *her* palms on my cheeks, as she holds my face and says she'll see me again. Ruefully, I see it's sized for a thin-wristed child, but I slip it over my fingers anyway.

The bracelet passes my thumb, my knuckles, expanding to circle my wrist as it once did in a long-ago forest. I stop breathing. It fits perfectly. What's more, it's *hot.* When I look up, I gasp. The trees seem wreathed in a web of silver, threads that intersect, branching off into root and leaf. My left wrist tingles where the silver touches it and I have a sudden urge to press my hand into the earth, to follow the weaving with my mind as it reaches out across the land. The temptation to lose myself is overwhelming. I feel it in my bones, my pounding heart.

A hoarse cry rips through the trees, and the silver threads vanish. I spin to stand, dizzy, gooseflesh spreading across my skin. The space between my shoulder blades prickles and I search the copse for movement, feeling watched.

A gull takes flight in a ruffle of wings.

5

RIVA

His name is Myrdhin and he is a magic man.

Drewydh, they call him, when he calms storm-stricken horses with a word; when he commands the wind to blow coastal raiders off course; when his stories come to life and fill our hall with selkies or elves, or the long-perished heroes of Éire.

He's only ever spoken to me twice: once at three when he told me not to fear, and once at thirteen when he told me not to die. Mother had struggled at Keyne's birth. My sister arrived feet first, as if eager to stand on the skin of the world, but then she'd come no further and the midwives' faces were grave. Myrdhin happened to be passing – at least that's what he claimed. But he saved both their lives that night.

Afterwards, Father took him into his counsel. Now whenever Myrdhin visits, he eats the choicest food, sleeps in the best quarters. He has his pick of new-forged tools and weapons, though he carries only a knife. Another man might take advantage of such hospitality. But Myrdhin trespasses just a sennight at a time, sometimes healing, sometimes advising, or dispensing stories like honey cakes around the hearth. And after seven days, he is gone again, and our world is the dimmer for it.

Of course Father sent out riders for him when I had my

accident. My burns were terrible, had thrust me into a sleep of shadow and hurt. Sometimes I remember snatches of those fever-days, when I walked the border of life and death. I'd glimpsed fading silver threads and Sinne's little white face. I'd dreamed of Roman cellars, filled with broken stone. None of the images made sense. And none of my family's words reached me – the fever took them all. But Myrdhin's words were stronger than the fever. *His* voice found me in the hinterlands. He told me to live and I lived.

We haven't seen as much of him in recent years. We're obviously not the only people he visits. His skin is weathered and brown as walnut wood, as if he travels to lands where the sun scorches instead of warms.

It isn't the first time I've thought of him, as I wash after church, seeing my scars unclothed. I've tried tonics and unguents, cantrips and prayers; nothing works. But Myrdhin brought me back from the brink of death; surely *he* has the power to restore my hand and foot. I will never marry otherwise.

Do I even want to?

If Gildas has his way, I will become a nun, retiring to a Christian convent to drown my days safely in scripture. That will keep me far from *his* hold, far from being able to practise my small powers on his newfound flock. In older times, I could have been a priestess, a true healer. But I'm coming to realize that Father fears Gildas and his foreign religion, spreading like a plague across this country. He fears the return of Rome and maybe this keeps him in check. Years have passed since he last went to the nemeton, bearing offerings for Woden, Lugh and our other gods – resplendent in his crown of sunlight.

I throw down the cleaning rag with more force than is necessary, calling for Locinna to come empty the bath. Drying myself on rough linen, I pull on my underdress before she glimpses my scars. They say Roman Isca had communal baths, where everyone washed together. I shudder. Keyne would hate it, too. She never lets anyone see even a scrap of her – not us, not Locinna. That won't go down well when she marries and I feel a pang of sorrow for my sister. Somehow I can't see Keyne as a wife, not even in my head. I can't see her tucked away in a convent either. And Sinne behaves as if she expects to be whisked away by a foreign princeling. I smile to myself. We might be rogue daughters, but I'm proud of my sisters all the same.

Our post-winter rations can hardly be called a feast, but Mother postpones it until Keyne is found, and I am ravenous by sunset. The worry twisting my gut makes it worse. Father has sent men to the woods, armed with bows against the possibility that she's been snatched by bandits, though no one has seen her leave the hold. Mother paces the women's quarters, clenching and unclenching her hands, as if she can't decide whether to throttle or embrace Keyne if she returns.

When she returns. I miss her, but I know my sister. She often seeks her own company, and I suspect she hates the idea of Candlemas even more than I do. Like as not, she's hidden in a haystack, quietly sneezed the day away and is now too scared to emerge.

'Where do you think she is?' Sinne asks from the open door of the women's quarters. It's started to rain, big fat drops that soak a person in seconds.

'You could scry for her,' I say out of Mother's earshot, nodding to a pail of fresh water.

'In a *bucket*?' Sinne shakes her head. 'That sounds silly.'

I try on one of her impish grins. 'A bucket wouldn't matter to a great seer such as yourself.'

'Now I wish I'd never told you.'

'Too late,' I say, enjoying being the sister doing the teasing as opposed to the one being teased.

Sinne does a good job of looking affronted before her lips start twitching. 'Oh pass it here,' she says finally and holds out her hand for the bucket.

Before I can fetch it, raised voices reach us. Two guards are escorting a struggling man up the steps to our hall. I frown – no, not a man, but Keyne. My sister strains against their grip, twisting like a wild thing in a snare. I hear Sinne snatch a surprised breath.

Mother pushes past us. Before I can think to stop her, she draws back her arm and slaps Keyne hard across the face.

A sound escapes me, half gasp, half cry. There is blood on Keyne's mouth; both she and Mother seem shocked by it. Mother's furious expression wavers, but then a shadow falls over her, made longer by the sinking sun.

Gildas's steps are slow, unhurried, his dark eyes fixed on Keyne. My sister pales. There is something terrible in the priest's gaunt face, like the chill of deep winter. They lock gazes.

'Lady Keyne.' His words are soft, but they carry. 'You were not at church.'

Keyne says nothing.

'Where were you?'

Her eyes flash to her left wrist and back again so fast I almost miss it. I follow her gaze and think I spot a bright gleam. Gildas waits, but she still doesn't answer.

'Do you perhaps consider yourself above the law of God?'

'Gildas,' Mother says, a hesitant reprimand. The priest ignores her, his eyes never leaving my sister. My gut twists further. I don't like his look. Beside me, Sinne is trembling with some pent-up emotion. I find her hand and hold it tight.

Keyne licks the blood from her lip. 'He is not *my* god,' she says.

For a moment, I think Gildas will strike her too, but his anger is a cold thing. Slow to come, slow to leave. Instead he smiles and I like it even less. Suddenly I fear for Keyne, held immobile before the priest.

Gildas circles her, his hands clasped piously. 'This clothing

does not become a woman, particularly a woman of royal blood.'
He addresses his next words to my mother, 'Why do you let it
continue?'

My mouth is dry. So, it seems, is Mother's. 'I . . .' she starts.

'Do you not think Lady Keyne should wear garments befitting
her station?' He purses his lips. 'She appears as a peasant.'

It isn't true. Keyne might wear a man's garb, but it's finely
made – by her own hands, no less. My father wears similar, as do
half the wealthier men in the hold.

Mother finds her voice. 'Surely it hurts no one.'

'On the contrary,' Gildas says. 'It hurts Lady Keyne herself. It
hurts her reputation. It hurts the reputation of this hold and of its
lord.'

The words are carefully chosen, a whisker shy of offensive.
Mother's eyes stray to the men holding Keyne, trying their best to
look as if they can't hear. Then a mask comes down over her face.
'Locinna,' she calls and our old nurse steps out of the shadows.
'Take Keyne to our quarters. Strip these clothes and burn them.'

'No,' Keyne gasps. 'Mother, *please* . . .'

'Ask others to help you, if need be.' My mother has to raise her
voice over Keyne's outraged shouts as the men drag her towards
the women's quarters. Sinne and I jump hastily aside and I wish I
could help my sister, somehow. My silence feels like a betrayal.
'And find her something sensible to wear,' Mother adds to Locinna.

'No!' Tears stain Keyne's cheeks now. The men holding her
turn their faces away. 'Mother, you can't.'

'Do not presume to tell me what I can and cannot do,
daughter.'

Keyne's shouts change in pitch as she is hauled into the depths
of our quarters and the women take charge of her. Before I shut
the door behind me, to at least hide the horrible scene from the
curious, I see Mother sink onto the step outside. Her head is in
her hands.

'You acted piously,' Gildas tells her. 'Do not regret your decision.'

'Leave me,' Mother says. Though iron coarsens her voice, I hear tears too. With a respectful nod, Gildas turns and walks into the darkness. I think of the morning: remembering Siaun's plea, his wife's cries as he was hauled away. I think of the anger in the church and of Mother's guilt-pale face as she ordered the men to leave.

Hatred for the priest blossoms in my chest.

Keyne wouldn't want me to watch, so I stay behind my screen, eyes wet, as five women strip the clothes from her back. She never stops fighting them. But when it is done and they finally leave her, I wait for the lamps to go out and then I creep across to her pallet. Sinne is already there. We do not speak. We only lie silently on either side of her stiff, curled body, together through the long night.

6

SINNE

I've never heard it so quiet, as if someone has died. Mother's
women sit with their sewing, hardly saying a word, while the
younger handmaidens exchange gossip behind cupped hands. I'd
like to hear what's being said, but they clam up whenever they
spot me. Hardly fair – I'm not Keyne, after all. Perhaps they think
I'd report back to her.

I would, of course, although I can't help thinking Keyne
brought this upon herself. My innards squirm a bit, but it's true.
What's so terrible about wearing a dress? I suppose Gildas used
her clothes as an excuse to punish her for not attending Candlemas. *Interfering old crow.*

Face stinging from the morning's chill, I push into our quarters,
blinking at the gloom. The windows are high up at either end,
small and fogged with smoke. They let in barely any light; just
enough to see Keyne curled against the back wall. Her grey dress
is stained and I tut to myself. A dress is hardly a punishment.

'Leave me alone,' she says

'Why?'

Keyne turns her head a fraction. Her face is a twist of misery,
cheeks pale, eyes red-rimmed. I can't hold her gaze. 'You should
really stop it,' I say to her knees.

'Stop what?'

'Sulking. Mother didn't even whip you.'

'Go away, Sinne.'

'It's no fun when you're like this.' I skip closer. 'At least tell me where you went when you should have been at church.' I pause, grinning. 'Gildas is really annoyed, you know.'

I'd hoped to coax a smile out of her, but she doesn't respond. So instead I crouch down and whisper, 'If you've found a good hiding place, you ought to share it.'

'Why won't you leave me be?' she growls.

I shrug. 'Because I'm your sister and I want to know what you were doing all day.'

The pallor starts to fade from Keyne's cheeks, replaced with a flush. 'I don't see why I should tell you.' Her hand goes to her left wrist, as if it has a will of its own. My eyes follow. There's something beneath her cuff.

'What's that?'

'What?' Keyne snatches her hand away.

'On your wrist.'

She glares. 'Nothing.'

'If it's nothing, why don't you show me?'

'Don't touch me, Sinne.'

I honestly can't see what all the fuss is about. 'Just a quick look,' I say, and grab for her arm.

Keyne jumps up with a snarl and *something* pushes me back. I didn't see her hand move, though, so perhaps I imagined it. '*Keyne!*' I protest.

'I said, leave me alone.' She throws herself after me, but the hem of her dress catches and sends her crashing to her knees.

I wince. 'Sorry.' Guilt at needling her makes me bend down and offer a hand. Keyne ignores it. 'But you don't have to get so upset.'

'What's going on?'

I whirl to see Riva making her way towards us. 'Nothing,' I say innocently, knowing that Riva's eyes are already flicking between the two of us. Keyne is a picture of anger and shame, stumbling ungracefully to her feet.

Riva immediately takes her arm to help her. 'What have you been saying?' she shoots at me.

'I only asked her what she'd been doing instead of Candlemas.'

Riva levels a severe look at me and I huff to myself. If there's a side to be taken, it's always Keyne's over mine. 'She doesn't have to tell you, Sinne.' But she is plainly interested too. We both look at Keyne.

Now that she's standing and I can see her properly, even I have to admit she looks . . . wrong like this. She folds her arms across her chest, hunches her back as if it pains her. The dress falls to her shoonless feet and its shape doesn't sit right on her either. Abruptly I really am sorry I provoked her. 'I just wanted to see what you were hiding,' I tell her. 'I'm not going to run to Mother or anything.'

Riva frowns. 'Hiding?'

'I was in Cēd Hen,' Keyne says suddenly.

My eyes widen, Riva's too. 'How did you get out of the fort?' Riva asks, and there's a new sharpness in her tone.

Keyne is still holding herself; her hands noticeably tighten. 'There's a secret way,' she whispers.

'Secret?' I feel a spark of excitement. 'Secret as in old magic secret?'

Keyne shakes her head. 'Not magic. Just a passage.'

'That's not *just* anything.' Riva's voice is sharper still. 'Does Father know about this passage?'

Keyne lifts her chin. 'Of course not.'

'Then you have to tell him.'

'Riva, *no*.' I've rarely heard Keyne so vehement. She's been like a ghost these past few seasons, drifting from room to room with scarcely a word. 'He'll block it up, you know he will.' She swallows. 'It's my escape.'

'He should block it up,' Riva says, but her expression wavers. 'You realize how dangerous it is? If the Saxons found—'

'They won't.' Keyne drops her arms, eyes imploring. 'It's *really* well hidden. You'd have to know it was there to find it.'

Riva doesn't answer. She's the eldest and I can see duty warring with love for Keyne in the tense set of her shoulders.

'Please,' Keyne whispers. 'I need it.'

Maybe Riva is moved by this new passionate Keyne because the breath leaves her in a rush. 'All right. Keep your secret. But if the Saxons start to push at our borders, you *have* to tell Father about it. Or I will.'

'I promise.'

'Wait.' I hold up my hands. 'Don't *we* get to know where this secret passage is?'

'You'll tell Father,' Keyne says immediately with a blink of her wasp eyes.

'I won't.'

'Leave it, Sinne,' Riva says.

'Fine. Be like that.' I know it's childish even as I turn, with a sweep of skirt, and head back out into the morning.

The sky is forbidding; clouds having gathered while I argued with my sisters. I tut at them, as if those boiling giants can hear my displeasure. Now *that* would be something. The mention of magic, however brief, has filled my head with wild thoughts. Imagine if my moods could influence nature, in the way of gods or magicians? One tut from me could bring lightning arcing across the heavens. A raised eyebrow could dispel thunder. I walk aimlessly – stretching out my arms, palms up – pretending I'm someone to whom the world listens. Wind catches my braid and I laugh at the imagined delight of it.

'What's funny?' a voice shouts.

I glance down. My feet have taken me to the short cliff above the wharves, where rough red steps tumble to the sea and the fishing boats bump against the swell. Bradan is looking up at me. Feeling mischievous, I spring lightly down towards him. He watches me come, winding a coil of salt-stained rope about one arm. I wrinkle my nose, despite being well used to the smell of fish. 'I have a fancy,' I say when I reach him, eyeing his calloused hands, his shoulders broad from hauling in the daily catch.

'A fancy, aye?' he says with a grin. He always grins when he sees me. I make sure of it. 'And what would that be?'

I stretch out my arms to the sea like Gildas's Moses, as if commanding the waves to rise and part. 'To be a god.'

Bradan frowns. 'You ought not to say such things, Sinne.' But I can tell he's pleased to be talking to me at all. 'What if that priest heard you?'

'Gildas doesn't frighten me.'

'He does me,' Bradan says, finishing his coil and stuffing the neatly bundled rope in a crate. 'The way he glides around like a wight. Always behind you, he is, ready with those Latin words.'

It's an accurate image. 'Ready with *words*,' I reply airily. 'Words can't hurt.'

'Can't they?' Bradan mutters, dropping his gaze. He picks up another rope and begins to coil it, shifting under my gaze, while I consider him.

'Put that down,' I say finally.

He glances at me, raising pale brows.

'Come here.'

It's funny to watch the emotions do battle on his face. I told Riva I wouldn't do it any more, this little trick of mine. *It's not nice to meddle with people's feelings, Sinne.* I huff silently. Sometimes she can be as preachy as Gildas. A small glamour never hurt anyone.

I crook a finger and Bradan drops the half-coiled rope. Keeping my will on him is not difficult – I'm only fanning the desire he already feels. It's not as if I could turn hate to love or anything. It's not as if it's *powerful, real* magic – like Father could do.

When he's a step away, I reach out and pull him close. No one is around; most boats are out to sea. He swallows, the lump in his throat bobbing nervously. Enjoying myself, I place his hand on my waist, right over the knotted belt which cinches the dress. A small sound escapes him. I tilt my face up to better watch the war between disbelief and desire in his eyes. His hand tightens on my waist. He leans down.

When his lips are inches from mine, I rest one finger against them. 'Maybe later,' I say and let my will fall away.

For a moment he freezes, then he blinks and backs off, a ruddy mix of hurt and confusion flushing his cheeks. I laugh and dart back up the steps, leaving him there with his ropes and his fool-ishness. Probably wondering what came over him. I snort. It's his own fault really – the glamour wouldn't work if he didn't think he had a chance with the king's daughter.

My smile fades as I walk through the hold, watching dull people go about dull tasks. Is this my life now – casting charms on boys? What's the point of me having magic if that's the only thing it can do? I'm sick of being ignored, powerless to change anything. I'm tired of sitting here, waiting for Father to marry me off. My eyes are drawn to the great hall. He'll be inside, listening to petty petitions, his crown leaving a wide red band across his forehead. He looks older these days. Weary.

To cheer myself up, I go back to work on the dream, filling in the gaps with my own colourful imaginings. He is a foreign prince, of a certainty. Important, wise even – but not above play-ing the odd trick or too. That's why we'll get along. He'll listen to me, unlike my parents. Even my sisters . . .

'Have you tried an invocation to Lugh or Brigid?' a woman's voice says.

Startled, I open my mouth – and close it, blinking at my surroundings. I'm relatively alone on the lowest terrace; whoever spoke isn't addressing me. So, curious, I step over a puddle and head towards the voice. This is where most of the common folk live and I spot the ragged figures of two women huddled in a doorway. The hut behind them seems dreadfully small. Dense smoke crawls from the hole in its roof.

'Of course I've tried,' the other woman says, as I flatten myself against a wet wooden wall, just out of sight. 'It's always worked before.'

'Always?'

'Well, its effects have been growing weaker for a while, but the invocation has never completely failed.'

Something is raising the hairs on my arms – maybe the note of panic in the woman's voice, buried beneath her frustration.

'My sleep charm failed too,' her companion says quietly. 'An old chant to Andraste used to make the babes sleep soundly. Now none of the children . . .' She trails off, sounding ashamed.

'Since *he* came.' The words are now so soft I'm forced to inch closer, ears straining.

'Hush your mouth. If someone hears you—'

'This is *our* home and these are our ways, Nia. And what will fail next? Master Myrdhin hasn't been seen in six seasons either.'

'Ach, but he's a law unto himself.'

'Until the priest gets a hold of him.'

I slip away, mind turning over the women's words. Does Father know that even the most basic charms are fading, withering away? In Dumnonia, you don't need to have royal blood to perform the simple magics. Or at least you never used to need it. I shiver, understanding the reason for the women's discretion. *Worse since he came.* Their words border on treason these days, but it's not as if I'm going to report them. I hate Gildas as much as my sisters do

because we aren't supposed to speak of magic now, let alone practise it, and a world with no magic is no world at all.

Riva talks loudly about her poultices and potions when she
heals, though I know that's only a part of what she does. If Gildas
found out about my glamour . . . It's just petty magic, but he'd call
it blasphemous all the same.

My steps slow. Up ahead, people are gathered around something on the ground. A hubbub of concerned voices reaches me.

'I said I'm fine.' Folk draw back as a man stands unsteadily,
holding onto another's shoulder. It's Siaun – the one who stormed
our Candlemas ceremony. The back of his tunic is stained, blood
seeping through the cloth.

At my side, my hands curl into cold fists. My stomach churns,
and not just with horror for Siaun. *The king will hear of this*, my
mother said. If Father ordered Siaun flogged for interrupting a
ceremony, what might he do to me – if he knew I was playing with
forbidden magic?

7

KEYNE

I wanted to die. Feeling their hands on me, pulling at my clothes, stripping away the layers of who I am. Who I'm trying to show them I am. My throat is still raw from screaming. But my fear and rage have gone now, leaving me sore, scarred and sick from the memory.

Walls and too many people press upon me, suffocating. I cannot stay here. I can weather their disdain – haven't I done so for years? But their lack of understanding is so much worse. It means they will never *see* me as I see myself. To them, I am merely the shell of a king's daughter. A shell is lighter than a person, lesser, and if I do not escape, that's what they will make me.

I cannot stay here. But if not here, where? I sit in the shadows of the women's quarters and I turn the bracelet on my wrist. It grows warmer with each turn until it's hotter than my skin. I have no other home to go to and how could I leave my sisters without a word? But I have to get out, if only for a time. I turn the bracelet again. If I wear it into the wood, will I find the witch there? And if I do, will she still offer to help me?

As I wait for dusk, I wonder what tales Father's guards might have shared about me. I can't recall the faces of the men who held me as I struggled, who dragged me to Mother's women to suffer at their hands in turn. Even the thought causes a shudder, or maybe it's the chill wind that finds its way through every crack in the wall.

Those women took my tunic and trousers away, those I'd painstakingly sewed for myself. All except for one set, a fine set, which I'd hidden just in case this happened. I will keep them hidden. For now. But I hate the spidery brush of the dress against my legs; each draughty step swaying the skirts. It's a constant reminder of who – or what – they want me to be, of the prison they're desperate to lock me in. At least I have my shoon, the ones with the good soles. Else the forest outside the fort will cut my feet to bloody strips.

I don't want Riva asking questions, so I make my move after she leaves for supper. She whiled away the noon trying to talk to me, and though I know she means well, I didn't listen. I am not for listening now. I am for doing. The silver on my wrist glints in the veiled moonlight as I creep my way to the eastern end of the hold, and for a moment I think I see *her* face in its curve. Is this the old magic or just another fancy?

Wear it when you are ready to find me again.

I wasn't ready to find her back then. I buried the bracelet like a Christian body, like a curse. I don't remember why. Fear, perhaps: of the unknown, of the ancient magic and what I could do if I sought it. But it isn't fear I feel now, it's a strange sort of excitement.

I steal through the gloom, knowing which buildings cast the longest shadows, keeping to their smoke-stained walls. I hold my breath as a group of men march past, coarse voices raised, heading to my father's hall. My heart hammers as I imagine being caught. I am already banned from leaving the women's quarters unaccompanied. What worse might follow?

It isn't long until I spy it: the earthwork and its spiny passage to the outside world. The gorse feels sharper without my thick tunic and trousers. I expect it to leave red weals on my flesh, but I don't slow – I can't risk it – so I bite my lip as my hands bleed and a bramble snags my cheek.

I emerge covered in scratches, but I'm beyond the walls. The now-familiar copse lies before me and I plunge into it, willing the grey moon to shine upon the path. I will follow it past the old yew to field and forest. There I will lose myself, as I did once before, and hope the witch finds me again.

I head past the old yew and deep into Cēd Hen, trusting the wood to guide me. The further I venture, the brighter gleams the bracelet and I start to see things I've never seen before, though I've walked the copse many times. An owl calls; a vole squeaks; a tree creaks in the cold. Ordinary sounds, but with the silver bracelet on my wrist, they take on shapes too. The cry is a streak of crimson, a promise of ending. The vole's tiny voice pops in the dark like bubbles on wash water. And the trees – their voices surround me, a chorus. I can hear the sap beneath their skins, the slow draw of water through roots. Again I think of the earth and how much of it lies beneath me. How the Christians suffocate their dead in it instead of giving them to the fire. The forest crowds in upon me, but I don't mind. It does not judge as people judge. I am just another thing, one of many, part of the breathing night.

'You *see* it now,' she says.

I spin around, heart hammering. The witch is as I remember. She's a small woman, dressed in a robe that would surely lose a battle with the cold. There are holes in it, the suggestion of bare skin. My mouth dries.

'I knew you'd put on the bracelet.' Her eyes, blue even in the gloom, flick to my wrist. 'Though I expected you sooner.'

I feel affronted. 'How could you have known to expect me at all?' Of their own accord, my fingers go to the silver. 'I decided you were just a story. And I buried the bracelet.'

She smiles, none too warmly. 'If I am just a story, why did you unearth it? Why did you put it on?'

I don't answer aloud. Because it is too painful – what they did to me at Imbolc. All I know is that it changed something: a line crossed; a trust shattered.

Maybe she can read my thoughts because her face softens. 'Come,' she says.

I remember last time and the invitation I turned down. Now I hesitate only a second before taking the hand she offers me. Her palm is rough and cool, and it soothes the ruffled sea in my chest.

A cottage appears through the trees, heady smoke drifting from two openings at either end, like an infant version of our quarters in the hold. Yet, however ordinary it seems, it wasn't there a moment ago and I say as much.

'Of course it was,' she declares, pulling me towards it. For a second my mind reels with stories of witches shutting children in cook-pots, but I am not a child and – though the thought pains me – I'd find more welcome in a witch's home than in my own right now.

I step into the cottage. *No turning back.* I'm familiar with thresholds and their power to entrap. Once crossed, they can never be uncrossed. But the inside is like any other country dwelling. Pans and dried herbs hang from the ceiling, just within reach. Crockery on dressers. Fresh reeds on the floor. A fire crackles and I can't help flinching at the sight of the cauldron set over it.

She follows my gaze. Laughs. 'Ah. All the better to boil you in.'

Her laughter is contagious. It gets into my throat, itching, until I'm forced to laugh too. I can't remember the last time I laughed. I feel lighter when it leaves me and the witch's eyes sparkle. 'What is your name?' I ask.

'You can call me Mori,' she says, turning to one of the cupboards.

On the back of the door hangs the beribboned cloak I once

mistook for moths' wings. I take a bit of it between thumb and forefinger: just cloth, though the ribbons sewn onto it are finer than I've ever seen, shimmering shades of bark and leaf. 'What is this fabric?'

She glances over. 'Silk. That's a rhymer's cape.'

'What?'

'It's the mark of a master storyteller.'

I tear my eyes from the silk to look at her. 'You're a storyteller?'

'That's what I said.'

I consider this. 'I've never met a woman storyteller. Do you know Myrdhin? He tells wonderful stories.'

Her mouth quirks. 'Does he now.'

It's not a question so I don't reply. Instead I ask, 'Where does the silk come from?'

She waves a hand over the cauldron; small leaves tumble from her fingers. 'Far away.'

I frown. 'As far as Rome?'

'Oh, child.' She chuckles. 'Rome might indeed be far, but it is far from farthest. No, it comes from silkworms in Sinae.'

'What?' I look incredulously at the strip I'm holding, this one dyed like dark honey. '*Worms* made this?'

She stirs the pot, once, twice, her wrist moving to an unheard rhythm.

'*Worms?*'

'Why not?'

She's certainly jesting. Inspired by the silk, my roaming eyes start to spy more things that don't belong in a humble cottage. The mantel holds a bustle of painted vases, as fine as Mother's best. Semi-mythical warriors frozen mid-fight; a Medusa-haired figure holding a man's severed head; a tangle of sea nymphs. The detail is breathtaking. I'm about to turn away when a gleam of gold catches my eye: a graceful cup near the end of the shelf. It seems to show some sort of religious ceremony. I frown, peering closer. At first glance, the participants resemble women, although none has a female body shape. My breath catches. On the other side of the cup is a Greek vase crowded with Amazons – the bellicose daughters of Ares. But beside them stands a figure just like those on the golden cup and this time it's titled ΕΝΑΡΗΣ. My Greek is not as good as my Latin, but I think it says –

'I see you've found the Enarees,' Mori remarks with eerie timing. 'I had a feeling they might interest you in particular.'

My head snaps around. 'Why would you think that?' I try to keep the alarm out of my face, but beneath my skin, my blood is racing.

Mori doesn't answer. When she turns, she's holding two steaming bowls and my traitorous belly rumbles at the smell. She smiles as she places them on the table alongside dark bread and a wheel of yellow cheese. Despite the sudden panic that she knows exactly who I am, I can't help thinking it looks wonderful; I haven't eaten all day. Then I remember the leaves falling from her hand and I eye the stew suspiciously. Was I meant to see that?

With a sigh, she retrieves a little pouch, opens it and pushes it across the table at me. 'Herbs. For flavouring.' She cocks her head. 'Do you still think me a witch?'

'Maybe,' I say, sliding into a chair and pulling the bowl towards me. One sniff is all it takes before I'm raising a wooden spoonful to my lips. The stew is a panacea, dispelling all thoughts of poison or enchantment – even a good deal of the fear that she sees what I hide in my heart – and before I know it, I'm using bread to scrape out the last drops. Mori watches me with an amused glint in her blue eyes. They stare from an unusually dark and weathered face. 'Where do you come from?' I ask.

Her mouth creases. 'I was born on these shores, same as you.'

'But you don't look like—'

'The people you know? Ah Keyne, one cannot gauge all from

a single point of experience.' She raises an eyebrow. 'Surely *you* understand that.'

I'm on alert again, the delicious stew churning in my belly. It takes me a minute to realize she's called me by name and my breath hitches. I didn't share it with her. *Witch.*

'Come with me,' she says abruptly, pushing back her chair. It scrapes across the wooden floor and I shiver, unsure. 'We're not going far,' Mori adds with a half smile, 'and I mean you no harm.' She leads the way outside and, after a few fretful seconds, I follow.

It's fully dark now, the moon torn by clouds. Mori swipes upward and comes away with a piece of it in her hand. I blink, but it's not illusion. Pale light glows between her fingers, shining on an overgrown path I hadn't noticed. I can't stop staring. What would Father say if he knew a witch lived so close to Dunbriga, openly clutching magic in her hand? And it's the magic of old, the type that cannot be harnessed by a simple cantrip.

'Your face tells a tale,' she says, her own silvered by moonbeams.

Eyes drawn like moths to the captured sliver, I whisper, 'I haven't seen real magic in years.'

Without another word, Mori sets her feet on the overgrown and forgotten path. Tangles of briar twitch respectfully aside for her. I steel myself and follow, wincing as twigs snap beneath my boots. Mori moves as quiet as a wildcat. After a few minutes, I realize where we are. There's a symmetry to the trees here, the bowed oaks twisted and ancient. Mori brushes one as we pass it, sighs and shakes her head. 'I am sorry, children,' she says.

'This is the path to the nemeton.' I am remembering my family's processions there, the little pilgrimages, weighed down with precious things. The songs we sang as we walked, the sun lighting the veins of the leaves. Now I am silent and empty-handed, placing my feet in a witch's prints.

I almost don't recognize the sacred glade when we reach it. In my memory, it's a clearing with clean moss to cushion toes and the trees regal as lords beneath a perfect circle of sky. They hid our rituals from all but the gods. Now weeds and creepers strangle the oaks and the moss is rough with debris: old gnawed bones and bramble. The skulls of our enemies, carved with symbols of power, are gone, scattered by wind and neglect.

Mori sinks to her knees, pats the moss beside her. 'Sit, Keyne.'

I do, tentatively. She is a cool rounded shape in the darkness, the moon growing fainter in her hand. After a while she says, 'I have been away too long.'

'What do you mean?'

'When was the king last in the nemeton?'

I think for a bit. 'Years ago . . . five, maybe. Why?'

'Do you know where power comes from, Keyne?'

I feel a flicker of frustration. She answers questions with questions. 'The gods,' I say after a moment.

She makes a sound in her throat. 'The gods.' Her eyes glitter. 'There are no gods, child.'

I go very still. 'But Brigid, Andraste, the Horned One—'

'Are just names.' Mori places her palm on the moss. 'Names folk have given the land and its many faces.'

I stare at her, robbed of words. We have *never* questioned the gods. 'Then why do we do it?' I ask eventually. 'Why do we make offerings, send up prayers and cantrips? Who answers them if not the gods?'

'The land answers,' Mori says and I hear a distant animal cry. 'Or it used to.'

'Used to?'

'You spoke of offerings and prayers. Tell me – who does the king pray to now?'

The silence is thicker in the aftermath of the cry, suffocating. I lick dry lips. 'The Christian god. I don't know his name.'

Mori sits back on her heels, and uncurls the hand holding moonlight. Now it's no more than a wisp. 'A chasm will open in the king's heart if he doesn't listen to the land. The king and the land are one. That is why the magic is weakening.' She pauses. 'Give me your hand.'

I've a mind not to, but the bracelet pulls on my wrist, as if it knows its mistress is close. When Mori touches my skin, the silver bracelet flares, almost painfully. Without warning, she presses my hand to the earth of the glade.

Nothing happens. Mori is gazing down intently. Maybe she too is holding her breath, poised on the edge of something like hope, something like fear.

'What—' I begin, before a surge of heat makes me gasp. Silver threads spread from my fingers, burrowing root-like through the earth. They cross the clearing, climb the ancient oaks, gilding each ridge and whorl. And then I cannot see them at all.

Because I *am* the threads. I fall to earth like rain, seep into stone. Beneath its surface is a web branching off into darkness. But where I go, I carry the light. I am the water and the rock. I am the blind things that live on the underside of the world. I delve further. I am the ore, the years, the blood and the bones. And as below, I am above. We are connected. I burst from the yawn of a cave a league away, find myself in reeds. There is a willow and a fox, an owl, a mouse. I open one of my throats and become the nightjar and its song.

It is too much. I can feel myself unravelling and a part of me wants this, to live in every body and in none. Far away I sense the people of Dunbriga. Breathing, talking, loving. They are like candle flames on the verge of flickering out.

'Enough.'

My stomach roils. It takes me a moment to realize I *have* a stomach, just one, a single brain, a pounding heart. So little of me after so many. I open my human mouth, but the words are a long while coming. 'What was *that*?'

'The land,' Mori says, sounding satisfied. We stare at one another. She is holding my hand tightly, away from the ground.

'It's fine,' I say, guessing her intent, trying to force my pulse to slow. 'I won't touch it again.'

'What did you feel?'

'I . . .' *Everything.* 'It's all connected.'

'It is a pattern, Keyne: the earth, air, the sea and the people. I am sorry. I didn't think it would take you so far.'

Her face seems older than the oaks in the gloom; primal, like the pattern she showed me. I feel a twinge of deepest fear and pull my hand away. 'I don't understand,' I say. 'Who are you? Why are you here?'

'I am here now because I have not been,' she murmurs. 'I am here because this land and its people are dying.'

8

RIVA

'I don't know where she is, Locinna.'

The old woman wrings her hands, eyes lost in a heap of worried wrinkles. 'She's not in her bed.'

'Maybe she went for a walk.'

More hand-wringing. She's probably thinking of Mother's last words to her – not to let Keyne out of her sight. My gaze flickers over the nurse's shoulder to Keyne's bed. Not slept in, I wager, but I don't plan to tell Locinna that. My sister is in enough trouble.

'Queen Enica will have me for this,' Locinna frets, hurrying outside. I make my slow way after her, pausing only to peer around Sinne's screen.

'Have you seen Keyne this morn?' I call at the bundle of girl.

Sinne grunts, rubbing the sleep from her eyes. 'What . . .?' she says, but I don't answer; raised voices pull me outside.

My heart begins to thump. I think of the terrible scene on Imbolc night and make for the courtyard, cursing my gait. My foot aches today; that's how it is – some days are just worse than others. I reach the courtyard with a bellyful of dread, expecting to see Keyne clawing at guards, Gildas hovering over her like a dreadful omen.

I do see Keyne, but she's alone, holding a basket of eggs. She blinks at our harried faces, taking in my hasty dress. 'What's wrong?'

'You little *fool*.' I do not realize how angry I am until the words are out. Keyne flinches.

'Why did you leave the women's quarters?' Locinna scolds her. 'Your mother forbade it without an escort.'

Keyne's hurt expression cools. 'I went to the hens,' she says stiffly. 'It's hardly a crime.'

It is if Gildas sees you, I think, but I don't say it aloud. Instead, I hiss, 'Are you stupid? Why give them further opportunity to punish you?'

Before Keyne can open her mouth to retort, Locinna seizes the basket. 'I will turn these into breakfast, just as long as you go back inside, Lady Keyne.'

My fierce sister looks as if she wants to argue, but she holds her tongue, her eyes sweeping the open space before our quarters. Perhaps she's remembering Imbolc too and the rough grip of the guards. 'Very well,' she says, relenting. I lead her inside, the rising sun on our backs, trying not to look at the snags in her dress or the mud that cakes its hem.

'All right,' I say when Keyne has reluctantly changed into clean clothes, 'where have you really been?'

'Been?' Sinne chirps from where she sits, poking a needle morosely into linen. 'What do you mean?'

'I told you,' Keyne says, not meeting either of our eyes. 'The hens.'

'Dung,' I snap, and the word might as well be a slap for the way she jerks back. 'You dirtied your dress.'

'I tripped,' she says, blank-faced. 'It was still dark.'

Sinne and I watch her. Keyne fidgets under our combined gaze, but she doesn't confess. Her face is haunted, a look I've never seen before. 'Fine,' I say. 'But don't expect any more warnings from me.'

I just want to protect her. So why am I so angry at her?

Is it because she has a secret way out of the hold, or do I envy her courage – when I have none? For freedom, she risked Mother's wrath a second time, chanced bruises or worse from the guards and exposed herself to Gildas's castigation. Cold grips my chest. If she is caught, then next time, I am sure Keyne's punishment will be in strokes, not words.

Fleetingly, I wonder if I could find the secret passage too. *Where would you go?* whispers my own mocking voice and I look askance at Keyne. Where does *she* go?

'Ouch,' Sinne snarls, breaking the silence. She sucks on a finger, and throws the stitching down in disgust. 'I hate it.'

'*Sinne*,' I said.

'Do it yourself if you like it so much.'

'Are you ever going to grow up?' I retrieve her work, unable to swallow a tut at its slapdash appearance.

'Stitching is hardly a sign of maturity,' she retorts, getting to her feet. 'I'm going out. There's a ship just in.' She straightens her skirts. 'Maybe they've brought some cloth from Armorica.'

'What good is cloth if you don't know how to sew it?' I call. Sinne gives me a look and slams the main door behind her. 'She's getting worse,' I remark to Keyne. With some difficulty, I kneel beside her on the rug, where she's been absently stroking its rough strands.

My sister has that haunted look on her face again. 'What?' she says and rubs her finger and thumb together as if holding something unseen.

'Sinne. She pines after beautiful clothes, but won't learn how to make them.'

'Hmm. What do you know about the land?'

I poke her. 'Are you even listening?'

'The land,' Keyne repeats, returning abruptly from wherever she's been. 'Our land.'

I stretch out, hoping to ease the ache in my foot. 'What about it?'

'It's where the magic comes from.' I can see vistas in her eyes. She speaks the words like a spell, the way I speak my charms.

'The magic comes from the gods,' I say with a frown. 'Or it used to, anyway.'

She shakes her head. 'I saw it, Riva. In the wood.'

The truth sounds strange in Keyne's mouth. I can tell it isn't a lie by the way my heart beats faster, by the sense of . . . rightness at her words. 'You saw *magic*?'

'It's all around us, in the earth. It's beautiful. And terrible too.' Keyne looks down at her hand tracing the rug's threads. 'And it's fading away.'

In the silence, I swallow, thinking of my healing, of the spark I feel in my veins. The spark that's slowly been weakening. 'I know,' I whisper at last.

Keyne's head snaps up. 'You believe me?'

'Although I've tried hard to hide it, you know I use magic in my healing. But it *has* been fading.' I lower my voice because I know that what I'm about to say is probably treasonous – so deep does the priest's influence run. 'Maybe Gildas is to blame.'

'*Gildas?*'

I don't know why Keyne sounds shocked. I suppose normally I wouldn't dare speak out against a person Father publicly supports, but Gildas is becoming bolder of late. I glance around, reassuring myself that we're not being watched too closely. The few women currently in our quarters sit weaving at the opposite end, and the soft *clack* of the loom covers the sound of my murmur. 'He's always condemning magic, telling us it's wicked.' I feel sick at the thought. 'It could be his fault.'

'Our bond with the land is breaking, Riva, eroding.' Keyne taps the rug beneath our knees. 'The bond is where the magic comes from.'

'How do you know this? I can heal and Sinne likes to brag about her glamours. But *you've* never spoken of magic before.'

Keyne immediately closes up like a clam shell, and I sigh. 'Very well, keep your secrets. But we mustn't go throwing accusations around without proof.'

My sister just nods and we sit in silence. After a while, I feel her eyes on me. Without warning, she says, 'They still hurt, don't they? Your foot and your hand.'

I stare at her warily. 'Why ask that now?'

Keyne hooks a dark strand of hair out of her eyes. She usually wears it pulled back in a warrior's braid, but it's mussed this morning, perhaps from her sojourn outside. 'Just . . .' she hesitates. 'I wondered why you haven't healed them.'

'Don't you think I've *tried*?' The women's loom falters, but I hardly notice, suddenly so overwhelmed with anger that it chokes me. I want to lash out at my sister's lack of comprehension. How can she ask me that? How can she see so little? When I am trying so hard to help her – to protect her from Mother, from Gildas? I take a deep breath, striving to regain some control. No one understands. Why would they? I feel a flash of guilt at the thought of Arlyn – he's always shown me kindness. He'd made my shoon himself, moulding the left one so that it doesn't chafe. But with kindness comes pity, and that is pressure on a bruise, a constant reminder of what I have lost.

Keyne's hand moves to comfort me, but falls short, uncertain. 'I'm sorry,' she says – and I'm relieved to hear none of that hated pity in her voice. Her gaze moves from my misshapen hand to my face. 'I've been thinking of myself too much lately.'

I open my mouth to agree, but something stops me. Perhaps the memory of Keyne's screams as her clothes were stripped – as a dress was bundled roughly over her head. I look at her face, at the way she holds herself, as if protecting an injury. 'I'm sorry too,' I say. 'For what they did to you.'

Shadows gather on her brow as she sits there, letting the silence stretch. Before either of us dare to break it, the door bangs open.

'Lady Riva, you must come at once.'

We turn. A girl bobs in the entryway, her cheeks flushed. 'I mean,' she adds belatedly, 'I beg my lady to come with me.'

'Of course,' I say, stirred by her distress. 'But what is it?'

'My brother. He's bad. Needs a healer.'

An icy creature stirs in my stomach. 'You're Siaun's sister.'

She nods frantically. 'Twin sister. Please, Lady Riva. He's taken a turn for the worse.'

'Let me get my bag,' I say, but Keyne is already handing it to me. We share a last look. *It's all around us, in the earth. And it's fading away.* I have no doubt that she's right about magic disappearing, but to claim it comes from the land and not the gods . . . I don't know. She's challenging the foundation of our beliefs. And our beliefs are being shaken enough.

The girl is impatient at my slowness. She keeps darting ahead. I try to ignore the pain in my foot and push myself faster. 'What's your name?' I gasp as we run through the hold, followed by curious eyes.

'Eldruda.'

'Can you tell me what happened?'

'You *know* what happened,' the girl growls before remembering herself and adding, 'my lady. He was flogged for interrupting the priest's ceremony.'

I know, believe me I know. 'I meant, what are his symptoms?'

'Fever. Weakness. He can't walk. And the wounds smell bad.'

I grimace. Poisoned wounds are hard to heal. I watch Eldruda's bobbing head, her scarf loosened by the way she keeps turning to check I'm still there. It was brave to run to me so openly with

Gildas around. Out of habit, I send up a prayer to Brigid, hoping no one reports us. The irony of trying to heal Siaun with the old magic is not lost on me; in fact it feels darkly significant and foreboding rumbles in my chest.

Siaun's home is tiny, just a hut on Dunbriga's lowest terrace. I almost gag at the stench of illness and the animals huddled within. No wonder his wounds have turned bad. I think uncomfortably of my own clean pallet, scented with flowers and cedar, trying not to see the dirt in the corners of the hut, on the face of Siaun's wife. I recognize her from the church. Does Father know how this family live? The peat on the fire smokes more than burns and I begin to cough. 'Open the door,' I say. 'Let some light and air inside.' They do as I ask, but the hut looks even worse in daylight. *Father knows*, I think with a shiver of guilt. How can he not?

Siaun lies moaning on his front. 'We've tried to keep the straw clean,' Eldruda says. 'But there's not much to go around this time of year.'

I crouch beside the pallet, opening my leather bag. 'Boil water,' I say, before steeling myself.

I peel Siaun's tunic away from his back. He lets out another moan of agony and even my healer's stomach wavers at the sight of the festering wounds. Deep parallel gashes weep blood and pus, as if some beast has sunk its claws in and torn downwards. Worse, red lines branch from the wounds: a sign of blood poisoning.

'Gods,' I murmur.

'Will he be all right?' his wife asks, biting a knuckle. 'Can you help him?'

'I don't know,' I say, unwilling to lie. 'I will try my best.'

With Eldruda's help, I force some willowbark tea into Siaun and then set about cleaning the wounds. She smiles when his pained gasps begin to ease, but I don't. His eyes are closed, his breathing very shallow. I will need something stronger than herbs.

I close my own eyes, shutting out the hut and the tear-stained women, sinking down inside myself – searching for the spark. I am sure Siaun will die without the aid of magic. The darkness within me feels quiet. Too quiet. Far away, I hear voices, but I do my best to filter them out. Where is it? I extend every sense, seeking the familiar silver glow, one I can take into myself.

There. Weak like moonshine at night's end. But weak or not, I need it and reach out.

A weight comes down on my shoulder. Heavy, burning. Mere inches from me, the light withers. 'No!' I cry involuntarily, alone in the darkness once more. With a shuddering gasp, I open my eyes. The hut spins and I have to steady myself against the pallet. The weight on my shoulder is a hand, oddly hot and heavier than a hand ought to be.

Gildas.

'Lady Riva,' he says softly. 'I am surprised to find you here, of all places.'

'Let her work,' Eldruda hisses, though I notice she has her back to the wall, as far from the priest as she can get. 'Everyone knows she's a healer.'

'I do not see much healing,' Gildas replies with a cool look. 'What were you doing, Lady Riva, with your eyes closed and your hands so still?'

'Praying,' I say stiffly, while my heart pounds behind my ribs.

'Praying.' In the priest's mouth, the word rings with condescension. 'To the Lord Our Saviour, I hope?'

'To *my* gods,' I snap, forcing down the fear in me, 'who have always been with our people.'

Gildas's look is long, considering. Then his eyes move to Siaun. 'They do not appear to be with you today.'

'What do you know—?' The rest of Eldruda's words are masked by a cry, as Siaun's wife falls to her knees beside him. And I realize that quietly, in the space between our breaths, Siaun's heart has stopped.

'I came to perform his last rites,' Gildas says into an awful silence. 'But I am too late, it seems. His soul is already lost to darkness.'

'Get *out*.' I am on my feet. A torrent rushes through me: not the healing magic I'd sought, but rage, white-hot. I should curb it. I should be silent. *He has Father's support, Mother's trust.* But Keyne's words have woken something in me, are feeding the conviction that Gildas is latched onto us like a bloodsucker and is slowly draining us dry of magic. I hear myself say, 'You are not welcome here.'

The priest's eyes glitter. 'Take more care with your words, my lady. Your parents would be . . . displeased to hear you speak so.' He addresses Siaun's sobbing widow. 'I will send for the body. It is the queen's wish that he be given to the ground, not burned on a heathen pyre. Our Lord, in His infinite mercy, may one day raise him up.'

When neither of Siaun's relatives reply, Gildas extends a slim finger and runs it over the nearest surface. It comes away dark and he grimaces; an expression that seems to take in the hut's entire filthy interior. When he speaks again, it is almost to himself. 'One cannot expect a people to awaken to the light if they live in dirt and darkness.' He raises his voice. 'I will have words with the king about the condition of this house, which is fit only for animals.' He nods at the scrawny goat tethered in the corner and his gaze meets mine. 'Poverty is not a sin. Perhaps I can help this family in other ways.'

I am acutely aware of my fine clothes, my clean skin. The women stare at me over Siaun's body and beneath the ache of loss in Eldruda's face, I see despair. My own mirrors hers; guilt at my failure to heal her brother makes it as thick and bitter as tallow. Before I can say anything, Gildas turns and is gone, melting into the dying day.

9

SINNE

Ēostre – the spring festival

I hear his name shouted from the gates.

Before anyone can stop me, I'm haring down the hall steps, scattering yellow flowers in my wake. I've been making dilly chains for the Ēostre festival, just two sennights away, practising on the older flowers growing beside the herb garden. It's late in their season; I'll have to go into the woods to pick fresh ones. I shiver at the thought – I don't like the woods.

I gather my skirts in one hand, grinning as I dart between buildings. *Finally something good.* I hope he stays for Ēostre. Shouts carry on the wind that's been blowing steadily for the past week and I increase my speed. I see others making for the gate, but I outpace them all.

His name travels like a rumour from person to person. 'Myrdhin, Myrdhin!' I too am shouting his name like a battle cry and when he sees me, he smiles. Opens his arms.

I jump into them before I realize how unseemly it is for a maiden to throw herself at a man. But Myrdhin is different and he's laughing. 'Lassie, how you've grown,' he says and I step back, my nose itching with the spicy smell that always clings to him.

'You've been gone years,' I say. It's a bit petulant, I suppose, but he *has*. And I've missed him.

'I am sorry for it,' he says, blue eyes twinkling. Dimples deepen as they take up his smile. 'You will have to fill me in on everything.'

'You're staying for Ēostre, then?' I almost squeal.

He laughs again, ruffles my hair as he did when I was little. If anyone else did that, I'd be mortified, but it's fine because he's Myrdhin and his next words fill me with joy. 'Yes.' He grins. 'I suppose I am.'

'Master Myrdhin, I take it,' a cool voice says.

People part for the crow and Gildas glides through as if he's Father himself. His black robes swirl in his wake, incongruously pristine given our muddy pathways. I chance a glance at my hems and wince.

'That is indeed one of my names,' Myrdhin says pleasantly into the sudden silence.

Gildas raises an eyebrow. 'A single name is honest. Only a liar has need of more.' No one makes a sound, but it's as if a sigh passes through the gathered people.

'Names have power,' Myrdhin ripostes and I realize with a twinge of thrill that this is a duel. 'As you and your god well know.'

More come to watch the exchange. The priest's smile is the opposite of Myrdhin's: a mirthless curve. 'He is not my God, but all of ours, whether Britain's people hearken to Him, or not.'

'And do they?' Myrdhin asks, a crack spidering across his casual smile. It looks a little more like Gildas's now. 'Because I've heard of you and the cunning whispers you pour into powerful ears. Tell me: is your great work bearing fruit?'

I frown. What great work? The priest's attempt to convert us?

Gildas is about to frame an answer when a shout booms out. We're all so tense, we jump as one. It's Father, of course, striding towards the gates. He's accompanied by his first sword, a wiry wolf of a man, who takes every chance to leer at me. I look away.

'Ah, Myrdhin.' There is true pleasure in Father's voice and Gildas scowls when he hears it. 'You've finally returned to me.'

You'd be forgiven for thinking Myrdhin Father's bondsman, the way he speaks to him, but I know the magician doesn't mind. I glance between the three men, enjoying the discomfort on Gildas's crow-face. He knows he can't cross the Dumnonian king and Father is looking very kingly today, with the wide gold band across his forehead and his great shoulders covered by a vermillion cloak. Fine wrinkles at the corners of his eyes are the only sign he's nearing five and forty.

'As usual, I see my youngest daughter couldn't restrain herself,' he remarks. I'm not sure if I hear rebuke or amusement, so I gift him with my demurest smile and a small flutter of lashes.

Myrdhin's chuckle dispels what's left of the tension. 'Lady Sinne could turn even the bitterest posset to honey.'

'Don't I know it,' Father mutters, but his glance is a fond one. 'Come then,' he says with a belly laugh of his own, throwing one arm about Myrdhin's slim shoulders. 'Let's retire to the warm where you can fill me in on your latest adventures.'

'Do you have new stories?' I call after them.

Myrdhin taps a finger to his temple. 'Safely locked away in here, little mistress.'

Riva is as delighted as I am. Even Keyne looks less dour than usual. 'So Father supported Myrdhin publicly?' Riva asks, putting her mending aside.

I shrug. 'I guess so.' I am already thinking of tonight and the joy of gathering in the great hall, watching rapt faces as Myrdhin strums his harp, pulling castles from the air. I wonder what story he has planned.

'Sinne. What did Father say?'

Her voice jerks me back to the women's quarters and I huff. 'Is it that important?'

'Yes,' Riva says with the kind of exaggerated patience I hate. 'It's important in that it sends a message.'

'What message?'

'Gildas is not as welcome as he thinks.'

'Oh.' That pleases me. Maybe the crow will fly away now Myrdhin is here. I twist a lock of hair around my finger. 'I wish Myrdhin would stay.'

'I thought you said he was,' Riva says, plucking it out of my hand as she always does. Goddess knows why it bothers her.

'I meant forever,' I reply. 'I wish he would live here.'

'Well, he might be staying longer this time.' Riva picks up a shawl to cover her shoulders. It's still as cold as Imbolc two months ago, despite the blossom now garlanding the trees. 'I overheard him say he won't be lodging here. He told Father he has a dwelling in the woods, near Cēd Hen.'

Keyne looks up sharply. 'He does?'

'Myrdhin said it needs airing out, and repairing before it falls down. Father's offered him some men to make it habitable again.'

'Sounds like he *is* intending to stay!' I exclaim with a clap. Everything's better with Myrdhin around. And perhaps his presence will attract merchants or travelling scholars seeking his wisdom. Maybe this place will become a proper beehive again.

Keyne looks troubled for some reason, but my good mood carries me right through the afternoon to suppertime. When the trenchers of mutton are cleared, we gather in the main hall, our whole household and a scattering more, to hear Myrdhin's tale. Our storyteller settles on a bench before the fire, built up to a crackling height. Most of the torches have been put out and the vast timbered space feels like a dragon's cave, the fire a hoard at its heart. I watch the flame-shadows dance across faces – we listeners are eager, attentive. The usual bickering over the best perches dies down as soon as Myrdhin raises a hand.

'What should I tell tonight?' His gaze strays to Father, who rarely misses a story. 'A tale of a king, perhaps –' his eyes move to Keyne – 'and his princely sons? The choices they made –' those blue eyes touch Riva before finally meeting mine – 'and the fate that befell them?'

It's not really a question. When Myrdhin decides on a particular story, not even Father requests he tell another. 'Sit still then, listeners,' our storyteller declares and he sweeps an arm through the air. A vision unfurls in its wake and we all gasp our astonishment. A rich green valley and sparkling river appear within a ring of fang-shaped mountains. The impression overlays our hall; I can just make out the fire crackling beneath. I glance around for Gildas and let go my breath in a rush when I don't see him. Instead I seek Father's face, worrying that he'll put a stop to this blatant use of magic. But Father's eyes are strangely wistful as they explore Myrdhin's illusion. The magician isn't part of our hold, or one of the king's subjects, after all. Besides, who would dare tell such a man that he couldn't do magic?

Myrdhin smiles and takes up his small harp. He strums a chord to accompany the story, a haunting note with a hint of threat. 'I will tell you of the sea god, Lir, and his children.'

The Five Rivers of Lir

When the land was young and boundless, there lived five princes and they were the sons of Lir. They dwelt together on a mountain slope beneath the stars and each had everything his heart desired: bounty, love, a warm bed of linen in a tower that overlooked gardens wild and rambling. Merriment they had in plenty; their halls rang with song, and people danced there.

And yet the princes' hearts were sick. The ailment was not bodily, for each man stood in his prime. What troubled them came from the mind and its ceaseless recitals. One thought hung about them like a curse: though the earth had endless years in its bosom, they must bend to death and pass beyond all sight of life.

So consuming was this thought, so sour was their mortality, that the five sons of Lir left their bright court and gardens. They left their people and the merry cries of their children. Bitterest of all, they left their wives – five women who were to become rulers in their absence. Their ears blocked to five protesting voices, eyes turned from five angry faces, the princes mounted and rode from the kingdom.

On pale beasts they journeyed, mythical creatures of claw or hoof or snout. Swift as unfettered winds, they made for the sea. 'Father will allay our fears,' the eldest declared, clinging to the mane beneath his fingers. 'He will grant our wish.' The other sons murmured agreement. They would return to their people as princes indeed: good, just and immortal. They would rule jointly, free from death forever.

The beasts made light work of journeying. Before a sennight passed, the five sons of Lir beheld the ocean. Each was struck by his father's majesty, his many aspects. Lir's mackerel hair washed up around their feet, shining in the last of the moonlight. His limbs touched the coastline, sometimes in anger and foam, sometimes in gentle ripples, for his moods were changeling. As they stood on the shore, a white-tipped wave gathered itself and rose, but did not fall upon them. Instead a voice spoke from its heart, black as the sunless depths, blue as coral. And the princes rejoiced, for they recognized their father's tongue.

'Glad am I to see you,' Lir said, and his wave trembled on the brink of breaking. 'It has been long since you visited.'

'We are sorry, Father,' the eldest prince replied. 'We have attended to the business of living.'

'You have ruled well,' shrewd Lir said then, 'but this does not

mean your hearts are without fault. For I see you are distracted, unsatisfied with your lot, and ask questions of the stars.'

'They do not answer,' said the youngest prince and watched a sorrowful smile dampen his father's mouth. 'So we have come to you.'

Lir answered, 'I know why you have come.' His cheeks churned and his hands tumbled down, and the princes were suddenly afraid.

'But, Great Lir,' said the eldest, whose heart was bolder than his head, 'do we not deserve to share your power, to also rule our lands forever? You know we are just and kind. Our kingdoms prosper under our care, and our people are happy.' He paused, for a crafty thought tickled his will. 'We do not ask this boon for ourselves, but for our people. If we died, they would scatter into the hills like lost sheep. A tyrant wolf may steal from the woods to kill and maim them, to fill their hearts with terror.' He gazed around at his brothers. 'We would not see that happen.'

Lir was silent. The ocean stilled and gulls paused in their shrieking flight. He regarded his eldest son, whose desire to cheat death so consumed him. Then Lir turned his many eyes on the other princes. 'Share you your brother's feelings?'

'We do,' responded the youngest. 'We wish to live forever.'

'So be it,' Lir said and the princes heard his despair – as an evil tide that drags men down to die. Fear again flashed hot, but it was too late to unvoice their wish. Their mighty father reared until he towered a league above the land, and his words were heard in every corner of the earth.

'You will run as the deer run, but no legs will bear you. You will sing as the thrush sings, but no throat will carry your voices. In your arrogance, you have asked for that which no mortal can comprehend. Perhaps when you have flowed for as long as I have worn white caps, you will understand. Carve your kingdoms well, my sons.'

Five bodies fell to merge with the earth. Such was their father's mercy: they would live forever, as long as the world turned and the moon moved the waters. And Lir gave each of them a land to shape, lessons to erode from stubborn stone, enlightenment to coax from caverns that had never known the sun.

The brothers roiled and cursed, but they had no tongues to lash their father. They poured from him in torrents, swallowing the fields so diligently tilled by their people. Animals cried out for them to stop, but the angry waters drowned them. Birds shrieked and humans cowered and ran. The brothers separated. Each flowed away from the sea, far from their father. They spread across lowlands, into the fens of the east and the steep hills of the west. They swam north until their reaching hands became ice which held them fast. They turned south, spent their anger foolishly in deserts where the hot skies baked them into sand.

Nile is the eldest, sire of great civilizations. Thamesa is the youngest, an unwilling pawn in the wars of men. They cannot bear to be near each other, reminded of their father's curse and his blessing. For he kept his promise and they live still, as long as the world turns and the moon moves the waters.

A shiver skitters across my skin like little moth feet. The great wave that was Lir collapses in on itself, leaving us dry and word-less. All is silent in the aftermath of Myrdhin's tale. Then the fire pops and with it the hush is broken. A log settles, people wake and start to clap, banging their mugs on the long tables in appreci-ation. I sit still, feeling the shiver pattering over my shoulders, down my arms. Usually I too would be clapping, but the story unnerves me and I can't get the horror of being a river out of my mind.

'Wasn't that cruel of Lir?' I say to Myrdhin before I can stop myself. 'They were his sons. Surely he could have said no instead of punishing them.'

Myrdhin looks at me, one eyebrow raised. 'Cruel, you say? Well, perhaps. But the princes got what they wanted, no?'

'The cost was too high.'

'Do you believe immortality should be without cost?'

I hesitate. 'No . . .' but I can't think of an argument.

'Ah child,' he sighs, 'don't mind me. Lir *is* cruel – all gods are.'

I catch movement at the edge of the firelight, the swirl of a black cassock, the soft tread of retreating feet. Myrdhin must have heard too, but he doesn't spare the lurking priest a glance. Instead he smiles a jester's smile. So Gildas was here after all. I watch him go with a twinge of dread, knowing this won't be the end of it.

'A valuable lesson indeed,' Father declares with a thump of his mead. Some sloshes over the rim and one of the dogs lumbers over to lap it up. 'But let's have a merrier tale now, old friend.'

Myrdhin gives as elaborate a bow as he can while seated and gestures for a refill. 'When my throat's a little wetter, I'll be happy to oblige.'

Sleep ought to find me with a head full of Myrdhin's lighter stories: majestic beasts, magical stones and boys who challenge giants, all brought to life by the lilting strains of his harp. But what I think about, as I lie on my pallet that night, are the rivers that used to be men, voiceless and betrayed.

10

KEYNE

'Have you ever seen Sinne so white?' Riva says to me as we return to our quarters after the final story. 'She just ran off.'

I murmur agreement. I admit it was unusual, seeing my younger sister hurry out before the rest of us. Even Myrdhin didn't receive his customary post-story embrace. But Sinne's always been flighty. Sometimes I think her head must be a place of butterfly thoughts, darting this way and that so she doesn't know which to pursue.

'What did *you* think of the story?' Riva asks.

Though the moon is veiled, it's bitterly cold and the earth feels like rock beneath my heels. 'Clever,' I say, 'when the boy pretended his cheese was a stone and tricked the giant.'

'I meant the story about Lir.' Riva's eyes glitter in the torches spaced at intervals throughout the hold.

'I knew how it was going to end,' I say.

'With them becoming rivers?'

I shake my head. 'Just that they would be punished for seeking more than what they were due.'

Riva seems to contemplate this. Then she says, 'When Myrdhin said all gods are cruel, do you think he wanted Gildas to hear in particular?'

'So you saw him too.'

She nods. 'He was lurking in the shadows – as usual. I didn't think he'd come. He doesn't like Myrdhin.'

'Maybe he wants to keep an eye on him. And his magic.'

'Wasn't brave enough to say anything to Father, though.' Riva's smile is fierce.

Inside our quarters, Sinne's screen is pulled across her pallet; she must have retired already. I snuff out most of the lamps and head for my own alcove. Talk of Myrdhin has stirred up my earlier unease. This ramshackle house of his sounds too near Mori's cottage for comfort. I realize I feel protective of the witch woman; it makes a difference knowing I have somewhere to go outside the hold, someone to talk to who doesn't know me. Though I'm starting to suspect she knows me all too well.

A horrible thought occurs and I stop in my tracks. What if Mori has been using Myrdhin's house? A moment later, I shake my head. No, Mori's cottage might be simple, but it isn't dilapidated. I have to warn her. Myrdhin will make for the woods tomorrow with a troop of Father's men. *He* might not harm Mori, but if the men catch sight of her . . . My heart clatters as I wait for the sounds of women bedding down to subside. Remembering my gorse scratches, I find my best and only trousers and pull them on, tucking the dress into them and wrapping my lower legs in leather. I grab mitts to shield my hands and a thick cloak to keep out the chill.

Finally it's quiet. I ease my screen aside, double-checking the room. The banked fire glows in the middle, casting its light over a slumped Locinna. The old woman's dozed off before reaching her pallet again. I tiptoe past her, holding my breath. Once outside, I let it go in a long white huff. The clouds are helpful gaolers – with the moon imprisoned I need not worry about its light.

I turn and walk straight into Gildas.

I manage to swallow a yelp of surprise but only just. Before I can run, the priest's hand closes around my arm. Why is he hovering near the women's quarters? It is surely past midnight. We look at each other in the dark. I haven't spoken to him since that awful night, careful to keep my distance.

'Lady Keyne.' Is that triumph or scorn in his voice? 'What might you be doing out on a night better suited to brigands and thieves?'

'I could ask you the same,' I retort, hoping he can't hear the pounding of my heart. *I have to get away, warn Mori.*

'An impertinent answer, but one I have come to expect from you.' He is not letting go. When I tug at my arm, his grip only tightens and his gaze dips to my exposed legs. 'I see your mother's people weren't diligent enough in removing these inappropriate garments.'

All at once I remember my strange burst of will that pushed Sinne away, just as she was about to discover my bracelet. The memory is foggy. I don't know how I did it – I was so angry at the time. I don't even know what had happened, really. But with the priest's hand around my wrist, I can't summon even a flicker of that same defiance. I try to slow my heart, refusing to let him frighten me. 'What do you want?'

'Only your soul.' He pauses. 'For God.'

'I think your god has enough souls already,' I reply, more bravely than I feel. 'I doubt he will miss mine.'

'You misunderstand.' How are his hands so hot in this chill? 'It is not for Our Lord's benefit, but your own.' His eyes are dark pools beneath the lightless sky. 'I seek only to save you from damnation.'

'I have seen no proof of this damnation you speak of,' I say, ceasing to tug against his grip, planting my feet more firmly. 'No endless dark, or burning halls.' But as the words emerge, I remember the dream I had on Imbolc eve, of hoofbeats on a long road, of a boiling black storm.

'No?' Gildas says softly. 'Your eyes tell me different.'

With a great wrench, I pull free. Cold rushes in to replace the heat of his fingers and I realize I'm shaking. I retreat to the women's quarters, the one place he cannot follow me.

'Think on my words, Keyne.' I should be affronted at his informality, but it's not enough to stop me fleeing. 'You know it is coming.'

I hurl myself inside, slamming the door behind me. Locinna jolts awake, but I'm already behind my screen, shutting Gildas out. I can't shut out his words, however, or the images they conjure.

I *did* dream of darkness that night. It will come from the east.

Despite my gnawing fear that Mori will be discovered, a sennight passes before I find another chance to escape Dunbriga. With Ēostre a week away, Mother keeps us busy with preparations: new customs ordered by Gildas, who insists we add crosses to our sweet buns. We haven't exchanged a word since the night he found me out of bed, but I feel his eyes on me sometimes. I can't forget his warning – or my dream.

Riva and I manage to slip in a few of our regular Ēostre practices; she stitches another hare into the great hanging we put up for festival, a traditional way of honouring the goddess. Although if Mori speaks truth and there are no gods, I suppose it's not Ēostre we're venerating, but the land itself, the spring. The idea feels right to me now.

I collect eggs to boil and simple dyes to turn them into jewels. Sinne's been oddly quiet since Myrdhin's story, but she's perked up now Ēostre's upon us. I see her adding fresh daffodils to her chains of flowers, which she drapes over doorways. I can't help smiling at their cheerful yellow; it makes the abnormal cold a little more bearable.

Apparently, Myrdhin's house is all mended now; it's where he spends most days. He comes often to Dunbriga to sup with us, riding a beautiful white mare called Nimue. I tell myself Mori is fine, and she can surely look after herself. But all the same, when a pre-dawn chance finally comes my way, I slip off to make sure.

It has become my habit to check for lurking priests. I won't let Gildas catch me out again. I sweep the narrow alleys between each building to be certain they're clear before I slip down them. When I reach the wall, I wait for the night guards to change. One yawns as he descends the sentry ladder and I wonder whether he'd fallen asleep. The rumour of Saxon raids is still only a rumour and it doesn't take much to blunt caution on a dull night.

I wait for him to pass and then I'm through the gorse tunnel and into the copse, going faster this time. I'd know if Mori had been discovered – a witch so close to Dunbriga would be a feast for gossips. Still, my heart only calms when I finally spot smoke through the trees and the silver bracelet warms on my wrist.

Mori is in her garden, harvesting herbs. She doesn't look around when I skid to a halt, panting from my run and the tightness of the linen around my chest. 'So you're back, are you?' she says, bending to a sprig of mint.

'I was worried for you.'

She chuckles; it's more of a cackle, actually. 'Because of the men passing near? Bah, they only see what they want to see.'

'Mori, your house isn't inconspicuous.' I gesture at the smoke curling up. 'They couldn't miss that.'

'You'd be surprised,' the witch woman mutters, straightening with a groan. 'I suppose you'll be wanting to break your fast.'

A stubborn refusal forms on my lips, but my belly betrays me, growling as if I haven't eaten in days. I redden.

Mori laughs again. 'You're in luck. I've some pancakes fresh from the griddle.' She gives me an appraising look. 'Bring some eggs next time.'

I follow her inside, eyes resuming their journey over the walls.

I wonder how long it's taken her to collect these objects and how she managed to bring them all here, especially the delicate vases.

'Here you are, you growing thing.' Mori gives a pancake a final toss and slides it onto a trencher in one smooth movement. There's a pot of honey on the table and I've half emptied it before I recall it might be her only one.

'Sorry,' I mumble around a mouthful. 'I can bring more.'

She waves the offer away. 'If a little honey is all it takes to buy your company, then it's a small price.'

There's a lump in my throat that isn't pancake. I blink at her and stupidly feel like crying. I can't think of anything to say, and I'm suddenly glad of breakfast, which fills my mouth so words don't have to.

Back turned, Mori is busy with the herbs. Perhaps it's not *my* company she likes, I tell myself, just company. She must be lonely living out here, no one to converse with save the wind and leaves. 'Thank you for breakfast,' I say, and I take the trencher outside to wash in the stream.

She is sitting at the table when I return. 'A patchwork outfit,' she says, taking in my dress and trousered legs. 'Wouldn't a tunic suit better?'

'They took my clothes away,' I say before registering the dangerous question and where it might lead.

'Ah,' Mori clasps her hands on the tabletop. 'I was wondering why you hadn't come to see me. Have they been watching you?'

I repress a shudder at the memory of Imbolc night. 'Yes. Especially the priest. Mother's orders.'

'Yet here you are.'

'They aren't so vigilant any more. Besides, everyone is busy with Ēostre.'

The silence stretches and I remember our awkward conversation two moons ago when I sat in this self-same chair, replete after a different meal. I glance at the golden cup, at the figure labelled

'Enarees' on the Grecian vase next to it, as enigmatic and compelling as ever. Mori wants truth, but no one else does. Because my truth is a language they do not speak.

'Did *you* do this?' I burst out suddenly, having no words with which to frame it. I wave a hand at the dress, at the body beneath it. 'When you gave me the bracelet in the forest?'

Mori doesn't ask what I mean. She seems to know. 'Do you really believe that?'

Moments pass. 'No,' I whisper.

I knew I was different before I met her. I think I've always known it, that I wasn't like my sisters. Close as we are, this is something we do not share and that they cannot understand. It is something I've never found the right words to express. Abruptly I think of Lir's wave; it is where I am now, balancing on its crest. What will happen when it falls?

Mori starts to frame a reply, but freezes. A crease appears between her brows. 'Strange,' she says. 'We have company.' She rises and pads fox-footed to the window with its hide covering. 'Ah,' she breathes. 'I think you had better hide.'

I shoot up, fear spiking at the memory of being dragged through the hold. I shouldn't have come – I've led Father's guards to Mori. What will they do to her?

What will they do to me?

'Child,' she snaps, pointing at a curtain. 'Hide.'

The hanging conceals her bed, set back in an alcove. The blankets appear scented with spices and a heady sweetness fills my nose. I sneeze just as there's a knock on the door. The sound of knuckles against wood is hesitant; perhaps guards haven't come after all. I can hear Mori's hasty steps, though I can't see what she's doing. The knock comes again, louder.

A creak as the door is opened. A cough. 'Good morrow,' a woman says.

I swallow a gasp. The voice is Riva's.

11

RIVA

I know she's up to something as soon as I see her sneaking across the yard.

I'd woken early, while dark still ruled the sky, from muddled dreams of men and rivers. Perhaps that story of Myrdhin's had taken root inside my head. In any case, I'd risen and dressed, wanting some air to dispel it.

It is only luck that I see her in the gloom: a cloaked figure flitting from shadow to shadow. From her practised grace, I can tell she's done this many times. I don't know what possesses me to follow her; I'm not reckless like my sisters. But Keyne's harried movements draw me. This is dangerous; Mother will surely miss her. She'll miss *me* if I follow.

Foolish girl, I berate myself as I pursue Keyne across the hold. My foot won't let me go swiftly; I almost lose her twice and then spot her crouched in the lee of the guard post, waiting. Her gaze is riveted to the guards coming down from night watch. As soon as they pass, she darts out . . . and throws herself headlong into a gorse bush.

The thorns close over her like swamp weed. I wait, but Keyne does not emerge. The gorse hugs the outer wall here; have I found her secret exit? Before new guards come by, I hurry over. Broken thorns litter the earth: clues for any who know how to look. But why would they? I feel a reluctant smile tugging at my mouth. Clever. How did she find it?

A man laughs somewhere behind me and, instinctively, I dive for thorny cover. Every scratch inspires new respect for my sister, and new worry. She must lacerate herself to earn her freedom. On the other side, I look at the wall that towers above me, and feel a swell of nausea. It's my duty to tell Father of this breach. If an enemy finds it . . . But I remember Keyne's begging, in her eyes the pain of being shut away, and know it will kill her to lose it.

A trail of crushed grass leads straight into the copse. I could go back now, cover for her if anyone asks. If both of us are missing, won't it raise greater suspicion? But another part of me is desperate to know what she does with her gorse-won freedom.

So with rare recklessness, I follow.

The night's rain helps me; the wet woodland mulch holds Keyne's prints and I feel like a hunter reading the deer trails.

I cannot go fast; half an hour passes. Hampered by my bad foot and skirt, I struggle on, despite the fact Keyne's footprints are starting to merge with the earth. Just as I begin to doubt the wisdom of following her, I see smoke through the trees and stop.

It comes to me. *Myrdhin.* Of course, this must be his house. But what possessed Keyne to risk coming all this way to see him when he so often shares our supper? I inch closer to the cottage, lichen-stained but with a roof bearing evidence of recent thatching. An open area rings it, cleared of trees. Keyne is nowhere to be seen.

I loiter in the shadow of an elm, wondering what to do. I could go in and ask after my sister, but if she *is* in there, she might be angry that I followed her. And there is Myrdhin himself to consider. But Keyne has almost certainly been this way before and he hasn't betrayed her yet. Does that mean he won't betray me either?

The sensible option is to retrace my steps through the wood

and try slipping back into the fort, unnoticed. It will be hard; the sun is well into its climb now, but if I'm careful . . .

Shivering, I face the cottage door. Smoke curls into the air, woody and sweet; it looks so warm, so inviting and my foot hurts. It would be wonderful to sit down a while. Surely Myrdhin won't say anything incriminating to Father? And if Keyne is here . . . well, we'll just have to keep each other's secrets.

Before I can change my mind, I set off across the open ground, grasping nervous fistfuls of skirt. When I raise my hand to knock, it trembles.

The door opens at my second tap; Myrdhin appears, greying brows raised. 'Good morrow,' I say faintly.

'Lady Riva,' he replies and I know I've surprised him. 'What are you doing here?'

It's a good question. *What* am *I doing here?* Surreptitiously, I peer beyond him into the cottage, searching for my sister, but finding it empty. 'I was –' I change answer mid-flow – 'just out for a walk.'

He frowns. 'Do your parents know you're here?'

'No,' I say guiltily, and then raise my chin. 'But I am a woman grown and go where I like.'

'As you say,' Myrdhin answers politely. 'Some refreshment then?'

I ought to leave. Keyne isn't here and our joint absence will almost certainly have raised suspicion by now. But I am weary from my long pursuit through birdsong and bramble and the cold is making me ache.

I nod and follow Myrdhin inside.

My gaze goes immediately to the fire, my old enemy, but it is banked and tamed. Only then do I let my eyes explore the cottage properly. Myriad things clutter Myrdhin's home, some mundane, others which I am unable to name . . . I pass over a cluster of vases on the mantel and dried herbs strung from the rafters, pausing at a ragged but colourful cloak that hangs from a peg. A scrubbed table dominates the single room and a curtain hides what I assume is a pallet bed. Myrdhin certainly lives frugally. Father would be horrified if he saw; he'd probably order quarters prepared in the hold.

'Please sit,' Myrdhin says.

As I do so, it occurs to me that I shouldn't be alone in a man's house, even if that man is a trusted friend of my father. But what can I do about it now? So I take the mug he offers, lured by its steaming contents. A sniff reveals mint – with maybe nettle or burdock. I murmur the names of the plants aloud, questioning.

'You have a healer's nose.' Myrdhin smiles. 'Have you considered it as a profession?'

I gape at him before realizing it looks undignified 'A *profession*?'

'Why not? If you're interested, I can guide you more closely in the art.'

'I – I am a king's daughter. I am expected to marry well, to bear sons, to command a household . . .' I stop. The sound of that fate, recited in my own voice, inspires a wave of dizziness and I clutch the table with my good hand. Is this really still my destiny? Is Father still planning to marry me off – scars and all? I blink at Myrdhin. What if there is another path? One which would let me practise my healing openly?

Myrdhin watches, blue eyes unblinking. 'Is that what *you* want?'

I take a deep breath, smoothing my face over the turmoil his words have woken in me. 'What *I* want doesn't matter. Mother taught us that for royal girls, it's marriage or a convent.'

'It's a waste, is what it is,' Myrdhin says. 'Especially for one able to draw on the land's magic.'

I am in danger of gaping again. *The land's magic* . . . This is what Keyne spoke of – could she have discussed such a thing with

Myrdhin? I can't suppress a shiver when I think of Father and how he'd react if he heard this. Any talk of magic is forbidden now, with Gildas here. I look at Myrdhin with new eyes, warmed by the tea, shaken by his words and his daring. I haven't allowed myself to imagine it recently, but perhaps I do have a future that doesn't involve being married off to a man of Father's choosing. What if I can be a true priestess of Brigid, of the old religion? Would Myrdhin really help me?

'Thank you . . .' I say, after a moment.

'For what, lass?'

'For saving my life all those years ago.'

His eyes travel over my burned hand resting on the table and, self-conscious, I hide it in my lap. 'That's not what you said to me then,' he replies.

It's true. I had screamed into the face that had saved me, sick at the sight of my own mangled limbs. Death, I'd thought, was better than this half life, where everyone I saw wore dismay or pity. Or tried to hide their disgust with varying degrees of success. Mother had wrung her hands, weeping at the disfigurements that would make it hard to find me a husband.

'The most important parts are still there,' Father had snapped back at her, expressing his hurt in the only way he knew how. 'She's a fine-looking girl who can give him heirs. That's what a man will care about.'

He and Mother had fought well into the night, and I heard it all from my sickbed, my burns throbbing in time with their traded insults.

The memory settles on me like a grey dawn that promises only rain – dampening those sparkling vistas I'd imagined. 'Master Myrdhin,' I whisper, unable to meet his gaze. 'Can you make me . . . as I was before?'

He waits for me to look up before he says, 'Lass. Like you, I have some healing skill. But it is not all-powerful, especially against wounds caused by wildfire. The kind of healing you seek can only come from in here.' He touches his fingers lightly to my temple.

I stare at him. There is no hated pity in his eyes, and nothing in his face to anger me. Yet the rage boiling up inside is almost hotter than the fire that had near stolen my life. *Wildfire.* I want to ask him what he means, but the rage jerks me to my feet instead. 'Are you saying I can *think* my injuries away? Imagine them gone – and it will be so?'

He is infuriatingly calm. 'Of course not, Riva. I am saying that despite everything you have suffered, you are still *you* – nothing can change that.'

I open my mouth and close it; the anger choking me. 'Did you even save my life?' I demand eventually. 'Or did you let me struggle alone and simply took credit for the fact I didn't die?' My hand gropes for the door behind me.

He shakes his head ambiguously, in a way that only stokes my fury. 'Why shouldn't you believe that? Why not believe that you saved yourself?'

So is he *admitting* it – that he really didn't lift the fever? Or are his words a fiction designed to 'help' me? My lip curls at the thought.

'Riva.' There is no hint now of Myrdhin's earlier casualness. 'I know this is difficult. It might seem impossible. But the only thing stopping you from finding peace is you. I will speak to Cador about your healing—'

I do not let him finish. 'How *dare* you say this is my fault? *Mine?*'

'I am not—'

I don't wait for him to finish. My flailing hand finds the latch and pulls. Before Myrdhin – gods curse him – can say another word, I am out in the cold and running, uncaring of tree or thorn. Twigs slap my cheek; I feel skin tear. Heedless, I run on, my gait slow and stumbling – and he said *I* am supposed to heal this? Or am I supposed to accept my scars? Which is it? My confusion only fans the flames of my anger. I am no Christian saint to cure the blind or make a lame man walk. I am not god-touched like Jesus or one of his disciples. I am no magic man and neither, it seems, is Myrdhin. For all his illusions, he is nothing but a liar spouting platitudes. I swear that Father will hear of it.

I run and run until I can't recall what I am running from. All I know is that I have to get away. From Myrdhin and his poisonous words. Eventually exhaustion makes me slow, breath ragged and cold in my throat. My foot is agony, but I use the pain to clear my head. Gradually the furious mist lifts and I can see again. But the sight is unfamiliar; I am surrounded by trees and pathless ways.

I turn, heart hammering from fear this time, not anger. Where am I? Which direction have I run in? I can't remember now. This is surely still the copse – but a closer look at the trees sows doubt. They are taller here, gnarled like trolls. Their menacing expressions tell me what I already know: I am lost and a long way from home.

12

KEYNE

Can you make me as I was before?

She'd spoken in a child's whisper. The broken child she'd been on the morning she woke, alive but scarred in body and mind. We all remembered that day. Riva's words shocked me, the way she'd snarled them at Myrdhin. For a moment, they overshadow even the question I am desperate to ask. But the curtain is drawn aside and there stands Myrdhin: magic man, counsellor . . . stranger. I burst out, 'What have you done with Mori?'

It's stupid, but I have to ask it. Because the answer staring me in the face is too unbelievable for me to accept.

'Even you, Keyne?' he says and offers me a hand. I hesitate before taking it and almost gasp when I do; it soothes with the same dry coolness as Mori's, he has the same calluses. His dusky skin is the same shade of brown, his eyes that incongruous blue. But how can *he* be Mori?

He shows me.

It is more than trappings, more than the act of donning a woman's skirt and shawl. He is standing in a different way, holding himself differently too, one hip slightly out, weight shifted onto his forward leg. Shoulders inch forward, back slightly rounds. One hand on his waist, the other loose at his side, an amused tilt of his head . . . or rather *her* head because it's not Myrdhin I'm looking at now, but Mori, the witch.

'Shape-shifter,' I whisper, taking a step back before I know it, shivers running down my arms.

'No,' Mori says. 'Suggestion. Magic lets me run with the deer, hunt with the eagles, even swim with the fish. It does not let me change my shape.' She sweeps her hand through the air as if casting a charm. 'In a world full of people who see what they expect or wish to see, suggestion is sometimes more powerful than any magic.'

Her voice carries the same timbre as Myrdhin's – how could I not have heard it before? *Because I wasn't looking for it.* 'Who are you . . . really?' I croak out.

'I am Mori,' she says unsmiling. Then one blooms on her lips and it's the smile of Myrdhin on the cusp of a story. 'I am also Myrdhin.' She pauses, looks at me carefully. 'Perhaps I am simply me.'

I want to rage and run like Riva. I want the witch I thought was Mori to show me how she is two people. Paralysed by conflicting desires, I stand brimful of words. The most painful ones make it out. 'You lied to me.'

'Ah, Keyne.' She sits at the table, suddenly weary-seeming. 'Is this a lie?' She touches her face. 'Are these?' She raises her hands. 'When have I ever pretended to be someone I am not?'

'You –' but she's right. She's always been Mori with me . . . and Myrdhin at our hold. She's always been both. 'Why?' I ask instead.

'Because I am who I am.' She places a hand over her heart. 'In here are Mori and Myrdhin and each one is me.' She grimaces. 'I am glad of it these days. Because there are places Mori would be burned if she did the things Myrdhin does. And there are those who would withhold their trust if Myrdhin spoke to them as Mori speaks.'

'All right. But why weren't you Myrdhin when we first met?' I demand. 'When you gave me the bracelet? I wouldn't have been so suspicious, if I'd recognized you.'

'And you wouldn't have kept it secret,' Mori says with a smile. 'Cador and I have history. There are things I prefer him not to know.' Her smile fades as she taps the bracelet on my wrist. 'This is between you and me.'

Before I can ask what exactly is between us, Mori adds, 'I would have liked to show you the truth in my own time. But your sister forced the issue today.'

I grasp at the lifeline that allows me space to think, a chance to round up all my scrambling thoughts. 'I didn't know she followed me here. I can't believe she dared.'

'Even those we think we know best can surprise us,' Mori says. 'I worry for her. There is anger in Riva that will consume her if she cannot let it go.'

'You're asking a lot,' I say, sliding into a chair. The air feels heavy, like the sky before rain. 'She's lost so much. I'm not sure I'd be any different.'

'You and she must both stop thinking in terms of loss.' Mori pours herself more of the herbal brew from the pot. 'What about the skills Riva has honed in adversity? What about the strength of spirit that saved her life?'

A chill spikes through me. 'So she was right? You *didn't* save her?'

'Maybe I did, or maybe I didn't. She needed someone to tell her to live.'

'We've *all* told her that.'

'She needed someone to tell her she could live with her injuries at the time. That they were not the end of her, or her dreams.'

'But what if they are?' I whisper. 'What if she never marries?'

Mori sighs, and takes a sip of her brew. 'Is marriage all she can hope for? I am surprised to hear that from you.'

'Why?' I flare. 'It's what Father has planned for her.' *For us.* 'There's never been anything else.'

'And there won't be, if you confine yourself to other people's plans.'

'You don't know what you're talking about,' I say, nettled. 'You are free to be who you want, go where you want, *wear* what you want –' the words are coming now, like the threatened rain, and I can't stop them. 'You aren't a king's child. You haven't been schooled to obedience. You aren't thought of as a woman, called one, treated like one every single day. You don't have to live a lie.'

Tears sting, but they are like a raindrop to the ocean rising inside me. Lir's wave threatens to crash down, the foaming torrent of the last few years ready to wash all my defences away. I am shaking. I am angry. I am *terrified* of what Mori will say and where it will lead.

'You have a great capacity for caring, Keyne.' Mori's voice is quiet. 'It is why you suffer so.'

I turn away. It is easier to stare at the wall. What I see instead is the row of vases. The Enarees gaze out at me from their immortal terracotta, and the gaze seems to say, *I am truth.*

I gesture at the vase and the golden cup beside it. 'Tell me about the Enarees.'

'Have you heard of the Scythians?'

'Yes,' I say to the cup after a second's pondering, still not turning to face Mori. 'I think Herodotus said they were a tribe notable for their warriors?' I pause, feeling a flicker of a smile. 'Some of them were women, too.'

'They undoubtedly were.' Mori sounds pleased. 'That old fool managed to get some things right. But he was unforgivably fanciful when it came to the Enarees. Simply put, they were Scythian shamans, men who donned feminine dress and did not conform to either sex.' Her voice reaches me across a distance, as if she's speaking from a land well beyond our rocky shores. 'And they are not the only ones. The followers of the goddesses Cybele and Astarte are also known to have transcended their given sex.'

My mouth dries. I sit absolutely still. 'How is that possible?'

'Because their worship gave them a space in which to be themselves. And they did whatever was necessary to feel like themselves, to show the world who they were. They weren't forced to abide by what the Christian Church now considers male and female.'

'*Were?*' I ask. 'So they're not around today?'

'The priests of Cybele were once politically powerful. But that ended when Rome officially adopted the Christian religion.' I feel her eyes on me again. 'And the arms of that Church are long and stained with the blood of people they do not understand.' She sounds sad and angry too, a darkness of tone that suggests a darker memory. 'The point is, though: you are not alone.'

I whip around, heart pounding. 'How . . . What do you know of me, of my life?'

'Just what I know of mine,' Mori says. There is no condemnation in her, only acceptance; I don't know whether I'm ready for it. I've become so used to hiding, to being constantly on the defensive. I never dreamed I'd tell someone my truth and that they'd react without fear or disgust. It is too much to take in.

Will you help me? The question is almost an echo of Riva's and I don't say it aloud. But Mori seems to hear it regardless because she says, 'I will help you.'

That first morning, she teaches me to stand.

There is a world of meaning in a stance and the way we hold ourselves, in how we give the world what it expects to see. In Mori's cottage, I am taller. My head near brushes the lowest beam. How long have I spent hunched over, trying to hide myself? An unfamiliar ache ripples across my shoulders and I wince. 'It will pass,' Mori says with a sparkling glance up at me. I hadn't realized how short she is. 'If I had a mirror, I would show you the difference.'

'You act as my mirror,' I say boldly, 'until I am ready to look.'

She laughs and tilts her head in acquiescence.

The ache is also the easing of a burden I feel I've carried forever. Outside the cottage, the sun moves across the sky. But I don't want to return to the fort because I know this freedom is only temporary. The world is waiting to force me back into the shape it is used to seeing, no matter how false it is and how bad a fit for who I am. I know I can't ignore it forever; there is Riva to consider. If she saw me leave Dunbriga, who knows what she might have told Mother and Father?

Before I go, Mori presses a parcel upon me. It is a bundle of clothes like the ones Mother's women burned – and I swallow anger and tears. 'They won't let me wear them.'

'Things will not always be this way, Keyne,' she says and I'm drawn to the bright silver bracelet jingling on her wrist too. 'But the world won't change unless you work to change it.'

I shake my head. 'Outside this cottage, I'm no one. I don't have a voice to change a thing.'

'You are stronger than you think,' she says, laying a hand on my arm. I usually hate being touched, but Mori is different and I don't flinch. 'And the world is not made of stone. There's some give in it yet. Remember –' she moves her hand to the silver on my wrist. It heats and for a moment I see the pattern I saw before, the web that connects us all. 'Remember, Keyne. The land woke at your touch.'

13

SINNE

Keyne's lying. She does this rapid blink when she's fibbing, so quick you'd miss it if you weren't looking. But I don't miss it. When Father asked her why she'd gone out alone, she said she was looking for Riva. In his worry, he let it go. I don't.

'You might be able to trick Father, but not me,' I say when I have her cornered in our quarters. It's dusk now and still no Riva. 'Where did you really go?'

Keyne regards me, her gaze a warning. 'I'm not lying. I *was* looking for her.'

'Horseshit,' I say and watch shock bloom across her face. She had no idea I've learned such words, or dared to use them. It makes me grin inside. 'You've been somewhere you shouldn't, haven't you?'

'Aren't you worried about Riva at all?'

'Of course not,' I say airily, but now it's my turn to lie. Although Riva can be a terrible bore sometimes, she's still my sister. It's unlike her to go off without telling anyone. That's what Keyne does. The thought raises a new and intriguing question. 'I wonder how she got out of the hold,' I say slyly.

Keyne's face is carefully blank. There's something different about her tonight, but I can't think what. 'Bribed the guards?' she suggests.

We both know Riva would never do that, but I see I'm not getting anywhere. 'Father's men will find her.'

Keyne's expression hardens. She's probably thinking about the night she herself was dragged through the hold, fighting her captors. It was all anyone talked about for weeks, but they've forgotten now that everything's back to its monotonous normal.

The sun brings morning, but not Riva. We're breaking our fast with pottage when Myrdhin strides into the great hall. He tips Keyne a wink and I feel an odd surge of jealousy as her face lights up. *I've* always been his favourite. I like it when he calls me *lass* and *little mistress*. He used to swing me around as a child, but I am too big now and it wouldn't be proper.

'I heard the news,' he says to Father, who looks pale despite the eggs he's shovelled in. 'She's still missing?'

Father wipes his mouth on the back of his hand and rises. 'Since yesterday. We've searched Dunbriga from top to bottom, so she must be outside the walls. God knows how no one saw her leave. I don't suppose you . . .?' He gazes at Myrdhin as if the magician might produce Riva from a fold of his cloak, if he asks nicely. 'Can you . . . find her?'

We all know what he really means. He thinks Myrdhin can use the old magic to spirit Riva home, despite his own rule forbidding it. Myrdhin scratches his beardless cheek. 'I will try.'

'That's all I ask,' Father says, collapsing back into his chair with a sigh. 'I've men out searching, but we don't know which way she might have gone, or why.'

I swear Myrdhin's eyes meet Keyne's for just a moment, as if they share a guilty secret. I scowl. 'What if she's been captured?' I say loudly.

'Sinne,' Mother gasps from where she's seated beside Father. He narrows his eyes at me.

'Well, we've all heard the rumours,' I say. 'What if Saxons found her?'

'If the Saxons were that near, I'd know,' Father snaps. 'There are guards on the walls day and night, and scouts combing the perimeter of our land.' His face darkens as he looks at me. 'I do not wish to hear such words from you, daughter. Let men worry about Saxons.'

My cheeks flame. He makes me feel like a thoughtless child.

'Lady Sinne does, however, have a point,' Myrdhin says and I raise my head. 'If Lady Riva became lost, my lord, she might have inadvertently strayed beyond the bounds of your land. If so, it is not only Saxons we have to worry about, but King Vortipor or even King Maelgwn who might seek to hold her to ransom.'

Father shakes his fair head. 'I have agreements with both. They would not dare touch my children.'

Myrdhin shrugs. 'But how well do those kings know their southern lordlings – their subjects? An enterprising noble might seek to gain favour with their king by offering up a Dumnonian princess. Or a fortune-hunter might consider ransoming Riva back to you if you will pay to have her returned unharmed.'

Father seems to age with every word. He scrubs his hands over his face. 'Yes, you speak true as usual. Let us hope our allies are not involved. I can ill afford squabbling amongst the tribes when we all face the threat of a Saxon invasion.'

'I still cannot believe no one saw her leave the hold,' Mother says. Her brown eyes sweep over Keyne and me. 'Are you *certain* you didn't see her? She didn't tell you where she was going?'

Both of us say no, but I can see the stiffness in Keyne's shoulders; she's terrified I'll give away her escape route. I might have to, if Riva doesn't come back. My stomach clenches at the thought. *What if she really doesn't return?* I can't imagine it. Even when Riva was burned, I didn't believe she'd actually die. We belong together. There have always been three of us. There always will be.

'Might I speak with Lady Sinne?' Myrdhin asks.

'Sinne?' Mother shoots me a glance. 'Whatever for?'

I grind my teeth. She doesn't even bother to hide it – she clearly thinks I'm useless. But Myrdhin simply says, 'If I'm to find Riva, I need one of her sisters, one of her blood, to help.'

'Take Keyne then,' Mother replies with a curl of her lip, as if she finds even the merest suggestion of magic distasteful. 'Sinne still needs to finish her needlework.'

Suddenly, there is an odd atmosphere in the hall, as if the air has become as slow and thick as honey. Spoons are raised to mouths at a quarter of their usual speed. Kindling spills from a servant's arms, one stick tumbling end over end until it hits the floor a full five seconds later. 'I am sorry, my lady,' Myrdhin says and he *does* sound apologetic. 'But I have to insist.'

Keyne is staring wide-eyed at Myrdhin, knuckles white as her fingers clasp her left wrist. She, Myrdhin and I seem able to move and speak normally – and I have the fleeting feeling that we are the only real ones here. Everyone else is a mirage, a memory on the face of the land. Mother is frozen entirely, the ghost of refusal still on her lips.

But Father is blinking, holding his head as if trying to calm a dizzy spell. Is he trying to shake off this strange magic? Myrdhin gazes at him, seeming sad. Then he raises a hand and time resumes in a rush. Mother is now saying, 'I must go to Gildas and ask him to pray for Riva's safe return.' She sweeps past us without a second glance and my mouth falls open. Did Myrdhin really make her forget that she'd forbidden him to take me?

'Come then, Sinne,' Myrdhin says. In a softer voice he adds, 'Prayer will be of no use here. I can teach you something better.'

When Keyne makes to follow us, Myrdhin holds up a hand. 'Apologies. This is something only Sinne can do.'

Hurt narrows my sister's eyes and I smile to myself. Let's see how *she* enjoys feeling left out. There's a new skip in my step as I trail Myrdhin to Dunbriga's gates. 'King's business,' he says to the guards, who look confused to see me standing at the magician's side. Before they can open them, a cold voice rings out behind us.

'You truly wish to taint the soul of an innocent?'

Gildas. I roll my eyes. Myrdhin does not turn around and the priest is forced to circle us in order to bar our passage.

'I suppose it's too much trouble to ask you to move aside,' Myrdhin remarks.

Gildas extends his hands, palms up. On anyone else, it would seem a peaceful gesture, but on him it's threatening. 'You ask me to stand aside when evil is being done?'

'The only evil I see here is intolerance.' All warmth has fled Myrdhin's voice. The ribbons on his cloak snap like whips in the wind. I stare between the two of them, half of me thrilling at the confrontation, the other half fretting over what will happen if Father hears we crossed the priest.

'The king has been gracious,' Gildas says. 'He, like many other wise lords across Britain, has opened his doors to the light.' His gaze meets mine and though I flinch inside, I lace my fingers and stare straight back as if I hadn't a care. 'I will not permit you to corrupt one of his children.'

'And I will not permit you to stop us,' Myrdhin replies. 'What I do here, I do on his orders.'

For the first time, Gilda's face flickers. 'The king would never condone your . . . methods.'

I snort. He cannot bring himself to say the word, *magic.*

Myrdhin gestures behind us. 'Feel free to ask him yourself.' Then he narrows his icy blue eyes. 'In the meantime, *stand aside.*'

Gildas stumbles back, as if thrust by invisible hands. Gasping, he lifts a trembling finger. 'You may have the king's ear, conjuror, but I have his trust. We will see which is stronger.'

'I am sure we will,' Myrdhin mutters, watching the priest stride off in the direction of the great hall. The magician seems weary now, rather than angry.

One twitch of Myrdhin's brow is all it takes for the guards to open the gate. I put my shoulders back and march through, enjoying the attention.

'There's no need for smugness, lass,' Myrdhin chides once we're clear of the hold. 'It doesn't become you.'

I feel a pang of shame, only for a moment. What will he ask me to do? Maybe he's going to teach me some magic. Imagining it, I want to laugh for sheer joy. At last something exciting, something new. *Remember Riva*, a little voice whispers. *She's missing – that's the reason you're doing this.*

I huff. I suppose I ought to take this more seriously. But I can't suppress a grin as I tramp through the foliage, following a path I can barely remember. The day is darkening, as if some huge hand is drawing a blanket over the sun. With the clouds comes wind, hissing through last year's leaves. I must have been nine or ten the last time I came this way. And when we reach the glade, it looks different. I have a hazy memory of torches and skulls gazing ghoulishly down upon us. But there's nothing like that here any more. A scrap of tune surfaces and I find myself singing under my breath.

'Keepers of the Dreamtime,
Keepers of face and form,
The roots of the mountain,
Silent, asleep.
Shapers of stone, of earth and wheat,
Shapers of the land beneath our feet—'

'Hush, Sinne,' Myrdhin says sharply. 'You know not what you may wake.'

My song cuts off. I hadn't realized I'd been singing so loud. The great oaks seem to have bent towards me with a sigh and I stumble back. Then Myrdhin's hand is warm on my shoulder. 'No worry, lass. They sleep still. But songs have power – remember that.'

I swallow. 'I will.'

'Good. Now, sit with me.' We find a patch of moss clear of leaves and sit cross-legged, facing each other. The magician takes my hands and I feel a niggle of foreboding. How strong his magic must be, to convince my parents to let me out of the hold – after my Mother had challenged and refused him too. *You wanted to learn magic*, I remind myself. It's true – I do. But still I eye Myrdhin uneasily. He used to smile more than this, used to laugh with his whole body. Maybe I'm remembering him through a child's eyes.

'What do you know about the old magic of the land?'

I frown. 'Riva says magic belongs to the gods, not the land.'

Myrdhin sighs. 'This is something your father ought to have told you.' Thunder growls in the distance. 'Cador has forsaken his bond with the earth . . . and I am too late to help him mend it.'

The approaching storm whips the wind before it like a chariot. It sweeps into the grove, lifting my plaits and Myrdhin's dark, grey-streaked hair. The trees groan. 'What does *that* mean?'

'It means, Sinne, that Dumnonia has lost its greatest protector.'

'Father?' I ask. 'Because he doesn't come to the nemeton any more?'

'That is part of it, yes. But the land no longer lives in his heart.'

The listing trees create pockets of shadow where they touch, and in one of them I imagine a tall thin figure. One blink and it's gone. 'And Gildas?' I whisper.

'He is part of the severing. He and the religion he brings, that turns people's eyes upwards instead of into the earth that gives them life. But all things are subject to change, Sinne. And this change is a march even I cannot stop.'

His words make me feel small. 'What can *I* do, then?'

'Firstly, you can help me find Riva. All three of you carry Cador's blood. Together you may be enough to restore the land to its people, before the bond is broken forever.' Myrdhin straightens. 'Are you ready?'

'Of course,' I say, a little overwhelmed by it all. 'But I still don't understand what *I* can do to find Riva.'

'You and she share a connection I do not.' He squeezes my hands in his. 'Do you not also have a gift for seeing?'

My earlier excitement flares back to life. He senses it. 'Yes. Well, I think so . . . But I don't know how to use it.'

'You use the glamour easily enough,' Myrdhin says and I flush because I *did* try it on him once. 'Glamour, however, is the least part of it. For a short time, you can make people see what you wish them to see. But with training, I believe you could start to read the pattern of things to come. Far-seeing.'

Far-seeing. Although my blood races at his words, it's not all exhilaration. 'Yes,' Myrdhin says, seemingly reading my thoughts. 'It is curse and blessing both. And a great responsibility. Because seeing the future sometimes allows us to change it. And other times, it does not. You must learn to read people as well as you read the pattern of their days – and impart only a fraction of what you see.' His face is serious. 'It will take a lifetime to master fully.'

I openly deflate and Myrdhin laughs. 'Cheer up, lass. You've a great gift. Nothing worth having should come without a bit of honest work.'

'I suppose so,' I agree glumly, but my disappointment seems to fill Myrdhin with new zest.

'No time like the present to start,' he says. 'Now, close your eyes. Focus on Riva.'

Although he tells me to shut out the world, I can't ignore the cruel wind, or the thunder behind it. I shudder at the damp creeping through my skirt – it's one of my best, too – and the scuffling of dead leaves. It's the storm's fault. Who could think of anything with that gale in the background?

'Concentrate,' the magician snaps.

'I'm *trying.*' And I do try. I picture my lost sister, her brown locks and hazel eyes and abruptly I miss her more than ever. I imagine her sewing. She likes to sew. She used to make my dresses for me when I was younger. She always knew I liked blue. Knows.

I don't notice when the pictures shift from memory into something else. She has leaves in her hair and her cheek is bloody, one eye swollen. The smell of must and loam overwhelms me; she's crawling through the woods and abruptly I'm seeing through her eyes, as she uses fingers and fist to pull herself along. The sky above is thunderous and the trees are twisted and wild. Where is she? An iron taste floods my mouth. On my left, the sun hangs heavy and low in the sky. Silver threads run through the earth beneath Riva, brighter where her body touches it.

Oh, goddess. She's hurt. She could be dying. I can't stop myself reaching out to her.

Without warning, the forest transforms into rough walls. They are familiar – this feels more like a memory . . . but not my own. Because it's hot here, too hot. I would have remembered heat like this. I want to run, but there's nowhere to go. Unnatural flames skip across bare stone, jump hungrily onto my boot. The leather smokes and I yell, scrabbling at the laces, the skin on one hand blistering. Air, sweet and smelling of the sea, comes through a crack in the door, but the door remains closed, locked. The fire is *everywhere*: in my throat and my hair, shrivelling the strands. The crack in the wood darkens – someone is outside, framed against the sky. Someone small and shocked. I scream for help, over and over, the fire burning out the words. And that figure is frozen in place, transfixed. Her hands are so little. Maybe they are not strong enough to open the door.

'Sinne!'

Choking, I fall sideways, feeling moss beneath my cheek. Fingers are stroking my forehead. 'Sinne, you're safe,' a voice says. With a huge effort, I open my eyes and the fire is gone.

'Oh, Myrdhin.' My throat is scorched from imaginary flame. 'I . . . What happened?'

The magician helps me sit up. 'What did you see?' he asks intently.

'Riva. She's in a forest I don't recognize, the setting sun to her left. She's on the ground, hurt, but she's moving. And then . . .' My voice trails off as I remember the suffocating heat, the stench of my own burning flesh.

'Then?'

'I remember fire,' I say and a shudder goes through me. 'I was b-burning.'

A shadow passes across Myrdhin's face. 'I think it's time we returned to Dunbriga, Sinne. You need rest.'

'But what does it mean?' I ask as I stagger to my feet. 'What about Riva?'

'Sun on her left? It sounds as if she's at the northern border of Cador's land. I will ask him to send riders.'

It's not an answer. Where did the fire come from? That vision was far stronger than the one which had shown me Riva in the wood. It was wild, more real, and more terrible. And I am certain . . . I am certain it *was* a memory.

14

RIVA

The Lord's Prayer tastes bitter as a winter root.

Badly scratched and starving, it's the only thing I have left. I've prayed to Brigid of the warm homestead. I've prayed to Andraste of the guiding moon, to Epona of the horse-feet and to Ēostre, whose festival we are about to celebrate. I've even prayed to the Horned One, aware that he reigns in the forest. But none of them answers me.

We honour you, I think, throat too dry to speak. *You are supposed to protect us in return.* Maybe I am delirious with hunger and thirst, or maybe the leaves rustle and I mistake them for voices. But the sounds of the forest form an answer of sorts.

You turned from us, they say. *Now you worship another.*

You leave me no choice, I cry back, but the wind dies and the trees are silenced.

How long has it been? Four days? I'm not sure. I've long since lost the strength to walk on my bad foot. Now I drag myself through the dirt like an animal looking for a place to die. Something sparks in my chest at that thought. *No, I am still alive, I will live.* But I don't know how. I am lost. The forest is vast. I can barely see the sky through its twisted limbs. Once I hear water and alter my course to meet it. But instead of a stream, I find an unwholesome bubble of a brook seeping out of the earth. I drink from it anyway, but it makes me sick and that makes me weaker.

I am going to die here, wherever here is.

So I pray. Whisper words to Jesus and His Holy Father in Heaven. I pray for salvation and forgiveness for the things I said to Myrdhin, who has only ever been kind. I pray for my sisters, my parents and Locinna. I pray for Dunbriga and our people. I even pray for Gildas, who's only come because he believes in his god and wants others to do the same.

He says Jesus will be merciful and caring to those who take him into their hearts. So I do. There in the forest, I do. And the prayer grows sweeter as I speak it, less bitter, and I imagine I feel a little strength return, enough to open crusted eyes and see light.

It isn't sunlight or an end to the forest. It is a formless glow, roughly circular, darting from tree to tree. I hold my breath as it comes closer, too weary to feel afraid. Only when it hovers before me, and I see how it pulses like a heartbeat, do I whisper its name. 'Wisp.'

My voice is dry as a sun-scorched heath. I've seen them only a few times, long ago on the path to the nemeton. They help the lost and lead the wicked astray, so it is said. With the taste of Christian prayer upon my tongue, I wonder which I am. The wisp bobs before me a few times before striking out to the right.

One direction is as good as another. With a groan of effort, I use a tree to haul myself up. My legs shake violently, but I grit my teeth and take one step, then another. Tears score my cheeks, precious water I can't spare. The wisp keeps ahead, always just out of reach, and when I have to rest, it waits.

I lose track of time. It could be morning or night. Darkness closes in at the corners of my vision and I cling to the sight of the wisp as if it is life itself. Perhaps it is, after all, because a new light begins to grow in the distance, one which doesn't dart and skip.

I've spent my tears, so all I can do is choke with relief. Daylight. An end to the forest.

I drag myself towards it. The wisp drifts around my head and I reach out to it. My fingers sink into its bright heart. *I do not know why you helped me. But thank you.*

When I pull my hand back, a dark little kernel comes with it. The wisp convulses once, before its light fades, and I gaze at the black acorn in horror. 'I'm sorry, sorry –' I am gabbling the words, half delirious still, trying to push the kernel back into the wisp. But it is gone, sputtered to nothing and I am slumped alone on the edge of the daylight.

A shadow falls over me.

The shadow has four legs and it snorts, breath billowing from unseen nostrils. I try to scream and manage only a whimper. The Horned One has sent retribution for my blasphemy. I hear words, human words, though I can't make them out. Something thumps to the ground. Raising my head, I see metal-shod hooves and think, dazedly, *a horse. Just a horse.* The voice speaks again. A new shadow falls over me.

'Gods, it's a woman. Osred, come here!'

This time I understand. Hands touch me, brush a bramble away from my eyes and I see with new clarity a face looking down at me. It is framed by curling hair with high cheekbones, an unshaven jaw. A stranger. I try to sit up, to get my legs beneath me. Weakened by thirst, they refuse to obey.

'Stop,' the stranger says. 'You'll hurt yourself.' I watch his eyes stray to my scarred hand. Then he lifts me as if I am a child. My heart hammers in my chest, the terror of dying replaced by a much more immediate one. I know what men do to a woman alone. Rape is not only the province of Saxons.

'Please.' I struggle, but he just tightens his hold. We step into sunlight, blinding me after days of shade, and he lays me down on a blanket. 'No.' I try again, urging my exhausted body to move. 'Leave me alone.'

'I'm not going to hurt you.' He must see the fear in my eyes because he retreats, reaching instead into one of his saddlebags. He comes up with a water skin and, forgetting all else at the sight, I grab at it. Cool ale trickles down my throat and I feel as if I am returning to life after a spell in the underworld. 'Steady,' he says as I gulp more. 'You'll make yourself sick.'

He speaks Brythonic with a slight accent; he isn't from these parts. It is only a flicker of a thought; my attention is focused on the drink. Gradually I become aware of another man watching me, big and broad-shouldered, and I lower the skin, fear cramping my belly again. 'Who are you?' I ask.

The stranger who carried me gives a prince's bow out of the old stories: flamboyant, reckless. Curls cling to his neck, a rich auburn in the sunlight. I've never seen that colour on a man before. 'My name is Tristan,' he says, 'and this one beside me is Os.' He elbows the other man. 'Friend and reprobate.'

Os's fair hair is cropped short, his knuckles scarred. And when he grins and mouths a silent rebuttal, I see with horror that his tongue is missing. 'Yes,' Tristan says, noticing my gaze, 'he cannot speak. Raiders cut him when he was small.' Something seems to pass between the two men. 'I wouldn't trade his company for the world,' Tristan adds, 'but by all the gods, our travels are quiet.'

'That is a terrible crime,' I whisper, shrinking back.

'One we've yet to repay,' Tristan says darkly. His smile reappears a moment later. 'But enough. Who do we have the pleasure of addressing?'

I straighten as best I can while seated. I don't think my legs can take my weight and I have no wish to fall flat on my face in front of strangers. My face . . . I lift my hand, black acorn still hidden in my palm, and trace the scratches on my cheeks. A lump rises above my eyelid; I dimly remember a hard fall. Sweet Brigid, I must look a sight. 'I am Riva, firstborn of Cador, Lord of Dumnonia.'

Only after the words emerge do I realize my foolishness. It hasn't occurred to me to lie; I've never had to hide my identity. I watch the light spark in Tristan's eyes and wonder whether I've made a terrible mistake. These men could be bandits. They could hold me to a huge ransom.

But then Tristan kneels before me. 'My lady . . . forgive me, I had no idea.'

'You were not to know.' *Hush, I chastise myself. You've already given away too much.* I press my lips together.

'What are you doing out here?'

'I was lost,' I say. What other reason will he believe? 'I went for a walk and . . .' *Ran like a child*, a nasty voice prompts. What a mess I am in.

'The forest is a trickster,' Tristan says kindly, as if it could happen to anyone. 'How long have you been wandering?'

'Some days. I do not know exactly.' Giddiness sweeps me and I have to steady myself against the ground.

'Os, bring me that loaf from your saddlebag.'

The man grunts a protest.

'You're big as a boar already,' Tristan says, but with fondness, and I find a weak smile on my lips. 'Her need is greater.'

Os passes me the bread. I surreptitiously slip the acorn into a pocket before I begin tearing pieces off. I try for some decorum, but all I want to do is stuff the lot into my mouth. It is hard and stale, and the best thing I've ever tasted.

'Are you strong enough to ride?' Tristan asks.

I swallow another mouthful of bread. Only hunger has kept the fear at bay and now it surges back up. 'Where are you taking me?'

'To your home, of course,' Tristan says. 'What kind of man do you think I am?'

'I am not sure,' I answer, 'since I know nothing about you save your name.'

'Apologies, my lady. Os and I hail from Dyfed.'

I blink. 'You're King Vortipor's men. What are you doing in our lands?'

Tristan is still kneeling in front of me, which calms me somewhat. The ground is dampening his trousers. Despite the state I'm in, I note they are well made, of good thick fabric. These men aren't bandits, then. 'Nothing nefarious, I assure you,' he says, holding his hands up. 'We've had word that Gildas has ensconced himself in Dumnonia and we ride to seek his counsel.'

'He is known to be well-learned,' I admit, suppressing a swell of dislike. Gods, I *prayed* for him in the woods. What was I thinking? 'What does your king wish of him?'

'Ah,' Tristan gives a regretful sigh. 'That is a subject upon which I'm not permitted to speak, even if a pretty woman commands it.'

It's a cruel thing to say. I know I look half dead. 'Flattery is a poor way to hide evasion.'

'True,' he says with a laugh, 'but it's always worked before.'

I frown. Grudgingly and in the safety of my head, I concede there is something likeable about the man. I'm not so sure of Os. Perhaps it is his silence, or the lingering horror of his maiming, but I can't hold back a shudder when I look at him. His features are blunter than Tristan's, but there might be a resemblance in the shape of their mouths and noses. 'Are you two related?' I ask, looking between them.

'Ha.' Tristan snorts. 'No, Os is merely my countryman.'

Despite the other man's agreeable nod, something about their interaction speaks of master and servant, not equals.

'I'm afraid you will have to bear our company for at least a sennight,' Tristan says. 'Unlike you, we must circle the forest. There isn't space for the horses.'

A weight settles in my chest: the strain of being far from home and safety. Of course, I'd barrelled and bruised my way through; it was the wisp that had led me to the forest's edge. It had saved my life. And I had killed it for its trouble . . . Remembering my prayer, I feel sick, the ale churning in my belly. How easily I turned to the Christian god when my own did not answer. But the old magic had saved me in the end. What did that mean? 'Do not trouble yourselves,' I tell the strangers. 'I can find my way back from here.'

'My lady,' Tristan says, and it sounds like an apology. 'You barely have the strength to sit upright. And you admitted you were lost. I can't in good conscience let you strike out alone.'

'I will be fine.' But we both know it for a lie.

Tristan has to help me stand. I notice he is careful where he puts his hands. Perhaps he doesn't want to frighten me again. 'Surely your horse can't bear two of us,' I say.

Tristan slaps the beast's dark flank. 'He's a strong one. His name's Nihthelm.'

'I don't know that word.'

'It's Saxon,' Tristan says with an ironic grin, 'meaning *night*. He bears down on their warriors like the shades of darkness.'

I eye the gleaming stallion; he really is very fine. The name suits him. 'You've seen battle?' I ask. 'Has the Saxon advance spread even to Dyfed?'

'Not quite so far, no,' Tristan says, a distant look in his eyes. 'But it will.' After a moment he seems to recall himself. 'Os and I went to fight at Old Sarum.'

'I heard it fell to the Saxons.'

'It did.'

'You were lucky to escape with your lives, then,' I say.

'It was rather too close,' Tristan admits. I watch as he tightens his saddle girth. 'But no more talk of war, my lady. You are safe here in the west.'

'I don't know about that . . .' I am thinking of our traditions, of the way we're slowly abandoning Brigid and the other gods, of the rumoured Saxon scouts. And this unseasonable cold. Is it all a punishment for shunning the old ways? For being complacent in our security?

I shake myself. These thoughts are a distraction. I ought to be worrying about *my* security, alone in the wild with two men. But I sense no evil intent in Tristan. Even when he speaks of war, he appears at ease. And what choice do I have? He's right; I can't walk, let alone find my way back through the woodlands that almost killed me.

'Come, then,' Tristan says. 'The afternoon wears on and I'd like to cover a few more leagues before sundown.' He hefts me into the saddle; my skirts – or what is left of them – snag around my legs. I've never sat such a tall horse. Our own animals are several hands shorter. 'I'll have to go in front,' Tristan says. 'Ni doesn't like anyone but me at the reins.' Once settled, he adds, 'Hold onto my waist.'

I can't. My bad hand throbs, bloody and scratched. He doesn't want to see that every time he glances down. When I don't move, Tristan twists around. 'What's the matter?'

'I . . .' I feel ashamed, wordless, my hand curled against my chest.

'Oh,' Tristan says. 'Does it pain you?'

'You . . .' My cheeks flush. 'You don't want to see it. It's . . . ugly.' Each word is like thrusting a knife into my own flesh. I can't meet his gaze.

'I've seen worse injuries, Riva,' Tristan says. Perhaps it is his use of my name that makes me look up. 'It isn't ugly. It's like a battle scar. And you are no more or less because of it. In fact I'd say you are more for learning to live with the use of a single hand, where everyone else has two. The world can be an unforgiving place. You must have been strong to weather it.'

I stare at him, unable to think of anything to say. As his impossible words sink in, my mouth dries and my heart pounds. *I'd say you are more.*

15

KEYNE

I make my way to Mori's house.

I think of her as Mori more often than Myrdhin. I suppose it's because she was Mori when I first met her, as a lost child in the woods. But I see both now, and can hear one in the other's words. It's comforting to know there is someone so near who might understand me. Someone unafraid to be who they are.

I had to wait until full dark before using my secret passage. Guards are on constant alert for signs of Riva – or Saxons, despite Father's claims that none are near. And there's no moon tonight, so I move with care. I open my eyes as wide as they'll go, trying to follow my own trampled path through the copse. I don't want to make Riva's mistake and miss the cottage, losing myself in the wilder forest beyond.

Riva. She is an ache in my temple, a churning in my gut. I'm worried sick about her. She's been missing for days and now Ēostre is on the overmorrow. If I hadn't left the fort, she wouldn't have followed me. I know what Mori would say. *It's not your fault. You cannot blame yourself for her decisions.* But I can. I should have been more careful. I imagine her lost as I was once lost, fearful of the trees. I imagine her bones beneath them and a lump rises in my throat. Tears will not help her.

Warm light wells through the dark. I knock and open the cottage door to find Mori at her table, primed, it seems, for my arrival. 'You're here at last,' she says.

'How did you know I'd come?'

'Really,' she answers. 'You do ask some foolish questions.'

There's a retort on my lips, but I let it go. I haven't come to argue with my only ally. Instead I fold into a chair. Fear for Riva escapes as a heavy sigh. 'What are we going to do?'

Mori crosses her arms. 'Sinne and I have done what we can.'

'You said you'd sent riders north. But they're not back yet.'

'Sinne knows Riva is still alive.'

'How?' I demand. 'She won't tell me what you were doing.'

'She had a fright.' Mori frowns. 'She's never used her abilities in that way before. But she saw Riva in the forest.'

I stare at her, breathless. 'So she's really a seer?' My fingers go to the silver bracelet on my wrist. It's warm. It always is when I'm near Mori. 'Why didn't you let me help? I wanted to.' Although I try, I can't quite keep the accusation out of my voice.

'You have a different journey before you,' Mori chides me. 'And there are many things you still need to learn. Magic, or your connection with the land, is only one of them.'

I feel a bit wretched at her words. Just when I learn that magic is still alive in the land, Mori seems to dismiss it. I shouldn't care; magic hasn't done me any good, hasn't done me any bad. It shouldn't mean anything to me. But somehow it does. I can't forget that night in the sacred glade when I *was* the land, felt its very spirit, ran with its creatures. When I sensed the chasm between it and my people. For the first time, I felt I might have a purpose – if only I could grasp it.

'I . . . You . . . I don't understand.' The question blocks my throat. *Why did you show me my bond with the land, if it didn't matter that much?*

Mori sits quietly through my internal struggle. After a while she raises an eyebrow and says, 'Are you done?'

'No,' I growl, but I don't know how to ask this question. I am scared of the answer too.

Mori shoots up without warning, her eyes on the door, and my stomach flips. Was I followed? I twist towards it . . . and so miss the dagger she tosses. It smacks me on the shoulder.

'Ow!' I clap a hand to it, but there's no wound, no blood. She must have thrown pommel first. The blade skids to a stop on the wooden floor while I hold my uninjured shoulder and gape at her.

'Tsk. You're easily distracted.' She sighs. 'Well then. Pick it up.'

I stare.

'The dagger, Keyne.'

'I don't understand.'

Mori puts her hands on her hips. 'If you say that again, I will throw you out.'

'That's hardly fair,' I grumble. 'I thought you were trying to kill me.'

She gives a hearty laugh, straight from her belly. Myrdhin's laugh. 'I thank you not to insult my aim. This close, I could have put it through your eye.'

'Why did you throw a dagger at me?'

'Why do you think? To teach you how to use it.'

'I don't think you're going the right way about it,' I say before her words sink in. 'Wait. Me? You want to teach *me* how to use a dagger?'

'To start with. Then we might move on to the sword. But if you don't want to learn, it's no skin off my nose.' There's another weapon in her belt, I notice. She fingers it as she speaks.

I hesitate. 'Why?'

'I thought you might like to learn how to defend yourself. How to fight.'

'*Fight?*'

'By the gods, you are slow tonight.' Mori shakes her head, as if disappointed at my response. What did she expect? In the hold, I am a king's daughter. Daughters aren't taught to fight.

A gust slips through the smoke hole and the fire fidgets in its grate. On the floor, the dagger catches the light, sends it sleeting across the blade. 'I thought you were going to teach me magic, not weaponry'.

'I am,' Mori says infuriatingly.

I try to put the two together in my head and fail. 'What has fighting got to do with magic?'

Mori sighs. 'Do you remember what you felt when you touched the land?'

'How could I forget?'

'And do you remember how it felt at the end, just before I pulled you back?'

Mouth open to answer, I pause, remembering. *It is too much. I can feel myself unravelling.* 'Yes,' I say softly.

'You need to learn control.' Mori clenches a fist. 'The land is *power*, Keyne. It resides in life's beginnings and endings, in fire and rain and wind, in the seasons. The land supports a million lives and a million deaths. It is bones, seeds and breath. And it can rip you apart if you're not careful. I won't let you anywhere near it until you learn control. Mastery over self. Honing the muscles hones the mind.' Her expression eases into a grin. 'Besides, not all situations call for magic. Sometimes a pointy object will do just fine.'

I try to take it all in. Me, fight? My palms tingle, as if handling an invisible blade. I feel a smile curve my lips.

'That's what I thought,' Mori says. 'Now, are you going to pick up that dagger?'

All in all, I think I make a decent go of my first attempt. 'You're quick,' Mori admits as I finally manage to disarm her – though I wonder if she let me – sending her blade cartwheeling across the room. The weapon falls with a hollow thud.

After an introduction to the basics of a blade, during which I accidentally sliced my fingers, she produced two wooden practice daggers and we fought with them instead. Everything else became distant – even thoughts of Riva, as I lost myself in the quick steps, thrusts and counterthrusts while night crawled towards dawn.

Now, bent over and panting, I lean on my thighs, victorious grin fading as all my worries rush back into the void left by the practice. 'Here,' Mori says. She hands me a dagger, a real one. 'Keep it with you.'

I curl my fingers around the grip. 'Thank you.' I don't think any gift has made my heart swell like this. Before Mori, no one has ever given me anything of real use. A moment later, that warm glow falters. 'How am I to wear it? Mother would take it away if she saw.'

'We'll just have to ensure she doesn't.' Mori roots through a chest and sundry items soon litter her floor. Eventually she gives a satisfied grunt and emerges holding a scuffed piece of leather.

I blink at it. 'What's that?'

'A sheath,' she says. 'Seen a bit of use, but it's none the worse for it.'

'Didn't you hear me? I can't wear—'

'It's not made for your waist.' She tosses the leather and this time I'm ready and catch it. She's right – it's far too small to work as a belt. 'The dagger I gave you is called a pugio. Roman legionnaires carry them in addition to a sword. Strap it to your forearm or thigh,' Mori adds, tapping her own sheathed blades. 'Then you'll never be without a backup plan.'

I eye her narrowly. 'What do I need a plan for, let alone a backup plan?'

All traces of humour fade from Mori's face. Her hand tightens on the hilt at her hip. 'I am no seer. I don't possess Sinne's gift. But

I've learned to trust my intuition and it tells me that surviving what lies ahead will be up to you, Keyne, you and your sisters. All three of you must grow up fast to meet it.'

'*What* lies ahead?' I ask, joy sputtering out like a spent candle. Inexplicably I think of Gildas, his hand hot on my arm. And I remember the dream I had, the darkness in the east. *This land and its people are dying.*

'I fear war is in our future,' Mori says, 'and little chance of victory if we do nothing. If *you* do nothing.'

I stare at her. 'You mean the Saxons? They'll come here? What can *I* do to stop them? Surely *you*—'

'While the king and the land were one, no hostile intent could touch this earth.' Mori fixes me with a blazing look that's hard to hold. 'But Cador has turned his eyes and his heart elsewhere. He does not believe in the old magic. He believes in hard iron, walls and warning bells. But those are the Saxon's weapons, not his. And it is too late for him to recover what was lost.' She pauses. 'That falls to you, Keyne. I can guide you, but I cannot win this war for you.'

'This is hardly the time to be cryptic,' I protest, chilled by her words. 'Guide me how? I don't understand.'

Mori twitches. 'All right. *Out.*'

Before I know it, she's hustling me through the door. 'Mori—'

'I told you I'd throw you out if you said you didn't understand *one more time.*'

'But . . .'

'It's dawn and you'll be missed, boy. Get going. We'll speak again.'

I'm halfway across the clearing before her words catch up with me. I look back at the closed cottage door. *Boy, she said.* Despite Mori's warning and her elusive talk of war, I find myself smiling.

16

RIVA

I think about Tristan's words all that day. Akin to a battle scar, he'd said of my injuries, but they don't feel that way. I didn't earn them bravely defending my people, by swinging a sword at an enemy. My memory of that day is hazy – I was only thirteen. All I remember is arguing with Sinne and running off to hide in the smokehouse. Afterwards, Mother told me I'd been stupid and careless, and that it was only Arlyn and his master's quick actions that had stopped the fire spreading. If Tristan knew the truth, he'd never have said what he did.

I grow nervous as night comes on. Dusk lies like a geas on the land, determined to hide the rolling hills that give my people our name. Os shadows us on a big bay mare, constantly checking our surroundings, but what do we have to fear on the borders of Dumnonia?

'Who is Os watching for?' I ask as Tristan reins in and dismounts. 'You said we were safe.' My good hand has cramped in the chill, and my arms are stiff from grasping his waist. My legs ache too, unused to riding so far. I grimace to myself. If I feel like this after one day of travel, how will I feel after a whole sennight?

'Can't be too careful.' Tristan's hands are on me before I know it, lifting me down. He takes them away as soon as I have my feet and I feel an odd flicker of disappointment – alongside the affront that he touched me without permission. 'Rogues still roam the wild places.'

I take a step and my fire-scarred foot rolls, pitching me head first onto the grass. Or it would have done if Tristan had not caught me before I fell. 'Careful,' he says, setting me down on his cloak. 'You're still weak from the forest.'

It's true, but – 'No,' I murmur. 'My foot was burned too.' I regret the words as soon as I utter them. What possessed me? He doesn't want to hear about my injuries, the way they ensure I can't run like Keyne or dance like Sinne. Even unspoken, my sisters' names taste strange. They feel very far away. Tristan is looking at me, not at my foot. His lips part.

The jingle of harness breaks the moment. Os looms out of the darkness. He makes a series of gestures and Tristan nods, seeming to understand. While they are distracted, I finger the acorn in my pocket. I can't throw it away, however much I want to. The wisp had saved my life, then died because I'd taken it.

'Thanks, my friend,' Tristan says to Os. 'Get a fire going and warm up.' Perhaps he sees my flinch because he adds, 'A small one, mind. Don't want to draw too much attention.'

Gratitude wells. It's foolish, really. I'm still alone with two strangers, still in lands I don't recognize. But here, outside the hold, I am not the damaged daughter, a lodestone for pity. There are greater concerns than my comfort or lack thereof. This feels *real*, bigger than days spent confronting the tragedy of my own story.

I find myself smiling at Tristan as the small fire crackles between us. It catches in his auburn hair, gilding it, and I think bizarrely of Jesus – the way an entire religion is bound up in just one man. I've always been too angry to consider any part of his story before. Of course, Gildas would have us believe Jesus the son of god, but the Christian stories seem to emphasize his human acts, not the divine ones. Maybe that's why people believe in him.

'Are you a Christian?' I ask.

'Ah, well . . .' Tristan hands me a slice of cheese on stale bread. He doesn't mention that I am used to finer fare and neither do I. 'Christ's teachings seem good to me. I try to follow them. But my people have our own gods too, and it's no small thing putting a god aside.' His grey eyes narrow on my face. 'As I'm sure you yourself know.'

I look away, stung by the memory of the forest and my own infidelity to the gods. 'Yes,' I whisper. 'It is not easy.'

'Living never is. But that is part of its appeal.' He grins when I turn back to him and it's catching – my smile returns too.

It must have rained upriver because I wake to the sound of water.

The men lie wrapped in their bedrolls, apparently asleep, but I am sure I feel Os's gaze as I clamber quietly to my feet. Has it ever been possible to heal an injury like his? To regrow something the body has lost? I itch at the thought, wanting to try. But I only have to glance at my hand to remind myself I've tried before . . . and failed.

Through the grey dawn, I make for the babble of water over stones and find a little stream tucked beneath an overhang. I dip a hand to drink. It tastes of leaves and earth, fresher than the pitchers we have in Dunbriga. With a glance to check I'm alone, I strip a layer at a time and wash myself, sloughing off dried blood and dirt like the daub our warriors wear into battle. I'd like to wash my clothes too, but the stream is cold and, with the wind rising, I have no wish to get a chill.

Gasping at the water's bite, I plunge my bad foot into the stream, hoping to take some of the swelling down. When I pull it out, the sky has lightened and my flesh is white with cold. Still, it appears a bit better. I generally avoid the sight of it, covering it with stocking and shoon, pretending it isn't there. But here in the wild, it is somehow easier to look. I touch the skin where it ridges like the coastal dunes, flesh piled up in drifts by fire, not water. Out here, it seems the only disgust I will find is my own.

I pull my shoon back on, feeling more alive than I've done in days, and set about my tangled hair, crooking my fingers into a comb. Swirling the dark ends in the stream, a few small leaves are borne away. I have nothing to pin it back, so I let it lie wet on my shoulders.

The men have already broken camp by the time I return. Did they think I would run? Under their eyes, I am suddenly afraid again, made naked by the absence of dirt. But Tristan comes forward, stopping just shy of touching me. 'Forgive me, lady, for calling you pretty before. You are nothing short of beautiful.'

I gape at him in what is surely a most unbeautiful way before I recall myself. 'I only washed off some mud.'

He is still staring and it's beginning to unnerve me, though I can't suppress a small glow of pleasure. 'Shouldn't we be away?'

Tristan glances at Os and then offers me a hand to help me mount.

I feel a tension in him as we ride. At first, I try to keep a respectable distance between us, though what about this situation can be called respectable? My chest presses into his back, my thighs brushing his. It isn't unpleasant. But what would my sisters say, and my parents? Best they never know the details.

We stick to the edges of the forest, circling it from the east. This is wild country, ancient heathland that hasn't yet felt the farmer's touch. The glow inside me begins to fade as morning drags into afternoon. Father must have men out looking for me. Or has he given up hope? He will think a woman in the wild stands no chance at all. Especially a woman who has lived all her life behind high walls.

'Will you tell me about your home?' Tristan asks as we ride.

'Well, it's larger than Dintagel, which we sometimes visit in summer. Not as big as Caer Uisc, of course, but we abandoned that years ago.'

I can almost feel his frown. 'Why? Surely a Roman civitas would offer more comforts than a hill fort.'

'Yes, if you have slaves and coin to work them. But we aren't made of silver like the empire and Father doesn't approve of labour without recompense. Roman comforts come at a price. Others we just don't understand. For example – it's said they had the means to heat their floors.'

Tristan rumbles agreement. 'And it's not as if the Romans are going to come back and show you.'

I draw a breath. 'You think they've gone forever?'

'Well, they refused to send legions to Britain when we asked for help to fight the Saxons,' Tristan says with a hint of amusement.

'That's funny?'

'Only because they spent so much time subduing this country. Why expend the energy – and lives – only to abandon your gains?'

I think about it while the silence stretches. He's right. We might never have felt the full yoke of Rome here in the west, but we still knew we were part of something larger once. 'It's not so funny,' Tristan concedes after a moment. 'More sad than anything.'

'Tell me about *your* home,' I say.

He speaks of plains and rambling woods, where deer are plentiful and the waters run cold even in the hot heart of summer. But his words are vague and his mind clearly elsewhere, turning over thoughts he isn't sharing. Perhaps my question has dredged up homesickness.

'Sorry,' I murmur. 'You sound as if you miss Dyfed.'

He glances back. 'You could say that. I've been away for a long time.'

'Dyfed isn't that far. Can't you return after seeing Gildas?'

'I've a few other duties to attend to first.'

'Like?'

'You're very talkative today, my lady.'

I feel myself flush. 'It's . . . it's just that the usual strangers we see in Dunbriga are traders. They talk only of ships and goods and bad seas. You are something of a rarity.'

He chuckles. 'Well, I hope Os and I don't disappoint. And if I may say it, you are something of a rarity yourself, my lady.'

My heart beats a little faster. 'Me?'

'Other women of this country are not so bold. You speak your mind and you speak it eloquently. It's . . . refreshing.'

I am thankful in that moment that he isn't looking at me; my cheeks feel even hotter. 'I am no one special,' I manage.

'On the contrary,' Tristan says. 'I do not believe I've met a woman your equal in beauty or in spirit.'

I want to brush off his words, or make some witty remark. But surprise stills my tongue. He sounds as if he means it, so I don't say anything and the horse's grass-muffled hoofbeats fill the silence instead.

17

SINNE

On Ēostre morning it snows and the snow is black.

Shouts shake me from slumber. People are calling to each other, voices frantic, and I spring out of bed so fast I almost fall over. When the world rights itself, I can hear Locinna's voice and Mother's, then the deep tones of Father. Frowning, I step into view. Even Father's not supposed to enter the women's quarters.

Chaos reigns: women rushing out, others rushing in and colliding with them. 'Sinne!' Mother pulls me into a rare embrace. 'You're well. Thank God.'

'What's going on?' I say into the stiff cloth of her shoulder. 'Is it Saxons?' Mother draws back, her cheeks pale except for a smear of ash. 'Have they set fires?' I ask, alarmed upon seeing it. Panic is starting to build in my chest at the thought of our home burning, of all my things burning. Of Father being killed and us womenfolk taken by the wild men of the east – to be roughly used until we die. Suddenly I can't breathe.

'Not Saxons,' Mother says and leads me outside to see.

My relief at it not being Saxons fades when I see the snow. No . . . it's ash, falling like snow from a hellish sky. It swirls down around us, settling in a travesty of snowflakes, building up against the sides of houses, turning the thatched eaves into old men's beards. It sticks in my throat until I start coughing and Mother pulls me back inside. People are tying rags around their faces in an attempt to keep the fine stuff out. It's in my unbound hair, smearing ashy fingers on the nightdress I'm still wearing.

'Where –' I cough violently. 'Where is it coming from?'

Mother shakes her head, then looks to Father. 'Cador?'

'I have sent for Gildas.' His lips are set in two grim lines. I notice the sword at his waist and bizarrely want to laugh. Blades won't cut ash.

When Gildas arrives, he looks unruffled, though I think his face is graver than usual. No one seems to care that we're standing in the women's quarters and I'm just in my nightdress. 'What's happening?' Father asks bluntly.

'It is the shadow I predicted. I warned you . . .' the priest says. His gaze flickers briefly to me before returning to Father. 'A punishment for the unrighteous.'

Despite everything, I roll my eyes. I can see Father struggling to believe too. He embraced this new god because it made Mother happy, though I suspect the real reason is because the Christian god is popular in Armorica, and we trade more with there than with anywhere else. He's always been a practical man. Will he truly ever come to believe in Heaven and Hell, in a man born from a virgin, and righteous punishment from above?

'What's to be done?' Father's fingers stroke the hilt of his sword; he probably doesn't realize he's doing it. 'How do we stop this?'

'It stops when the Almighty wills it,' Gildas says implacably, still a picture of calm. It's because he thinks his god has shown himself, I bet. He thinks the ash proves he's been telling the truth about Jesus, the Bible and everything in it.

Father bites his lip. He wants action not words. I can't see him just sitting this out in church, praying for salvation. But that's what Gildas says we must do. 'Come then,' Father sighs heavily.

His gaze alights on my nightdress. 'Put some clothes on, child. Have you no shame?'

That stings. Mother didn't exactly give me time. I hurry to pull an overdress out of a chest. However, I've barely struggled into it and shoon when fresh shouting reaches me. *What now?* I grab a hooded cloak and scarf to combat the ash and make for the door.

No sign of my parents or Gildas. The shouting must have called them away. I hurry after, following the brutal clanging of the sentry bell. Fear of Saxons takes me again, but none of the faces I pass wear alarm. Ash is turning the muddy streets into slurry. My shoon will be ruined.

I reach the main gates. Through the swirling grey, I can just make out two figures on horseback. No, *three* figures – one is hidden behind the first. They're being escorted by scouts wearing our colours. As they ride closer, my father bellows, 'Declare yourselves,' but ash muffles his voice. I turn to see guards with nocked arrows on either side, their deadly heads pointed towards the riders.

Obediently the newcomers rein in. All three are cloaked like us to keep off the ash, which I suppose is why I don't recognize her sooner. 'Stop!' a woman's voice calls. 'They're friends.' She dismounts inelegantly, refusing her companion's aid. She stumbles towards us and flings back her hood.

'Riva!' Mother runs towards her. She throws her arms around my lost sister, no longer lost, and warmth wells in my chest. Riva's eyes somehow find me in the crowd, and a knot that's been tightening inside me ever since she disappeared unravels. She looks different, scratched but smiling confidently, as she returns Mother's embrace. Father calls off the archers and only then do I realize I haven't seen Keyne since it all began.

Riva escapes Mother's arms and goes to kiss Father's cheek. I stare. I can't recall her doing that, not ever. Father looks equally shocked, but Riva is gone again before he can react. She limps back to the unfamiliar riders as they dismount and stands in front of them almost protectively. 'Father,' she says clearly, 'these are men of Dyfed, Masters Tristan and Os. I owe them my life.'

'Then be welcome,' Father replies. But I can tell he's sizing up the newcomers, his gaze sweeping over their fine horses and the swords strapped to their sides, wrapped snugly in leather. 'If my daughter speaks true, I am in your debt.'

'Please, my lord,' says a voice. 'It is my honour to aid so noble a lady.' One of the men pulls off his hood and a cascade of fiery hair tumbles free. His eyes are as grey as the falling ash. A shiver of light runs through me from head to toe as I stare at him, unable to take my eyes from his face. His hands are gloved, but I *know* they are slender and deft. I can feel them on my skin. He's the man from my dream – still as fresh as the night I dreamed it two months ago.

Father blocks him from my sight and I'm released. *Goddesses*. I feel as if I've run a Lammas race, having poured every breath into winning. What will happen when our eyes meet? I can hardly keep from capering. I want to laugh. Because I saw him, and he came. I truly am a seer. I have magic. And he's my future.

A gasp sounds behind me. Keyne is standing in the shadow of the stables. I barely register the fact that she's wearing trousers again. Instead I look at her face and my joy falters. She is white, staring at Riva's fire-haired rescuer as if she's seen a dead man rise.

18

KEYNE

The stranger isn't looking at me any more. But when our eyes met, so very briefly, the bracelet grew cold on my wrist. Then I saw what lay beneath his horse's hooves – a void darker than the dark at the root of the world.

Dizzy, I cough ash and draw my scarf up to cover mouth and nose, breathing in musty closet instead. What does it mean? I realize I've become used to glimpsing the veins of the land, flickers like the silver tails of fish from the corner of my eye. But this . . . Where the newcomers tread is only absence. Is it because they're not Dumnonian?

Father strikes out for the main hall. In all the excitement, people seem to have forgotten the ash. Now that the gates are swinging shut, however, a small group surrounds Gildas. They are snatching at his hands, their voices a babble of fear and hope.

'Prayer is your salvation,' the priest calls, avoiding their grasping fingers. 'The Lord's door is always open to those who seek to absolve themselves.'

Most folk are hanging back, unstirred by the sermon. But some follow Gildas, trotting at his heels as he heads for the church. Many are young couples, children clinging to their waists, little faces smudged with grey. I want to stop them, to tell them that prayer is useless – but what can I offer instead?

I glance up with a shiver and get ash in my eyes for my trouble. Blinking fiercely, I hurry after Father's party before they're too far ahead, mind churning with the morning's shocks. First the grey rain, then the strangers returning with Riva. I can see my sister now, head held high despite the ash that streaks her hair. She walks close to the man with the auburn locks and I just make out her nervous smile, one I haven't seen before. I follow, feeling conflicted, as they wend their way up through the fort's terraces to the shelter of the main hall.

It's a relief to escape the ash. It's drawn a curtain across the day, making it almost as dark as night. The stench of spent embers fills the air. Today was supposed to be a celebration – and I guess it is, with Riva returned. But the last of the daffodils hang limp and it's hard to believe summer will ever come.

I choose the gloomiest corner, where shadows cast by the firelight cluster thickest. The darkness is an unwelcome reminder of the void the strangers brought with them. But it's not so pronounced now, beneath their feet, and I wonder whether I half imagined it. Nobody looks my way. As I lean against the wall, Mori's dagger presses reassuringly against my thigh.

'Make yourselves at ease,' Father says, gesturing to benches before the raised fire pit. Instead the auburn-haired man goes down on one knee and his companion follows suit.

'King Cador.' His accent is not one I've heard before, but then I've never been to Dyfed or Gwynedd. 'My name is Tristan. And this is Os. It is an honour to meet the Lord of the Dumnonii. We are envoys of Vortipor, come to speak with the priest, Gildas.'

'Vortipor,' Father muses aloud, a hand in his short beard. 'What does he want with Gildas?'

'Forgive me, my lord, but the answer to that question should be aired in private.'

Father's eyes touch on Mother, seated beside him. 'Of course. For now, you will have food and drink and whatever boon you desire for returning my daughter.' He snaps out a set of commands and refreshments start to appear in the hall. Despite his words, Father doesn't pay any attention to Riva at all.

She can't take her eyes off Tristan either. I don't think I've ever seen her wear that expression. It's more than simple gratitude and I wonder uneasily what might have happened in the wild. But there's nothing distraught in her manner; on the contrary, she shines in the dim hall like a full moon on snow. All at once, jealousy creeps through me – that a stranger can make her bright when I cannot.

The door creaks and Gildas glides in, his cassock speckled with grey like a fledgling's down. 'Ah,' Father says, rising from his seat. 'I am glad you're here. These men have travelled a long way to speak with you.'

From the safety of my corner, I watch as Tristan introduces himself. 'It is an honour, holy one.'

Gildas's attention sweeps over Tristan and Os and a slight frown appears between his brows. 'Likewise,' he says finally, though it sounds less than sincere. *Goddess, he really doesn't care for anyone.* 'From where do you hail?'

'Dyfed. We both of us serve Vortipor.'

If Tristan means to impress Gildas, it has the opposite effect. The priest's face tightens. 'A pard who sits on a throne of guile. I have warned him to change his ways in his twilight years. Tell me, men of Dyfed, does your king still consort with the sins of murder and adultery?'

A deathly hush falls. I realize I'm biting my lip – not from shock at the insult, but from trying to suppress a laugh. Tristan, so glib, is clearly at a loss for words. 'I . . .' He stumbles, seems to recover, but there's a high flush in his cheeks. 'I could not say, holy one. A king's business is his own and not my place to judge.'

Father's looking askance at Gildas. Perhaps he's wondering whether the priest thinks equally excoriating thoughts about *him*.

'A fair answer,' Gildas says, 'and the only one possible to give.' A sigh in the room as everyone lets out a breath. 'We will speak later. First, I entreat the court to come to church. This is a holy day and God is still displeased.'

Of course, the ash is our fault, caused by countless nameless sins and our adherence to the old ways. 'Certainly,' Mother says into the uncomfortable silence. I wonder whether she too heard a *demand* for us to follow when Gildas said *entreat*.

'King Cador.' Myrdhin stands in the doorway and I let out a relieved breath at the sight of him. Perhaps he too senses the void beneath the boots of Tristan and Os. If he does, nothing shows on his weathered face. 'There is no need to go to the priest's church. I can offer an explanation for the ash.'

Gildas's black robes rustle as he turns, an oddly unpleasant sound. 'The king requires no explanations, conjuror. The signs are quite clear. The skies weep a warning – I have seen it before.'

'As have I,' Myrdhin says coolly. 'On the shores of a different island where the very earth burns from fires underground.'

Gildas smiles and I feel a chill. 'That you have walked the borders of Hell does not surprise me. What does, however, is your readiness to admit it in front of the king.'

'You need not go so far to find mountains that smoke and belch ash,' Myrdhin says, narrowing his eyes. 'It is a natural phenomenon, as I am sure you know. This land was once protected from such things. The old powers would have swayed the wind, carried the cloud far out to sea.'

'I will not have my ears filled with your blasphemy,' Gildas snarls. The air seems to crackle between the two men. 'Take your lies elsewhere.'

'I do not lie.' Myrdhin fixes my father with his hard blue gaze. 'Ask the king whether I speak truth. Ask him why he does not go to the nemeton. Ask him why his harvests are poor, why his people are thin, his walls brittle—'

'*Enough.*'

Father's fists are clenched. 'None will interrogate me in my own hall.' He steps towards Myrdhin and abruptly I'm frightened for the magician, although I've no doubt he can defend himself. 'Even you, old *friend.*' The word is harsh, and not at all affectionate. 'If you have a grievance, you may air it in private. For now, my family and I will go with the priest. I have a duty of care to my people. If we have somehow offended God, I must make amends.'

Myrdhin stares at my father, stony-faced. But I've been around him long enough to recognize the twist to his mouth as sadness. 'As you wish, my lord,' he says softly.

I can't bring myself to watch as Gildas sweeps past, triumphant. Mother beckons Riva and Sinne, and I shrink further into the shadows. Even the two strangers fall into line. Soon the hall is empty but for the servants and Myrdhin, who stands alone. We look at each other – and I see that any last, faint hope he might have had for my father is gone.

I catch Riva on her way back from church. Even three hours of prayer haven't been enough to vanquish her smile. 'So you managed to miss it,' she says, on spotting me. Her eyes rake over my clothes. Although I'm wearing the garments Mori gave me openly, no one has spared me a glance, too preoccupied with Tristan's arrival and the ash. Then again, I've been careful to keep out of the way.

'What happened?' I ask, before I feel the urge to draw her into a hug. It's the first time we've been alone since she returned. She squeezes me back and we stand for a moment, as if we're both reflecting on what could have happened.

'Well.' She pulls away. 'I became lost, following you.'

I have to feign surprise. 'You followed me?'

'It was an impulse. I wanted to see where you go when you escape.'

'And did you see?' I ask, wondering whether she'll admit to visiting Myrdhin.

'I . . .' She looks as though she might confess, but then her face closes up. 'No. I lost sight of you and then must have strayed too far.'

Would she be horrified if she knew *I* knew she'd asked Myrdhin for healing? That, on being denied it, she'd raged and run? Riva is proud. She hates to admit weakness. So instead I ask the question she clearly wants to answer: 'How did Tristan find you?'

From closed and furled, her face blooms. 'I must have looked awful, half-dead and raving. But he was kind and gave me food and drink. He made me feel safe.'

The ash is still falling. We snug our hoods more tightly, feet speeding us towards our quarters. Inside, we shed our outer garments and Riva reaches up to brush ash off my collar. I can feel my eyes widening at the gesture. Where is my reserved sister with her serious smiles and measured words? Her flushed cheeks are the final piece in the puzzle. 'You *like* him.'

Her flush deepens. 'Keyne!'

'You do. It's clear.'

'I . . .' She swallows. 'He saved my life is all.'

It's not all. She's behaving like Sinne over a make-believe prince. Part of me wants to be happy for her – Riva could do with some light in her life. But I can't stop thinking of the void I saw. 'Be careful. You don't know anything about him.'

Her face cools. 'I know plenty, Keyne. We travelled together a sennight.'

'Father might not allow you to marry an outsider he hasn't picked.' Void or no, there's something about Tristan I don't like. Perhaps it's envy – again I feel a flash of it – that he's so easily able to make her smile. Truly smile.

'Really, Keyne.' It's a brave attempt at carefree, but it falls short. I know my words have touched a nerve. 'Who said anything about marrying?'

'No one. Riva,' I catch her arm before she can vanish behind her screen, 'don't get too close. We still don't know why Tristan's here.'

'He returned me to Father. And he wishes to speak to Gildas.'

'Or so he claims.'

She stops pulling against me. 'Why would you say that?'

'I'm being realistic. You only have his word.'

Riva studies me, a cold expression I don't much care for. 'Are you jealous?' she says. 'Do you wish he'd look at you the way he looks at me?'

I can't help but laugh. She's right but not in the way she thinks. And as for *liking* Tristan – 'I thought you knew me better than that,' I say.

'Sometimes I don't think I know you at all, Keyne.' Before I can reply, she wrenches free and vanishes behind her wooden screen.

19

RIVA

It's a strange feeling, this heaviness in my chest. Finally I recognize it as disappointment. Disappointment! A sennight ago, all I wanted was to be home and safe. Now I long for the wild, where there are no soft pallets, or rich food, or shelter from passing squalls. Just Tristan and me riding through the days, talking idly of our likes and dislikes, sharing ideas about religion, politics, philosophy. No one has ever spoken with me like that. Father lets me read his codices, but he never asks me what I think of them. In terms of our education, only languages seem to interest Keyne, and Sinne prefers to torment boys than read.

'Beautiful *and* learned,' Tristan had said near the end of our journey, chuckling at my blushes. 'Your betrothed is a lucky man.'

'I don't have a betrothed.'

Beside me, in the firelight, Tristan shook his head. 'I find that hard to believe.'

'You . . .' I faltered, glanced away. 'I should be married already. Mother says it's because no man wants a-a damaged wife.'

The words hung in the air between us and I wished I could take them back, no matter how true they were. I couldn't bear to look at Tristan, but he didn't give me a choice. He took my chin and tilted it towards him. My skin warmed beneath his touch. 'A man would be beyond fortunate to have you as his partner,' he said firmly. 'I have never met your equal, Riva, and more leagues have passed beneath my feet than I can recall. Do not lessen yourself.'

I was wordless then as I am wordless now, remembering. But I've barely spoken to Tristan today – he's been spirited away by Father, leaving Os behind. The man gave me a smile far closer to a leer as soon as Tristan wasn't around to see. I shudder. Keyne would do better to suspect Os of something nefarious, rather than Tristan. *How* can Tristan enjoy his company?

My hand strays to my pocket, fingering the wisp's acorn. Pulling it out, I study it in the lamplight. Apart from its ebony hue, it looks and feels like a normal acorn. Myrdhin will surely know what it is, but after our last meeting, I don't feel much like asking him. Instead I think about the wisp. It led me to Tristan . . . didn't it? What does that mean?

The door to the women's quarters crashes open and I nearly jump out of my skin. I shove the acorn into my pocket just as Sinne rushes over and throws herself on my pallet. She is a whirlwind of golden hair and flushed cheeks – two high spots of colour as round and red as apples. 'Tell me about him,' she demands.

I open my mouth to ask her to leave, but something stops me. Her eyes are overly bright, almost feverish. 'What's the matter with you?'

'Nothing.' Sinne lays the backs of her hands against her cheeks, as if she's surprised to find heat there. 'Go on. Tell me what happened.'

And I do. Not because she asks, but because it means I can talk about Tristan, have his name on my lips. I don't tell her what he's said to me, just how he found me near death in the forest, how he showed me kindness and brought me home.

'And he said he's well-travelled?'

'It seems so. He fought the Saxons at Old Sarum and he's been over the sea.'

'Where?'

'I don't know, Sinne.'

'And his horse is *black*?'

Her questions come like an arrow storm, but with no discernible pattern. I frown. 'Yes. His name is Nihthelm.'

'He didn't kiss you, did he?' Sinne asks, sounding oddly anxious.

It's my turn to blush. 'Sinne! Of course not.'

'It's unfair,' she declares. 'Why do *you* get to have the adventures? You don't even like adventures.'

'Dying in the forest didn't feel much like an adventure, I assure you.'

'Well no. But being saved by a handsome stranger, sitting behind him on a horse, galloping through the wilds, facing down bandits . . .'

'Sinne, there were no bandits.' I don't think she hears me. Her eyes have that faraway sparkle whenever she imagines herself in one of her stories. I sigh. 'Can you leave me be now?'

My little sister shivers as she returns to a present that is no doubt far less exciting than the one in her head. 'You are such a bore. It should have been me.' She flounces out.

For once her teasing doesn't needle me, perhaps because of the warm glow in my chest. 'Well,' I whisper to the closed door, 'it wasn't.'

I don't see Tristan again until the next morning. The ash is still coming down, but less thickly. Perhaps the Christian god really is listening to our prayers. As soon as I think it, I feel guilty, remembering Myrdhin's words. But I don't understand his explanation either. If there *are* islands built on fire, why doesn't this happen all the time? And how did the ash even reach us? Surely the wind can't carry so much so far. What's more, Myrdhin said it was *Father*'s fault . . . I shake my head. Too many questions without answers.

Tristan comes to kneel beside us in the cold church and I wonder whether he is trying to impress Gildas, who doesn't seem to care for him. 'That's not unusual for Gildas,' I reassure Tristan as we leave afterwards. 'He genuinely doesn't like anyone.'

'He *is* rather free with his insults,' Tristan replies easily.

'Aren't you angry that Gildas spoke ill of your king?'

He barks a laugh. 'The priest wasn't far wrong.'

I stare at him, half delighted, half scandalized. 'I'm not sure Vortipor would agree.'

'He can't very well hear me say it.' Tristan bares white teeth in a grin. 'Besides, he's probably buried between the thighs of his mistress as we speak.' I choke on my next words, cheeks hot as the sun. 'Apologies, my lady,' Tristan says contritely. 'I ought to think before I speak.'

'No.' I wave his words away, but am not so successful with my blushes. 'I'm not as sheltered as all that.'

'Still,' he says. 'I forget myself.'

We walk in awkward silence before he stops. 'Would you perhaps show me around, Lady Riva? Only if you feel recovered enough, of course.'

I have no intention of turning down such an invitation. The ash is easing more still, though the sky clings desperately to grey. 'It would be my pleasure,' I say and watch as a smile lights Tristan's face. *Sweet Brigid, when he stares at me like that . . .*

We begin at the stables and walk sunwise around the hold. My foot starts to throb, but I forget the pain, busy answering Tristan's questions. 'How many live here?' he asks.

'Well over a thousand at last count.'

'I've heard great things about the warriors of Dumnonia.' His smile buries the little white scar that runs diagonally from nose to chin. 'They were crucial to the Britons' victory against the Saxons at Badon Hill.'

'Yes.' My brow furrows. 'We probably have five hundred fighting men here at Dunbriga. But Father can call upon the whole province in times of crisis. With enough warning, he could likely raise several thousand.' I smile back at him. 'We are as prepared for any Saxon attack as it's possible to be.'

'I don't doubt it,' Tristan says, looking about him with interest. 'Is that your master smith?'

I follow his gaze and see the bulky frame of Arlyn bent over the anvil. Sparks fly from the metal as he hammers away at it. 'That's his apprentice. Farrar is our blacksmith. He provides us with most of our metalwork.' As if he feels our combined gaze, Arlyn glances up. I wave at him, but he doesn't return it, his attention fixed darkly on Tristan.

'Seems a surly fellow,' Tristan remarks.

'He isn't usually.'

'Well. Jealousy can turn a man.'

A slow flush creeps back over my cheeks. 'Arlyn's not jealous.'

'No?'

Suddenly uncomfortable, I say, 'Let's move on.' We leave the smith's apprentice to his work. I feel his eyes on me until a corner hides him from view.

I lead Tristan down to the wharves where the fisher boats dock, as well as the occasional merchant ship. The smoky ember smell that accompanies the ash isn't so pronounced here, lost in salt and sea air. I take a deep grateful breath and say, 'We might seem to live at the end of the world, but it's really just the edge. We trade with peoples all over the continent, not just Armorica.' I am not quite able to keep the pride from my voice.

'We can hardly say the same,' Tristan replies. 'Diplomacy doesn't suit our king. He has a habit of taking whatever he wants without due consideration of the consequences.'

'Is that why you're here?' I say shrewdly. 'In the name of diplomacy?'

Tristan doesn't answer and I curse myself for being so bold. Twice now he's said his words are for Gildas. 'I'm sorry, I didn't mean—'

'No, you are right.' His good humour is back in place. 'That's a large part of my role here. We are a fractured kingdom, hoping to strengthen ties with our neighbours instead of weakening them.' The wind that ruffles the water also tousles his hair. Beneath it, his skin is several shades paler than mine and Keyne's, inherited from our mother. Tristan looks more like Sinne.

I force down unreasoning irritation at the thought of my sister and say, 'Does that mean you wish to strengthen ties with us too? You're not just here for Gildas?'

Tristan turns from the sea to gaze up towards Dunbriga. 'I fear the time of being a fractured nation is nearing its end. We separate kingdoms have to unite, or risk losing our lands one by one. I asked your father if Os and I might stay amongst you for a time, so we might build an alliance.'

With a prickling unease comes hope. 'And what did he say?'

The capricious wind catches me too, tugging a lock free from my braid. Before I can pin it, Tristan takes the dark strands between his fingers. I freeze, hardly daring to breathe as he gently hooks them behind my ear. 'He said awhile,' he murmurs, grey eyes on mine. 'He said we might stay here awhile.'

20

SINNE

Beltane – the festival of fire and the start of summer

I thought I could forget my dream.

I mean, there was plenty to distract me: the black snowfall, Gildas's increasingly strict rules and the grudging return of the sun that meant we could finally plant. I don't usually pay attention to farmhands and their dull talk, but you couldn't go anywhere without hearing their groans of worry.

It's almost Beltane now and I still haven't forgotten.

Whenever I see him around the hold, it's like a beesting. When our eyes unexpectedly meet, it's a nettle bite. I had pictured our hands touching. There should have been lightning, or a song, a swelling harmony as both of us realized we were meant to be together. Instead there was . . . nothing. Polite introductions. Courtesies exchanged. Riva's little sister.

I am a child to him.

Then why did I dream of him before, as if he were already mine? I clutch myself, cold-fingered. *Seeing* is cruel. I did not know my gift could be cruel. What's worse, he hangs around Riva so. They're always in each other's company. The sight stirs something dark within me. This is wrong. It's wrong.

Instead, I go and talk at Os. Riva doesn't like him, so I make it my business to feel the opposite. He doesn't frighten me. Being tongue-less is no worse than Riva's hand or limp – surely she of all people should sympathize. Os might not care much for me, but he doesn't send me away. Even as a silent stranger, he's one hundred times more interesting than anyone else in the hold.

Except Myrdhin. 'Why are you spending so much time with him?' I hiss at Keyne over supper one night. I know she is – I've seen her slipping off on more than a dozen occasions. She *must* be going to visit him. 'What are you doing there?' *I used to be his favourite – didn't I?*

'Talking,' Keyne says. She blows on a spoonful of broth. It's not very good. The rabbits are stringy this year. Perhaps our huntsmen cannot catch anything larger without the aid of magic. Incantations to send children to sleep are not the only things we've lost.

'About . . .?'

'Things.'

I huff. 'I hate talking to you.'

'Then don't,' Keyne says, but she says it with a smile. She smiles more often now and has gone back to wearing her boy's clothes. Mother hasn't bothered her again and neither has Gildas, though I notice Keyne's careful to keep out of his way. I suppose they have bigger concerns right now.

'What does he see in her?' I mutter, staring at Riva and Tristan sitting near the fire. She seems better able to bear its heat, if he's with her. They both hold cups of cider; the brightness in my sister's eyes hints that she's unused to drinking.

'Are you jealous of her?'

'Of course not,' I say quickly. I can't exactly tell Keyne about the dream. But it rubs me like coarse cloth. 'I just don't think they should get too close.'

'They shouldn't,' Keyne says and I glance round in surprise.

'You agree with me for once?'

'I told Riva not to entangle herself. When Tristan leaves, and he has to eventually, she'll be hurt.'

It's not that I don't want my sister to be happy, but *I* saw Tristan first. I saw him for a reason, I know it. 'I'm going to talk to Os,' I say, abandoning my broth. Keyne gives me an odd look as I stump, dispirited, from the table.

Sometimes I think Os is just as annoyed by Tristan and Riva as I am. As usual, I find him in the smithy, watching Arlyn braid leather over a hilt. He comes here so often that I wonder whether he's a blacksmith himself, missing his work. But he never offers to help and Arlyn never asks. Perhaps some unspoken custom between smiths?

'Oh, Sinne, it's you.' Arlyn grunts as he pulls a leather strip tight. He has nice shoulders, better than Bradan's, but for some reason he's particularly resistant to my glamour.

I settle near Os. '*He's* with Riva,' I say. 'They're drinking.'

Arlyn makes a sound in his throat, but doesn't look up from his work. Os, of course, says nothing. The firelight flickers over his short hair and beard, picking up the blond in them. On an impulse, one day, I asked him to teach me his hand signals. I didn't expect him to agree, thought he might even take offence, but Os didn't seem to mind. 'What do you sign for fire?' I ask him now. After a short pause, he lifts his hands, palms facing and wiggles his fingers. 'Like flames,' I say. He nods when I copy him and it makes me marvel – such a simple action really does convey meaning.

'And water,' I say. 'What's water?'

Os dips and waves one hand in front of his body, like the sea.

'All right, what about a doing word – singing?'

He thinks for a bit. Maybe it's not something he's ever had to say. Eventually he lifts his hands before him and cycles them outwards. 'I suppose it looks a little like a melody,' I concede. 'What about dying?'

'Sinne,' Arlyn snaps. 'He could do without being mocked.'

I look at him, stung. 'I'm not mocking!' *And how dare he chide me?*

'You're making light of it. This is just an idle pastime to you. But it's the way Os speaks to the world.'

Os's eyes are narrow and unreadable. I can't tell if I've upset him or not. 'Sorry,' I say, feeling a wriggle of guilt and trying to smother it in annoyance. Everyone's an ember coal these days, ready to burst into flame at a moment's prodding. Before Arlyn can chastise me again, I jump off the stool and lose myself in the early summer twilight. Trust the smith to ruin my mood. Not that it needed much more ruining.

I start as a shout halloos from the direction of the sinking sun. A man passes me – Bradan's father – running for the great hall. There's more shouting in the distance and I head towards it, following the ebb and flow of voices to the cliff above the beach. Immediately I see what's caused all the fuss. Dark fingers jut from the waves: broken spars, a snapped mast, the exposed ribs of a ship. More people cluster about me as I fight forward to get a better look. It must have washed in with the tide and now the sea's turned and left it here.

My breath catches in my throat as a tall figure pushes his way through the crowd, Os at his shoulder. Riva is there too, but Tristan's long strides have left her behind. I smile to myself as I make room for the two men beside me. 'It's a wreck,' I say – stupidly because it's obvious what we're seeing. Tristan spares me a glance before returning his gaze to the dead ship. I could have sworn he smiled. Perhaps I've judged the situation too hastily. After all, Myrdhin said nothing worth having should come without honest work. Perhaps all Tristan needs is a little work . . .

A ripple precedes Father, and the crowd quiets. Even Gildas is here, no doubt pulled from his evening prayer by the shouts of alarm. 'Must have been quite the storm,' Father says, eyes flitting from spar to broken spar, as if he's watching the disaster play out before him. 'Have any bodies washed up?'

'It wasn't a storm.'

The words fall into the grim silence left by Father's question. For a moment I don't recognize Keyne's voice – she so rarely draws attention to herself. But now she's standing on the perilous edge and she's pointing at the mast. A scrap of sail clings to it, eaten away – and not by the sea, I realize. The edges are blackened. 'Fire,' says Keyne.

Perhaps the word is magic because I suddenly spot other signs of it; black smoky stains on the hull and the bit of deck we can see. 'And there,' Keyne says. I follow her pointing finger to an arrow buried so deep in the mast that even the tossing sea hasn't torn it loose. *His cheeks churned*, says Myrdhin's voice in my head, *and his hands tumbled down, and the princes were suddenly afraid.*

So am I, looking at the arrow. A piece of weed is caught on its fletching. 'What ship is that?' I ask, the words a tremble on my lips.

'Briton,' Father says, 'from the high prow, but not one of ours.' Then a new silence steals over us. Everyone's staring at the arrow, proof of an act of war.

Tristan says it because no one else wants to. 'Saxons.'

Lying on our coast's red sand, the wreck is a carcass in the setting sun.

21

KEYNE

My bracelet throbs. The moment I saw the wreck, I knew war had brought it here, not nature. Mori has been teaching me to feel the edges of something she calls the pattern. We are part of it, strands on a great web that exists all around us. The hard part is recognizing individual threads like fire and water, and picking them out of the throng. But I've seen fire before – it was the first strand Mori showed me, the first piece of the pattern.

As I stare at the shipwreck, a misty echo of flame unfurls towards me like an open hand. I shrink from that searing grip, knowing it means war, the end of everything I've known. Yet I have a perverse desire to take it too, to let myself be changed. What new world might rise from the ashes? What new me?

I blink, letting my concentration lapse. I stand above the beach, watching as Father directs men to dismantle the ship, to salvage what they can. Unexpectedly he switches his attention to me. 'You've good eyes on you, Keyne.'

I'm unbalanced. He hardly ever speaks to me. 'No better than anyone else's,' I say. 'I just spotted the signs first.'

'Perhaps because you were looking for them.'

He's right. I *was* looking for them. I never believed for a moment that this was the work of a storm. Is it Mori's warning or Gildas's threats of damnation that have me so on edge? 'Perhaps.'

Father sighs, and rubs a hand over his face as he's wont to do when troubled. He has big knuckles, knuckles he could use to strike us when we misbehave. He never has. 'I feel it coming,' he says.

I stare at him. Is this a flicker of who he was before? When he was one with the land, when he recognized the great pattern and knew the true names of fire, air and earth. When he wore a crown of light and danced in the nemeton, singing the songs that made us the strongest kingdom in Britain. 'What's coming?'

'The ash and the cold . . . I fear they are not the worst we can expect. And it will be a difficult winter if the crops fail.'

'We'll weather it.' I'm surprised at the calm in my voice. 'We have suffered bad winters before.'

'A bad winter *and* Saxons on our doorstep?' Father gestures at the wreck. 'Not both at once.'

'You underestimate our people,' I say. 'We've lived with threats for years now. It is nothing new.'

'Maybe not. But what if those threats are realized?'

It's almost dark, too dark for the men to work. Tristan has taken over – I hear him calling out, telling them to reconvene on the morrow. When I don't answer, Father seems to recall himself and remember who he's talking to. 'You should return to your quarters, Keyne. This is no place for you.' But his look is considering where it used to be blank. I don't know what that means.

I'm up before dawn to practise in the old barn.

Close to the shore and its sea salt spray, it's only used for storing tools now. Mother deemed it too damp for grain and she's the mistress of such things. Once, that would have been my future too – navigating the domestic matters of my own hold. My situation hasn't changed, but I can no longer imagine it. I suppose I never really could.

It's quiet here and safe enough to take the dagger from its hidden sheath. I run through the positions Mori's been teaching me – defence, offence, drawing with stealth, how to grip the blade differently for throwing – though she promised me a set of properly weighted knives for that. Moving smoothly from one form to another, I forget the world outside. For a while I even forget the world inside.

'Impressive,' says a voice.

My speed surprises even me. My arm whips back and the dagger spins through the air to *thunk* into the wooden wall beside Tristan's head. We both freeze as the hilt shudders to a stop. Then he pulls it free, tilts it appraisingly, and casually tosses it back. I catch it, thank all the gods, and clasp it tight in my sweating palm. What is he doing here?

'You are Riva's other sister.'

I can't hold in a wince at the statement. In the weeks Tristan has been here, I've managed to avoid speaking with him alone. We only see each other at mealtimes and exchange no more than a glance. I don't know why exactly, except that the closer he and Riva grow, the more I want to distance myself from them. I don't trust him with my sister and I don't trust my sister with him.

'You don't much care for me, do you?' Tristan says.

The barn is dim. It's hard to make out his expression. 'I haven't an opinion either way,' I say mildly. 'I do wonder why you're still here, however.'

Instead of answering, Tristan walks closer. And for the first time, I don't just see but *feel* that absence beneath his feet. It wants to smother me – like a hand clamped over my mouth. I can't help it. I take a step back.

'Keyne, isn't it? A strong name.' He looks me up and down. 'I must say the Dumnonii produce some remarkable people.'

If it's a compliment, it doesn't sound like one. The glib cast of his face is just the surface we see: thin ice on a pond. What lies beneath? The thought makes me say, 'You seem practised at hiding your feelings.'

'My work demands it.'

'And what work is that?'

Tristan smiles. 'You are not like your sisters.'

'I'm not,' I agree, inwardly marvelling at my own composure. I couldn't imagine talking like this half a year ago. Mori's influence, no doubt. 'And you haven't answered my question.'

'True. Well then, I am a servant of my king.'

'We're all servants of our kings,' I say, gritting my teeth against the feel of that wasteland beneath his feet where no magic lives.

'Also true,' Tristan concedes. 'But I report directly to him and no one else. I am his eyes and ears. Sometimes, when he requires it, I am his hands.'

'You're a spy, then.'

He barks a laugh. 'I am a bondsman, Keyne, a king's man. I go where he cannot because of time, distance and responsibility. When he needs answers, I find them.'

'And he needs answers from Gildas?'

'Some, yes. For example, how much influence has Christianity amassed in these provinces – and what are its followers' intentions?'

'Why does Vortipor care about that?'

'It is a king's job to study the way the wind is blowing. Ask your father. All leaders look to make powerful friends, and there are few friends more powerful than those in an ascendant church.'

Tristan's words ring with the metre of truth. 'And us? What friends are you hoping to make here?'

He considers me, that irritating smile still balanced on his lips. 'I did not come to make friends, Keyne.'

'Then what—?'

'I didn't come to make friends,' he says over me, 'but I've found myself making them all the same.'

I narrow my eyes. 'You mean my sister.'

'She's beautiful,' he says with a nod, 'intelligent, compassionate, all fine traits. But you've many fine people here. My countryman Os spends a good deal of time with the smith's apprentice – Arlam?'

'Arlyn,' I correct. I've seen them together on a dozen occasions, it's true. Tristan's silent companion seems to enjoy watching Arlyn and his master at work. But it's Riva who concerns me more. 'What are your . . . intentions regarding my sister?'

Tristan holds his hands up in a gesture of peace. 'Strictly proper, I assure you. We are simply friends.'

What would Riva say if she heard him? Anyone with eyes can see she adores Tristan and not in a 'friendly' way. Does she think he feels the same?

His attention shifts to my dagger. 'A pugio is a useful thing,' he says, pulling Riva from my thoughts – perhaps deliberately. 'But it won't hold off several attackers alone. You need a sword too.'

'I'm happy with my dagger, thank you.'

'I can show you, if you like.' Without waiting for an answer, he draws his sword and I tense. The light catches it, a slender glint in the gloom of the barn. The pommel is inlaid with gold. 'Your training with the dagger will help – and I won't ask where that came from – but you have to compensate for a longer blade with a greater reach.' He holds it at a slant across his body. 'Your opponent may well have a shield –' he extends his free hand – 'or might, when compelled, use the sword two-handed.'

I'm listening, despite my distrust, tracking the path of his hands. No man in my hold would think to show me such things. Tristan must know that. Is this his way of charming me, as he's charmed so many others? I can't deny its effectiveness. My fingers itch to hold the sword, to feel its weight and balance. I have a sudden vision of me throwing open the doors of the great hall, weapon on my belt, armoured in leather and helm.

But until I find out what Tristan's really up to . . . 'Thanks for the offer, but I can't accept.'

'Think on it,' he says. Smoothly, he sheathes the sword and pauses at the door. 'You could be a great warrior, Keyne. You've the reflexes for it.'

Is he mocking me? He's gone before I can decide.

22

RIVA

Beltane dawns bright and warm. It's a joy to stretch my arms to the heavens, to feel the sun on my skin after months of cold. I go to help smother the fires, proud of my calm heart and steady hand, of the way I do not break into a sweat. Sinne loves Beltane. I did too, before my accident. The day is sacred, representing renewal. The festival bonfires grant a household protection, but fire has become anathema to me. How can I revere a force that almost took my life?

Now I clean out the old winter ashes and lay fresh kindling. We'll relight the hearths from the Beltane bonfires later. Or others will. Handling ashes is one thing, but I'm not quite ready to bear a flaming brand aloft. Maybe one day, with Tristan's help.

Before I can follow that thought to its logical conclusion, he appears before me and kisses my hand, ash-smeared though it is. He looks very fine today, in a white shirt under a deep green tunic. I feel his smile in my trembling knees, and in my belly, the way it flutters. It is like this every time I see him.

Are these feelings love? The only love I've heard described is in Myrdhin's stories – when pining youths ask birds for songs, or girls dream fondly of love letters. I dream now too, but not of poetry. Nowhere in those stories is there mention of hands or lips or other things one doesn't discuss in polite company. Mother's women talk often of men – their foibles, faults and infidelity mostly, but also of the things a couple might get up to when alone. I feel heat building in my cheeks.

'What are you looking at me like that for?'

'Oh.' I can't think what to say. 'Nothing.'

'"Nothing" doesn't tend to make a lady blush,' he replies slyly and I jab an elbow into his side.

'Let's go and see if the bonfires are ready.'

'Certainly.'

He offers me his arm and I take it, appreciating his strength, the firmness of muscle under cloth. Sweet Brigid, I am getting as bad as Sinne.

In an effort to dispel my blush, I ask, 'Do you celebrate Beltane in Dyfed?'

'Of course,' he answers. 'But, being on the road, I've missed it the last few years. It will be nice to see it again.'

'How long have you been away from home?'

Tristan screws up his face, as if unsure. 'Four years? You lose count after a while.'

'I can't imagine that.' But then, I've never left home – save for the time I lost myself and he found me. Trips to Dintagel hardly counted – it's well within the borders of our territory. I look side-long at Tristan. What will I do when he finally returns to Dyfed? Will Father let me go with him? He'll surely see the sense in having marriage ties to a neighbouring kingdom. It will be the best way to unite us against invasion.

What am I doing? My thoughts have run away with me – I've known Tristan mere weeks. As we reach the unlit fires laid in a space on the second terrace, I shake my head, trying to rid it of foolish musings.

At least eight cubits tall, the bonfires tower over me, great pyra-mids of birch, and I can't help flinching at their imagined heat.

Beside me, Tristan squeezes my arm. 'I always forget how large they are,' I say.

'They will burn bright and sweet,' he replies, 'and you need not stand close. But I think you are braver than you admit.'

I grimace. 'I'm not. I can barely look at a fire without fear.'

'And yet you've spent the morning with them.'

'That's different. They were out.'

'There you go again,' he chides me. 'Have some pride in yourself, Riva.'

'There will be dancing,' I say to change the subject. 'And fire-jumping when the bonfires slump.'

'Now that's something I'm looking forward to.' Tristan gives me a wink. 'I might give it a try myself.'

I look at him, wide-eyed. 'It's dangerous. You could get burned.'

'What is life without a little danger?'

'You're impossible.'

'Only when I'm around you,' he says.

I turn to wave at Sinne before he can catch me blushing again. She is already clothed for festival, her golden hair half braided, the rest trailing over her shoulder. She's wearing a new dress, blue as the summer sea, embroidered with flowers I know she didn't sew herself.

When she shines her dimpled smile on Tristan, I regret waving her over. He's staring at her and my heart sinks. 'Happy Beltane,' Sinne trills. 'Have you come to see the fires being lit?'

'We have,' Tristan answers with a glance at me. He must register my stormy expression because his smile fades and he reaches for my arm. It's petty but I draw him away, unwilling to watch Sinne toying with him. If she even *thinks* about trying out her glamour . . .

A crowd is gathering now, eager to see the torch-bearers open the festival. Not all faces wear excitement, though. Farmers gaze at the bonfires with gloomy hope and I know they are thinking of their crops and the cold, the possibility of failure. But today we'll drive the animals out to summer pasture, blessed by fire, and with luck they will grow fat and healthy and the crops will flourish. It is why we celebrate Beltane, after all. Gildas has been vocal in his disapproval, but even he hasn't managed to put a stop to it.

Hands beat skin drums and the rhythm thumps in my ribcage. A great 'Halloo!' comes on the wind: the sign to touch torch to kindling. When the bearers retreat, hungry flames lick at the base of the bonfires, leaping from branch to branch with a crackling *whoosh*. The halloo again – and now the cattle are being driven towards us up the dirt street, figures chivvying them along. The crowd edges back to give them room.

Farmhands steer the cattle, but I recognize two others in their midst: Myrdhin and Keyne. My sister is hallooing with the rest, clapping hands and keeping the animals in neat formation. The shaggy cows approach the fires, stiffening at the flames. Keyne shouts something to Myrdhin and he steps close to the animals, his lips moving.

Whatever magic he whispers seems to work; the cattle pass meekly between the bonfires then down towards the gates of the hold, where farmers take charge of them.

'Does your sister make a habit of herding cattle?'

I glance at Tristan. 'No, I've never seen her do it before.'

'She's . . . unusual.'

'She's Keyne,' I say, and feel a touch of pride.

'Are you angry with me?' he asks after a moment.

I study him. The sun is at his back, lighting his auburn hair and leaving his eyes in shadow. 'I'm not,' I say truthfully. 'Besides, it's unlucky to be angry on Beltane.'

'Later,' Tristan says, taking my unburned hand and kissing it again – I shiver at the touch of his lips – 'I hope you will dance with me.'

'Dance?' I gesture at my foot. 'I haven't danced in seven years.'

'That's because you've had no one to dance *with*,' he says, winking.

I laugh, but it rings into a sudden silence. The crowd has fallen quiet. All I can hear is the crackle of the flames as they eat their way towards the sky. Gildas has arrived, cutting a stark figure against the backdrop of bright tunics. He stares at the bonfires and the torch-bearers still carrying their brands before he turns on the rest of us.

'You invite the Devil amongst you?' He has no need to raise his voice. 'You light fires to welcome him inside this hold that I have sanctified to *God*?'

No one answers.

'What evil urge compels you to summon one who will lead you into sin?'

'This is not evil.'

My stomach feels full of lead as Keyne faces Gildas across the fire. 'These flames are sacred,' she says, 'part of a pact we share with the land. It keeps us safe – and strong.'

The priest's lip curls as he regards Keyne. '*You* already walk a damned path. There is no need to take innocents with you.' He points at the flames. 'In the Lord's name, let this fire be quenched.' And amazingly, the bonfires shrink, withering under the weight of that condemning finger. Gasps reach me. A few people are on their knees now, hands raised to faces in shock. Keyne's own face is white.

It takes me several moments to realize someone is laughing: Myrdhin stands doubled over on the edge of the crowd. Shoulders shaking, he turns to Gildas, and I see the mirth doesn't reach his eyes. 'Look what you did,' he says, still chuckling. 'And you call *me* a liar.'

'You speak in riddles,' Gildas replies.

'And you in hypocrisies.' Myrdhin tilts his head to regard the priest, something of the falcon in his look. 'Do you know what it is you do when you call on your god's power? Or do you tell yourself it is his will working through you?'

I think I see the priest tremble. 'Do not mock me, magician.'

Myrdhin clicks his fingers. The fires surge up again with a roar and Gildas staggers back, as if struck. Beside me, Tristan hisses in a breath, his eyes wide on the flames. 'Do you want to try again?' Myrdhin asks coldly. 'Perhaps you were not devout enough in your prayer –'

Gildas turns on his heel and leaves, walking quickly. Those on their knees rise, some going to Myrdhin, others to the fires, clearly relieved. Have we really just seen the will of the Christian God? Did Myrdhin really oppose Him? The magician gazes after the priest, an indecipherable furrow between his thick grey brows.

They begin arriving at noon for the festival: Dumnonian nobles from surrounding holds and their retinues. They bring Father tribute – all sorts of things, from honey and barrels of salt to wooden carvings and fine leather saddles. I spot Keyne eyeing a brace of knives and the bandolier that holds them. She even runs her fingers over their hilts, until Mother stops her with a word. Sinne is more interested in a bolt of green cloth and a little wooden sparrow, so real it seems it will fly at a moment's magic. My own hands itch for a couple of codices gifted to Gildas from Banon Bedeu, master of Moriduno, a settlement to the north-east. 'They will be safer with you, good priest,' the ageing man says. 'Saxons are known to be free with their torches.'

'You fear an attack?' Father asks, brows coming together.

'We would be foolish not to worry. Badon Hill was fought near half a century ago and Gewisse raids are spreading further west. It's that damned son of Cerdic who's been leading them the last few years – Cynric.'

Father frowns. 'Those are not Saxon names.'

'Cerdic's mother was a Briton, it's said. But the rest of him's as

Saxon as they come. And his son is worse. They're busy building themselves a kingdom in our lands. The whole of the east has fallen to them, from Glevum to the Isle of Vectis.'

'We saw evidence of fighting at sea,' Father admits. 'A ship wrecked off our coast.'

'Then it has already begun.' The old man hangs his head. 'I hoped I would not live to see war renewed.'

'We will push them back,' Gildas says, looking even paler than usual. I haven't seen him since the events of the afternoon. 'This is a Christian land, where their heathen gods are weak. If Our Lord wills it, and if the people are pious, we will build a new Israel here in Britain.'

It is too merry a night for talk of Saxons, though. The doors of the hall stand wide so all can see the people carrying fire from house to house, relighting their hearths with fair fortune. Myrdhin goes with them and I wonder whether he means to keep Gildas away, in case the priest plans to interfere. We eat the first of the fresh cheeses with rhubarb pies and early raspberries still a little green from the bush. Meat roasts, cider flows and men bang cups on tables, forgetting talk of war.

And at some point in the evening, when I've drunk too much to refuse, Tristan asks me to dance. Lyres and fiddles carry a lively tune – I know a few of the songs, but other players have come with our guests, plucking refrains I haven't heard before. It isn't quite dark outside, the May dusk drifting through the open doors, woodsmoke on the wind.

Before I know it, his hands are on my waist and he is lifting me effortlessly, my toes brushing the ground. I laugh. I can't help it, with cider in my veins. Supported, I spin with barely a stumble and entirely forget to blush. The melody is in us both. We seem of one body, each knowing where the other's feet will be, when to part and when to come together. I am aware of people around us, but little else – save for Tristan's earnest gaze and the half smile he seems always to wear, as if he finds the whole world a jest.

It feels as if we dance for hours before the music pauses and I realize my heart is fit to bursting with exertion. Even Tristan's cheeks are pink, so with a gentle tug I draw him outside, appreciating the cool air on my skin. The players strike up a new tune behind us and the sweet strains of the lead lyre catch on the wind. They swell out to us, as we rest beneath the boughs of the old oak growing beside the hall.

We lean against its trunk, spent, until our breath returns to us. 'Thank you,' I say when I can. 'I haven't danced like that in . . . well, ever, really.'

'It's been a while,' Tristan agrees, still a little out of breath. 'Work rarely affords me time for merrymaking.'

'A shame, for you are good at it.' My cider-tongue is running away with me, but I decide I don't care. Not tonight.

'As are you,' he says with a light touch on my arm.

I laugh. 'Sinne wouldn't agree. She spends half the time telling me I'm a bore.'

'That's a sister's job, is it not?' He doesn't wait for me to respond before adding, '*I* don't think you're a bore.'

'Do you have a sister?' I ask, rather quickly.

Tristan shakes his head. 'I'm my father's only child.'

'That must have been lonely growing up.'

'We were always on the move. I didn't have much of a childhood.'

'I can't imagine that,' I say, staring into the dusk. 'Apart from Caer Uisc, I've always lived here.'

'I can think of worse places to live.' Tristan gives me a gentle nudge. 'And you had a real magician to entertain you.'

Something about his tone makes me pause. 'Do you mean you've never met one? Never seen magic?'

'Even the word sounds exotic,' Tristan says. His eyes gleam in the torchlight. 'What can he do? I mean apart from summon fire?'

'Oh, not as much as he claims, I bet.' It comes out sounding caustic. Am I really still so angry with Myrdhin? 'But he tells excellent stories and his illusions are marvellous.'

'And what of your father?' Tristan asks. 'It's long been rumoured that the King of Dumnonia is a magician himself.' When I don't answer immediately, he adds, 'Apologies. That was rather personal. It's just I've seen no sign of King Cador's abilities. Are the rumours false?'

When I was a child, my father wore a crown of light. The spirits of the ghost fence used to stand at our borders, fighting for us against raiders, sparing our men. Our harvests were so rich we fed half of Durnovaria as well as ourselves.

'The rumours are false,' I say softly, remembering my attempt to heal Siaun and the fading spark of my power. 'Myrdhin is the only magician here.'

For a while we watch the bonfires one terrace below us, safe beneath the shadow of the great tree. Figures dance around them, waiting until the flames are low enough to leap.

'I don't want you to leave.' The words have been on my tongue for days, but I've always managed to hold them back. Now the dancing has freed them – and the night.

Tristan turns to look at me. With the bonfire behind and below him, the tips of his hair seem like stray sparks. I ache to touch them and raise my fingers, dream-slow.

He catches my hand. 'You don't know what you say,' he whispers.

My heart pounds – from the drink, from his nearness. I feel his touch as a shiver low in my belly. We stare at each other and I wonder only fleetingly what he sees. Then his hand is against my cheek and his mouth covers mine in a rush of heat.

I've dreamed of this moment, but now that it is here, I have no idea what to do. One arm hangs useless at my side, my other hand still caught in his. But Tristan holds me close when my knees threaten to give way, easing his lips over mine, sweet and insistent. My back presses against the bark of the tree and all of a sudden it is too much, too fast. He pulls away and I don't know what I want more – half of me wishes he'd take up kissing again while the other feels like fleeing to my room, hiding my flushed cheeks in a pillow. What would my parents say if they saw?

'Apologies, my lady,' Tristan says a touch shyly. 'I forgot myself for a moment.'

'I think I did too,' I murmur, still battling opposite desires. Tristan makes the decision for me by stepping back, and now I can hear the swelling crowd as voices call out to summon friends to the fire. The drummers take up the beat again. 'Are you really going to leap it?' I ask.

Tristan follows my gaze. We have a good view from up here. I watch his eyes alight on a single figure, standing with rolled up sleeves. 'Of course,' he answers, 'I can't very well be outdone by your sister.'

23

KEYNE

I'm watching the girl.

I think she came with Banon Bedeu, but I can't be sure because I haven't plucked up the courage to speak to her. She's finely dressed – perhaps a niece or cousin of the old master. I lean against the wall, half in shadow, while the revelry clatters on around me and the girl dances with Bradan then Arlyn and half the other young men of the hold.

'There you are.' Sinne thrusts a tankard at me, foamy with ale. 'Drink up and stop skulking. It's Beltane.' She doesn't sound too happy about it, though. Her eyes stray from me to the space cleared for dancing. I think she's staring at the girl too until I spot a couple turning dangerous circles and scattering other dancers.

'She's like a scarecrow,' Sinne remarks.

There *is* something haphazard about Riva's dancing. I suppose it's because she's seven years out of practice and hampered by her foot. From the look on her face, I can tell she doesn't care. Mother is watching her with half-speculative eyes, and suddenly I fear she'll intervene.

The music ends and I square my shoulders. Time to give Mother something else to worry about. But as I walk towards the girl, my stomach flips and I feel as if a tiny sun has come to shine directly on me, lighting my intentions to the room. It's too late now. The girl has seen me. Her gaze travels over me, over the fine set of clothes I'd hidden away: a black tunic and undershirt, trousers and shoon, my calves wrapped in leather. The outfit feels a little tight on me now – Mori's training has strengthened the muscles in my arms and back. It hurts to hunch as I used to, so I walk straight, trying for confidence.

'May I?'

The words come out gravelly with nerves, but she blushes a little and nods, and surprise gives me the courage to ask her name.

'Gwen,' she says, no more. I don't need more. The name suits her soft brown curls and eyes. Arlyn, her last partner, gives me a startled look, words on his lips. But I glare at him until he shrugs and moves away. I watch him settle in my old place against the wall, eyes on Tristan. They are hard and narrow.

Gwen and I stand opposite each other in line with the other dancers. As the harp strikes up, I wonder what she sees. My dark hair is pulled into a warrior's tail at the nape of my neck. In a room full of beards, my face feels very bare. What am I doing here? Mother will be furious. But isn't that why I did it? So Riva can enjoy her dancing undisturbed? I suspect the real reason might not be quite as altruistic.

The steps are complicated; I am taking the man's part, of course. However, Mori's quick footwork aids me and I fall into the rhythm as if it were a second heartbeat. I feel a brief terror at touching Gwen's hand, of her own on my shoulder, but the dance demands it and we follow along. My blood races at my daring.

She is soft, softer than I'd imagined in her dress of fine red wool. For a mad moment, I allow myself the fantasy of kissing her, here in front of everyone. The way she's looking at me . . .

When the music ends, we stand panting, our hands still joined. I can't help noticing the fullness of her, the hint of breast and curve of hip. There's a light sheen on her skin; the hall is hot with fire and food and the plucking of strings. We are staring into each other's eyes and I am barely aware of those preparing for the next dance.

'Lady Keyne!'

I turn my head with difficulty. There's a serving girl bobbing at my side. 'Lady Keyne,' she says again. 'The queen wants you.'

In an agony of slowness, I watch Gwen process the words. Those brown eyes widen and she steps back, sweeping them over me anew, searching me out. 'Gwen—'

'You're a . . .' She stumbles back a few more steps, her cheeks flushed with shame. I am sick to see it. 'What do you think you're doing?'

'I'm sorry. I didn't mean to—' She doesn't wait to hear what I didn't mean. Without another word, she loses herself in the ebb and flow of the hall and I am left thinking that in fact I *did* mean to, all along.

Riva and Tristan have disappeared. That's something, I suppose. I follow the serving girl on a winding path to Mother, who has chosen as discreet a corner as possible to receive me.

'What do you think you are *doing*?' she hisses at me as soon as we're alone and it's a horrible echo of Gwen's words. 'Making a spectacle of yourself in such a way.'

I don't answer. I can't stop seeing Gwen's expression, the way it curdled like bad milk.

'Well?'

'What do you want me to say?' I ask dully.

The question seems to stump her. She gazes at me, at my clothes and hair, at the only trappings I have to tell the world who I am. They are not enough. They have never been enough.

'You are my daughter,' Mother says then. 'Not my son.'

I stare at her in a kind of icy shock. That she would even put it into words. I am ill prepared for this conversation, I realize. No time to marshal my arguments, my feelings. And I am too muddled by Gwen, blown off course by our encounter. 'I . . .' I croak.

'All I ask is that you remember it.'

She's gone before she risks hearing my answer, and I am alone once more in the trembling shadows. 'How can I forget?' I say to her retreating back.

Anger is rising in my veins, desperate for freedom. *Have to get outside.* I skirt the hall, avoiding people, pushing past them when I can't, leaving a trail of irritated whispers in my wake.

Night has ridden in on the clouds while I danced and the Beltane fires burn like the eyes of Gildas's devil in the darkness. Much of the crowd follows me out, spilling raucous songs to the sky, to any gods who might be listening. As we descend towards the fires a terrace below, a rolling clap begins, emboldened by drums, summoning those brave enough to leap the flames.

The fire is kin to the anger in my blood. It calls to me. Some instinct turns my head and there at the crowd's edge stands Myrdhin. His eyes meet mine.

Before any of them realize what I'm about to do, I kick off my shoon and step into the cleared space, facing the fire's heat. It's been burning for hours, a veteran blaze, and I am just a novice in its eyes. Still, I plant my feet, feeling the muscles contract in my thighs. I fix my gaze on the flames, searching out their pattern. It's chaotic, all fire is. Not fluid like water, or stable like earth. Even air has an order, Myrdhin says, blowing with the wind, hanging in the heat.

Pipes and lyres join the drums, wild timbrels that seem to leave trails of light in the air. I remember standing in this place as a very young child and watching a great figure, horned like the old god, green-shouldered and bearded. He bent to scoop a handful of fire in each hand. He was laughing, head tipped back to the stars. He was my father.

I raise my foot and stamp it hard on the earth.

Silver answers. It bursts out, spanning the gap between the bonfires and I follow, dancing between them, the bracelet hot on my wrist. I'm only dimly aware of the gasps of the crowd and the light dripping from the soles of my bare feet. It is a wild dance. The magic is wearing me like a skin; there's a glow beneath my palms. Words reach me as I spin around the great bonfires, borne on the strains of the lyre. A sweet voice like a bird, like a brook: Sinne. Of course it would be Sinne.

> 'I go as wren and come as hawk,
> I sing as thrush and die as dusk,
> I rise as dawn and fall as rain,
> What, pray tell me, is my name?'

Other voices take up her song; it's an old one, the oldest Beltane tune. I can still hear hers amongst them, soaring the highest. My sister's voice calls to me as powerfully as the fire. *I rise as dawn.*

> 'I swim as trout and howl as wolf,
> I shine as moon and fear as mouse,
> I hunt as owl and fish as crane,
> But who amongst you knows my name?'

It is like the night in the forest when Mori pressed my hand to the earth. As I dance, I am suddenly with them, all Sinne's creatures, lives lived in the bosom of the land. I open a thousand eyes, but what I see is a desert. Apart from the magic I am calling up through the fire's pattern, the land's veins are faint, fading.

> 'I am as light and am as dark,
> I am as birth and am as breath,
> I am as flesh and bone and brain,
> Look inside and know my name.'

Haunted by my glimpse of devastation, I see a pause in the fire's pattern and run for it, my soles beating the earth, body flying for the brief gap between the flames. It's hot, a shade away from pain. I feel as if the fire lifts me, sends me hurtling over and out, as if eager to be rid of me. I land and roll and spring to my feet on the far side, the heat inside me abruptly quenched.

I straighten to see watching faces.

For someone used to shadows, the attention is blinding. So is the silence. The drums have ceased. Instead I am the centre of a storm of eyes. I spot Sinne's golden hair amongst the watchers. We look at each other, the echo of her song between us. There is something in her expression I cannot read.

A single slow clap rings out and I turn with everyone else, searching for its maker. Tristan steps into the space, still clapping. With a nod to my unscorched clothes, he calls, 'I should think some applause is in order for the first to brave the flames.'

He is answered by a half-hearted smattering of hands. I shake myself. It feels as if I'm waking from sleep, tatters of dream clinging to my mind. Roused now, people are beginning to mutter and I realize no one has danced with the fire since Father himself.

'What is this power?' Tristan asks me, eyes like dark mirrors.

'The land,' Myrdhin says, coming forward. He looks frail next to Tristan, the night leaching his cape of its bright hues. 'The Dumnonian birthright.'

'Remarkable. I've never seen its like.'

Riva joins us, colour in her cheeks. 'Dyfed has no magic at all?'

After a heartbeat, Tristan says, 'I am a warrior who knows only the blade.'

A slight movement snags my eye. Someone is there, a figure in the shadows, almost escaping my notice. When I meet that hidden gaze, the figure turns away. But not before I catch the glint of gold upon my watching father's brow.

24

SINNE

I can still see it; the memory is like a stone around my neck. The way their lips came together, his hand on Riva's chin to tilt it just as he did in my dream. My stomach lurches; what if it wasn't my dream, but Riva's? What if I saw him through her eyes all along? I don't know enough about far-seeing to answer my own tormented questions.

The unfairness leaves me sick. The jealousy is worse. I tell myself I don't care, as I lean against the stable wall, watching others take their turns at leaping the fire. Tristan has a go, launching himself just before his foot touches the smouldering edge. Even I see he's timed it badly. He spends a moment wreathed in fire like some avenging spirit; the next he's rolling on the ground, trying to smother the flames in his clothes. Men rush forward to help, but Tristan is up and thrusting his fists into the air to a roar of cheering that should have been Keyne's.

That last great leap of hers was stupid and dangerous but oh – the faces! After the first shock, I'd looked around at all those gormless expressions and laughed to myself. I've no idea what Keyne's up to – dallying with that girl, throwing herself across fires – but she makes life interesting. And her dance . . . I'd thought only Father could dance with the fire.

I hear voices. The tone of them draws me: sober when others are drunk on ale and revel. It's getting late now, past midnight, and I wonder who could still be up. Locinna has been looking for me, but I don't feel like sleep. The moment I close my eyes, I know what I'll see. I'll see *them*. So I follow the voices instead, scurrying behind a cart divested of its kegs, peering around it.

Keyne stands eye to eye with Gildas. The crow is almost invisible in the darkness – born out of night itself. I strain my ears.

'If you have come to scold me for my actions, you need not bother,' Keyne says and even I'm shocked at her presumption. I've never heard anyone speak to Gildas like that. Except Myrdhin.

Clearly neither has he: his brows draw down until he looks more like a carrion bird than ever. But instead of chiding her, he says, 'I have come to ask a favour.'

Keyne looks as surprised as I feel. I'm sure she expected fire and brimstone. 'A favour,' she repeats in a tone of disbelief.

Gildas lowers his voice even more and I struggle to pick out his words against the backdrop of other sounds: drunken yells and clanging, the odd hoot of an owl somewhere above. '. . . sent a message to Vortipor,' the priest is saying.

'Why?'

'I wish to know the real reason behind Tristan's presence.'

'This – favour – is about Tristan?' Keyne says.

'Do not play ignorant, girl. The entire hold has seen him with your sister.'

'Do not call me "girl",' Keyne snaps back. 'They are just friends. And why does this investigation of yours involve Riva at all?'

'Because she must *know*.' Gildas raises a robed arm, shakes it in the general direction of the church. 'For all his talk of seeking me out to discuss holy matters, the man spends little to no time in my company. Your sister seems to have his undivided attention.'

She does, I think bitterly.

'It doesn't necessarily follow that he would confide in her, or share his intentions,' Keyne replies. I can tell she's uncomfortable from the set of her shoulders, but she faces Gildas head-on. She's braver than I am, I admit. I wouldn't want the crow looming over me like that.

'It matters not,' Gildas says after a moment. 'Vortipor will tell me the truth.' Remembering his scathing attack on the adulterer king, I'm not so sure. Gildas isn't the sort of person to hide his opinions, even from kings. Especially from kings. And that doesn't gain their favour. 'In the meantime,' he continues, 'will you do as I ask? Will you watch him?'

'I won't do anything for you. Do you think I've forgotten what you did to me at Imbolc?'

They regard each other in hostile silence, the tension like an imminent storm between them. 'You are a godless creature,' Gildas says without malice. 'So I cannot tell you that aiding me is His will. But you are well placed to watch Tristan. You possess certain . . .' he is clearly struggling with something, 'attributes.'

'What attributes?'

For a moment I don't think the priest will reply, but reluctantly he says, 'You have talents that stem from your blood. Do not pretend otherwise – I saw what you did tonight. It is why Myrdhin takes an interest in you.'

'He certainly does. But don't frighten the boy.' Heart in my mouth, I whip around. Myrdhin is standing right next to me and I swear his eyes dip to my hiding place before they return to Gildas.

'She is no boy,' the priest spits, but his face has paled at the sight of the magician.

'He is who he is. The world cannot change that and neither can you.' Myrdhin's natural humour is gone. I've never heard him sound so serious, even when Riva was missing. And what he said about Keyne . . .

'I have nothing more to say to you, pagan.' That pallor is still in Gildas's cheeks. He's easing back, I notice, away from Myrdhin. 'I should have known better than to ask anything of heathen witches.'

'What do you see when you look in the mirror, priest?'

Myrdhin's words are simple enough, but they have a remarkable effect on Gildas. His steady retreat turns into a stumble. 'You cannot run from it,' Myrdhin calls after him. The wind snatches at the magician's cloak, whirling its myriad ribbons like a bee swarm. 'And you betray your own by denying it.'

'What was that about?' Keyne asks Myrdhin when it's clear Gildas has gone. 'And why does he want me to watch Tristan? Is it to do with the void I feel beneath Tristan's feet?'

I find myself frowning. What void?

'Tristan is not tied to the land,' Myrdhin says. 'What you're sensing is a lack of Dumnonian heritage.'

'Then why don't I feel a void beneath Gildas, or you?'

Myrdhin raises his voice. 'You can come out now, Sinne.'

I emerge guiltily. 'What are you doing here?' Keyne demands. 'Were you spying on me?'

'No . . .' Well, of course I was. I look to Myrdhin for help, but he just shrugs, and I feel a flicker of resentment that he gave me away. 'I happened to be passing,' I say with a shrug of my own.

'Little point arguing now,' Myrdhin says before Keyne can voice her obvious scepticism. 'Better to ask Sinne what she thinks of Gildas's request.'

What *do* I think of it? 'You heard him,' I say. 'The priest is just jealous that Tristan is spending time with Riva. Most people come here to talk to *him*.'

'I don't think so.' Myrdhin gazes into the darkness after Gildas. 'It's clear he mistrusts Tristan. I wonder why.'

'Do *you* trust him?' Keyne asks.

'I have a healthy distrust of most people.'

I feel excluded, as if they're discussing a secret right in front of me. First Tristan and Riva pair off, now Myrdhin and Keyne are confidants. I'm sick of it. 'I am going to bed,' I say coldly, turning on my heel and stalking off before they can stop me.

The conversation is still bouncing around my head the following morning, when I bump into Tristan and Os outside the women's quarters. It's another fine day for once and I've a basket on my arm, ready to fill with winkles now the tide is out. Locinna blinked in surprise when she saw me, but I'm not going because of the work. I woke with the imagined rush of the sea in my ears and a desire to stand knee-deep in the swell, feeling the sun on my hair. Perhaps Lir will make my troubles seem smaller. I smile to myself, but it's a smile that comes with a shiver. I still haven't forgotten the princes.

'Oh!' Tristan's chest knocks the exclamation out of me – and the basket out of my arms – as he rounds the corner.

'Apologies, lady.' Tristan scoops it up with a flourish. 'The fault is mine.'

It is, but I won't say so.

'Is your sister still abed?' he adds.

I glare at him. How *dare* he ask me? 'I've no idea,' I say, attempting breeziness. 'I have winkles to find.'

'Well then.' Tristan glances at his companion. 'Why don't you take Os with you? I am sure we'd both feel safer. The sea's a treacherous maiden.'

'I do not need a minder. I am no child.'

'I can see that,' he says with a lingering sweep of his eyes. I am wearing an apron over my blue dress this morning and have not bothered to braid my hair. For a moment I feel pleasure and a smile threatens, but then I remember why he's here and who he's waiting for and pique usurps it. What gives him the right to ogle me when he wants Riva?

'Excuse me,' I say, pushing past. Though I walk quickly, it's not long before I hear footfalls and Os catches up. 'I told you I don't need a minder,' I snap at him.

He just shrugs. Then, after a moment, he gestures upward. 'The sky?' I say, drawn to his miming despite myself. 'The sun?'

He nods, pointing to himself then out in the direction of the sea. 'You want to see the ocean?' Os smiles and I feel a different kind of pleasure, that of being able to understand him. 'All right,' I say, as if I've given him permission, but we both know he would have come along anyway. He always obeys Tristan.

'He likes to order you around,' I voice it aloud as we walk and Os looks pained. After a moment he gestures at himself then back at the women's quarters and puts a hand on his heart. I frown. Is he referring to Tristan and Riva? He seems to sense my question because he thumps his own chest repeatedly. 'You're . . . sworn to him?' I say and he nods. 'But he treats you like a servant.'

Os extends his hands, tips them palm-up in a half shrug.

'He does sometimes,' I conclude. 'And you don't mind?'

He shakes his head, puts his hand over his heart again.

'You follow him willingly.'

Os's arms fall to his sides. He looks away from me.

I don't know if this means 'no' or not because we need all four of our limbs for the descent to the beach. I'm hampered by the basket and my skirts. Os offers to carry it, but I just toss it down ahead of us, watching as it bounces and rolls to a stop on the shingle.

Once on the beach, I tie two knots in my skirt, hoisting the material to knee-height so the surf won't drench me. I suspect I'm embarrassing Os because the man's just standing there, big hands hanging uselessly at his sides. 'You might as well help now you're here,' I say, and when he looks blank I add, 'Haven't you ever picked winkles before?'

He shifts – uncomfortably I think – and points to me, the basket and then to himself pushing his hands away in an unmistakable no. It takes me a moment to puzzle out what he means. 'It's women's work?' I say under a raised brow. Os nods.

'Well since there's no one to fight here except crabs – oh, and grab any you find, by the way – you can learn to pick winkles. It's easy.' I point to a cluster of rocks, seaweed-slicked. The receding water has left little pools behind and I spot a crab almost immediately. 'Os – there.' Obediently he lifts the creature but drops it again with a grunt. I laugh. 'Avoid the pincers. *How* have you never done this before?'

The sun steals across the sky and the sea is as blue as a kingfisher's wing. It makes a nice change from its usual choppy red when wind churns up the sand to dye it bloody. I pluck the little winkle shells and feel a tugging from the water, as if it longs to carry me away. 'Have you travelled much, Os?'

He ambles over with his own handful of winkles and tips them into the basket where they sit like beady black eyes. He points to the sea and spreads his arms wide. 'I know the world is large,' I say. 'But how much have *you* seen?'

Os makes the same gesture, this time tapping his chest. 'So you've been to many places?' I ask.

Again that odd twist of pain furrows his face. He nods. I wonder if it means he'd rather be home. 'Do you have anyone waiting for you in Dyfed?'

Os stares at the ocean, watching the tide beginning to foam and turn towards us. Eventually he shakes his head. I wonder at that. Perhaps he had a woman and she died or went with another man when he left to fight? I decide to drop it.

After another half hour, the sea has reclaimed all the rock pools. I find a large flat stone and sit down to rest. The beach slopes sharply on my right, water flowing into the dip there. I stick my salt-stained legs out in front of me on the rock. The sun is hot on my neck, the wind cold in my ears, so I loop my shawl into a hood. I feel Os settle too, his silent presence somehow reassuring. I don't know why.

All I can hear is wind and water, a soothing melody. What was it Myrdhin said in the wood? I have to concentrate if I want to *see*, quiet my thoughts, still my body. I close my eyes, but I've nothing to picture this time: no Riva to find. I'd rather not think of her at all because then I have to think of Tristan too and the roil in my chest is as rough as the sea. I can't swim, never managed to make my arms and legs move in time with each other. And water isn't to be trusted, full of undercurrents and stones and wriggling creatures.

The sun is hot. I think of it instead, that big ball of fire in the sky. I like to stand in its warmth, my face tilted up to the light, but it turns me red. It burns. I struggle against the vision that reaches out to grip me, but it's no use. My skin is peeling, cracking, blackening in a small space, so small I can't get out – and it's hungry, this sun. Or is it something else? Its tongues scorch, turning my screams to smoke. Beneath my blistering hand, the latch melts, useless. And there is the figure, oh so small, perfect unburned hands raised to cover her face, blue eyes wide and terrified.

'No!' I roll desperately, trying to smother the flames that have taken root in me like weeds. They crawl and push through my body and suddenly I can smell the sea. I reach for it and fall, banging my hip on something hard. Water closes over my head.

The next moment, my eyes are stinging – from smoke, or salt? There's fire in my throat, but it's salty too. Arms are lifting me up; seawater cascades from my dress. I retch, spitting out more salt. The flames are gone; the water must have put them out. Someone is making a sound, a whine and when I blink I see Os, sopping wet, carrying me away from the sea's edge and the rock where we'd rested – back to the safety of the shingle. The tide is higher than it was.

'I . . .' it comes out as a croak. The fire wasn't real; it's the same vision as before. I must have thrown myself into the sea, or fallen from our rock perch while struggling to escape the images that overwhelmed me. Thank all the goddesses for Os. I look at him as he lays me down. 'You saved me.'

There is a question in his eyes. I don't know how to answer it, or whether I even should. Myrdhin told me not to speak openly of my power, now that Gildas has Father's ear. And some power . . . it almost killed me. I swallow. Will this happen every time? How am I meant to practise if all I see is the fire? I will have to talk to Myrdhin, find out what's causing it, who the little watcher is. I swallow uneasily. Do I even want to know?

Os gestures to the sea and then to my clothes and hugs himself. I nod. He's right: I will catch a chill if I don't change. But I'm wobbly on my feet and I don't want to leave the basket behind. Before I can tell him I'm fine, Os scoops me up in his big arms. I'm too relieved to feel embarrassed. The shingle rolls beneath his boots and twice I almost drop the basket of winkles, but we make it away from the shore.

Os lowers me to the wharf and I yell for Bradan, my throat still sore and salty. I can hear him grumbling as he comes, but he stops dead on seeing me. I watch his eyes move from my wet dress to Os and back again and suddenly I realize what this looks like.

'What have you done to her?' Bradan says, thunder in his eyes.

'Os saved my life,' I tell him quickly, moving in front of the big man. 'I fell in the sea picking winkles.'

Bradan takes a threatening step forward and despite the fact he has it all wrong, I admire his courage in facing a man twice his size. 'Get away from him, Sinne.'

'Aren't you listening,' I snap and it makes me cough. 'He didn't hurt me. He *saved* me.'

Bradan's frown only deepens. 'Can I have a word with you, Sinne – alone?'

'I need to change out of my clothes.'

'Please,' Bradan says with a dark and meaningful glance at Os.

'Very well.' I turn to Os and it crashes down on me: what would have happened if he hadn't been there to pull me from the water. I'd have drowned, fire and water in my lungs. 'Thank you, Os,' I say more seriously than I've ever said anything. 'I am in your debt.' The big man shakes his head, looks as if he wants to tell me something, but Bradan has seized my hand and is pulling me away.

I break free as soon as we're around the side of the smoke-house. 'What's wrong with you?' I demand. 'You should be thanking him.'

For a moment Bradan just looks at me. Then he says, 'You ought to be more careful, Sinne.'

I am at a loss. 'Careful? Of what?'

'Of *him*.' Bradan stabs a finger at the place where we left Os. 'You shouldn't be alone with a stranger.'

'Os isn't a stranger,' I say, nettled. 'He's my friend. He just proved it.'

Bradan's brows draw together. 'Don't be naive, Sinne. Men like that – they only want one thing from a girl.'

'Oh, and what's that?' I say, determined to make him voice it. He has it completely wrong. Os isn't like that at all.

'You know what I mean.'

'I couldn't possibly imagine.'

Bradan's sigh is almost a snarl. 'Don't play games, Sinne.'

'Don't tell me what to do.' I straighten aching shoulders. The wet cloth is heavy and all I want is to shed it and sleep. 'I am the king's daughter.'

'You're a spoiled child is what you are,' Bradan says. 'And a foolish one.'

My mouth falls open, shock robbing me of words and breath. All I can think is, *How dare he?* My stinging eyes prickle.

Bradan bites his lip and takes a step back. 'I just don't want you to get hurt,' he adds quietly.

I finally find my voice. 'You're wrong about him. Os would never harm me.' Before he can muster a reply, I turn on my heel, wet skirts slapping my legs as I break into a run.

25

RIVA

It's becoming dangerous. As the summer turns wetter, I lose count of the times we've almost been caught: the times Tristan seizes my arm as I pass, bundling us both into the shadow of a building. I've never thought Dunbriga especially small, but it seems so now. Eyes are everywhere. Even pressed against Tristan's chest, his lips trailing kisses along my neck, I feel watched.

Yet I can't stop myself. The merest glance lights something between us: over supper in the hall or in church, his thigh touching mine. I am almost glad when Gildas declares it proper for women to sit on one side, men on the other. I can barely concentrate on the sermons as it is, my head full of the things I'd like to do if Tristan and I were fully alone. Our kisses have become much more, accompanied by an urgency that both thrills and frightens. I don't feel like myself; the old Riva wouldn't have dreamed of behaving in such a way. But she is gone and in her place is a creature Gildas would surely call sinful.

I don't care.

'I want to talk to you,' Mother says on yet another morning of rain. Distracted as I am, even I can't ignore the rumblings of farmers now, as crops struggle to grow in the constant downpours. Beltane should have brought the sun. Instead, the berries are drowning on the bush and Keyne's fire dance, though wondrous, is a distant memory.

We are alone in the women's quarters and Mother looks especially serious. Her dark hair is pulled back in a severe braid and a pallor overlays her tanned skin. 'Are you well?' I ask before she can open her mouth.

'A little worry,' she replies. 'It is hard for me to sleep.'

I have trouble sleeping too – for an entirely different reason. As if she plucks the wicked thought right out of my head, she says, 'Do not think I haven't noticed, daughter.'

'Noticed what?' I keep my tone light, but a weight begins to settle in my belly.

'Don't play coy.' She shakes her head. 'I always imagined I'd be saying this to Sinne, never to you.'

'Really, Mother, I've done nothing wrong.'

'You spend too much time with him, Riva. People are starting to whisper.'

'So?' I feel a rising anger. 'People always gossip.'

'You are the daughter of a king.' Her hands clench on the needlework in her lap. 'Certain behaviours are expected of you. Dallying with an outsider is not one of them.'

Through gritted teeth, I say, 'I am not *dallying*. We're friends.'

'Men and women cannot be friends, Riva. Especially not when the woman is young and unmarried, and the man is a foreigner.'

'That's ridiculous. Father always says how proud he is of our trade with foreign peoples. Besides, Tristan is hardly foreign, Mother. He's a Briton like us.'

The delicate needlework tumbles to the floor as she seizes my arm. 'This will *cease*, Riva. I don't want to see you with him again.'

I break free, an angry sob in my throat, and dash for the door – praying my foot won't betray me.

'Riva, don't you dare.'

I hurl myself out into the rain, which drenches me in seconds.

I let it, desperate to get away, to put distance between her words and the pain they awake. The thought of abandoning Tristan makes me sick and cold. She doesn't understand what we have together.

A pair of hands catch me. As if summoned, Tristan's face appears out of the grey, auburn hair hanging in sodden curls. I don't question why he is outside, or how we've managed to find each other. I just push him hard against a wooden wall, and I kiss him none too gently. His lips are warm against mine, an antidote to rain; we taste each other hungrily and I let my hands explore his chest. He cups my breast through my dress and a moan escapes me. When he hears it, Tristan draws back to look at me, staring intently into my eyes. 'What?' I breathe.

He doesn't answer. Instead he says, 'That was unexpected. Nice but unexpected.'

I blush. I am not sure what to do with the heat we've created. I ache to hold him again, but we're standing in full view of any who care to look. Luckily the rain has driven most of the upper terrace folk indoors. 'Mother told me I wasn't to see you.'

Tristan's smile fades. 'What did you say?'

'Nothing. I just had to get out. She made me so angry.'

He touches my cheek. 'Did someone see us?'

'No. She just said people are talking.'

Tristan frees himself and I feel a swell of regret. But I know he is right – we are too exposed here. 'I wish we had somewhere to go,' he says. And though the words themselves are innocent, his tone turns them into something that makes me blush harder. 'Somewhere we need not worry over prying eyes.'

'I know a place,' I whisper.

'Where?'

'Outside the hold.' *Stupid.* I am used to hearing my own disapproving voice in my head by now. *Remember what happened last time you left the fort.*

Tristan throws up his hands. 'The gates are too closely watched.'

'No.' I catch one of them. 'I know a way out. A secret way.'

'What?' His eyes widen on my face. 'Unguarded?'

'Yes. It's small and full of thorns, but it means we could reach the woods unobserved.'

'Why didn't you mention this before?'

It's Keyne's secret. 'I . . . I didn't think. And besides, it wasn't my secret to tell. It still isn't.'

For a moment I fear I've angered him, but it's only a trick of the rain. His eyes are full of light. And mischief. 'Show me.'

We make it a game, darting from one building to the next, flattening ourselves against walls, or crouching behind barrels, laughing like children. I quite forget the ache in my foot, too focused on watching the extra guards Father has stationed on the walls.

'We're nearly there,' I whisper, lips brushing the back of Tristan's neck. He shivers a little and I smile. 'See those bushes? The passage is behind them.'

'I see them. Wait for that man to turn the corner.'

The rain has become fine drifting mist. We wait, breathless, gazes fixed on the guard. As soon as his back is turned, Tristan seizes my arm and pulls me into a sprint. Or as close to a sprint as I can manage. Still it's the fastest I've run since the accident. When we reach the gorse, I wrap my unburned hand in my cloak and thrust the branches aside.

Tristan hisses through his teeth. When he looks at me, his face is alight. 'And no one knows?'

We slip into the gorse-roofed tunnel. 'Keyne does,' I admit. 'She found it. The land must have weakened here.' The rain has made a muddy soup of the earth and soon my skirts are caked in it. Luckily it's not long before we break free into open grass and I pull Tristan down again while we check the walls.

After another mad dash, we are safe beneath the trees and

collapse, laughing. 'Incredible,' Tristan says when we find our breath. 'You can't even see it from this side.' He turns back to me. 'Why haven't you told King Cador?'

'Keyne – she says she needs it. She begged me not to tell.' For a fleeting moment, I feel an echo of my earlier worry and squeeze Tristan's hand. 'You must promise not to say anything.'

'I promise,' Tristan says seriously, kissing my hand in turn. 'You have my word.'

'Thank you. Come on.' I set off into the woods. 'Let's escape for a bit.'

As our heartbeats resume their normal rhythm, we walk with fingers intertwined, all haste forgotten. After a while, the summer sun breaks free and goes to work on the mist. I can almost see raindrops rising from the leaves. It's warmer here too, everything a riot of green.

I don't realize I am leading us to the nemeton until we step into the sacred glade – and then I marvel. What deep instinct let me open the way? We stop and even Tristan seems at a loss for words. A kind of forsaken beauty rules here now, like the fallen Roman temple on the road to Dintagel. I remember the peace of that place, quietly forlorn in the setting sun. Real vines had snaked over their carved stone cousins and a family of foxes had made their home beneath the altar.

'What is this?'

Tristan's question brings me back to myself. He is staring at the glade, at the strewn and weathered skulls, the twisted oaks. 'We used to come here,' I say, forcing down sadness at the sight. 'When Father still made offerings to the gods.'

Tristan turns over a jawbone with the toe of his boot. 'And what did they grant him in return?'

'Power,' I say.

He looks at me sharply. 'What kind?'

'Every kind. Power over harvest and sea. Power over the hunt.' I pause. 'Power over our enemies.'

Tristan nods at the skull. 'That's one of them, I take it?'

'Yes. The skulls of those deemed worthy were added to something we called the ghost fence. Their spirits protected us from invaders. And the wisdom of our fallen enemies made us stronger.'

'I wonder if I'd have been found worthy,' Tristan says.

'You're not an enemy,' I exclaim, horrified. 'Ignore Mother. She's just overprotective.'

He seems to be having trouble taking his eyes from the skulls, so I shake him gently. 'Tristan. It's gone now, all of it. The magic is gone.'

A sharp snap. I jump and let out a cry – but it is only a gull, a brittle twig in its beak.

'You're right, it's a bit eerie here.' Tristan laughs. 'But this moss looks comfortable.' And without further ado, he begins to strip off his clothes. My cheeks heat. 'What are you doing?'

'Hanging these up to dry.' He throws tunic and shirt over a branch and then sits to pull off sodden shoon. I just stand there, heart back to thumping, unable to stop my eyes from straying to his bare chest, his shoulders. The unforgiving sun picks out the scars on his skin, some faded to pale, others still angry grins of red.

'Oh.' My healer's gasp escapes before I can stop it and Tristan glances up.

'I told you before, I am no stranger to injury,' he says.

'But you have so many . . .'

'Such is a warrior's lot, I'm afraid. I have fought numerous battles and cheated death many times.'

In an effort to stop staring, I strip off my muddied cloak and overdress with some difficulty and hang them beside his clothes. My shoon are fair-ruined so I take those off too, relishing the feel of the soft damp moss. Tristan has spread his cloak in a patch of sun and I sit on it beside him. 'It's good to be out of the hold.'

'It is,' he agrees. Though his eyes are on my face, I feel as if they are elsewhere too, as if they see all of me, or hunger to do so. I think briefly of Mother and her warning and have to swallow a grin – she'd have an apoplexy if she saw me now.

'What are you smiling about?'

So I haven't managed to hide it after all. 'Mother,' I admit. 'She told me I wasn't to see you only an hour since.'

'Lady Enica is a formidable woman,' Tristan says. 'I'm half anticipating a similar visit from her.'

'I don't think she'd dare. I am her daughter, so she can say what she wants to me. You're a man and not of our people.'

'Does that matter to you?'

Suddenly his tone is no longer light. I feel the shift like a wind change. 'You know it doesn't,' I whisper.

He leans in closer. 'But it does to your parents.' I notice his lips are chapped in places, as if he worries at them. Before I think too closely about it, I lift a finger and touch the tip to one of the sore spots, wishing I could heal it.

'Riva—'

'Shh. Stay still.' If Keyne is right and magic lies in the land, perhaps it's strongest here – beneath the oaks, on ground where kings have danced. I close my eyes. I don't have my healer's bag, the potions and salves so carefully prepared. Siaun is in my mind and Gildas too; he stopped me healing Siaun before. I lock them both away.

Instead I think about the oaks and their roots that run deeper than the hills. I think about the moss I kneel upon, the ring of sky above. I consider the seashore, where earth meets and mingles with water. And this time, I do not seek the spark. I let it come to me.

Something hums against my chest; the little black acorn. Not knowing what else to do, I strung it from a cord to wear beneath my shift. Now it grows hot and the heat spreads: down my arm, into the hand I hold to Tristan's lips.

I feel despair and joy. Despair because the magic is so very weak, joy because it hasn't died. Tristan makes a startled sound. When I open my eyes, I can see his lips through my hand, silver-limned, translucent. They need only a little magic; a little is all I have.

My heart beats like an animal cornered, wild and breathless. When I take my hand away, Tristan's skin is whole. The heat in the acorn fades, but I sense it's still there, waiting to be called up again.

Tristan raises his own hand to his mouth; a slight tremble as his fingers touch the place I healed. We stare at each other. 'You . . .' he whispers. 'I thought you said the magic had died.'

'I thought it had.' Wonder turns to giddy mirth. 'I thought it had!'

His eyes are very wide. 'You never told me you could heal.'

'I couldn't – not like that. Not without my herbs to help, at least. It's this place.' *And the acorn.*

'This is . . . I have no words. Riva –' I can't read his expression, it is a jumble of feelings all tumbled together: shock, awe, disbelief – 'the things you might do.'

Before I can confess that healing a split lip seems to be the limit of my abilities, Tristan catches me up and kisses me.

That shift I'd felt earlier in myself is in him too, an insistence in the lips I have just healed. Something is different, as if we've crossed a boundary. The midsummer sun beats hot on my hair; an answering warmth races through me, rougher than the touch of magic, tingling in my fingers and thighs. It is sweet and terri-fying and I still don't know what to do with it – save follow where it leads.

I lie back on the cloak and draw Tristan down to me. His lips seek my neck, the hollow of my throat. When he kisses me there,

I dare to let my hands explore him. My scarred flesh seems at home against his; we have been marked by the world, and it isn't a crime or a tragedy. It is victory, as he says. Something we share, that makes us stronger. I throw my head back as he pulls at my dress, hearing cloth tear. I don't care, not with his mouth on me. His breathing is ragged. When he cups my face in his hand, he has that same intense look in his eyes, seeking out something in mine.

I am conscious of the thin layers between us. How can I not be – with him pressed so close against me? Even in a mist of want, something trembles, almost a fear of him, for I know it's too late to stop this. And I don't want to, not when his hand slides beneath my skirt, stroking its way closer, towards the heart of me. I arch against the ground; his fingers are inquisitive and gentle and urgent all at once. He takes my good hand, guides it between his legs, and teaches me to feel, to push aside the last bit of cloth between us.

'Tris—'

'You are so beautiful. Riva.' He breathes my name, eases his lips over mine – just as he stretches his body over mine, making us one.

The pain is sudden and shocking – even buoyed by desire, I can't hold back a small cry, buried in Tristan's shoulder. I feel it travel through him, through us both. Locinna had warned us of pain like this. She'd taken me and my sisters aside the moment we were old enough to ask such questions, but I had expected it to be lost in my own need. Foolish. I hold onto Tristan so tightly that my nails leave crescents in his flesh. And as he moves, I squeeze my eyes shut.

I never imagined it this way. His breathing is harsh amidst the birdsong. With my eyes closed, I can hear every scrap of the woodland, every tiny crunch or sigh – as small claws alight on branches, or paws patter like rain on leaves. We are the trespassers here. It is *our* sounds that don't belong.

It seems to be forever before Tristan gives a shuddering groan. For a few moments he lies panting on my chest before drawing back to look at me.

I think I've been careful to hide my tears, but when he wipes one from my cheek, I realize I've failed. 'I'm sorry,' he murmurs. 'They say a woman does not enjoy it the first time.'

It's ridiculous – considering we are still bound up in each other – but the words make me flush. 'I'm . . . I am fine,' I manage. Tristan eases off me and I can't stop myself from reaching down. I think to find a lot of blood, but there is hardly any at all.

Tristan looks at my fingertips. 'We will try again, Riva,' he says. 'It will get better.'

'I know.' Of course I don't. I am forcing confidence, ignoring the sting, the shock and the disappointment. Even with Tristan, trying again is the last thing I want to do right now. It takes a while for the implications of his words to sink in. When they do, I tug my dress down over my hips, suddenly cold. 'They can't find out about this.'

Tristan brushes a damp strand of hair away from my eyes. 'We'll be careful.'

I don't know what to say to his casual acceptance. I am ruined now, in my parents' eyes, in the eyes of the hold. 'We will have to marry.'

'In time,' he replies.

I stiffen. 'What do you mean?'

He strokes my bare shoulder, but I pull away. 'Tell me.'

'I have business to see to, Riva. I cannot afford to settle down just yet.'

A flutter of panic. 'Are you saying you don't want to—?'

'Hush.' He lays his palm against my cheek. 'Of *course* I want to marry you.' His finger moves, vanquishing another tear. 'But I have responsibilities, duties to dispatch. When I said we'd need to be careful, I only meant it would be better to keep this from your parents for now. But just because we can't be seen together in public, it does not mean we cannot spend time together here.'

I shiver. The wind has picked up and brought more clouds, slowly sucking the sun away. Abruptly, I feel watched, judged. 'We ought to return before we're missed.'

The brief sunlight has done little to dry our clothes. I shudder into mine, hating the cling of clammy material. Tristan takes my hand as we walk and I am glad of it; my foot hurts from our mad run, sending tremors of protest up my calf, and I am sore. What we've done has birthed a litter of questions – like whether Tristan even has the means to support us. I have no idea how high up in Vortipor's court he is. He has a fine horse and carries fine weaponry, but does that mean he owns a holding?

I slide him a surreptitious glance. 'All right,' he says, catching it. 'You have something on your mind.'

Although mine is a reasonable question for a bride-to-be, I still feel awkward asking it. 'I was wondering where we'd live. Do you have a holding?'

Tristan's mouth quirks. '"A holding" is a quaint expression, isn't it?' On seeing my face, he raises his free hand. 'I was jesting. Of course I have somewhere. I don't know whether you'll like it, though.'

'If it's yours, I will,' I say, more to convince myself.

He pulls us both to a halt, just shy of the treeline. 'No one has ever shown such faith in me,' he says, turning so we are face to face. 'I promise you I will return it, Riva, one day.'

I don't much like the sound of 'one day' but I let him kiss me a final time before we have to become strangers.

26

KEYNE

I stare at the blood and feel sick. Not because it's blood, but because of what it means. I admit I've been feeling happier since I met Mori. Not *happy*, just more at ease with myself. And then the month turns, the bleeding comes again and it's a culmination of everything that is wrong. I sit frozen, unable to move for long minutes. I can't even bring myself to go through the motions of cleaning up and fetching linens.

Things will not always be this way, Mori had said.

But they will, I tell her silently. Although I've touched the magic of the land, I am no shape-shifter. I can't change this body, only hide it, and never from myself. I can't hide it from my parents, my sisters or the hold either. They will always see me one way. Maybe the only path to some semblance of freedom is by embracing the wild and the foreign, passing anonymously through far-off streets, where people see what they expect to see – no more, no less.

I might have sat for hours if Riva hadn't called, 'Are you finished, Keyne?'

I've been perching on the rim of the large basin we use for bathing. When I'm forced to move, I feel wooden, stiff. I push the concealing screens aside with numb arms.

A little feeling trickles back at the sight of Riva. 'What happened to *you*?'

'The rain caught me.'

She's wearing more mud than cloth, split shoon in her good hand. 'The rain,' I repeat.

'What?' Riva throws them down.

'Have you been outside the fort?'

She flushes. 'No.'

I consider her. There's something guilty in the way her shoulders hunch, in the way she can't quite meet my eyes. 'You used the passage,' I say, unable to keep accusation out of my voice.

'I . . .' She looks up. 'Yes.'

'Why?'

'Tristan. Mother said I wasn't to see him again.'

I swallow my first reply. I can see she's in no mood to hear it. And there's something more far more pressing. 'You showed *him* the gorse passage?'

'I'm sorry, Keyne.'

Anger thaws my frozen limbs. '*You* were the one who ordered me to tell Father.'

'You can't,' she gasps, seizing her bad hand with her good as if she wants to wring them both. 'It's the only way we're allowed to see each other, alone.'

'You told me it was a dangerous secret to keep.'

'I know. Keyne, I'm sorry. It was the only thing I could think of after Mother forbade me. And Tristan swore to me he wouldn't tell Father.'

'I don't trust him.'

Even I'm surprised at the hostility that erupts in her face. She drops her hands. 'You've nothing to base that on. You don't know him.'

I think of the conversation I had with Tristan in the barn. 'That's exactly why I don't trust him.'

'He's only ever shown us courtesy. He helps around the hold –' there is an odd sort of desperation in her face – 'he even helped dismantle that wrecked ship.'

'Courtesy is not honesty,' I say.

'I don't have to listen to this.' Riva pushes me aside, grabs the bathing screens so violently that they creak in protest, and drags them closed behind her. I stare at them, listening to her harsh, angry breathing until Locinna stumbles in, carrying two steaming buckets of water.

'Help me, child,' she says and I take them, wondering all the while whether I'd imagined the glitter of tears in Riva's eyes.

'I don't know what she's thinking,' I tell Myrdhin later as we spar in the old barn. The exercise is the only thing that helps take my mind off the cramps. 'I can't reach her. And she refuses to listen to any criticism of Tristan.'

Myrdhin's wooden blade comes down on the back of my hand and I yelp. 'Never let your thoughts distract you,' he says reprovingly. 'Even the greatest warrior can be undone by a stray musing.'

I rub my hand where already a red welt is rising. 'As you've said before.'

'Clearly I need to say it again.'

After a moment I ask, 'Is control the only reason you're teaching me weaponry?'

Myrdhin looks at me through those blue, blue eyes. 'Patterns of movement echo patterns of thought. You are beginning to see them, aren't you?'

I remember Beltane and the feeling of fire in my bones. 'Since the festival, I can pick out fire, but other strands are harder. And I'm not sure what the point is. I can't do anything *with* the pattern.' I pause. 'Not like when you relit the bonfires.'

Myrdhin plants his hands on his hips, practice sword still

clasped in one. It's a gesture I'm more used to seeing on Mori. 'I merely gave it a prod, just as the priest did.'

'It was still impress—' I stop as his words catch up with me. 'What, Gildas? *Gildas* did something to the fire?'

'You didn't believe his little trick was divine intervention?' Myrdhin says, raising an eyebrow.

'I didn't know what to think,' I protest. 'You're saying *he* did it? With magic?'

'He will never admit it.' There's an odd sort of sadness in Myrdhin's eyes. 'He really thinks the magic is his god working through him.'

I feel winded, recalling the priest's words to me – *heathen, damned, godless.* 'How dare he?'

'He dares because the truth is too terrible. He has been raised to believe a drewydh, a magic-user, is a creature of Satan. To admit that he is one of *us* . . . his fear has forced him to invent a narrative wherein his powers are god-given.'

'But how can he have magic? I thought it came from the land and he's not of Dumnonia . . .' I trail off, struck by the obvious. 'Neither are you.'

'Only your power is drawn through the land, lad. Not ours. And the land augments it. Here, you are more powerful than I or the priest will ever be – or could be so.'

I shake my head, confused. 'I don't feel powerful. You were the one who summoned the magic, back during Imbolc.'

'Not summoned. Showed. The summoning was all you.'

'Then how do you do what you do?' I demand. 'Where does your magic come from?'

Myrdhin's smile is enigmatic. 'Everywhere.'

'That's hardly an answer.'

'It's the only one I have for you.' He stuffs the sword into his belt. 'Some few of us are born with the ability to see the web that holds the world together – the great pattern of which I spoke. Even fewer can actually touch that pattern, altering certain strands of it to suit their needs – like I did with the fire.' His smile fades slightly. 'But with power comes peril.'

His words raise gooseflesh and I rub my arm with the flat of the wooden blade. 'I'm not sure I understand. Are you saying it's dangerous to alter parts of the great pattern for your own ends?'

'Very dangerous. Which is why Gildas is a fool for meddling without foreknowledge.'

We stand in silence a moment while my thoughts creak and whirl. 'So when I see the silver in the earth – the veins of magic – am I touching the great pattern too?'

'Yes,' Myrdhin says, 'through your bond with the land. And you'll recall I told you to be careful. Because when all is said and done, we are both simply human. The pattern is as old as the universe itself.'

'Will I still be able to touch it if I leave Dumnonia?' *Why did I say that?*

Myrdhin scrutinizes me. 'Perhaps. Perhaps not. For now, as you are in Dumnonia, trust in your blood. It is that which allows you to use what folk call magic. Same for Riva and Sinne.'

Both of us have run out of words. We stand in silence while the seconds pass, crawling towards dusk. Here, Myrdhin says I am stronger than him, but despite his explanation, I can't bring myself to believe it. Eventually I say, 'Gildas thinks you're teaching me hellish magics. What would he say if he knew we spend more time sparring?'

Myrdhin meets my eyes and it feels as if the world . . . stops, as I wait for his answer. The woodlice in the rotting beams are still, as are the spiders spinning their quiet webs, even the draught that frets and harries its way inside the barn. 'What I'm showing you is far worse than hellish magics, lad,' Myrdhin replies, 'to men like him, anyway.' I see a shadowless expanse in his gaze. 'Bit by bit, I am teaching you to recognize the truth.'

*

I am still turning over Myrdhin's words when I hear a light tread behind me. My feet have taken me to the sea and its oily, dark waves. I watch them crumble into foam against the shore and I think of Sinae, Constantinople and Gildas's Holy Land. I imagine their peoples and wonder whether they are anything like us . . . anything like me. My feet itch to carry me further still, right into the sea itself and across until I find land again.

When I realize I am not alone, these bright vistas flicker and take flight. My visitor is not wearing her red dress today. Instead her skirts are sober, matching my new mood. She did indeed come with Bedeu; she's his ward, I hear. He left her when he went back to Moriduno, saying she'd be safer with us. I've been avoiding her, unable to forget her lips and their mirrored curves of happiness and horror. My mouth is dry, even now.

'I'm sorry,' she says, a near-whisper.

The word catches me out, the last one I expected. When I say nothing, Gwen laces her fingers, looks down at them. 'It was rude of me to run away. At Beltane.'

'I should have . . .' But what I should have done, I do not know. Is it my duty to share my truths with all who meet me? As if they've already earned a right to know me? So I stop. I cannot be sorry that I didn't tell her. I cannot be sorry that who I am caused her to run. She could have stayed.

'You dance well,' she says, with a shy glance up, and once again I am disarmed by her large brown eyes.

'So do you,' I manage. By the gods, this is awkward. I am always uncomfortable in my skin, but her proximity makes it worse. I might have suspected a trick if it wasn't for the open discomfort that causes her shoulders to hunch, her gaze to stray. So I say, 'You are Banon Bedeu's ward.'

'He is my uncle.' She unlinks her hands. 'My mother died of a fever and my father too. Or maybe he died from grief. Either way, he wouldn't stay for me,' she adds bitterly and bites her tongue a moment later.

'How long have you been a ward?' I ask.

'Five years.' She shrugs. 'My uncle will be searching out a husband for me soon.'

The awkwardness returns threefold. I might ask her if she's looking forward to marriage, but the words stick in my throat.

We are both silent. The moments stretch until Gwen says, 'Why do you wear those clothes?'

This time when I look at her, she's looking back. If she has the courage to ask, I have the courage to answer. 'Because most men do.'

'But you are not . . .' She falters and suddenly I don't care about being polite, or whether she'll find my truth upsetting.

'I am.' I say it more firmly than I have ever said anything. 'In here, I know myself, and I am. That is the only thing that matters.'

'Then I think you are very brave.'

She still hasn't looked down. I stare at her, off balance. She has caught me out again.

'Can we be friends?' she asks. And with a small smile, 'I do feel terrible for getting you into trouble with your mother.'

You are my daughter, not my son. 'That wasn't your fault,' I say. 'I was the one who decided to "make a spectacle of myself".'

Her mouth creases. 'Is that what she said?'

'Amongst other things.'

We're silent again until Gwen murmurs, 'So can we? Be friends, I mean.' She's picking a stray thread on her dress, but her gaze is sure and steady. I search for the horror she wore at Beltane, for any trace of mockery. Finding none, I hold out my hand – Gwen makes a sound halfway between surprise and pleasure – and we grasp wrists like kinsmen.

'Yes,' I hear myself say. 'I think I'd like that.'

27

SINNE

Riva thinks she's being clever, sneaking out with Tristan. She's ever alert for guards and other eyes that would report her to Father, but not for sisters. *I* could report her if I chose. Sometimes I don't know what stops me.

I know what stops Keyne. If they end Riva's trips outside, they end hers too. I suppose I'd be betraying both my sisters if I were to tell. So I don't, I can't. Instead I watch and I talk to Os.

I'm sure he wants to tell me something, something too complex to communicate with gestures. From the way his chin drops, the way he glances at me when his fingers grip the edge of his bench, instead of hovering in front of him ready to shape words – that's how I know. And maybe it's a secret, this thing he struggles to share. A secret that's too dangerous to reveal, even to a young woman with no real say in anything.

Riva would grumble that I'm letting my imagination get the better of me. Perhaps she would be right. But no one understands Os as well as I do . . . save Tristan, of course.

He finds us in the stables one wet afternoon that bears no resemblance to summer. Rain drips from the hem of his cloak, darkens his auburn hair to brown. He looks no less handsome for it, I think, hating the way my heart races to see him. It's as if it's still in thrall to the dream. Now more often than not I dream of fire.

'My lady,' Tristan says in his courteous way, a quick bend of his spine. I wish he didn't sound so distant. Then he turns to Os. 'I need you to take a message.'

Os seems troubled. He raises his hands, makes three quick gestures – so quick I miss them. 'This is important,' Tristan replies. He glances at me. 'Lazing in this hold's not good for you. It's time you were back in the saddle.'

I watch Os's eyes narrow. Slowly he taps his chest and then points straight out, palm up. *Where*, I think he's asking.

'I'd like this report in our king's hands before six sennights have passed.' Tristan pauses. 'The Sarum road is fastest.'

When Os looks at me, I can see from his face that he doesn't want to go.

Tristan can too. 'Really, Os. I'd never have expected to see you so comfortable in a fort. You've always preferred the open road. I'm sure your mare would agree.'

At this, Os reaches out to pat the animal's neck. She nickers softly at him. 'There,' Tristan says as if the horse does indeed agree. 'I'm only sorry Ni won't have a decent run too.'

Os looks up at the sky, shrugs.

'You can leave at dawn, yes,' Tristan says. He hands over a sealed scroll and Os pockets it.

I've been silent through the exchange, skin prickling at the tension simmering between the two men. I can't remember it being there before. 'I'll miss you, Os,' I say truthfully and the big man turns to me. He smiles the smile that scares Riva so, and taps his heart.

'He says he will miss you too,' Tristan remarks with some amusement.

'I know,' I snap. 'I understood.'

Tristan moves closer to me, the flickering torches leaving him half in shadow. 'You must have spent a good deal of time with him to learn.'

'We're friends.'

'So I see. Well, I hope you'll consider me a substitute in his absence.' Tristan raises a hand to my unbound hair, picks up a lock. I stop breathing. It lies like coiled gold in his palm, and the image pleases me.

Then Os knocks Tristan's hand away. With a growl, he steps in front of me, blocking my sight of the other man. His arms move; I can't see what he's saying.

But Tristan just laughs. 'Don't forget, Osred,' he says, 'who you swore to serve.' When I peek around the edge of Os's leather-clad shoulder, he's walking away, his laughter still ringing through the gloom.

We watch him go. I can hear Os breathing: short and sharp as if he's angry or in pain. I lay a hand on his arm. 'I'll be fine. You're the one who needs to be careful. Please don't get killed by Saxons.'

He looks down at me, faint humour curving his lips. His hands have uncurled and he uses them to say something like, *I will try my best.* Then before I know it, he's swept me into an embrace; the kind of embrace a father gives a small child. The top of my head barely reaches his collarbone. His leather tunic smells of sweat and horse, but I don't really mind. Oddly, it makes me feel safe.

His smile has faded by the time he lets me go and he stares in the direction Tristan has gone. I think the last thing he says to me – looking into my eyes – is, *Be wary of him.*

It's quiet without Os around. Quiet in the sense of . . . there being an absent presence is the only way of describing it. And Os has such a large presence. Not being able to talk like the rest of us doesn't change that. Truthfully, the only other person who's sad to see Os go is Arlyn. 'I'm used to him sitting here,' he admits to me, after Os has ridden his bay mare away. 'He's comfortable to have around – you know what I mean?'

I nod. I know what he means.

Arlyn's silent a while. I am too. There's an empty space in me, which I hadn't known Os filled. I'd only befriended him to spite Riva, after all.

'Do you think . . .?' Arlyn stops.

'What?' I say, staring morosely into the fire. Despite everything, sometimes I wish Tristan and Os had never come here at all.

'Riva.' Her name sounds like it hurts him. 'Do you think she loves him? I mean – truly?'

I look up. There's colour in Arlyn's face, and misery, and the picture is abruptly complete. I always wondered why I couldn't charm the smith's apprentice. '*You* love Riva.'

Arlyn starts pounding on a shapeless mass of metal. 'It's that obvious?'

The truth is like a surge of seawater. Is everyone in this place obsessed with Riva? What has she done to merit any of it? She's boring and dour and reads too much. She has that awful limp. Her laugh is too piercing. She natters on about the old ways, but hasn't the courage to refuse Gildas and his stupid church outright.

Wings thrash in my chest. I don't know why, but I need to get out. I'll go and see Os; his languid gestures always calm me. But then I remember Os is gone, perhaps for weeks, perhaps forever. I have nowhere to go.

I burst from the smithy with a nameless cry, part anger, part hurt. And I listen as my cry is taken up, hallooed over the wooden rooftops, leaping from throat to throat until enough sense comes back to me to wonder why. There are other sounds now: the pounding and shuffling of many feet; the creak of gates. I break into a run.

Someone catches my arm as I hare into the lower terrace, jerking me to a halt. 'What's going on?'

I'm affronted until I realize it isn't some stable boy hanging onto me, but Keyne. I blink up at her. When did she grow so tall? There's a thin sweat on her brow as if she's been running too. 'I was about to find out,' I say peevishly.

'Let's go then.' Before I can think of a suitable response, she's pulling me along in her wake like so much flotsam. Her grip on my arm is almost painful and I find myself remembering Beltane – and Myrdhin's words. *He is who he is. The world cannot change that and neither can you.*

He is who he is.

I look sidelong at Keyne. What is the difference between a girl in boy's clothes and a boy in boy's clothes? Huge, I realize, for Keyne. It goes deeper than clothing – that is just the thing we see. Is this what she's been trying to tell us all these years? No wonder she confided in Myrdhin. We haven't been listening at all. Still aren't listening. The understanding hits me as an almost physical pain.

We reach the main gates and I'm distracted by a flood of people entering: two or three hundred, mostly women and children with very few fighting men amongst them. Faces are haggard, some bloodstained. I see packs on shoulders, but a number walk unburdened save for the look in their eyes. Keyne and I can only stand and stare. Why are they here and where have they all come from?

Father is there, talking to a man I recognize as Banon Bedeu. Another two separate themselves from the mass of bodies and join them. 'Let's get closer,' I suggest. 'I want to hear what they're saying.'

Keyne doesn't argue, just nods, and we both scurry around the side of the tanner's workshop to crouch in its shadow. 'I had to bring them here,' Bedeu is saying. His hair and beard resemble a silver haystack, unkempt, and he looks as if he's worn the same set of clothes for weeks. 'There are too many for me to shelter and, besides, Moriduno cannot hold off a concerted Saxon attack on its own.'

'Lindinis has fallen,' one of the newcomers says, an old warrior by the looks of him. 'And these that follow me are the only ones we could save from Durnovaria before the Gewisse Saxons swept down on it.'

'So the whole of Durnovaria too is lost?' Father asks. His face is pale as old ash.

'It surely will be by now, lord.' The veteran glances at the people still streaming through the gates. His head dips. 'The Durotriges are broken. We ask Dumnonia to offer us shelter.' In his eyes, there's something more. The way he looks at my father is hopeful, almost expectant. Has he heard of the drewydh-king of Dumnonia, of the power Father can wield over land and sea? *Used to wield.* What will he say when he realizes we're nothing special? I feel cold remembering Myrdhin's words. *Dumnonia has lost its greatest protector.*

'When did this happen?'

It's the other stranger's turn to answer my father. He appears more farmer than warrior in his scuffed and tattered apron. 'Lindinis fell at Imbolc. We didn't have the numbers to hold it. Our enemies are canny, had surprise on their side. But I fear they'd have won without it all the same. That thrice-damned Cerdic must have the gods in his pocket.'

'He can't be leading the campaign, surely,' Father says. 'From all reports, he's seen more than fifty summers, at least.'

'He's still a formidable warrior.' The man shakes his head. 'But it's his son who commands his armies. Cynric.'

'You have been travelling since Imbolc?' Father looks over their heads at the people still filing between his gates. 'That's four moons gone.'

'Leading a group as large as this through the wild is no easy task. Saxon scouts forced us to take a circuitous route. We lost many along the way.'

'Have you seen Cerdic or Cynric? Met with either?'

The farmer shakes his head, but the old warrior gives a sharp nod. 'I saw him and his son from the walls of Lindinis. They demanded surrender.'

'I am surprised they offered you the chance.'

'They claim civility,' the man says and spits on the ground. His saliva is bloody and I look away. 'But in reality, they're little more than black-eyed butchers of babes. Oh, my lady. Apologies, I did not see you there.'

I hiss and pull Keyne deeper into the shadows, hoping Mother didn't spy us. 'There are a great many here, husband,' she says, eyeing the dispirited people flooding into our hold. 'We will struggle to feed them, especially if we must call up fighting men from the west to protect the hold.'

'I fear we will have to,' Father says heavily. He's not wearing his golden circlet today, I notice. It's left an echo on his skin, of kingship.

'Excuse us, sirs,' Mother says. 'My lord, may I speak with you a moment?'

Although it's phrased as a request, and politely too, it isn't one. I wonder what the men make of her tone, and of my father following her so meekly without argument. My parents move out of the men's earshot, but not out of ours.

'Cador, we cannot feed them,' Mother says. 'Our own livelihood depends on the harvest and it looks weak, if not entirely ruined by this rain.' She pauses. 'And our hunters bring in barely any game. It's as if they've lost all ability overnight.'

They have, I think, *but not overnight*. Even the greenest hunter could mutter a prayer to Cernunnos or Andraste to make their arrows fly true. But I know now it's not a goddess that answers:

it's the land itself. And the king and the land are supposed to be as one.

'We must ration, then,' my father replies and my belly gives a protesting rumble, which would have been funny if it wasn't full of dread. 'I cannot turn them away, Enica.'

'They are not of our people. You must look to your own first and foremost. As their king, it is your duty.'

'I know it,' Father shouts. He starts to pace, curling trembling fingers into fists. Keyne and I look at each other and I see my own worry reflected on the hard planes of her face. I wonder if she's remembering a time, as I am, when the king could make the sun shine, or the rain come. When we could afford to give half our shining pelts to the gods. A time when Father hunted bandits and didn't lose a single man.

And then my mother says, 'Keyne, Sinne. You may as well show yourselves.'

We share startled glances before we both do as she says. Father seems surprised to see us, but Mother is standing with hands on hips, not in the least shocked at our eavesdropping. 'As long as you're here, make yourselves useful,' she barks in a very warrior-like way. 'Sinne, go to Master Cadfan and request an inventory of the grain stores. Then do the same with Huntmaster Drem and Dinuus. Keyne,' she turns, 'ask Gildas to join me as soon as possible. And then see if you can find Master Myrdhin. There are injuries to treat.' She lowers her voice, says with a glance at Father, 'I will not have sickness spread amongst our people.'

Keyne makes a bitter sound at the prospect of being sent to Gildas, but we've both learned not to argue with Mother when she takes that tone. 'Keep quiet,' Mother adds, 'and do not gossip. A panic is the last thing we need.'

She seems far calmer than Father. He is still pacing distractedly, looking for all the world like a lost child.

28

RIVA

When we re-enter the hold, we conceal ourselves in the weary crowd instead of chancing the gorse. I was lying curled against Tristan's side, enjoying the warm ache in my belly when we heard the shouts. It is so much better now between us, more as I imagined it would be, but the memory of the first time stays with me. I wish it had been in a marriage bed, not a bone-strewn glade. I wish we didn't have to hide. I wish for the day I can stand beside him as his wife. Because until that day comes, I feel as if the earth beneath me might suddenly turn to bog.

We make it through the gates. Our cloaks drawn up, we are part of the faceless throng. But we move without the weight that bends their backs, that causes them to hack and shudder and clutch their small bundles tightly. They stink too – the cloying stink of unwashed bodies and bile. I hold my breath and then feel guilty for doing so. These people ought to be pitied, not shunned. A daughter of Christ would welcome them, tend their wounds and see to it that they are fed. But I am not a daughter of Christ, am I? I use pagan magic and dally with men in glades.

Tristan's face pales as he scans the crowd. The moment we pass the sentry post, he pulls me into a jog. I take great gulps of wind; despite the dung it carries from the meadows, it's sweeter than the stench of people. As we flit from smithy to tannery, I spy my parents standing with two strangers. I try to go to them, but Tristan squeezes the arm he is holding. 'Don't,' he says, glancing the same way. 'Your clothes are muddied and they will ask questions.'

My skirts are no more muddied than Mother's, but I let him steer me in the direction of the women's quarters. 'You shouldn't be with me,' I hiss. 'Why don't you go and see what's happened?'

'Later,' Tristan says tensely. He's wearing a look I've come to recognize, as if a tide mill turns behind his eyes.

I pull us to a stop. 'What are you thinking?'

He blinks and the wheel stops turning. 'Only that I wish I hadn't sent Os away. If I need to pass on another message, I may well have to take it myself.'

I am about to ask what message, but – 'Surely not?' It is almost a cry. 'Tristan, you cannot leave. No message can be so important.'

'Let us hope not,' he says, eyes flickering back towards the gates. Perhaps my distress is written plainly because he cups my cheek. 'Don't despair, Riva. I will not leave unless I'm forced to do so.'

I clutch at his hand, hating my own desperation. 'Promise me.'

'I promise,' he says solemnly, but adds a moment later, 'You must understand, however, a man's desire to protect his home.'

This is your home, I want to say. I don't. It's too soon. And Tristan is stubborn; I see the scars that prove it every time we lie together; I feel them under my fingers, blade-carved into his skin.

Gildas isn't happy about his church becoming an infirmary, but he can't exactly refuse. That first day, I help Myrdhin mix potions and poultices, their herby smell battling the stench of sickness as well as tackling the sickness itself. The church cannot house everyone, though, so Mother sets the stronger survivors to building shelters just inside the gates. Their supplies are pooled, counted and found desperately wanting. Mother's lips are pursed when I see her later, charcoal in one hand, a scroll in the other. I guess the inventory is not looking good.

I am careful with my healing magic. It is weaker outside the nemeton and weaker still in the church. But I can take it into myself if I close my eyes and concentrate. The acorn helps. I give a little to every patient: enough to make a difference, but not enough to invite questions. I don't know how many of these people are Christian.

'Riva,' Myrdhin cautions in a low voice when I lay a fingertip on a sleeping man's throat. I recognize him as one of the warriors who'd been standing with my parents earlier, the one from Lindinis. His breathing eases. 'Riva,' the magician says again when I don't answer, 'magic is unpredictable and healing magic harder than most to master. I asked you before whether you'd take instruction . . .'

'I know what I'm doing.' I am unsure why, but I don't want him to see the acorn. 'I've been healing all this past year.'

'Not without herbs, I wager.'

His blue eyes are horribly piercing. I avoid them, picking up a jug instead. 'It's none of your business what I do with my magic,' I hiss and turn away.

'Thank you, mistress,' a young girl says when I pass her the water. She drinks feverishly as I bend over her pallet, and I think of my own desperate thirst when I was lost in the forest. I take the jug back when she is done, watching as she wipes a drop from her lips. They are cracked and dry and her eyes are dull. 'I cannot tell you how sweet fresh water tastes,' she sighs. 'I've had little but ale, sour from the skins.'

'I heard you've been travelling four moons.'

She nods.

'From Lindinis?'

She nods again, her eyes clouding at the name. 'I have never seen it,' I say.

'She was beautiful, my home. Lendiniae of the lakes. When the sun rose, it set the waters to flashing. Like our tiles.'

'Tiles?'

'Of all colours. Our craftsmen are very clever. Were,' she adds in a whisper.

'What happened?' I ask gently.

Her gaze grows haunted. 'They came when we were supposed to be celebrating. I heard Isberir say that they killed our lookouts. The warrior who spoke to your king, over there.' She points to the man whose breathing I've just eased. 'They were so many,' the girl continues. 'A horde. They had archers and great shields and their eyes were –' she drags a hand across her own – 'masked with black paint. They looked like demons.'

I want to tell her to stop, but can't . . . her story fills my head with too many pictures. I think of the horrors I can't possibly understand: the horror of battle and blood, of seeing your home overrun, its sunlit streets clogged with dead. Suddenly, the girl lurches forward, seizing a fistful of my dress. 'They will come here,' she whispers and I recoil from her fever-breath. 'They will come and they will take it – all of Dumnonia.'

'You're wrong,' I jerk free. 'They won't. They couldn't. The king will protect us.'

She sinks back onto her blanket and turns her face away. 'We thought we were strong too.'

The man called Isberir dies in the night. When I arrive the next morning, it's to see Myrdhin shaking his head over the corpse. 'This shouldn't have happened,' he mutters to Keyne, who stands beside him. 'He was stable enough when I left.' Then he flicks his eyes to me. 'I thought you healed him yesterday.'

'I did,' I say with a shiver. I've seen the dead before now

but – apart from Siaun – only once they'd been washed and laid out for funeral rites, their limbs composed and peaceful. I see no peace here. Isberir's open eyes stare at something none of us can see; whatever it is has left its mark on his face. Myrdhin regards the frozen grimace, a crease appearing between his brows. He and Keyne exchange a look.

'Did no one see him pass away?' I ask.

'Apparently not.'

'He didn't look well, before Riva tended him.' Keyne bends to cover the corpse with a blanket. 'I saw him coughing blood yesterday. Perhaps the journey was too much.'

'Perhaps.' Myrdhin seems unconvinced and a prickle starts between my shoulder blades.

'You think someone helped him along?' Keyne says, putting the prickle into words.

I swallow. 'No one here would do such a thing. Besides, what reason would they have?'

'Maybe he knew something.' Keyne's dark eyes range over the church's other occupants. Soft groans can be heard and the occasional gasp of pain. 'Maybe he had information,'

'As in he was a spy? A Saxon spy?' I say, eyeing the blanket-covered corpse anew. 'But then someone would have to have known that – and it can't have been anyone in Dunbriga. We've never met him before. If one of the other survivors knew, why didn't they kill him in the wild?'

'Lower your voice,' Myrdhin warns. He beckons to us both and we leave the church. 'There's nothing more to be learned here. I'll send someone to move the body.'

Father doesn't take Isberir's death as badly as Myrdhin. 'It's a blow,' is all he says when we go to relay the news. 'We were to have met today. He's fought Cynric's men, so is certainly more familiar with Gewisse tactics than we are.'

'This is more than a blow,' Tristan says from the shadows. I start; I'd missed him, so dark was the day. Servants begin to move about the hall with extra torches, banishing the gloom. By their light, I see Mother watching me, and I force myself to face pointedly away from Tristan.

'What do you mean?' Father asks him.

'Do you not find the timing of his death suspicious, lord? Just *before* he could pass on his knowledge.'

I am acutely aware of the servants trying to look inconspicuous, as if they know they are witnessing something they shouldn't. Father knows it too. 'Out,' he barks at them and when the hall is empty save for us, he rounds on Tristan. 'Watch your words, man of the Demetae. Will you accuse my people of treachery under my very roof?'

'Forgive me, lord, for speaking so boldly,' Tristan says, coming forward. 'But these are not normal times. There is too much at stake to ignore even small oddities.'

'He speaks true, husband.' Mother lays a brief hand on Father's arm. 'We would do well to heed his caution. It disturbs me that this warrior perished inside our walls. Even more so after Master Myrdhin vouched for his health.'

I was the one who healed him, I find myself thinking resentfully.

'There isn't a need for panic,' Tristan says. 'But this man had information he can no longer share. At the very least we ought to ask ourselves why he died when he did.' He gives a short bow in Myrdhin's direction. 'I've heard Master Myrdhin is rarely wrong in matters of healing.' His eyes, however, flicker to me.

I am not sure what to make of Tristan's words. He clearly believes we have a spy in our midst. But why would they come here and what do they want? I rub a hand over my face. I've begun to feel tired lately, as summer drags on, without a hint of real heat. I need sunshine. It would help soften the long shadow of war stretching over us.

Tristan is watching me, a question on his lips, but I can't talk to him with Mother present. She is especially vigilant when Tristan and I are in the same room together. Sometimes I think she isn't fooled at all.

'Have the farmer sent to me instead,' Father says to Tristan, as if he is one of us – one of the servants perhaps. 'Echel, wasn't it? I can think of several things I'd like to ask him.'

29

KEYNE

Lammas – the harvest festival

There are no dances this Lammas.

We'd all seen the signs – the cold, the wet, even the ash rain. But no one wanted to believe they heralded anything other than a bout of poor weather. No one wanted to believe that this was due to our king's neglect. The price of change; the price of embracing a new religion and forsaking an age-old bond with the land. When I look up, the sun is bluish, as if frostbitten, and its light is veiled. It could almost be the moon.

Last year's harvest was disappointing, but it's nothing to the death I see in the fields now. It's the same story across the rest of Dumnonia. Riders have been coming and going from Dunbriga bearing the news: we walk on the knife-edge of famine. It touches us even in the king's house. Our stores are low and nothing is wasted. Our bread is thinner than ever, old flour eked out in an attempt to weather the coming winter. And we have the Duro-triges to feed too: two hundred mouths at last count.

'My household is an added burden on you,' Banon Bedeu says to Father. He speaks in a low voice, but I hear it, despite the fact I'm sitting a goodly distance away. It's one of the things I've started to notice, this increased strength of hearing – alongside keener vision and a greater clarity of mind. I think it's tied to mastering the patterns. I can pick out a dozen now: the wind's circle, the water's curve, the jagged angles of thunder. But I can't do anything with them.

Mori tells me it'll come in time. She has given me papyrus texts, incredibly ancient, which she insists I read. I'm terrified they'll crumble to dust when I touch them. They are mostly in Latin and cover all manner of things – from history to military tactics to depictions of peoples and cultures I've never encountered before. Although they are hard to understand, odd passages have a tendency to come to mind later, when I'm half asleep, as if I can only see them in that state. I wonder if they are patterns of a sort, captured in writing, teaching things I can't learn from the elements around me. Some of that knowledge settles behind my eyes, dormant, waiting.

'You are my kinsman, Bedeu,' Father replies. 'It is my duty to shelter you – and your household.' The only other people in earshot are Gildas and Tristan; the former sits with a codex on his lap, the latter with a sword and cloth. He's polishing the metal until it's a streak of silver in the gloom. Mother and her ladies – including my sisters – are tucked up in the women's quarters. It makes me wonder whether my garb bestows a kind of invisibility; whether Mori is right when she says people see what they expect to see. A sweep of skirt would surely catch the eye in a hall full of men.

'Still,' Bedeu says, 'I find myself thinking we fled Moriduno too precipitously. We have stores there, stores which I am loath to gift the Saxons.'

Tristan glances up, sword still in hand. 'A significant quantity?'

'When famine threatens, even a small bag of flour is worth its weight in gold.'

Father rubs his chin, staring deep into the flames. 'Are you proposing a foray, Bedeu? Into unsecured territory?'

'I suppose I am,' the old lord says. There is something brittle in his gaze as he studies the others. 'One I will lead.' He doesn't voice them, but I sense the words fluttering behind his closed lips. *Though it may be my last.*

Gildas snaps shut his codex. 'This is madness, surely. As King Cador says, the territory is dangerous. Who knows what you may find?'

'Dangerous, yes.' Tristan turns his blade; fire runs up and down its length. 'But not without potential reward.' He looks at Father. 'If you deem it worth the risk, allow me to lend you my sword in payment for your hospitality.'

Riva won't like this.

Father purses his lips. 'It's true, gifting any supplies to our enemies in a time of famine is foolhardy – if it can be avoided.'

'I do not pretend to have Isberir's experience,' Tristan says, 'but I encountered the Saxons at Old Sarum and have even led small sorties. It seems the best way to proceed would be to take just a few men – no more than fifty, say. That way, they could remain beneath notice or strike hard and fast if the situation demands it.' He pauses. 'We do not even know our enemy's position, or how much land they now control – land which lies on your very doorstep. Sallying out to gain that knowledge would be equally worthwhile.'

Father is scratching one cheek with his forefinger. So he's actually considering this. I've been following their debate for a while, but for the first time, I feel a stab of worry. It urges me to rise up and demand that they abandon this plan. We are not so badly off yet that we must risk our men's lives for flour.

'I admit I've longed to take the fight to our enemy, to bloody them as they bloody this land.' Father shakes his head. 'I've held off only because we are secure here, and I have no wish to throw lives away.' He looks at Gildas. 'What do you say, priest? Would such an action find favour with your god?'

'Our God,' Gildas corrects with a frown. His long fingers stroke the cover of his codex. 'The Saxons are sent to test us, to test our faith. They are not a godly people. They do not belong here.' He speaks his next words slowly, as if feeling out their truth. 'I agree. Spilling the blood of heathens is a worthy cause.'

He called me heathen too once. So he considers Myrdhin and me no better than our enemies, slaughterers of innocents. I can't say I'm surprised, but it makes my fists clench.

The only sound is the fire as it crackles on, uncaring of conquest or the lives lost in pursuit of it. Tristan's eyes gleam. So do Bedeu's. The promise of blood seems to have banished the old warrior's weariness, lifted his long-stooped shoulders. 'I will speak with my sworn lords,' Father says. 'I would seek their blessing. If they give it, I will lead this sortie myself.'

I can't help it. Some force compels me to stand and I'm dimly aware that my feet have carried me to the circle of men. 'This is not wise,' I hear myself say.

They jump in their skins like night creatures caught in the sun. I've startled them, appearing behind the central fire pit – which forces them to look through the flames to see my face. While they're still off balance, I add, 'The Saxons will expect a sortie. The threat of famine benefits them. It will make us desperate.'

'The longer we wait, the weaker our warriors become,' Banon Bedeu replies, clearly not realizing who I am yet. He's already lost in his campaign, excited by the idea of some small revenge on the people who have driven him from his home.

'Keyne,' Father barks. His eyes sweep the hall, as if wondering where I was hiding until now. 'What are you doing here?'

I ignore the question. 'The territory outside our hold is unsecured – you've said it yourself. You have no idea of Saxon numbers. And even fifty men leave traces of their passage.' I take a breath. 'If they catch wind of your presence, the King of

Dumnonia's presence . . . they will show no mercy. They will slaughter you all.'

There is silence. Father stares up at me and I can tell my words have struck a blow. Then he seems to remember how to stand and it's my turn to look up at him. 'I do not give you leave to speak to me so, child. You know nothing of warfare, or battling. This is my country and I will do what is best for her.'

'But it's foolish,' I appeal – of all people – to Gildas. 'To fetch supplies, you will need horses and carts. They move slowly, are easy to spot. Fifty men are not enough to guard a convoy.' Gildas is watching me and I hope he is considering my words, but it's Tristan's gaze that burns into me. He is wearing a half smile, a strange smile, and I do not like it.

'I won't warn you again,' Father says in a growl, coming around the fire to face me. 'Return to your mother and sisters and we will say no more of this.'

Abruptly I realize he no longer towers over me. I have to look up, yes, but only a little. It gives me the courage to say, 'No. I do not belong with them. I never have.'

He draws back his arm, quick as a striking snake.

I ought to take the blow, the first he's ever threatened. I should give him back the power I've so carelessly stripped from him before the eyes of other men. But my months of training won't let me. My feet steady instinctively. Quicker even than he, I move to counter and I catch the blow as it falls.

We stand locked, arm to arm. There are bells in my ears. I can feel his muscles straining as they struggle against mine. He is strong, I grant, and no stranger to violence. Although I am younger and have trained hard for months, my shoulder trembles. We are close enough to lock gazes too. And in his eyes, besides anger, I make out something else, something almost wistful.

It frightens me. My arm gives another protesting tremble. I break our stalemate, pull away, and turn on my heel. 'Keyne,'

Father says, but I am at the door, opening it, stepping out into the afternoon. Blood rushes to my face. I can still hear the bells.

'Well,' says a voice, 'finally.'

Myrdhin leans against the wall, arms folded. I'd have missed him if he hadn't spoken. 'Finally what?'

'You found sense and the courage to speak it.'

I feel a niggle between my brows. 'You heard?'

'Enough to agree that Cador's plan is foolhardy.' He sets off at a brisk walk and I hurry to join him. I don't want to be here when the group emerges. I am wrung out, as if I have spent a whole day's energy in that hall, standing eye to eye with Father.

We pass a house. Shouting reaches us through the thin walls, punctured by a baby's wail. I catch only a word or two, but I can tell it's about food. 'Supplies would be useful,' I concede, 'especially flour. There's little enough to go around.'

'Bedeu wants battle, not food,' Myrdhin pronounces darkly and I'm forced to agree.

'I heard his death wish,' I say without thinking.

Myrdhin pauses. I feel his eyes on me, but then he's nodding. 'Of course you did. He shouted it to the heavens for all to catch it – if they would.'

I cannot keep down a shiver. 'It worries me. They ride for the stuff of life, but carry one who seeks death in their midst.'

Again, that gaze is upon me. 'You have grown, Keyne,' Myrdhin says in Mori's voice. 'Soon you'll be needing another name.'

I blink at the person beside me. 'A name?'

'You will find the world eager to push them on you. But the only names that matter are the ones we take for ourselves.'

'It's too dangerous,' Gwen says later, as we sit together on the beach. 'I can't believe my uncle would risk going back.' The little cove is sheltered from the wharves by a shoulder of cliff. It's one of the places I like to come when it's all too much, to stare instead at the boundless, uncaring sea.

'That's what I told them,' I reply. 'But Bedeu wants revenge. I think he wants it more than the supplies.'

'He would,' she says distantly, gazing at the waves. They are red today, having taken on the colour of the cliffs. 'He's a proud man.'

'They are all prideful men. Too proud to admit they might be mistaken.' A little bitterly, I add, 'Too proud to listen to me.'

She lays a tentative hand on my arm. 'You did what you could.'

'It wasn't enough.' I am overly conscious of her touch, innocent though it is. I want to edge away. I also want to cover her hand with mine. I do neither and she doesn't remove it, so we sit there in silence while the waves tumble and crash. Their bloody colour feels like a portent. I can't help imagining it's the blood of our people, *my* people, as we're driven at last into the sea.

'Keyne,' she says suddenly. She looks at me, her gaze direct. 'What are you going to do?'

I sense more than one question. What am I going to do when Father goes to war? What am I going to do if the Saxons come here? What am I going to do if they don't – and Mother tries to force me down a path I could never walk?

I don't know the answer to any of these and perhaps it's a good thing. There is a freedom in choosing to live from moment to moment, safe from past and future. Mori taught me that when she showed me how to fight. Myrdhin taught me that when he revealed the patterns within the land. *Now* is a place where I can choose not to be afraid.

Instead of answering, I find myself saying, 'To my parents and my sisters, I am a woman in a man's garb. They have never seen anything else. They may never see who I am.' My gaze is as direct as hers. 'Maybe I can't blame them, but I also can't accept their version of me. Because it's not true.'

I haven't spoken so honestly to anyone. But Gwen is not of our hold. She has never known me as a daughter of the royal house. Her first sight of me was of *me* as I am. Perhaps that makes all the difference. I hope it makes all the difference.

Her hand tightens on my arm. And this time, I cover it with my own.

30

SINNE

I can't breathe.

Fire in my mouth and nose, fire in my eyes. When I scream, it roars down my throat, burning it, burning *me*. I stumble; the smouldering stone tears at my skin and the flames tear at my soul until I am nothing. I am nothing.

I can't breathe. My face is buried in the pillow. I roll away, gasping, tangled in a nest of blankets, which I flail at until I'm free of them. My heart's sprinting. For a moment, I barely recognize my dimly lit part of the women's quarters. And it's so quiet. A moment later, I realize why. I kick free of the nightmare as I did the blankets, yank on dress and overdress and fling myself out of doors.

This morning, Father rides for Moriduno.

It seems as if all Dunbriga has gathered to wish the men well. I dodge through narrow ways, muddying shoon and skirt. The nightmare is still with me, but dormant now, a sleeping dragon. I am trying not to think of it, trying not to remember what it felt like to burn. It must be the burden of being a seer; it touches me in the same way Myrdhin's story touched me – the story of Lir and his river-sons. I couldn't shake that one for weeks.

I elbow my way through the crowd. Why didn't Riva or Keyne wake me, or Mother? She's over there, biting her knuckle, something I haven't seen her do in years. She's always so collected. Now her eyes are on Father and I can't work out what's in them. It isn't love. It's closer to anger.

When I spot Riva, I almost feel sorry for her – for the look on her face as the men assemble before the gates. Almost. Because her eyes are fixed only on Tristan, handsome in his fine armour. She spares a glance for no one else, not even Father, and doesn't care who notices.

She's not the only one staring at Tristan. Mail coats are rare; Father has one, and a scant handful of his lords. 'It's been in my family for years,' I hear Tristan say when one of the men enquires. 'Passed down a few generations before it reached me.'

'And has it served you well?' Father asks him.

'My hide's still in one piece, so I should say so.'

I admit I'm looking at Tristan too but also at the other men, milling like dogs before a hunt. Their eyes are bright, almost feverish, their hands fingering hilts. The air is sharp with well-oiled harness and the steaming droppings of horses. I do a rough count – close to a hundred warriors are mustered here, each bearing spear and sword, shields lashed to mounts.

'Let us not waste what little daylight we have,' Father calls, swinging into his saddle. 'We ride for Moriduno!'

There are cheers and cries from many throats, the watching women adding their voices to the chorus. Some stand with wet eyes. When Tristan mounts his great dark horse, his mail catches fire in the sun and he could be mistaken for the king himself. My father seems to ride in his shadow.

Thank the goddess I put tokens in my dress last night. Hands plunging into its deep pockets, I run first to Father, offering up a posy of wildflowers I picked and bound with twine. He receives it solemnly. Next I dash to Tristan. Him I offer a single wild rose, rich and bloody red. When I spotted a bush growing in an unexpected corner, I knew one would serve as a good token. Tristan might be riding to battle, after all, if the Saxons already hold Moriduno.

He reaches out a hand, careful to avoid the thorns. I could have trimmed them, but where's the fun in that? Roses are meant to be barbed and beautiful. In the fleeting moment when we both hold the stem, I turn the full force of my glamour on him. The trances I practise have made me more susceptible to the fire-vision – but also stronger, more focused. Tristan's eyes widen. He blinks, as if seeing me for the very first time. I imagine it: he sees a girl, no – a woman, her hair tumbled gold in the sunlight. He sees her eyes, kingfisher blue. And her lips, a shade lighter than the rose. He wants to touch her skin, tilt her chin upwards. If only there weren't so many people watching . . .

Pain stabs and I gasp. His hand has closed tightly on mine, the rose stem still between us. One of the thorns is sinking into my palm, perhaps into his too, but I can see he doesn't care. His eyes on my face are narrow and dark. We are close enough for him to whisper, 'Is this really what you want, little girl?'

All I can do is stare at him, in pain, in horror.

'Because I don't think it is.' His smile is hard. 'I don't think you know what you're asking.'

He lets go before I can rip my hand free, thorns or no. Blood oozes from the centre of my palm. I stumble, can barely breathe through the pounding of my heart. Rose still in his hand, Tristan gives me a last scornful look. The bloom is especially striking against his pale skin. Then he turns, spurring his horse into a trot, and the gates swing wide to let them all through. My shoulders slump as I watch them ride off. I'm exhausted, as if I've danced day and night. I catch sight of Keyne, who looks desperate to mount up too.

I've gone only a little way, enough to distance myself from the women reluctant to leave the gates, when something slams into me from behind. I stagger, catching myself on the timber wall of the armoury. Heart hammering, I whirl around, straight into Riva's flushed glare.

Although she's not much taller than me, she looks it now. 'What do you think you're doing?' she snarls.

'You *pushed* me.'

'You gave him a rose.' She's shaking and the sight unsettles me. 'Why? Did you use your glamour on him too? *Did you*?'

I have a flippant response on my tongue, but I swallow it. 'No.' It's barely a lie. My glamour was useless. It's never failed before, but she's giving me no time to wonder why. 'I just thought a rose was appropriate.'

'In what way did you think a *rose* appropriate?'

'Well . . .' I consider repeating my earlier thoughts about thorns and blood, but I'm not sure how well she'll take them. And they suddenly seem rather childish in the face of her rage. My stomach squirms when I remember Tristan's words. 'Why are you so angry?' I ask instead.

Her wind falters a bit. 'I . . . He . . .' she draws a breath. 'You *know* how I feel about him, Sinne.'

I sense a peace offering. And I do know how she feels. It's plain to half the hold. But I must have a darkness in me because instead of taking the olive branch, I say, 'I know how you feel about him, certainly, but how does *he* feel about *you*?'

Some of the blood leaves her face. 'You don't know what you're talking about.'

'It's a simple enough question.'

'Tristan loves me,' she declares with only the tiniest wobble. But I hear it. I'm listening for it.

'How do you know? Has he told you?'

'Of course he has.'

It's a lie. Doubt crawls over her like a sea fret. 'And how has he shown it?' I needle. 'Has he asked Father for your hand?'

'He . . . We are not ready for that.'

'Either a man's *ready* or he's not.'

'What do you know?' she flares, regaining some of her colour. 'You're just a child!'

'A child whose hips he likes to watch when he suspects no one is looking? A child whose hair he coils in the palm of his hand?'

Her eyes go wide. 'What?'

It's cruel. I *am* just a child to Tristan and I have to force down fear when I remember his cold smile. But I'm still bitter about the dream where he was *mine*, and how Riva got her claws in him before I ever had the chance. I shrug. 'Just don't be so sure of him, Riva. He has eyes enough for other women.'

The next moment, my ears are ringing. Suns burst. The fire torments me, promising relief and then withholding it, burning, blackening my skin . . . I shake my head, coming back to myself in time to see Riva cover her mouth with her good hand. It trembles.

My own hand comes away from my face bloody. She *hit* me. In a mist of anger and shame, I still can't quite believe it. She can't either. Her eyes are huge, staring at the mark her hand must have left. 'Sinne . . .'

I whirl away before the sob in my throat finds a way out. She doesn't follow. I go through the hold like a storm, teary and raging. No one stops me. No one sees me. I keep to the quietest parts, until the sea forces a halt. Moving and unmovable. It would drown me if it could. At least it would put out the fire. The fire that's in my hands, my arms, that bursts from my shoulders like wings –

I gasp. There really *is* fire. It crackles out of me, leaping off my skin. But it's not burning me. How can this be? My breath comes fast. The fire is alive, jumping between my hands, familiar like a friend whose name I've forgotten. I don't want it to go. It's so beautiful, deadly beautiful. It's wild.

Wildfire.

I remember it. I've summoned it before. I can feel it inside me, laughing like the old lord whose mind, they say, was stolen by the moon. It's too strong . . . I can't keep it in the circle of my arms. I can feel its hunger, its want, and I start to panic. Because I'm losing control. It will burn the boats and the fishing nets. It will burn the seagrass and the rock beneath it. The very ocean will catch fire –

Slim brown hands close on my shoulders. The fire kicks and bucks. My earlier wonder has evaporated entirely into terror. But Myrdhin whispers nameless words that take root in my soul. I calm and the fire dwindles, leaving a smoky stain on my skin as it sinks back beneath it.

'Sinne,' he says and I cling to him, suddenly overcome and crying uncontrollably. I feel loss and fear in a terrible tangle. For a moment I had it back: the power that Tristan took from me. But it was too much. It almost escaped, as it did once before . . .

I freeze in Myrdhin's arms. Memory, not vision. Memory.

I pull back. 'This . . . This has happened before. I remember—'

'Sinne,' Myrdhin says again. I hear caution, but the gates are open now, understanding streaming through.

'Oh . . . *goddess*.'

'It wasn't your fault, lass. It was an accident.'

She was screaming as she burned, trapped in the little stone smokehouse I'd locked her in. Stone shouldn't burn. We'd argued. Something stupid. She made me angry – she's always been able to make me angry. So I burned her. I didn't mean it. The latch had stuck and the wildfire didn't care that I didn't mean it.

'What have I done?' I whisper, staring at my hands. They are white beneath the patina of smoke, and so small to cause such harm.

'If it is anyone's fault, it is mine,' Myrdhin says with a shake of his head. 'I should have taken you aside, found out what you could do and taught you the rudiments of control. Instead I left it to Cador, not guessing he could ever turn from the old ways.'

'You told me I'm a seer,' I whisper. I can't seem to stop shaking, imagining Riva's twisted hand and foot. 'This isn't seeing. This is . . . something else.'

'Yes,' Myrdhin agrees and he sounds worried. What has he to worry about? There's no chance of *him* burning his family whenever his emotions get the better of him. I could raze my home to the ground, while standing unmarked amidst the flames.

'Does Riva know?'

'I don't believe so,' Myrdhin says after too long a pause. 'She doesn't remember.'

'But she might, one day.' I squeeze my eyes shut. She thinks she was careless, had only herself to blame. But *I* was the one who ruined her life. My lip throbs. Riva's slap will purple and swell, then I will look terrible. I can't bring myself to care, not now. 'I'm a monster.'

'You are not a monster, Sinne. Never that,' Myrdhin says. 'You were born into a powerful heritage, and you should have been made aware of it. But the rot set in long before Cador stopped visiting the nemeton . . . and I was not able to see it.' He bends to look into my eyes – not much, I'm almost as tall as he. 'Wildfire is one of the primal patterns, Sinne. Your heart calls it and your blood answers. I will do what I can to aid you, but you must learn *not* to call it unless truly necessary. Meditating will help.'

I'm not so sure. It's when I'm meditating that the fire comes for me. A moment later, I shudder, realizing that I've been seeing it all through *Riva's* eyes. The horrors she suffered . . . my heart quails within me. If that's what it means to be a seer, I wish I'd never heard of magic.

'I fell on the rocks,' I tell Mother later, as she inspects my chin. Riva sits across from me. She's pretending to work, but I catch her quick glances. She wonders whether I'll spill everything to Mother: how she's in love with Tristan, how she's expecting him to marry her and whisk her off to Dyfed.

I could. Maybe I should, but I don't. Because now I know I owe her a terrible debt, one I can never reveal and can never repay.

31

KEYNE

The fact I didn't accompany the king's men is an itch, an irritation, one my fingers aren't long enough to scratch. It's there when I walk through the hold, mud sucking at my shoon. It lurks in the long shadows beneath the eaves. When I close my eyes, it's an imprint on the darkness, a fading slap whose sting I can still feel. Some deep instinct is telling me I should have gone. I stand on the steps of the great hall, facing east. Dunbriga is eerily silent this afternoon, three days after Father's departure. I can feel that departure like a wound that throbs throughout the night, giving a patient no rest. We're vulnerable, but the king and his men are more so. I can't help thinking they're riding into an ambush. *They know what they're about*, I try to tell myself. *Surely they are a match for any Saxon attack.* But again I see the bloom in Bedeu's eyes, his desire for vengeance even if it ends in death. And my father has never been tested against the Saxons, never been without the power of the land in battle. In times past, he would ride with the skulls of his enemies tied to his saddle: ghostly arms would wield ghostly blades to protect the living.

'I have to warn them,' I tell the wind, which snaps my cloak in a chuckle. 'Who else will help?' I say angrily. Nobody would believe my vague misgivings, and maybe they'd be right. But I cannot spend another night sweating on my pallet.

I am sidestepping the enormity of my plan. How am I to get a horse out of the hold? How will I know where to go? Perhaps the ground is soft enough to hold the shape of wheels and hooves. Not for much longer, though. And what will I do when I get to Moriduno? Despite Mori's training, I am no warrior. Untested, unblooded, the men would claim. What place do I have amongst veterans?

'It doesn't matter,' I say aloud to quiet my own rambling questions. 'I still have to do it.'

'Do what?' says a voice.

Slowly, I turn. Gwen is wearing red; the dress I liked so much on her at Beltane. But its soft wool is dark under the heavy cloud, a foreboding shade. I swallow. 'Nothing. I was just thinking aloud.'

'I am beginning to recognize that expression,' she says, coming closer, and too late I feel the lines dug deep into my brow. I smooth them, but she's already seen. 'You're planning something,' Gwen accuses.

'Why would you think that?'

She folds her arms. 'Because you're skittish as a colt, always pacing. I knew I'd find you here, staring at the horizon.'

I blink. She's been watching me. Another time, her words might've caused a slow flush to creep up my neck. But I am too full of fret.

'You're worried about your father, about the men.' She turns her face into the wind. 'We all are.'

Above us, the clouds boil and thicken. The northern sky is dark. 'It's more than that,' I whisper. 'Moriduno is a mistake. A trap.'

'This is fear talking,' Gwen says, coming to stand beside me. 'You can't know that.'

'I *do*,' I say fiercely and she actually sways at my vehemence. 'I feel it. I see it. If I don't warn them, they will all die.'

My words drop into silence. Thunder rolls along the distant hills.

'You cannot be serious,' Gwen says in its wake. She has paled. 'It's too dangerous, Keyne.'

'Maybe. But I couldn't forgive myself if I stayed behind walls.' I straighten, trying for confidence. 'Not when I can make a difference.'

'This is madness.' Red is fast replacing the pallor in her cheeks. 'There is no reason for you to go. None at all.'

'There are plenty of reasons, Gwen. I gave them before and my father wouldn't listen. Bedeu wouldn't listen.' My mention of her uncle pulls her up short. She presses her lips together. 'You know he doesn't intend to return,' I say quietly.

She looks away. Perhaps I've gone too far, said too much. She could easily betray me to my mother. Then I would be locked up to await the certain news of Father's death. 'Gwen,' I whisper. 'Please.'

'What do you want me to say?' She rounds on me. 'Give my blessing to a folly that will get you killed?'

We eye each other. 'I know it sounds like madness,' I say, 'and I can't explain how I know. Will . . . Will you help me?'

'Help you how?' The fire is still in her voice.

'I need to get a horse past the guards.'

She snorts. 'Oh, such a little thing. And then what? Do you even know where you're going?'

I look at her helplessly.

'All right,' Gwen says after a long pause, and my heart quickens. 'I will help you. On one condition.'

'Yes?'

'That I come with you.'

It takes a few moments before her words hit home. I stare at her wide-eyed. 'No. No, it's too dangerous.'

'But it's not too dangerous for you?'

'I . . .' My mouth is dry. 'I can defend myself, Gwen, if needs be. But you—'

'I'm a weak woman, am I? Too cosseted to hold a dagger?' She shakes her head; one brown lock pulls free of her braid. 'You need a guide and I know the way.'

'I couldn't forgive myself if anything happened to you,' I say through the dread churning in my belly. 'And what would your uncle do if he found out I'd put you in danger?'

'*You* haven't put me anywhere. I make my own decisions.'

I shake my head. 'Getting one horse out of the hold will be hard. Two impossible.'

'Myrdhin will help us, yes?'

I am running out of arguments. Desperate, I stare at her, but can't see any cracks in her stubborn facade. It's true, I don't know how I'll track Father and the others without a guide. 'Please,' I try one last time. 'Don't ask me to do this.'

'If you want to reach the king in time, this is the only way.' Her gaze is hard, harder than I've ever seen it. As we stand there in taut silence, the first drops of rain find us, flecking Gwen's cheek.

I feel my shoulders slump. 'I can't believe I'm even considering this. But –' and now it's my turn to regard her stonily – 'if there's fighting, you will stay out of it. Hide.'

To my surprise, she nods. 'Agreed.'

Thunder knocks again, a giant's knuckles on the hillside. I watch the rain sweep towards us and feel as if the steps beneath our feet are dissolving into sand.

Myrdhin dashes any lingering hopes I have of keeping Gwen at Dunbriga. Instead he studies us, blue eyes flicking between our faces: mine contorted with worry, Gwen's immovable. 'Yes, I think so,' he says and smiles. I ball my fists. How can he treat this so casually?

Something in Gwen's expression loosens. 'Thank you, Master Myrdhin. I don't know how we'll escape notice otherwise.'

Myrdhin narrows his eyes at me. 'You could arrange such a thing yourself, lad, if you had a mind to.'

'A mind to do what?' I ask murderously. Does he hold Gwen's life so cheap?

'There's no talking to him when he's like this,' Myrdhin says to Gwen, which coaxes a smile from her.

'I know,' she says lightly and I glare at them both.

Myrdhin sighs. To me, he says, 'If you want to conceal something, look to the pattern of air. A small manipulation. I'd show you now if you weren't sulking.'

Blood rushes into my cheeks. 'Do you take nothing seriously? Why are you letting Gwen come?'

The humour fades from Myrdhin's face. 'Is it my place to stop a woman from doing what she feels she must?' I hear Mori in his words. 'Gwen possesses her own mind. And if you wish to succeed in this, you'll need her help.'

At a loss, I look between them, feeling the fight drain out of me.

'It's just over a week's ride to Moriduno,' Gwen says. 'We'll need supplies. Warm cloaks and food for the horses.'

'Take my mare, lad,' Myrdhin lays a brief hand on my arm. 'Nimue will watch over you. And –' he slides a bracelet off his arm, a silver twin to mine – 'take this. You may need it.' I open my mouth to ask what he means, but Myrdhin gives a short shake of his head and I realize Gwen is looking at us, a crease between her brows.

I avoid Riva and Sinne as best I can while I prepare. Either one might read the intention in my face and start asking questions.

'Master Myrdhin requires his horse,' I tell the stableboys when I open Nimue's stall. 'He needs to visit his cottage for herbs.'

They share a glance, but don't question me. I know what they're thinking, though. None but Myrdhin would risk leaving the safety of Dunbriga alone these days.

Gwen waits for me on the lower terrace, holding the bridle of her own horse. I blink when I see her. She's wearing trousers and a tunic like mine, but clearly not as well made. Leather wraps about her legs and her hair is braided and tucked into a hood. She flushes a bit at my scrutiny, says, 'A dress won't do for a fast ride. Besides –' she lifts her chin defensively – 'you gave me the idea.'

'It's hardly an "idea" for me to dress as other men do.'

Her flush deepens. 'I didn't mean it like that, Keyne. I just thought it would be more practical.'

'Where did you get them?'

'I . . . borrowed them from one of the servants. Don't worry, I'll give them back.'

I imagine Gwen furtively shoving a bundle of clothes under her cloak and feel a smile tugging at the side of my mouth. 'Are you ready?'

She pats her horse's saddlebags. 'Everything except for food.'

'I have it,' I say, thinking guiltily of the food stores. Even so small a dent won't go unnoticed by Mother. I've left her a letter. I don't know what she'll feel on opening it. Anger, probably.

'It's sundown,' Gwen says with a nod to the greyish west. 'Let's go.'

My nerves are jangling like a locksmith's tools as we approach the gate. We'll slip out when the scouts return to the safety of Dunbriga before dark. I spot Myrdhin in the shadow of the wall. Although one guard passes within paces of him, he doesn't spare the magician a glance. I can see the strands he's woven around himself – a sheath of air that watchers' eyes pass over. 'There he is,' I whisper to Gwen.

She cranes her neck. 'I can't see.'

I don't have time to point him out before Myrdhin beckons us forward. 'This is it,' I say and step into full view of the guards, feeling the strands engulf us too. Part of me wants to pause and feel out the pattern, see if I too can pull it around myself like a cloak. But there isn't time. Nimue's coat is moon white, a beacon in the darkening day. Although I tense, no one looks our way. 'Hurry,' I hiss at Gwen. We mount, coaxing the horses into a trot. I share a last glance with Myrdhin as we pass him. He only has time for a single grave nod before we're through the gates and out into the farmlands beyond.

We put as much distance as possible between ourselves and the hold before full night forces us to halt. I spread our blankets in the lee of one of the great stone tors common in the land around Dunbriga. Gwen tethers the horses. We both of us work in silence and doubt suddenly drenches me. What am I doing here? My foreboding seemed so much keener in the hold, safe behind guarded walls. What if this is a mistake? What if I'm leading us both to our deaths?

'You're quiet. Are you regretting coming?'

I stare at her. We haven't lit a fire yet; the moon shows me the stubborn tilt of her chin. 'No,' I say. 'Just . . . It didn't feel real before. Now that we're out here . . .'

'It does,' she finishes.

'Gwen, you don't have to come.'

'I thought we'd been through this. Besides,' she adds wryly, 'it's a bit late for me to turn around now.'

I sigh. 'I guess so. Supper?'

'Hard biscuit, hard cheese, or hard meat?' she says, holding each one up.

I laugh and abruptly the dread isn't so consuming. 'Is there anything that isn't hard?'

'*You* were responsible for the food.'

'Huh.' I tear into a piece of salted meat and grimace. 'I tried to take things Mother wouldn't miss too much. Wish I'd been less careful.'

'You and me both,' she says, making a face at her cheese.

Later, we lie next to each other in the crook of the wild, sharing our blankets for warmth. An owl cries and Gwen jumps a little. 'I think we may both be fools,' I tell her after a moment, 'but I'm glad you're with me, Gwen.'

She finds my hand in the darkness. 'Me too.'

We keep to the wild country where possible, avoiding the roads. Father's party will be travelling more slowly, but they have three days' start on us. I imagine Mother's face upon discovering my letter and wince. No doubt a rough welcome awaits me when I return. *If* I return.

Every night, after an unsatisfying supper, we spar. Well, sparring isn't quite the right word, but I teach Gwen how to hold her dagger, just as Mori taught me, and we practise a few moves. 'I think you're picking this up more quickly than I did,' I offer, when she looks dispirited.

Gwen tilts her blade; the rising moon runs off it like water. 'I just wish Uncle had permitted real lessons. I had to bribe our smith to show me the little I know.'

'This is what I don't understand. In the old Ulster stories, Scáthach the warrior woman is accepted readily enough. She taught the legendary Cú Chulainn himself.' I scuff the dirt, irritated. 'And yet now men baulk at the very idea of a woman wielding a weapon.'

'Don't forget Boudica,' Gwen says with a flash of her teeth. 'She's not a story.'

'And yet she may as well be for all the difference it makes.'

Gwen is quiet a moment. 'It's as if by fighting, a woman is no longer a woman. In their eyes.'

I still. The hand holding the dagger falls to my side as I stare at her. It's because her words so closely echo something Mori said to me early on, after she explained about the Enarees and the Amazons. *A woman can fight and is no less a woman. A man can be a woman. A woman can be a man. And then there are those who choose to be both or neither. Do you see now, Keyne, how foolish are the names we force on people before they're even able to speak?* I remember the way her brows came together. *Your magic threatens Gildas much less than who you are – as a person. I fear this god of his is no fly-by-night. He is here to stay and people like you and me will have to fight all the harder to be heard.*

'But that does not mean we will be silent,' I whisper to myself.

If Gwen hears me, she does not reply. But she does step closer to lay a hand on my arm. 'Thank you for showing me what you know,' she says. She looks very serious in that moment and I feel it's not just swordplay she means.

'Tomorrow we'll see Moriduno,' Gwen tells me on our sixth morning out. 'We're about to cross into my uncle's holding.'

'We've made good time.' I lean forward to pat Nimue's neck. Myrdhin's mare seems untiring. Sometimes I catch her watching me. 'We must have closed the distance between us and Father considerably.'

Gwen slides me a look. 'What if Moriduno is already surrounded?'

'I'll think of something.' In truth, I have no idea what I'll do. I realize I've been counting on reaching Father *before* he's cut off. 'Maybe I'm wrong,' I say loudly half to Gwen and half to my own foreboding. 'Maybe we'll see neither hide nor hair of the Saxons.'

Gwen bites her lip. In my chest, the foreboding gives a hollow laugh.

As the day passes, I'm more vigilant than ever, seeking cover when possible, avoiding higher ground which would throw our silhouettes against the sky. As dusk stains the grey afternoon, Gwen reins in. 'We should stop now. There is little cover beyond this copse.'

We don't risk a fire, however small. Our supplies are running low too, so we make do with a single biscuit each. Gwen grimaces as she crunches through the thing; it's anvil-hard. After we've seen to the horses, we lie back on our blankets, doing our best to avoid tree roots. It's full dark now and the copse echoes with the sounds of the night: little scuffles and sighs, the creaking of branches in wind.

We're lying side by side again and, despite the threat of tomorrow, a small thrill courses through me at her nearness. I don't move. It's not that I haven't imagined it – I have. I remember what it was like to hold Gwen at Beltane, the shape of her beneath the soft red wool. But that memory is tainted by what came after, despite us being friends now.

We are making new memories, I tell myself firmly, listening to her breathing. Instead of Beltane, I think of Gwen cantering ahead of me, face turned back, cheeks rosy from the wind. I think of the courage with which she mounts her horse every morning, knowing we might be riding into battle. I think of her words during our journey, as she pointed out landmarks. She knows things about Father's kingdom that I have never considered.

Something fierce beats in my chest. 'I swear I will keep you safe tomorrow,' I whisper.

'And who will keep you safe?' she says, making me start. I'd thought her asleep.

I don't answer. Mori's fighting? Myrdhin's patterns? What else do I have to stave off death on the morrow? I think ruefully of the stories Myrdhin likes to tell after our training sessions. Can a story stop a blade?

The thoughts must have chased each other into sleep because the next thing I know the birds are up, their little chests full of carefree song. Dawn is creeping through the woods. Nimue eyes me from where she's tethered and her look seems to say, *You have work to do.*

'I know,' I tell her. My belly is too tight to eat, so I swallow some ale instead.

'What do you think we'll find?' Gwen murmurs as we ride towards the edge of the copse. We pull up our hoods as it begins to rain, but the material does little to keep us dry. I'm about to answer when the trees end and we come face to face with a haze of white. 'Not this,' I say, gazing at the fog. 'It's impossible to see more than a few yards ahead. 'Anything could be hiding in it.'

Gwen curses. 'Moriduno should be in sight, just. It's built on a promontory with steep cliffs on three sides.'

'How far?'

She screws up her mouth, thinking. 'Four leagues, maybe. But the land is flat the whole way.'

'No cover at all?'

'Scanty.'

'Well then. Perhaps the fog is a blessing.'

Gwen shoots me a dubious glance. 'As long as we don't end up going in circles.'

'I think we have to risk it,' I say. 'It might be our only chance to reach the fort unseen.'

The air thickens, the fog reeking of trampled green. Our horses' hooves make no noise on the shrouded grass of the plain. We ride for a long time and the day grows darker if anything. When I think we're veering too far east, I tug on the reins, but Nimue nickers softly, shaking her head and, after a moment's thought, I let her pick the route, trusting to Myrdhin.

'We should have hit the road by now,' Gwen murmurs, eyes sweeping the ground for some sign of it. 'Are you sure that horse knows where she's going?'

'No.'

'How reassuring.'

A shadow looms ahead of us. I jerk and yank on the reins. Nimue pays me no mind, however, and I realize the shadow is merely rugged stone, a cliff reaching far over our heads to vanish in grey.

Gwen utters a surprisingly dirty word. 'We've missed the road entirely. That horse has brought us to the base of the cliff. There's no way up.' She shoots Nimue an unfriendly glance. 'We'll have to circle back—'

I raise my hand to stop her. My sharpened hearing is picking up sounds in the fog, not the natural sighs of wind or grass or wild. Is that the clink of metal, a hushed word? I have to be sure. I dismount and drop into a crouch. Dragging off my leather glove, I hesitate before placing a hand against the earth.

Control. I hear Gwen's sharp inhale as silver light blooms between my fingers. When I close my eyes and follow it downwards, I don't follow blindly. This time I am looking for something. I flow past the small burrowers, the underground streams. The roots of the land cradle hewn bones, evidence of war. People lived, fought and died here long before Moriduno was built.

The silver convulses before its light dims so suddenly it almost takes me with it. I gasp, but there's no obvious cause. Just emptiness. My eyes snap open. There's someone here. Someone not connected with the land, with Dumnonia. It could be another tribe of Britons, but the only other tribe out this way are the Durotriges, and they're sheltered in Dunbriga now.

'What is it?' Gwen whispers.

'Stay with the horses.' I rise, moving my hand to the cliff wall for guidance. The fog swallows Gwen's warning and after a few more steps, swallows her as well. I steel myself, moving as silently as the ground allows. I'm wearing leather armour, the cuirass well padded against the cold. It doesn't give me away, whereas I catch . . . something creaking out there, shrouded by the fog.

The noises grow louder, surrounding me, and I pray my cover won't suddenly dissipate. A shoulder of the cliff juts ahead. I peer around it and immediately pull back. On the other side sit two men, black smeared across their eyes.

My blood races as I press myself tight to the stone. I hear movement and chance a second look. One of the men is now side on, the closest with his back to me. Neither seems alarmed and I ease out a slow breath.

The fact that Saxons are here should overwhelm me with terror, should send me pelting back to Gwen, the only thought in my head how to warn Father. But I find myself frozen, watching as the Saxons exchange companionable talk, words muffled by the white haze. I catch some of these, but it's not a language I know. The man sitting furthest from me is carving something. I squint. It's an animal, a horse, proud head flung back and captured expertly in wood. When he smiles and places it on the ground, I half expect it to come alive.

His companion says something, leans forward and picks up the horse. There is no doubt that it's a toy for a child. The breath catches in my throat as I watch the carver put away his knife and dust down his hands. After a moment he takes the horse back, studies it for a while and his eyes – his eyes beneath the black paint are full of longing.

I duck behind the stone before I risk seeing anything else to soften my heart. If the Saxons are here, they're here for only one thing: battle. It's them or us, I tell myself sternly, as I make my way back along the wall to where Gwen waits. 'What's wrong?' she whispers when she sees my face.

'Saxons,' I say and watch as her brows come together and her lips part in a silent snarl.

'They will *not* have my home.' Gwen mounts in one smooth movement, turns her horse. 'We must find my uncle.'

The fog has thinned just a little by the time we spot the road.

My head is full of the scene I witnessed and I stare at Nimue's bobbing ears, thoughts adrift. *She'd* taken me there, after all. *Do you want to make me doubt?* I ask her silently. The Gewisse Saxons have come to overthrow our kings, to take our land for their own. They are raiders who care nothing for my people. But I've never wondered about *their* families. I've never wondered why they left their own country . . . It's easier not to, I realize, and the thought makes me dizzy. It's hard to feel empathy for a people who have our blood on their hands. It's hard to imagine their hopes and fears – perhaps the same hopes and fears that live in us.

These thoughts plague me almost to the gates of Moriduno. 'Gwen,' I hiss just before we round the final turn of the promontory. 'What if the Saxons have already taken the fort?'

'If so, why are they camped out of sight of its walls?' she throws over her shoulder.

'We should make certain.' Cautiously, I urge Nimue forward. The steep side of the promontory rolls back and there are the gates: great wooden portals at least ten cubits high.

I hear Gwen gasp. They stand open.

32

RIVA

I thought Mother was angry when she forbade me to see Tristan, but her simmering rage on finding Keyne gone is worse. I feel sorry for the stable boys, blown into a corner by her shouts and curses. 'She said Master Myrdhin needed his horse,' one brave boy ventures from behind raised hands.

'And you didn't stop to wonder why in God's name Myrdhin would ride out at dusk?' Mother's cheeks are mottled red, a vein pulsing in her brow. 'Any fool would have known it for a lie.'

'Mother,' I try quietly. 'Myrdhin's a law unto himself. You can't blame them for not questioning. Besides, it's hardly their place to do so.'

She rounds on me. 'The girl then. Why did they let her take her horse out?'

'Mistress Gwen comes for her horse every day,' the boy says. 'She likes to walk him herself.'

Mother's nostrils flare and I realize her anger is a shield, one she can hide her fear behind. She opens her mouth, closes it, groping perhaps for someone else to blame. I could tell her Myrdhin isn't the only law unto himself; Keyne has always cared little for rules. But Gwen troubles me. I haven't spoken to the girl much, despite often seeing her sitting in the women's quarters. Keyne riding off somewhere I can believe. Not Gwen.

'She's sweet on Keyne, you know,' Sinne tells me, when I return to our fire-warmed hall. 'Your shoon stink of horse,' she adds half-heartedly. She's been quiet this past week.

I grind my teeth. Although Sinne's face still bears traces of my slap, I haven't forgiven her for the rose. She'd known perfectly well what she was doing. And what she'd said about Tristan . . . I want to slap her again for her poison. She's jealous. That much is obvious to me. And don't I know what it is to be jealous? I've envied her fair hair and eyes, her perfect limbs, her nightingale voice – envied them to the edge of despair. She draws the eye of every man she meets. She can have her pick of them. And yet she wants my Tristan, the only man who's ever looked at me and seen the woman, not the scars. Sinne is my sister. Can she not let me have even one thing for myself?

'Are you listening? I said Gwen's sweet on Keyne. That's why she went.'

'We don't even know *where* . . .' I begin before her words register. 'Sweet . . . on Keyne? Are you joking?'

'You'd have to be moon-addled not to see it.'

'Don't be ridiculous.'

'Why is it ridiculous?' Sinne tosses away her terrible sewing and leans back on her hands. 'Gwen doesn't see Keyne as a girl.'

I frown. 'But she is.'

'Has Keyne *ever* called herself a girl? Worn girl's clothing? Joined us women in the Imbolc procession?'

'She just doesn't like the ceremony, Sinne.'

My sister narrows her eyes at me. 'I've thought about this. It's not that Keyne doesn't like it. It's that a man wouldn't process.'

I stare at her, frozen in the act of pulling off my shoon. 'What are you saying?'

Sinne shakes her golden head. 'I'm saying that maybe Keyne is tired of being called a girl.'

The door bolt clanks loudly and we both start. Mother stands there, her cloak hem dark with mud. In her hand is a curl of lambskin, scraped clean for writing. When she holds it out, I recognize Keyne's wavy script. 'She's gone after him.' Mother's lips are white. 'She's gone after your father.'

'What?' I grab at the skin and smooth it out on a low table. Sinne's shoulders bump mine as she jostles to see.

Mother,
Father and Tristan are wrong. They are riding into an
ambush. I have to stop them before it's too late. I am sorry
for the food I took when it is scarce. I hope you will
understand. K.

'I cannot believe it.' Mother's cloak sheds mud all over the floorboards as she paces. She doesn't notice. 'They will both be killed.' I hear a catch in her voice that wasn't there earlier.

Sinne and I look at each other, my shock reflected in my sister's eyes. 'She *has* been distracted this past week,' I say, remembering Keyne's fractious roaming all over the hold. 'Perhaps she really did sense something wrong.'

'Nonsense.' It is Mother's response to even the vaguest mention of magic. 'This is to punish me for my words at Beltane.' She tugs at a loose thread in her cuff. 'She feels she has something to prove.'

Maybe she's tired of being called a girl. Sinne's voice echoes and I shake my head. 'No, Keyne wouldn't do this unless it was truly necessary.'

'You do not know what you say,' my mother flares, rounding on me. 'Why is it necessary to risk her own life and that of the girl? It is a whim, a foolish whim.'

'It isn't a whim,' Sinne pipes up. 'And –' she reddens – 'do you know the old barn by the cliff? Myrdhin has been teaching Keyne swordplay there.'

My mouth drops open. 'He *has*?' What else have I missed, with my thoughts wrapped up in Tristan? Goddesses, is my sister right and we've failed to grasp something so vital about Keyne? Guilt stabs me; I ought to know what it's like to be different – and to be judged constantly because of it.

Mother's pacing stops.

'So you see,' Sinne says quickly, 'Keyne's not defenceless.'

'How long has this . . . swordplay been going on?' Mother asks, that angry chill back in her voice.

'I don't know.' Sinne bites her lip, as if she regrets speaking. 'I only peeked once.'

'I will have words with Master Myrdhin,' Mother vows and is gone again before either of us can speak.

'Smoothly done,' I say to Sinne. 'Weren't you Keyne's champion a few minutes ago?'

She shifts away from me. 'I only said it to put Mother's mind at ease.'

'And see how well that worked out.' After a moment I add, 'Swordplay, really?'

Sinne grins. 'From what I saw, Keyne's really good.' The smile doesn't last. It fades as she stares into the fire and I wonder whether Sinne is thinking the same as I: that skill alone might not be enough to keep Keyne alive.

The days drag. Lammas is behind us now and autumn threatens to turn the trees. Every morning is a torment to me: waking to discover that neither Keyne nor Father has returned. I am often so sick with worry that I can't keep my breakfast down. That is a concern in itself since we have no food to spare. I break my fast later and later, waiting until the worry stops twisting my gut into knots. It never really leaves me, though.

Father's absence has given Gildas a new lease of life. I think our heathen enthusiasm at Beltane took the wind out of his sails, but now – with Mother's support – he's working harder than ever. I feel as if I spend half my life cooped up in the church listening to endless sermons. More people are turning to him, caught between fears of Saxons and famine. I've often seen Gildas amongst the poorest folk, sharing his meagre rations, helping to shore up draughty homes. It's no wonder they embrace his religion, especially now their charms and simple spells no longer work.

I grimace at the thought, fingering the black acorn I cannot throw away. But between the recited lines of Latin, I sense something growing, something forceful, unstoppable. A new God is opening His eyes amongst us. And I don't think they can be closed again.

Myrdhin, however, hasn't been idle either. Each night we gather about the fire in the great hall, building it up against the coming chill, and the magician tells stories to fill the void that Keyne and Father have left – of peasant girls and magic pools and the little folk of the hills. But if I am honest with myself, the void I feel most keenly is Tristan's. I hadn't realized how inseparable we've become, despite the way we carefully avoid each other in public. We are inseparable on a deeper level: he casts his shadow across my every thought. And despite Sinne's cruel words, I am sure I cast mine across his.

'I want to know more about this magic that lets you heal,' he said the last time we went to the nemeton together. We lay side by side on the soft moss and I'd long grown used to the broken skulls that watched us. Tristan propped himself up on an elbow. 'Where does it come from?'

'I used to think the gods,' I said. 'But Keyne says the gods are just faces of the land and it's the land that grants us power.'

'The land,' Tristan murmured, his palm flat against it. 'It's alive?'

'It gives us the harvest, doesn't it? But I know what you mean,'

I added before he could argue. 'You mean is it sentient? You would have to ask my father. The king and the land are one.' I paused. 'Or were.'

'Were?'

'As I said before, Father doesn't come here any more. He doesn't follow the old ways, doesn't listen to the land. He used to be able to do magic – he *was* called the drewydh-king.'

Tristan crinkled his brow. 'You told me those rumours were false.'

'Well they might as well be.' I shrugged. 'We're just like any other people now. Even the little magics no longer work.'

'So your healing is even more precious,' he said, running a hand down my arm. I shivered at his touch. 'And Keyne and Sinne. Do they have healing powers too?'

I shook my head. 'No. Myrdhin thinks Sinne is a seer, but she's more interested in casting foolish glamours.' Well, why shouldn't Tristan know? Sinne might still have tried to use it on him. 'Be on your guard. She could have all the men in Dunbriga skipping to her tune.'

'Not me,' he said firmly and I smiled. 'What about Keyne?' he added.

I sighed. 'Keyne . . . I don't know. She danced with the fire at Beltane and no one's done that since Father himself. I didn't think anyone could.'

We were both silent for a time before Tristan pulled me closer. 'I think it's safe to say I've never met a more remarkable family.'

Laughing, I reached out to play with one of his auburn curls. 'Tell me of *your* family.'

'Well,' he said, 'we may not have magical connections to the land, but my father –' here his eyes grew distant – 'he's a bear of a man, something special. And that's not just a proud son talking.'

I moved my hand to his chest, to the little arrow of skin framed by his tunic. 'Why is he special?'

'He's a great strategist, has a better mind for tactics than I do. He's won many battles against the odds, expanded our lands—'

'For Dyfed's king?'

'For the king,' Tristan agreed. 'Though I think my father would make a better one.'

'Why do you say that?'

'Most rulers think too small. They choose to stagnate rather than evolve, and that makes them weak, susceptible to being overthrown.'

I studied him. 'And what of my father? Dumnonia's king?'

'He is an enigma.' Tristan poked me gently. 'As are you.'

'Oh really?' I pushed him onto his back and climbed atop him. 'In what way?'

'You can't expect me to form a coherent answer when we're doing this,' he said and pulled me down for a kiss.

Is he even now bleeding out on the end of a Saxon spear? I shudder and clench my fists as if I can crush the thought into dust. I won't believe it. No news is good news, I tell myself. But at night my dreams are filled with horrors. Only news, one way or another, can bring me relief.

33

KEYNE

The sight of the open gates stops me short. Why would they be open unless the fort was already lost? I squint, searching for signs of battle. Instead, daring to ride a little closer, I see activity, men coming and going, bearing sacks on their shoulders. A wagon waits just inside, already half loaded. The wind blows me a shouted order and, with a surge of relief, I recognize my own language.

'It's them,' I tell Gwen and she gives me a shaky smile. I don't return it; a new dread is growing in me. Father must be unaware of the Saxons, or the gates would be fastened tight. I glance at the sky. The short afternoon is swiftly turning to evening. And with the onset of night comes a terrible certainty that this is what the Saxons are waiting for.

'Come on!' I cry, spurring Nimue. We gallop the few hundred paces to the gates, raising cries of alarm from the men there. 'Where is King Cador?' I demand, confidence bolstered by being on horseback. 'I have urgent news.'

'Gwen?'

The name is harsh with incredulity. I turn to see Bedeu hurrying towards us, gaze fixed on his niece. 'Uncle,' Gwen says and I wonder if it's only me who hears the trepidation in her voice.

'What?' Bedeu chokes on his question. 'By all the gods, what do you do here, child?'

'We've come to warn you,' Gwen says. 'There are—'

'*You.*' The old lord snarls at me and I flinch despite myself. 'This is your doing. How dare you put my ward in danger?'

'I didn't give Keyne a choice, Uncle,' Gwen starts, but Bedeu has begun to tremble, his cheeks purpling. His grey hair is matted with sweat and his eyes glare from dark pouches.

'Get down here and face me. Is this how you play at being a man? Putting innocent maidens' lives at risk?'

I am trying to keep calm, trying to remember the real reason I'm here, but Bedeu's words light a torch in the pit of my stomach. Nimue feels it, brings her hooves down hard on the earth. 'Where is my father?' I ask in a low voice, restraining my anger.

'Cador should have put a stop to this long ago.' Bedeu levels a shaking finger at my chest. 'You are unfit to bear his blood.'

I swallow. *He is not the enemy.* 'Get out of my way, Bedeu.'

'You dare threaten me now?'

'I am sure Keyne has a very good reason for being here,' comes a cool voice and Tristan steps into the semicircle surrounding Gwen and me. We lock gazes. He is as hard to read as ever, a slight smile playing about his lips. 'Do you not, Keyne?' he adds lightly.

'There are Saxons camped on the other side of the promontory,' I say. Tristan's smile disappears.

Bedeu scoffs. 'Lunacy. We have scouts upon the walls in each direction. They would have seen—'

'*Nothing* through this fog,' I snap. 'I tell you, the Saxons have used it to cover their advance. They are out there even now, awaiting their chance. I do not know their number, but there are surely more of them than us.'

Muttering amongst the men. I can hear my words borne back, as others enter the courtyard. Bedeu, however, only grows more livid. 'I do not care for your games, girl.'

'Why would I lie?' I shout, voice trembling with the outrage I am trying to control. 'If you don't leave now, you will all—'

'That is enough.'

It is Father at last, cloak billowing at his heels. The men hastily scramble aside to make room for him. I am still sitting atop Nimue, but now I dismount and give a formal bow, hearing Gwen do the same behind me.

'Keyne,' he says, eyes ranging over the horse, my armour, the weapon I wear openly at my waist. 'What are you doing here?'

'Trying to warn you,' I say, avoiding Bedeu's hostile eyes. 'There are Saxons out there, hiding in the fog.'

Father's stare is unblinking and I try not to shift beneath it. I straighten my shoulders. Eventually he says, 'True or not, you couldn't have known this when you left Dunbriga.'

It's the question I've been dreading. How to explain a feeling, a foreboding to men who now believe only in what they see and hear? How to explain that the magic which once protected our people is dying and it's the king's fault? A glance at Bedeu shows me he's ready to heap scorn on the idea. So I take a deep breath and say, 'Master Myrdhin had a vision.' I know very well that my friend is no seer – Sinne told me quite gleefully herself. But I'm counting on the mystery Myrdhin likes to encourage. A magician never reveals his secrets.

Father's face does not change. Bedeu opens his mouth to speak. Before he can, I say, 'A vision of a Saxon attack, an ambush in the dark. He saw the standard of Dumnonia fall. He saw our men slain and –' I swallow for effect – 'our king perish.'

Utter silence greets my words. The wind wakes, begins to batter the steep hill upon which Moriduno is built. Too late, the fog is dissipating, giving way to another cover: night.

Eventually, Father says, 'Then why didn't he come himself? In the event of such an attack, his power—'

'He is an old man. I am younger, faster and not without . . .

ability. As you see, he gave me his horse.' I turn to Gwen. 'Gwen heard it all too. I never wished to put her in danger, but I needed a guide if I was to reach you in time.'

'I insisted, King Cador,' Gwen says firmly, stepping forward and I admire her unwavering voice. 'I have a duty to home and kin. I did what I had to in order to uphold it.'

No one replies, but some men exchange furtive looks. Duty is something they understand. It binds us all. And then, to my astonishment, Father says, 'What do you propose then, Keyne?'

Over the surprised murmuring of the men, I say, 'Are the supplies ready to move?'

'Almost.'

'The Saxons will not wait for dawn. They're in place to strike tonight.'

Immediately Father is shaking his head. 'They would be foolish to storm a hold in the dark. No, any concerted attack will come at dawn when they have light on their side.'

'You're wrong.' This time the men do more than murmur. I know I am out of line, but the foreboding is so strong it's a sickness. I can't say why, but I look at Tristan. He's come to my defence before. But he doesn't speak, either for or against my plan. So I say, 'They will not wait, Father. You must begin preparations for an assault.'

'You will remember your place,' the king growls. 'So far, I have shown forbearance, more than is sensible for a man who has not seen the truth of your claims.'

'But—'

'I am king here,' he roars and the force of it rocks me. My mouth is dry. The knowledge that he's making a dreadful mistake churns and roils in my belly.

'It cannot hurt to send out sentries,' Tristan says, finally speaking up. 'If our enemy does indeed move on us tonight, we will have sufficient warning.'

'Very well,' the king agrees after a moment's reflection. 'I think it unlikely, but we will exercise caution.' He flicks his eyes at me. 'It will satisfy my impudent daughter, at any rate.'

I clench my fists. *Daughter*. Does he have even the remotest idea how deeply the word cuts me? Staring at his rigid face, I think not, and a flame that had begun to burn in my chest dies. It's the hope that he might believe in me. That he might look at me and see the son who has always been there.

I lead Myrdhin's horse away from the wagon, as the men continue to load supplies. Paternus, one of Father's sworn lords, is choosing sentries. With a pang, I watch the small group head into the darkness. The gates are closed and barred behind them.

'It's not enough,' I say to Gwen. 'Those men will be killed.'

'You don't know that. Perhaps the Saxons *will* wait for dawn.'

I swallow a retort, having no wish to argue with her. And she may be right, I tell myself. All I have to go on is a feeling.

Moriduno is small, about a quarter of the size of Dunbriga. As is typical of our settlements, it's built on top of a hill. And this one is especially defensible; three sides of it are sheer faces of craggy rock. There are the usual buildings: stables, smithy, tanner's yard and a cluster of homes, all surrounding the timbered hall at its highest point. Away from the gate, the wall that rings the settlement drops to waist-height – more to stop errant children falling to their deaths than to keep out an invading force. Presumably the steep cliff does that all on its own. Still I am drawn to its edge, peering over into the gloom.

'Why so pensive, Keyne?'

Tristan comes to lean on the stone beside me, clad in that gleaming mail. Its linked rings catch the torchlight and I wish for a set of my own. I shake off the desire, returning my gaze to the darkness. 'You'll think I'm moon-touched,' I say.

'Try me.'

'The king is wrong. The Gewisse won't wait for dawn. And –'

I hesitate – 'the more I think about it, the more I'm convinced that they won't attack the gates.'

Tristan twitches. 'What do you mean?'

'The cliff.' I wince as the words leave my mouth because they're so improbable. 'They were camped at the base there for a reason, not just to keep out of sight. I think they plan to scale it . . . somehow.'

Tristan raises an eyebrow. 'In the dark?'

Looking at his expression, I know I shouldn't have spoken. 'Forget I said anything.'

After a moment, he rests a hand on my shoulder and I try not to flinch. 'The king may not admit it, but you were wise to come here, Keyne.' His tone, however, belies the statement: cool, calculating, not warm with approval.

I eye him. 'You don't think it a folly?'

'Like you, I have learned to listen to my gut,' Tristan says, removing his hand. 'It's never led me wrong yet.'

I draw a breath. 'So you think there will be an attack tonight?'

'I could not say. But we ought to be alert.' An answer without an answer. I watch him walk away, readjusting the gold-chased sword at his side.

Despite the knowledge that there are men on watch, I do not sleep. I cannot, every nerve afire. While others rest, I pace up and down near the gates, my shoon crunching on the stony ground. Hours pass and no attack comes.

'Does your mother know where you are?'

I jump. For an armoured man, Father moves quietly. 'She will by now,' I say, not looking at him.

'I take it that you didn't inform her of your plans in person?'

The combination of weariness and tension makes me terse. 'Hardly. She'd have locked me up.'

Father chuckles and I glance at him, surprised. 'Quite,' he says. 'I cannot imagine she'd condone you riding off on a whim.'

'You think I'd risk my life – and Gwen's – on a whim?' I say hotly, forgetting to whom I'm speaking. 'I know you and the lords hold little regard for me. But that does not mean I lack the courage to do what my instincts tell me is right. It does not mean I turn my back on family.'

I watch my father's face cycle through expressions, as if the muscles have a will of their own. Finally it settles on something I have no name for. Perhaps it's anger, or hope. Pride, or shame. I do not know my father well enough to tell.

'Keyne,' he says quietly, holding my gaze. 'I am sorry for speaking so to you earlier, in front of the men.' After a pause, 'It must have taken courage to come here.'

I want to tell him I came because, despite everything, he is my father. That our home is unprotected without him. I want to tell him that denying his birthright will doom us – Saxons or no. I want to confess that I've touched the living heart of the land. *How* could he turn away from that? There is no going back from what I saw beneath the soil of Dumnonia. Not for me.

Before I can put any of it into words, the night erupts. It's so quiet that a shout sounds like a thunderclap. More voices join it, rising from the gates. I share a single alarmed glance with my father before we throw ourselves into the torchlit dark.

The area around the gates has become an anthill. Men rush, struggling into armour, belting on swords. I spot blood on the ground and follow its trail to see the heads of our sentries, hewn from their bodies then hurled back to us over the wall. Father's face is a mask of fury. I am too full of horror to feel any sense of vindication.

'Gwen,' I gasp, whirling round. I find her at the stables, helping saddle the horses. She doesn't appear to have slept either, her eyes bruised-looking, face pale.

'Have they broken through?'

'No. But they killed our sentries.'

'How many are they?'

'I don't know. I don't know what they plan.' But a moment later, a great crash echoes through the hold. A ram. 'Gods,' I curse. 'They're bringing down the gates.'

'They'll have their work cut out,' Gwen says with a tremor in her voice. 'Those gates are banded with iron. They won't breach easily.' She catches a stallion, saddles it. When she returns her gaze to me, there is no sign of an answering tremor in her face. 'But if they do, we'll be ready for them.'

Nimue shoulders the stallion aside, bumps me with her chest and I swing onto her back without thinking. 'I have to check something,' I shout down to Gwen. 'I won't be long.'

She nods, already turning to another horse. Nimue knows my thoughts. As one, we gallop up through the narrow dirt streets, hooves ringing in the dark. Not quite dark, I realize with a glance at the sky. Grey is already bleeding into the night. For some reason, this makes me spur the horse faster, towards the back of the hill – below which I saw the Saxon camp. My heart is pounding, a heavy thump like the ram against the gates.

I dismount at a place where the cliff is not so sheer and peer over the edge.

They cling like dark clumps of moss in the gloom, moving slowly, but inexorably up the face of the rock. Hooks and hands are the only things keeping them from a terrible fall. The nearest is just paces from me. We lock eyes.

I stumble back, straight into Tristan. He's holding the reins of his stallion.

'I saw you haring off up—' He stops on seeing my face. 'What is it?'

I was right. 'The cliff,' I choke out. 'They *are* scaling it. If they breach the gates too, we'll be caught in the middle.'

'The gods.' Tristan glances over. 'Go, Keyne. Warn the king.'

'What about you?'

Tristan draws his sword, a grating ring in the gloom. 'I'll hold them off as long as I can.'

I gape at him. 'Alone? You'll be killed.'

'I should have listened to you.' His face is set. 'Go.'

'But . . .'

'Don't waste time.' In his eyes, a stubborn glitter. He stoops to pick up a stone, an additional weapon. 'Someone has to warn King Cador. What good will it do the men if we are both slain?'

I don't waste another minute. I swing onto Nimue's back. I know Tristan is right, but I can't help feeling guilt as I ride away, leaving him alone at the cliff's edge with only stones to rain down upon the Saxons, and his sword as a last resort.

I reach the gates in seconds. Men brace against them while the rest are mounting up, ready to charge the enemy as soon as they break through. For all Gwen's claims, it's just a matter of time. Already I can see cracks in the wood. The pounding of the ram hasn't paused.

'Father, there are Saxons scaling the back of the hill,' I cry.

About to call out an order, he rounds on me. 'What?'

'They mean to catch us between two forces.'

'Arrows!' Father yells and a group of bowmen let fly a volley, high over the gates. There are multiple *thunks* as shafts hit shields beyond, but also screams. 'How many?' he barks.

'I couldn't see well. Two hundred at a guess.'

Nearby, Paternus and Luch exchange glances. Concern is carved deep into the faces of both lords. 'We don't have enough men to defend on two fronts,' Paternus says.

I take a breath, tensed for a rebuff. 'We came seeking supplies, not battle. When the gates fall, we must force an exit.'

'What foolishness is this?' My heart sinks as Bedeu strides up to us. Torch ash is smeared with sweat across his brow.

'We're mounted,' I say, struggling to be heard over the crash of the ram. 'The Gewisse are not – I heard the farmer from Lindinis say that their strength is in infantrymen. But their numbers are greater. If we wait, we'll be trapped between forces and overwhelmed.'

'I will not give up my hold without a fight,' Bedeu snarls, hand tightening on his sword hilt.

'You had already deemed it lost,' I retort. 'We're here for supplies to stave off famine. And only that. We must force an exit for the wagon, then ride for Dunbriga. It is the only way.'

'It is a coward's way. A woman's way.'

Sudden silence wraps us. I feel myself straighten. Everything is sharper, the reek of sweat and fear, the grunts of men at the gate, the first, unconcerned trill of a lark high above. When I raise my hand to point at Bedeu, my voice rings out, the silver on my wrist blazing. 'We are not here to sate your pride.'

His eyes widen, the red receding blotchily from his cheeks. And then, in a screech of hooves, Tristan comes hurtling into the courtyard. He is sweating and bloody, the sides of his horse heaving. Behind me, I hear wood splinter.

'I couldn't hold them,' he gasps at my father. 'Ride out now, before it's too late.'

Father gazes at me, at the shining silver on my wrists. There's a question in his eyes, but we both know there's no time to ask it. 'Mount,' he shouts.

'But . . .'

'Moriduno is lost, Bedeu,' the king snaps. 'I will settle for a smaller victory.'

'Keyne!' I turn to see Gwen riding beside the wagon and I am abruptly filled with fear for her. 'We're charging through?' she cries.

'*You* aren't,' Bedeu says. 'Get in the wagon, child. Stay under cover.'

'I can ride—'

'You are still my ward!' the old lord bellows at her. 'Do as I say.'

Gwen meets my eyes. As much as I hate agreeing with Bedeu, I nod at her, silently reminding her of our deal. *If there's fighting, you will stay out of it.* Gwen looks murderous as she slides from the back of her horse and hands the reins to the man beside her. 'Take care of him, Owain.'

'Of course, mistress.'

I feel better when the wagon's canvas covers Gwen. But when Father turns to me, words on his lips, I snap, 'Don't even think about it. I will not hide.'

'I was going to say, stay close to the wagon,' he replies, donning his helm. 'You've too much of your mother in you for me to argue.'

Now that no one's bracing the gates, the splintering is worse. I catch a glint of metal, the capped head of the ram. My guts clench at the sight and I have to force down a surge of dizziness. Is it the same for every man here? Have they grown accustomed to the churn of battle, the crushing fear, the possibility that death is seconds away? Or does all this return with each new fight? If my father feels it, his face betrays nothing.

Nimue is a solid, warm presence beneath me. I tear my eyes from the ram and lay my hand against her neck, guiding her into formation with the rest of the men. I hear Father giving hasty orders to his lords. First a charge to scatter the enemy, to force an opening for the wagon. Then we split, half to guard the wagon, the other half to fight – buying it time to flee.

'Now!' Father yells and Nimue springs away. The pounding of hooves is deafening, but my blood thrills to it. We thunder across the open space, reaching the gates as they swing wide. The impact of horseflesh meeting men shudders through the front ranks. Nimue shrieks a challenge to the sky just as the sun breaks free from the hill. Dawn's light pours across the land, revealing the Saxon host at last.

My thrilling blood freezes. The Gewisse are a plague on the green, a shadow in the sun; a void swirls beneath their feet. Their numbers are . . . I cannot even guess. On a low mound just out of arrow range, a standard is planted: a golden dragon, roaring at the return of the light. Beside it stands a figure: massive and armoured, helm tucked under his arm.

'Cerdic,' Tristan cries beside me. He is pointing at the man, his teeth bared, and the cold flooding my blood chills every part of me. If Cerdic himself is here, Cynric must be too.

I look back at the wagon, rattling in our wake. The man driving it shouts at the horses, urging them on. They're free of the ruined gates now and rumbling down the road behind us. One of Father's lords and his men close up, so that the wagon is ringed on all sides.

A guttural shout pierces the morning and from the corner of my eye, I see arrows nocked. 'Shields!' I hear myself cry, trying to raise my own in time. It isn't large enough to cover both me and Nimue. I can only hunch in the saddle as death whistles overhead.

The arrows find their marks. Screams, both human and animal, fill the air. Some riders fall away and all we can do is spur our mounts on, hampered by the slower wagon. If we get out of range –

All eyes are on Father, as if the men are waiting for him to call up the earth in our defence. Maybe he could once. Maybe he could pull the ground out from under enemy feet, blind enemy eyes with the sun. But I've seen how weak the land is, how little power flows through its veins of rock and water. Even if he could command that magic, its might is sorely diminished. Once, land and king strengthened each other. Now Father only has a general's knowledge, a common warrior's strength.

Yet the Saxons have mastered both; without magic to help them, these are their weapons. When I look at the whirling black beneath Gewisse feet, I realize I'm seeing more than a simple absence of magic. I'm seeing magic's opposite: a potent belief in human strength alone, a world where magic does not and cannot exist.

It is terrifying.

An arrow bursts through the throat of the wagon driver. The horses' eyes roll and they veer left as the corpse slumps sideways, reins still clamped in his dead hand. One wheel leaves the road entirely, jolting through the grass. If it comes loose, I know there's no chance of saving the supplies our men are dying to protect.

Before any of us can act, the canvas is thrown back and Gwen leaps out. My cry is lost in the wind. Bending low, she scrambles across crates and barrels to reach the seat. I can't bear to look and I cannot look away. Any moment now another arrow flight will come.

Unceremoniously, Gwen shoves the corpse of the driver aside, wrenching the reins from his hands. She shouts to the horses, pulls them back onto the road. I catch a glimpse of Bedeu's face. He's pale, but his eyes on Gwen are hard and fierce.

'Paternus, stay with the wagon!' Father yells. 'Trachmyr, Luch and Gormant to me.' I watch at least fifty men peel off, thundering in a half circle to face the Saxon host. I don't know why I do it: I yank on the reins and Nimue turns to follow them. In that moment, Gwen looks back. Our eyes meet.

And then I'm leaving her, my name fading behind me on the wind.

Their arrows stop, as Father knew they must: we are too close to the Saxons for their bowmen to risk another volley. Instead they level their spears at us, a bristling death. We don't slow. The sound of horse and metal meeting is the most terrible I've heard. There's a din of animal screams, tearing flesh, human cries – as men are ridden down and crushed under hoof.

My hands are sweating, one in Nimue's mane, the other clutching my shield. A Saxon lunges for my stirrup and I punch out automatically, sending him tumbling back into the melee. Gewisse warriors are dead and dying all around us, but that is a fraction of their whole, a tiny portion. If we are pulled from our mounts, it's over.

Bedeu swings at a man on the ground. The black streaked across the Saxon's eyes is mixed with blood from a scalp wound. But instead of falling under Bedeu's blade, the huge Saxon catches it and uses it to yank the old lord from his saddle. I hear my father cry his name, but it's too late. Banon Bedeu disappears under a forest of swords and his killer seizes the reins of his horse, swinging up and turning it, riding straight for the king.

The Saxon's teeth are bloody, his eyes alight with resolve. Uttering a battle cry, Luch thunders across his path, sword raised, but the man brings a spiked mace around in a sweeping arc to cut Luch from the saddle. I have to tear my eyes from the lord's face, disbelieving even as he dies.

Only Gormant stands between the Saxon and the king now. Father's facing away from the scene, busy hacking at the men trying to pull him from his horse. Everything is happening too fast. I spur Nimue towards them, but am forced to lash out with dagger and shield or risk being pulled down myself. I am too slow, far too slow.

It is agony to watch as Gormant fails to parry a vicious blow from the mace. Although he stays in his saddle, I can see that his arm is broken, reduced to mangled flesh. The Saxon doesn't wait to finish him but continues his charge towards the king, weapon raised, aiming for Father's unprotected back.

I do the only thing I can think of. I call the fire.

It answers; it shouldn't have done. The only fire here is in the sky, unreachably distant. But Myrdhin's second silver band is hot on my arm, matching the heat of the first, and I know this pattern well. A wall of flame roars up. It's ghostly – I have to dig deep to find a vein of magic in the land here. But it's enough to make the Saxon rider shriek and Father turns at the last possible moment.

The mace takes him in the jaw. Everything seems to slow and the air is thick with blood. It's not a killing blow, but Father reels back; only a death grip on the reins keeps him from falling. Rage mixed with fear in his snarl, the Saxon raises the mace again – as Gormant forces his way through, reaching for the king.

And then Tristan looms at Father's side. The look on his face is terrible. His sword gleams in the new morning, oddly clean, though gore stains his horse's flanks. He raises it over his head and, in that moment, terror takes me. Stark and nameless. I lose my hold on the pattern and the flames flicker and die. Tristan's eyes meet mine; I see a fierce angry light in them and something seems to pass between us. And I realize I don't know anything at all about the world, or those who inhabit it.

The sword falls. It cleaves the huge Saxon warrior from shoulder to waist.

Tristan turns back to the king, but Gormant is there. He steadies Cador, his good arm keeping him in the saddle. Father is still conscious, but his eyes are glazed, his face a ruin of blood. And then the lord is breaking into a canter, breaking out of the melee, taking Father to safety.

'Withdraw!' I roar. The silver still blazes on my wrist; I thrust a fist into the air. 'Withdraw!' Bodily, Nimue and I force our way through the crush of men, growing bloodier by the second. Not all the blood is Saxon. Only the pounding of my heart, the fire of battle, is keeping the pain of my wounds at bay. Both of my legs are riddled with gashes where the enemy has tried to pull me out of the saddle. I hadn't noticed them until now.

Although I'm still holding onto the vein of magic, I need to follow a pattern to use it. Gritting my teeth, I search for fire again. It's hard to hold it in my head when half of me expects another arrow storm. I turn to look behind and sweep out an arm. Flame follows in my wake, cutting off the Saxons, covering our retreat. It's less ghostly this time; I can feel real heat on my back and hear the screams and curses of the enemy.

The air becomes sweeter, fresher, as I leave the stink of gore behind. Between the leaping flames is a scene of carnage: the tangled legs of dead horses, severed human limbs and guts spilled as if across a butcher's bench. I swallow, holding in vomit.

A deep whinny precedes Tristan on his stallion. The horse looks none the worse for the battle; I wonder how many it has witnessed in its life. Tristan glances back too, as our mounts speed us out of arrow range towards the now-distant wagon. That fierceness is still in his eyes.

'What if they follow?' I gasp at him, throat raw.

'They won't,' he calls back.

'How do you know?'

'Because they cannot outpace us without mounts. And it is not their way. They will not run blindly into unknown territory.' He looks sidelong at me. 'Besides, I suspect your display back there put the fear of God in them.'

Not God, I think.

'What other tricks do you have up your sleeve?' Tristan shouts over the wind's whistle. His gaze is calculating. 'Talents you've been hiding?'

'It's hardly a trick . . . the land knows its own.'

He frowns. 'The Dumnonian birthright? Is this like Riva's healing?'

My frown echoes his. 'She told you of it?' Privately I wonder what else she might have shared and have to force down unease.

'She claimed the magic was gone,' Tristan says, at a more normal volume; we've slowed to a canter. 'But then she healed me.' His raised a hand to his mouth. 'It was . . . miraculous.'

That Riva told Tristan so much about our magic surprises me. To hear she actually used it on him too . . . I shake my head. I don't think I recognize my cautious sister any more. Yet she's always had a rebellious streak, one she tends to bury beneath duty. After a moment, I say, 'You saved my father.'

'I didn't save him. Gormant must take the credit for that.'

'If you hadn't struck . . .' I give up. I'm suddenly weary, wearier than I've ever been in my life. The fire is now a distant flickering line behind us and I let the magic fade, slumping against Nimue.

Father is up ahead. I keep my eyes fixed on him, as Moriduno recedes. Trachmyr and Paternus have taken over from Gormant, who is drooping in his own saddle now, teeth gritted, face white with pain. The king's head is lolling, blood still flowing from the terrible wound. My belly clenches – I cannot heal. Myrdhin is his only hope. Or Riva. But both are a good week away.

Though death has done its best to empty me, still I have no room inside to consider the fact that Father might die. I have never felt close to him, but I am beginning to see the threads of the pattern that connects him to these men, to the hold, to the whole of Dumnonia. Those threads are already weak; if they're cut, what will happen? Who will mend them?

We halt when we catch the wagon. The king is fading rapidly; space must be cleared amongst the sacks and casks for him. When Gwen sees me, she jumps down and comes hurtling over, throwing her arms around me despite the blood and the stench. 'Are you wounded?' I ask her.

She shakes her head. 'You?'

My legs tremble beneath me and I'm forced to hold onto Nimue. 'A few scratches.'

'Serves you right,' she says a little shakily. 'Riding off like that.'

'You can hardly talk. What happened to staying out of sight?'

Gwen shrugs. 'I wasn't about to lose the wagon.'

'It was bravely done.' I smile at her and she reddens. But then her eyes stray beyond me, searching amongst the men.

'Where is my uncle?'

I'm silent. Again I see Bedeu, pulled roughly from his saddle, trampled beneath boot and blade. He'd shown me not a shred of kindness in life, but I had not wished death upon him.

'Keyne?' There is a ragged fear in Gwen's eyes.

I shake my head. 'I'm sorry.'

She turns from me, her hands over her mouth, shoulders beginning to tremble, and I don't know what to do or say. He was the last of her family. Instead my eyes go to the king, to his ruined face, to the laboured rise and fall of his chest. Will I weep for him if he dies? Will I weep for my father?

34

SINNE

We're sitting around the fire in the main hall when the doors fly open and panic floods inside. It's carried by the sentry bell tolling madly . . . and Tristan.

My heart jolts and Riva stumbles up with a cry, forgetting herself. But Mother isn't paying attention. She's hurrying across the floor to seize Tristan's arm. 'What is it?' she demands. 'Where is the king?'

Tristan gently shakes her free, gazing around at us all. Fear looks back at him; I can see it in every eye and there are pins and needles in my fingertips. 'Speak, man,' Arlyn barks out. 'Are we under attack?'

'No.' Despite the word, Tristan's handsome face is grim. Rain slicks his hair. 'But the king is gravely injured.'

'Cador,' Mother cries and dashes into the storm. I can hear it howling like the eldest prince in Myrdhin's tale. Arlyn throws Tristan a dark glance, as if this is somehow all his fault, before leaving too.

'Come in and get dry,' Riva pleads, but Tristan shakes his head. 'I must go back and help. I came only to deliver the news.'

'What happened?' I ask, pushing to the fore of the small crowd that's gathered around him. 'How was Father wounded? Where is Keyne?'

'Keyne is well,' he says, a strange glitter in his eyes, almost unfriendly. 'But the story is too long to tell now. We must get the king into the warm.'

'I will fetch my herbs,' Myrdhin says and pauses to look over Riva and me. 'Why don't you two help me prepare the king's chamber? I could do with your help especially, Riva.'

I'm not too happy about being drenched, but it's the only way I'll get to see Father. Riva and I exchange a glance and hurry into our cloaks. Riva struggles with hers; there's a twist of pain on her face as she watches Tristan turn tail into the storm, without even greeting her. I might've gloated if I wasn't so worried about Father.

It's foolish, but the royal quarters scare me a bit. This is my parents' sanctum and I feel like a child again, shut out from the things that go on inside. The doors seem smaller now. I've always imagined them the doors to a fortress, their handle higher than my head. Now that latch is waist-high. Still, I feel a prickle of disquiet as I enter.

Mother's hangings drape the walls; the air is sweet with rose-water. There's a raised fire pit, a smaller version of the one in the main hall. The bed has a feather-stuffed mattress, finer than mine, and chests stand here and there. Trinkets lie on tables. Myrdhin leaves us shaking out blankets and returns with his bag of herbs and a serving girl, who is carrying hot water.

We prepare for the king in uneasy silence until the door bangs open. Rain patters on the threshold as three men bear my father across, Tristan one of them. Mother clutches Father's hand, but he doesn't seem to see her. His face is a ruin of blood.

Myrdhin's eyes grow as grey as the sky outside. The lamplight doesn't spare our feelings either; it glares down on the king as if angry at his wounds. His jaw is shattered. I glimpse bone and splintered teeth, and have to turn away before I'm sick. When I risk looking up, Mother's eyes are fixed on the dreadful injury, one hand over her mouth.

'Please take the queen outside,' Myrdhin says.

'No. I must stay with him.'

'Take the queen outside,' Myrdhin repeats, but then he raises his head, staring at something behind us. I wheel around.

Keyne is a shadow in the doorway. Tall, armoured, the glint of weapons catching the dying daylight. I cannot call this person my *sister*. It isn't the warrior garb alone; the word simply doesn't fit. Perhaps it never has and we just didn't see or want to see. I remember my words to Riva. Perhaps Keyne left so we could grow new eyes in the time he's been gone. I cannot stop looking and my heart patters in my chest.

'Keyne,' Mother gasps and staggers forward – and I see Keyne wince as he's pulled into an embrace. Is he wounded too?

'How did this happen?' Myrdhin asks, gesturing to Father.

'A mace,' Tristan says. Imagining it, I feel another wave of sickness. I can almost see Father caught off guard, face turning towards that dreadful blow. 'They were clever,' Tristan continues and his eyes flick briefly to Keyne. 'Scaled an almost sheer cliff in an attempt to pincer us between their forces. We had to charge their lines. The king fought valiantly.' He looks down at Cador, cheeks pale with anger. 'It shouldn't have ended this way.'

'Ended?' Myrdhin smiles grimly. 'It has not ended. And we will do all we can to ensure it does not.'

'Look at him. Even you, Master Myrdhin, cannot heal this.'

'Perhaps,' Myrdhin says. 'But I am not the true healer here.'

For the first time, Tristan's eyes go to Riva where she kneels beside Father. Something passes between them. It's strange to see that cold handsome face soften into tenderness, especially when I remember what he looked like when I gave him the rose. Seeing him is strange and painful. Although I feel little but fear now, I remember the dream-vision too. It's taken me a long time to understand that it wasn't ever *my* waist he held, wasn't *my* chin he tilted: it was Riva's. It's always been Riva. Perhaps the wildfire forged an awful bond between my sister and me that day, one I hadn't realized was there until now.

'Of course I will help,' Riva says, clearly forcing herself to move. Tristan too turns away. As he passes Keyne on the way out, the two of them exchange a glance and I wonder what happened at Moriduno.

Myrdhin mutters something I don't catch. I look back at Father, unable to see how his face can ever be healed. His eyes are closed now, his breath the shallow rasp of the dying.

'It's well he sleeps,' Myrdhin says. 'This will be grim work.' He looks around at me. 'Sinne, will you stay too? Riva and I will need some help.'

'I'll stay,' I hear myself say. I'm not sure why. Even looking at Father is making my gorge rise. But he's my father. And Keyne has done his part. I want to do mine.

When we leave Father, an hour later, we're all bloody and exhausted – at least I am. Father woke up with a gurgled roar as soon as Myrdhin began picking out the shards of shattered bone. He was using an implement that looked more suited to torture than healing. I struggled to hold Father as he thrashed, frightened by the way his eyes rolled up to show the whites. His laboured breathing turned into chokes and gasps. But Myrdhin forced a steaming drink down his throat and he calmed a little, allowing Riva to lay her hand on him.

Despite knowing how it feels to hold the power of wildfire – my shudder is equal parts fear and dark delight at the memory – watching Father's skin regrow took all my words away. Riva's own skin turned silver and translucent as she drew up magic from the land, murmuring old words. She slumped when she'd finished, but her eyes were bright and Father's jaw, though badly misshapen, was somehow whole.

We ask for fresh water to wash ourselves. Myrdhin rinses his hands and face in silence. 'Will he survive?' I ask quietly, with a glance at my sister. Riva stands at the door, letting in air to freshen the stench of blood.

'I don't know, lass.'

My stomach drops. 'But Riva healed—'

'For men like him, such a wound . . .' Myrdhin pauses. 'They sometimes choose not to recover.'

'Father is strong,' I say firmly, though his words have woken worry in me. 'He would never make that choice.'

'Time will tell. You should be prepared, however.'

'For what?'

He says nothing until the three of us set out for the main hall, hoods pulled up to shield us from the constant rain. Once we are unobserved, he says into the gloom of the day, 'If the king does not recover, who will take the throne?'

My mouth dries. 'Mother? But she would have to remarry . . .' I trail off, unsure. In some irrational way I'd thought Father would rule forever. It's so ludicrous I feel ashamed for even admitting it to myself.

Riva, stumbling beside us, is very quiet. She clutches her burned hand tight to her breast and I can't look. Every time I see it, guilt pierces me – alongside the fear of what she'll say if she ever remembers.

Mother jumps up as soon as we enter the great hall, a blanket around her shoulders. Keyne and Gwen sit opposite her, side by side, both freshly washed. 'Cador?' Mother asks, searching Myrdhin's face. 'Will he die?'

'It is too early to tell,' Myrdhin says and I hear the news borne through the hall on a wave of whispers. 'Riva did her best, but he certainly cannot speak yet.'

'How then shall we know his will?' someone calls.

Mother's blanket slips to the floor. 'Through me,' she says. 'If my husband cannot speak, I will speak for him.'

The silence returns. Everyone is looking at her, me included. It's not unheard of; she is queen, after all, but doubt is a prickle in the room. Mother must feel it because she straightens her spine. 'The king still has his letters. I will consult with him when he is fit to hold quill. In the meantime, I will hear reports of the battle. Master Tristan –' she beckons to him – 'where is Bedeu?'

'My uncle fell in battle,' Gwen says in a clear voice, though grief pinches her face. A groan fills the hall, as if from the walls themselves. I see Keyne take her hand.

'What of Paternus, Trachmyr, Gormant, Luch?' Mother says, reeling off the names of Father's lords.

I look at Keyne, but it's Tristan who speaks.

'Luch fell too,' he answers soberly. 'And Gormant was injured. His wound turned sour in the time it took us to return. Paternus and Trachmyr stand vigil over him in the church.'

'Have them sent to me,' Mother commands and one of the hovering boys braces himself before dashing out into the rain.

By summoning the lords, Mother has essentially called a private council of war, but no one seems inclined to leave the hall, as if remaining might somehow dispel the threat. Then Mother claps her hands and barks out orders, and suddenly everyone remembers she is Queen Enica. Arlyn and his master leave, though the smith looks resentful about it.

'Gormant lies at death's door, my queen,' Trachmyr says as soon as he enters the now near-empty hall, Paternus on his heels. 'He should not be left alone.'

'I will go to him,' Myrdhin says immediately. 'You can best serve by remaining amongst the living.'

The lords want to protest; I can see it on their lips. But Myrdhin speaks with a command that only a magician possesses, and they let him go. Now it's just Mother, Tristan, Riva, Keyne, Gwen and the lords. And me, of course, desperate to hear of Moriduno's fate. I take a seat near Keyne.

'Why are your daughters present, my lady?' Paternus asks, flashing a glance my way. I glare at him.

'They are present because I want them to be.'

'We cannot spare their feelings. Battle is a foul business, unsuited for female ears.'

'I assure you my female ears are equal to the task,' Mother says, a touch drily. 'And my daughters have seen their share of Cador's injuries.' Her voice trembles just slightly on my father's name. 'I do not ask you to spare us.'

Paternus bows. 'As you wish, my queen.'

The news is as foul as he says. Between them, Tristan, Paternus and Trachmyr paint a picture: how all seemed well when they reached Moriduno. No signs of looting. No signs at all of Saxons. Clearly, Bedeu had said, he'd let fear sway him when he'd left – so his people might not share Durnovaria's fate. A man's home should not be lightly abandoned.

They found the deep stores untouched and brought horse and cart, loading up with stale, weevil-ridden flour they'd have disdained in a time of plenty. But weevils, Trachmyr insisted, could be picked out or simply baked into biscuits and bread. I feel a bit sick at the thought.

'It is tempting to let your guard down when you've had neither sight nor sound of the enemy,' Paternus says. The fire burns a haggard crimson; he appears older than his forty-odd summers. 'It shames me that we were not more alert.'

Tristan takes up the story. 'I must bear equal blame. When Keyne and Gwen arrived –' he nods at them – 'they reported seeing a Saxon host hidden in the fog. It was Keyne who warned us they might scale the promontory and I didn't listen. It seemed impossible.'

Keyne's eyes narrow on Tristan's face.

'They attacked the front gates and also fell on us from behind. If we were to have a chance at saving the supplies, we needed to force an exit.'

'Thank the gods we'd saddled most of the horses,' Paternus says. 'We rode out, guarding the wagon—'

'Which we'd have lost without Gwen,' Keyne interrupts. 'She was the one who drove it to safety through a storm of arrows.'

Paternus presses his lips together, but nods an acknowledgement. Gwen glances at Keyne and I picture the scene, barbs pelting from the sky. I can only imagine the terror Gwen must have felt. I don't think I could have done what she did.

'Cerdic himself was there,' Trachmyr says, 'with thousands of men. Still it looked as if we might get away, but the king—'

'He was surrounded.' The lords are competing to finish the tale, as if some purging tincture is forcing it up and out of them. 'Cador fought fiercely, buying time for the wagon to escape.' Paternus meets Mother's eyes. 'A great king is he who holds his men's lives higher than his own.'

'A foolish king,' Mother snaps, but there is no real anger in it. Her sigh is resigned.

'Foolish or brave, it ended the same. The blow near took him from his saddle. The Saxon would have killed him with the next, if it hadn't been for Tristan.'

Tristan is silent.

'Gormant said he cut the fellow in two,' Trachmyr says, not without respect. 'We managed to speed the king away.'

Finally Tristan looks up. 'I think you ascribe me too much honour. If Keyne had not distracted our enemy, the Saxon's blow would have been a killing one.'

I have been trying to see it as a story, like one of the great battles in Myrdhin's tales, but Father's damaged face keeps intruding.

It's too raw to be a story, too new. And he is my father, as well as a king.

'I thank you for the service you have done my husband,' Mother tells Tristan formally. She nods to the lords and finally to Keyne, where her gaze settles. 'And for your part in bringing our men home.'

'We brought home fewer than half of those who left.' Paternus closes his eyes. 'A high price to pay for a few bags of flour.' Slowly he opens them, stares at the flames. 'If the king dies too . . .'

'Do not even voice it,' Mother commands, springing to her feet. 'Cador is strong. He will recover. I will not call down ill omens upon my house.'

'As you say, my lady.' But Trachmyr is placating her. I'm watching him carefully, seeing the looks he's exchanging with Paternus. The lords believe Father will die. Perhaps they, like Myrdhin, are wondering who will step into the breach. Perhaps they are wondering whether *they* might seize kingship.

Riva calls me a dreamer, a child, but I am not. I could tell them that Father's shoulders have slumped a little more each day under the weight of duty. When he saw the arrow in the wrecked ship; when he learned of Lindinis and Durnovaria; when Mother told him we must feed more people than our meagre stores could manage.

Keyne's dark eyes are sober, but when they meet mine, he smiles. I go to sit by him and I put my arms around his neck, abruptly brimming with gratitude that the land returned him to us.

35

RIVA

Tristan has been distant since Moriduno. Even when we're alone together, his hands caressing my bare skin, his lips making me cry out, I feel he isn't really with me. His heart still beats to blood and battle. His eyes still see Cerdic. No matter how many times I ask him what's wrong, all he says is, 'I'm sorry, Riva,' and kisses me again. But that distance always comes back.

I am glad when Myrdhin takes his customary place by the fire. Gormant died from his fever yestereve and Father still sleeps the sleep of the dead. People whisper of Saxons, autumn and empty bellies, and the only tales being told are horror stories of the bloody Gewisse leaders.

'Beast of a man, Cerdic is,' Bradan says that evening. 'I was talking to a Durotriges girl who had it from a tile-maker in Lindinis. Brilliant and brutal.'

'What else?' Sinne asks, leaning forward. We are fascinated, all of us, despite ourselves. Like deer sniffing at the leaf-covered pit that will doom them.

Bradan glances at her, smiles slightly. 'Well, they say he's won a hundred battles across the east, that the chieftain of Vectis all but surrendered his isle – anything not to fight him.'

'Heard that too,' Farrar growls. The smith sits in a corner, slowly drawing a whetstone over his knife. I wince at every scrape. 'Even the Mercians are checking over their shoulders now.'

'Well that's saying something.' Tristan has one leg up on the bench, an arm around it, looking a picture of ease. 'Since the Mercians are bloodier by far.'

'True or not, the Mercians aren't the ones threatening our borders.' There are murmurs of agreement.

'And Cynric,' I say, deciding to join in. I can feel Tristan's gaze on me, have to stop myself returning it. 'What do they say of him?'

'Aye, what do they say?' Tristan echoes and I can't help but smile at him. He smiles back. My heart skips.

'Twice the height of a normal man,' Bradan tells the room. 'A devil with a blade. Makes a habit of slaughtering babes.'

'A giant, you say? And what of his dragon familiar?' Tristan asks and it raises a few chuckles to dissipate the tension. 'They talk about nothing else in Dyfed.'

'The rumour mill does not require more grist, Master Tristan,' Gildas says coldly. 'Especially not grist from Vortipor's court.'

'As you say, holy one.' But I can hear the amusement in Tristan's voice and so can everyone else. There is muffled laughter.

Before Gildas can gather himself for a riposte, Mother says, 'The priest is right. Rumour can only do us ill. Perhaps Myrdhin might tell a story instead.'

I find myself staring. She is usually the last person to request such a thing. It's a mark of how dire our situation has become.

'I will not play storyteller this eve,' Myrdhin says, and groans go up, mine amongst them. But he lifts a hand for silence. '*I* will not be storyteller. But you will have a story.' Over our confused and muttering heads, he says, 'Keyne.'

We all crane to look. Almost hidden in a crook of the fire's shadow, Keyne has turned quite pale. 'Well?' Myrdhin prompts.

'I . . . I'm not ready.'

He waves a hand. 'Of course you are. Now come up here.' He

pats the bench. The room seems to hold its breath as Keyne weaves a passage through it, docile as a lamb for once. When Myrdhin uses that tone, I imagine even kings fall into line.

Our new storyteller doesn't sit, but stands regarding us all, eyes flicking from face to uncertain face. I frown. 'Master Myrdhin,' Mother says, echoing our thoughts. 'What game is this? Keyne is no teller of tales, real or otherwise.'

'You may be surprised, lady,' Myrdhin replies politely, but with the same firmness of tone. He passes Keyne his handheld harp.

'I will tell you of Herla, then.' Keyne's voice strengthens, fills the hall like a call to arms. I marvel at its timbre, low and rich as Myrdhin's. 'And of the promise he made to the King of the Dwarfs.' The next moment, a shimmering chord sounds and it seems we stand in a forest of deep-hearted trees. I can almost hear the wind in their branches and feel my eyes widen. I've never seen anyone perform illusions, except the magician.

The Herlathing

It is said amongst the northern people that a great leader once rose to command. He was named King Herla, the mighty and the honest. And one morning found him riding with soldier and servant through a wood that bordered his realm. As the company passed beneath the arms of a great yew, a figure took shape, as if it had crawled from the very bowels of the earth. Perhaps it had – for the stranger declared himself a dwarf, nay, the King of the Dwarfs, and he bade Herla stay a while.

None could doubt the creature's claim, for his dangling feet were as cloven as the goat's upon which he rode and a crown nested in his copper hair. A beard he wore, down to his saddle bow, and his eyes were dark and cavernous –as if they regularly gazed upon the deep places of the world.

'Great surface king,' said the dwarf lord, 'I would offer thee a pact. Let me and mine attend upon thy wedding day. We will bring great merriment and gifts aplenty, and thou shalt want for nothing on this most splendid of occasions. But in one year hence, when my own day comes and I wed the Queen of the Faery Lands, thou and all thy retinue shalt attend me in my halls, returning the favour I so generously bestow upon thee now.'

Herla, as I said, was an honest man, but the dwarf's speech perplexed him greatly. For no bride awaited him at home. No wedding lay on his horizon. So he nodded and held out his hand to seal the bargain, thinking little of it.

Imagine his surprise then, on returning home, to hear his ambassadors celebrating a treaty signed with the Frankish king. Even now, a princess sailed for Britain and there would be such a wedding – the bards would sing of it and the ladies reel with it and all in the kingdom would rejoice.

The princess had a head for figures, and Herla was well-pleased. As soon as the first wedding banners were hung, a party appeared at the gates of the hold. Herla had forgotten his meeting with the dwarf king – but here the creature was, retinue spread behind him, come to honour the pact they had made.

And the dwarf was as good as his word. His weavers brought cloth of gold and silver; his smiths shining swords for human hands. The hold glittered with decoration. An eye could feast on jewels and goblets; a nose on the dewy petals of flowers that grew only in darkness. For three days they celebrated and the dwarf king's party showered the hold in music and song – ballads never before heard by surface ears.

On the fourth day, they departed, and Herla's hold was sad to see them go. 'Remember your promise,' said dwarf king to human. 'I will return in one year.'

Seasons are as inexorable as tides. Herla's queen quickened with child, giving birth to a daughter in springtime when bells *of blue and white blessed the realm. And it was not long after that the dwarf returned and asked Herla whether he would keep his promise. Our king was loath to leave his wife and child, but a pact is a pact and a promise is a promise. And remember he was an honest man. So he gathered soldier and servant, kissed his family farewell and, laden with gifts, he accompanied the dwarf. They travelled to a sheer cliff face, rugged and seemingly impenetrable. But at a touch from the dwarf, a crack appeared, gaping like a hellish scream. If Herla felt dread, he did not show it, but rode bravely forward into that crevasse.*

They traversed cave and chasm, pathway and pit, and Herla feared to look over the edge lest he lose his mind to the fall. For sounds crawled up from the darkness, clawing and gnashing, and once a baby's wail was heard. Herla and his men averted their eyes. They looked instead to the light provided them, which burned like a will-o-the-wisp in the gloom.

Wonder replaced fear when they reached the dwarven realm. A cavern vaster than any they had yet encountered unfolded before them, lit with a thousand candles. All manner of creatures capered there. Herla saw dwarfs and piskies and men with the heads of beasts, and he knew that he had strayed beyond the boundary of the civilized world. But he and his party drew only courteous glances, friendly smiles. They were plied with sweetmeats and nectar, pale fruits soft as hareskin. And though their surface gifts could not compare to the bounty on offer here, the dwarf king's subjects cooed over them and were much pleased.

There under the false stars that winked above, the dwarf king married the faery queen, who had none of his look. Indeed her dainty feet were human-shaped and her skin as dark as a moonless night. For three days, the feasting lasted, and Herla heard and saw such things as no bard would e'er believe.

On the fourth day, the dwarven king returned Herla's horses.

The animals seemed different now. Their eyes gleamed ruby and their smooth hides sparkled as ore caught in stone. With the king's party mounted, a small bloodhound was passed up to Herla, which seemed content to drape itself before his saddle. 'Here is my gift to thee,' the dwarf king said. 'Do not alight – or let any of thy men do so – until the hound jumps down.'

'Why?' asked Herla with a frown.

'Times change,' replied the dwarf. And at that, Herla and his men found themselves inexplicably outside, the opening in the cliff grinding shut behind them.

'Let us make haste,' Herla said. 'I am eager to greet my wife and daughter.'

They had not ridden far before they came upon a shepherd. He gawped and gasped at the great party, dressed so strangely, with horses rolling sulphurous eyes. 'How fares the road ahead?' Herla asked and the man's eyebrows drew together in confusion.

'I am a Dane,' said he in broken tongue. 'And you must be a Briton, for I can barely understand your language.'

Now great anger seized Herla. 'What do you do in my lands, Dane? Why announce yourself so freely?'

'These lands are under the Danelaw,' said the shepherd, holding his ground. 'It is you who trespass here.'

'You are mad,' Herla declared. 'What of this land's queen, my lady Gisela? She would not stand to hear you speak so.'

The peasant seemed troubled. 'I recall the name. But you speak of ancient history . . . Gisela was the queen of King Herla, who disappeared into the mountain and was never seen again.'

A great cold seized Herla. 'How long ago?' he whispered.

'Three hundred years at least,' said the man and he thumped his shepherd's crook on the ground. 'These are Dane lands now.'

'You will not utter lies to the king,' cried one of Herla's

servants and he leaped from his horse, fists raised. But the moment his feet touched the ground, he crumbled into dust.

'Halt!' shouted Herla. 'No one is to dismount.'

But it was too late – the shepherd fled, crying tales of witchcraft and dead men riding. 'Let him go,' said Herla to his bowman, who had an arrow nocked. 'For he is right and we are cursed.'

From that day forward, they rode and they rode, for the bloodhound showed no sign of jumping down. Death came to all who glimpsed them and it was whispered that Herla stole those spirits to bolster his ghastly ranks. Immortal they are, neither alive nor dead, and they will ride until the end of time or until the dwarf releases them. For none can trust the little folk of the hill. Their hearts are of stone – and beat in slow time to other gods than ours.

I see it all. Keyne's words bring them into our hall, words and something more: magic. Herla's horse breathes down my neck and I whip around with a half gasp. Although the tale has come to an end, perhaps it is my movement that breaks Keyne's spell because – like a straw man in a storm – all the illusions come tumbling down.

People stir and blink. None of us have time to regain our senses before the doors fly back and wind surges inside. At first I think it's Herla himself; there can be no other explanation. Then the cold gust slaps me sensible. Those are our guards and the man who hangs between them, beaten bloody, bears the Saxon dragon upon his cloak.

The hall erupts. Although it is just one man – no possible threat – women gasp at the sight of him and men spit, attempting to hide their fear. That fear is like a great black beast stalking amongst us – as black as the paint that streaks the man's eyes. We can all hear its breath. Its paws shake Dunbriga on its cliff. It makes me curl my toes and want to scream.

Even in the grip of four men, the Saxon glares at us. Mother rises to her feet, flanked by Paternus and Trachmyr. I've always thought Trachmyr the kinder of the two, but now his face is set and bleak. He doesn't seem in the mood for mercy.

'We caught him on the northern border of Cēd Hen,' one of the guards says and my heart beats sickly. That must be where I'd clawed free of the forest, the day Tristan found me. Scant leagues from Dunbriga.

'What say you, then, Saxon?' Paternus demands. 'What were you doing in our lands?'

The man clamps his lips together as if in response, but I'm not sure he understands. Paternus nods at the guards and one kicks the captive in the ribs. I hear a crack; a low growl of pain fills the hall and I have to glance away. 'I asked you a question,' Paternus says.

To my horror, the Saxon gives a choked laugh, then spews forth words in a heavy tongue. The guards kick him again and blood spatters the boards. 'Speak so we may understand,' Trachmyr snarls.

The captive twists in the guards' grip. I catch a word that sounds like Gewisse but no more. Incensed, Trachmyr strides forward, foot already aiming for the damaged ribs, but Mother's clear voice stops him.

'Saxon,' she says, looking down at the man, her face hard. I have to admire her composure. 'You are not in a position to deny us. I will hear your masters' plans, or you will be put to the torture.'

I gape at her. He might be the enemy, but the idea of torture chills every bit of me. Is she serious? Perhaps the Saxon wonders the same because he is staring at her through bloodshot eyes.

Then he says in broken but recognizable Brythonic, 'I . . . tell no words, whore.'

This time the guard doesn't wait for a signal before punching him in the mouth. The man reels from the blow, lip split and spilling blood down his chin. The eyes that glare through the paint are full of hatred.

Mother lifts a hand, seemingly unruffled. 'Now I know you understand me, I will ask again. What are Cerdic and his son planning?'

'Answer the lady,' Paternus barks.

The Saxon coughs more blood. 'Where is your king?' He laughs, turns his gaze on Paternus and Trachmyr. 'To be led by a woman . . . sign of weakness. You will all fall.' The room freezes, including me. Such conviction in the face of death. I shudder, suddenly wishing I had never come here tonight. Sinne's wide eyes tell me she's wishing the same.

And then Tristan is rising, his face dark with fury. I feel myself recoil; in that moment I don't recognize him. He draws his sword. It rings in the gloom and the captive stares at it, whites showing around his eyes. Then he starts to gabble in his own language, as Tristan stalks towards him. He is consumed by terror, flailing like an animal in a hunter's trap.

Tristan doesn't hesitate. He slashes his blade across the man's throat so violently that he half severs the neck. I turn and stagger a few steps away, bile rising in my throat, forcing its way out in a great heave. It's all happened in less than ten seconds.

'No!' I hear Paternus cry, far too late. I wipe my mouth and look back, eyes streaming. The lord marches up to Tristan, but even he wavers at the rage that emanates from the other man; I can almost see it – like a ripple of heat across a summer field. 'We had questions for him.'

'He wouldn't have said anything,' Tristan retorts, breathing heavily. 'I've seen his kind before.' He spares a hostile glance for the body at his feet. I can't look at it. I can't look at him.

'Still, taking his life wasn't your decision to make.'

Tristan gazes at Paternus and then beyond him to Mother. 'For that I am sorry. What I cannot be sorry for is spilling his worthless blood.'

I am shaking. I have never seen a man killed and I never wish to again. And Tristan . . . how can he hold such rage in him, such violence?

'This is grim indeed,' Trachmyr says into the hush. 'If Cynric's scouts are this close, we *must* call in reinforcements from across the province. Give the order, my lady. And tell them to bring what supplies they can.'

The Saxon's blood is pooling, dripping between the cracks in the boards.

36

SINNE

Samhain – the festival that heralds winter

My hair is going grey.

'Don't be ridiculous,' Riva snaps. 'Of course it isn't.'

'It is. Look.' I hold out a lacklustre lock. 'It used to shine. Now it's all dull.'

'That doesn't mean it's going grey, little fool.'

She's terribly waspish these days, Riva. She's always been the mildest of us, so it's disconcerting to hear her snapping and snarling like that runt pup Arlyn saved from Dapple's last litter. The dog's nothing more than a scrap of flesh, but it trails after him adoringly, yelping whenever anyone approaches the smithy.

'It's because I haven't had any good things to eat,' I say, dropping my hair. 'No honey or berries, or cream that isn't sour.'

'You are lucky to eat at all.'

She's right, of course. 'I hate being hungry.'

'Imagine what the people in the camp feel like. You're the king's daughter. You get twice as much as they do.'

There's a riposte on my lips, but her mention of Father deflects it. I'd brought him soup the other day. He can't take anything more solid. All his food must be pulped like a baby's before he can swallow it. He's just a shadow now, as if some faery stole my real father away and put a sickly changeling in his place. When he tries to write, his letters shake, ink weaving across the lambskin like a stream.

'We haven't had a ship for ages either,' I say in an effort to dispel the image of Father. 'Can the weather at sea really be so bad?'

'It's more than the weather,' Riva replies darkly. She stabs at her stitching, curses, sucks a finger a moment later. 'More wrecks have washed up along the coast, stuck with Gewisse arrows.'

'Saxons,' I say with a shiver. 'Do you think they'll attack us here?'

'We would be foolish to believe otherwise.' She winces, moves her hand to her back.

'What is it?'

'My time of the moon,' she says quickly, taking up her stitching again. 'I'm uncomfortable is all.'

'Ask Locinna to make you some chamomile tea.'

'It doesn't help.'

I agree, it doesn't help with the cramps, but I always sleep better. I close my eyes at the thought of a hot cup and clutch my blanket around me. It's as unseasonably cold now as it has been the rest of the year. We're all wearing multiple layers. I hate how the extra cloth makes me look like a fluffed-out wood pigeon, but it's better than being cold.

'We'll have snow soon,' Riva says, noticing my shiver.

'As long as it's not grey again.'

'That was ash, Sinne, not snow.'

'I *know*.' She's so humourless. 'Can't you try to smile at least once a day?'

'And what do I have to smile about?' she cries, throwing down her work. 'If we don't starve or freeze to death, we'll die at the hands of the Saxons.'

I flinch in surprise, scooting away from her.

'Don't you understand? We are all going to *die*, Sinne.' She's still shouting, now on her feet. 'And you sit here making jokes and complaining about honey.'

My mouth is hanging open. I close it, also rising to my feet – only so she doesn't tower over me. 'What's *wrong* with you?'

Her lips part, but no sound comes out. After a few moments, she says in a harsh whisper, 'Everything, Sinne. Everything is wrong.'

I'm grumpy through the overmorrow, I've always argued with Riva, but something about this feels different. Perhaps because a part of me knows she's telling the truth. That I really am a fool for fretting over honey and hair. 'What else can I do?' I mutter angrily to myself, stamping through the hold. I don't have Christ's way with bread, and two fish won't feed a thousand. And there'll be more mouths soon. We're going to be garrisoning a great force, larger than any Father's assembled before.

What will they say when they see him?

The talk hasn't escaped me. I've heard everyone – from stable boy to cook – discussing the succession. Tears prick my eyes. It feels as if they've already given up on Father, despite the fact it's nearly Samhain and he's still alive. But he's not getting any stronger either.

What will happen if – I force myself to think it – if Father dies? Will the lords squabble for the throne until the Saxons burn it out from under them? Perhaps Riva is right and everything is wrong.

'You seem contemplative, my lady.'

Surprised, I glance up to see the Moriduno girl, Gwen. The basket on her arm is full of linen. 'I was just on my way to the infirmary,' she says.

I look around. I've let my feet wander where they willed and they have dumped me in the middle of the hold, near a glum pen of sheep destined for the table. How long have I been standing here like a gaping fool? I straighten. 'I have a lot on my mind,' I say, trying to claw back some dignity.

'We all do,' she agrees, and though her smile is worried, it's also friendly.

'I'm sorry about your uncle,' I say, realizing how little we've spoken during the past weeks.

Her smile dies. 'I am too.'

An awkward silence falls until Gwen shifts her grip on the basket. 'Would you . . .?' she hesitates, before blurting out, 'Has Keyne always been the way he is?'

I blink. But hearing *he* out loud is not so very strange, not when I'm starting to use it in my head. 'I guess,' I say, thinking back. 'Keyne's never been like Riva or me.' I feel a pang at the thought of Riva, our lost closeness. 'Even so, we used to do everything together. Now it seems the three of us are a thousand leagues apart.'

'You are all rather different,' Gwen says. Her fingers clench and unclench on the basket. 'But I've never met anyone like Keyne.'

I remember Keyne's face as he watched Gwen that night at Beltane. I remember them dancing, graceful figures in red and black. Gwen's flushed cheeks. They are pink now too. I narrow my eyes, amused. 'Why so interested?'

Her blush deepens. She tries to shrug it off. 'We've become friends, that's all.'

'But you didn't seem so eager to be Keyne's friend at Beltane.'

'Well, I was wrong,' Gwen says fiercely. 'I shouldn't have run away. I was just . . . surprised.'

The wind is picking up, whipping my braid painfully against my neck. I grab it, pull it forward. Seeing the fierceness in Gwen's face, I say, 'I'm glad you're his friend. He's changed so much this year – for the better – and I think you've played a part in that.'

If anything, Gwen reddens further. 'He is an easy person to . . . admire.'

Perhaps her nerve failed because I am sure *admire* was not the word she intended to use. Gwen coughs and lifts her basket of linens. 'I'd better get back to Master Myrdhin.'

'What you did at Moriduno,' I say suddenly. 'That was very brave.'

Gwen smiles again, but this time it's grim. 'It was a little thing. You'd have done the same.'

I wouldn't, I tell her as she hurries off. *I am not as selfless as you.*

The sentry bell clangs across the hold and it sounds as if all my fears are rolled into one awful chime. Even my amicable conversation with Gwen isn't enough to dispel it. I'd usually hare towards the gate, too curious for caution. But my legs are filled with shingle. I don't think I can stand more bad news.

And that's why I don't hear Os is back.

The moment I do, I dash, cursing myself, to the stable, hoping he's still there. He isn't – though his horse is unsaddled and curried, eating its meagre rations. So I chance the smithy, already flinching away from Arlyn's yapping pup – but the place is empty except for Os, warming his hands by the fire. With a wail that would have embarrassed me once, I fly at him. He catches me in his big arms and whirls me around just as Myrdhin used to do. But although he's smiling to see me, it doesn't reach his eyes.

'What's wrong?' I ask.

He places me back on my feet. Stares at his palms. I realize he's wondering how to express whatever it is with only gestures to help him. When he raises his face, I step back despite myself. He wears misery like a shroud; his mouth twists and opens, closes, grasping for words. The sight wrings my heart. 'Please, Os. Tell me what the matter is. What's happened?'

His hands start moving, but they tremble and I find them hard to read. 'You are frightened,' I say uncertainly. 'For . . . for me?' He nods. 'Why?' I ask. 'Is it because of the king? Do you have news about the Saxons?'

Os nods. 'Are they coming?' I whisper. When he nods again, ice steals through me, despite my layers. *They're coming.* 'How many? How long do we have?' Words come out in a gabble, a muddle of questions, and to my horror Os falls to his knees before me. 'Os.' I sink down too, unsure how to comfort him, unsure what to make of this. His hands grip mine, as if we can somehow speak through our skin.

'Ink!' I cry. 'Can you write, Os?' He releases my hands, is about to sign something – but then his ruddy face pales, eyes staring over my shoulder.

'The only language he can write in,' Tristan says, 'is one you wouldn't understand.'

I whirl to my feet, hearing Os rise behind me.

'And what would you have written, Osred?' Tristan continues. I can't see his face: he stands beyond the one open side of the smithy, silhouetted against the grey light. But when he ducks under the eaves, he's wearing a thin smile. 'What would you have told your young friend here?'

Os doesn't move.

'Would you have trusted her with our king's orders, his secrets?' Tristan comes closer. 'The orders you carry in your belt pouch.' With some irony, he adds, 'Which I think are addressed to me?'

Os's shoulders slump. When Tristan holds out his hand, the big man passes over a scraped skin scroll. Tristan unrolls it in front of us, reads slowly. I watch his eyes move back and forth across the skin. The fire glances off his hair, throws his lowered face into shadow. Perhaps I imagine it, but a tension seems to leave him. 'You've done well, Os,' he says finally. With a wry look, he flashes me the scroll and I glimpse runes, but not any that are familiar to me. 'See, Sinne. It wouldn't do you any good.'

'What language is that?' I ask. 'Or is it a code? What does Vortipor want to hide?'

'What *don't* kings want to hide?' Tristan retorts, pocketing the scroll.

I think on this, trying to ignore the imagined feel of spiders scuttling down my back. It's the light in here and the words. And Os's face, his open mouth, as if his soul is being sucked from his body. *Everything is wrong.* 'I don't know about kings,' I say slowly. 'But you . . . you are something strange.'

Tristan laughs. 'I may have underestimated you, Sinne. You are much more interesting than I thought.'

The smile he gives me – that smile used to make my heart race and my blood pound. It used to wake parts of my body that had never woken for anyone else. Now all I feel are the spiders, and the quiet despairing presence of Os standing behind me.

37

KEYNE

I have to accompany Mother to every meeting with Father's lords, every visit to the storehouses and armoury. When she asks questions, she looks at me, as if she's disappointed I didn't ask them first. She's trying to tell me something – or teach me – and I feel we've spent more hours together in the weeks since Moriduno than we have in my entire life.

I haven't forgotten her words to me at Beltane. But none of our conversations now feature attire, feminine pursuits, the proper way to sit – or any of her myriad other complaints about the way I live my life. Instead we talk of rationing. And since the Saxon captive's death, we talk of war.

I don't think Paternus likes being told what to do by a woman. But Trachmyr and the other prominent men in the hold recognize leadership when they see it. And they remember that even the king doesn't choose to cross Mother if he can help it. We have become familiar figures amongst the fighting men: Mother, grim in her skirts, and me wearing armour I bullied Arlyn into making. I am trying to master the sword too – though I still prefer a dagger. My presence in the training yard attracts its share of eyebrows and not-so-hushed whispers. It would be hard to bear if it weren't for the men who fought with me at Moriduno. They look at me differently now, though they rarely speak to me.

I am sweating when Gildas finds me one dark afternoon on the day before Samhain. I've been practising parries in the training yard, empty at this late-afternoon hour, and my bound chest hurts from snatching lungfuls of smoky air. Surreptitiously, I yank at the bindings through my shirt, trying to wrestle them into a more comfortable position. My mood is souring fast – that tight band is a reminder of wrongness, of my body's imperfect shape. In the *now* of concentration, I can forget, focusing only on the next lunge or retreat or flick of the wrist. Training bestows a kind of freedom. But when it's over, my life rushes back in like a god-held tide.

'Later,' I snap at Gildas when he asks to speak to me. 'I am going to wash.'

'No.' He doesn't spare even a glance for my muddied tunic. 'Now, Keyne. It is important.'

We stare at each other. The inches I've gained over the past year have put me eye to eye with him. Or perhaps his height was merely illusion, which I can see through now. He has a pattern too, of course. On the outside, it's ordered, almost military – but inside those rigid angles is a chaos of shapes, wool unravelled by a kitten's play. I wonder what he'd say if I described it. He'd probably call me a heretic.

I let him lead me away from the barracks, away from prying eyes and ears. He moves stiffly. 'I've finally had a rider back from Vortipor,' he says.

I dimly remember him sending a man out. 'And?'

Gildas takes a step nearer. For someone who despises me, he always stands too close. 'Vortipor knows of no men by the names of Tristan and Os.'

For a moment, I stand blinking. 'What?' I say stupidly.

'He claims ignorance of them.' Gildas shakes his head. 'He could be lying, of course. He has no love for me.'

I wonder why, I think, remembering his condemnation of the king. But I force myself to ask, 'Is that likely?'

Gildas takes a breath and I realize he's unnerved. The only other time I've seen him off balance was when Myrdhin challenged him over the Beltane fire. Even when the sky cried ash, he boldly declared it heaven's blight and simple prayer its cure. 'No,' the priest says eventually. 'I do not think he lies in this.'

'What if they *are* spies?' I press. 'Vortipor is hardly going to admit it.'

'Is that what you think?' He regards me. 'Have you been watching Tristan as I suggested?'

I *have* been watching Tristan, ever since the day Father was injured and our eyes met across the battlefield. I've been watching him for reasons I can't quite explain. But there's little enough to see. Although he still sneaks off with Riva, he can hardly do much spying if she's with him. 'He did say one thing,' I admit, recalling that afternoon in the barn. It seems a lifetime ago. 'He claimed to be a king's man, a bondsman who goes where his master cannot.'

'A bondsman,' Gildas muses and he begins to pace with fractious feet. 'But whose is he if not Vortipor's?'

It's a question to which I have no answer. Against the backdrop of war, it seems a small matter. I say as much.

'Perhaps,' Gildas replies. He stops to gaze out at Dunbriga's distant gates. 'But when one begins to discern the greater pattern of God –' I look at him very sharply – 'it becomes easier to see more mundane designs, the trails we mortals leave behind us. Something tells me all these things are linked. Tristan's lie, the famine, the Saxon threat.'

'If you're so concerned,' I say, still a bit taken aback by his mention of patterns, 'go to Father.'

'Do you not think I have?' Gildas turns to me. 'He dismissed my concerns.'

Perturbed, I shake my head. 'That doesn't sound like Father. What exactly did he say?'

'He assumes Vortipor's ignorance to mean that Tristan is a mere commoner. Even a petty criminal who stole a horse and fine weaponry, to appear noble, in order to gain admittance to this court.' Gildas clasps his long-fingered hands. 'King Cador told me that a man should be judged by his deeds, not his blood, and that Tristan has proven himself a person of integrity.'

The wind wails, as if in disagreement, but has no voice to express it. 'Tristan saved his life,' I mutter after it subsides into a chilly breeze. 'Father believes that proves his loyalty. Maybe it does.' But silently I think, *This explanation excuses Father from looking too closely into Tristan's identity.* Which means that he must have a reason for keeping the man around – does he wish him to stay on as an adviser, perhaps? A royal bondsman?

'I worry that his injury has affected his mind,' Gildas says – boldly, because this is the king we're discussing after all.

I narrow my eyes at him. 'Watch what you say, priest. You are still a guest here.'

Gildas ignores that and I bristle. 'King Cador believes that Tristan will share his tale in his own time. So I *must* have stronger evidence to accuse him again.' He pauses. 'Will you help me watch Tristan?'

I'd like to refuse on principle, but I nod. If Tristan is hiding something, I have to find out what. 'When Mother allows me time.'

'The men look at you with respect,' Gildas says after an odd moment, and is gone before I can decide whether he's surprised or disapproving.

'I never thought to hear the priest speak sense.'

Myrdhin leans against a wall, half in shadow. 'How long have you been there?' I demand, turning to face him.

'Long enough. He could have been one of us, before his god found him.'

I frown. 'Don't you mean before he found his god?'

'No. The Church specializes in hunting down vulnerable boys and filling their heads with nonsense.'

'You're particularly irascible today.'

Myrdhin ignores this. 'He is right, though. They do look at you with respect. The men.'

'If they didn't before, then I don't want their respect.' I take a breath. 'Does fighting make a man? Being able to swing a blade and cut out a life? Is that the only thing that commands respect in the eyes of men?'

'It commands it,' Myrdhin says. 'But so too does honesty. And leadership. That's what the men sense in you.'

The word stumps me. 'I've not led anyone or anything in my life.'

'Directing people or things is merely the outward part of leadership. The *potential* to lead is harder to see and is inside. I sensed that potential the moment we met, the day you were lost in the forest.'

'You've just said it yourself: I was lost. Lost is surely the opposite of leading.'

'You abandoned the usual path, that is all.' It is Mori's smile. 'You chose another. A better, if I am any judge of such things. One I am sure you will come to lead others down.'

We stand in silence a moment while I try to process the words. Then Myrdhin turns on his heel and beckons me. 'As long as you're wearing that mud, I have a task for you.'

'I'm not going to like this, am I?'

'Oh, I think you will.' He leads me back past the training yard on Dunbriga's first terrace, heading for the main gates. 'We've come to see to the defences,' Myrdhin tells the guards, hooking his thumbs in his belt.

'See to them?' one asks. 'We've already done all we can.'

'*You've* done all you can, true,' he says, smiling a drewydh's smile. 'Now it's our turn.'

The creak of the gate covers their muttering, as Myrdhin and I step outside. 'What are you going to do?' I ask.

'We're going to add an outer wall to the fort. Or more accurately, *you* are.'

'Me?'

'Yes,' Myrdhin says impatiently. 'Are you saying you can't do it?'

'No . . . but . . .'

'Good. Then come and kneel here.' He already has an audience: the guards are staring down at us. I do as he says, wincing a little at the chill mud. Myrdhin scoops up a handful of it and beckons me to do the same. It oozes unpleasantly between my fingers. 'You need a feel for the pattern.'

I close my eyes, trying to ignore my sweat-soaked clothes, the wind that's chilling me. Instead I focus on the earth in my hand. I see it immediately, a simple pattern for all the vastness it represents. Its point dives into the ground, towards the heart of the world – while its top corners stretch to north and south, linking the fragile surface with the deep. Using it, I can sense the entirety of my father's lands – from Pennsans in the west to the Parrett in the east – though the eastern edges are dim now, the magic dying beneath Saxon feet.

'Good,' Myrdhin says again. His voice is distant, tiny compared to the pattern I hold in my head. 'The silver I gave you will amplify the connection, help you shape the earth.'

It had been relatively easy to call the fire at Moriduno; I'd just pulled it formless out of the ground to block my enemy. This is altogether harder. I can feel the pattern, yes, but it seems fixed, immutable, and I am barely more than a feather. 'Remember the land, lad,' Myrdhin says. 'Remember how it answered you before – in the glade and at Beltane.'

I think of the glade. That rush of being swept out of my body and into the heart of the magic. Earth had been the greater part of the vast silver pattern that caught me up and ran with me through stone, hill and valley. We had been one. We are one. I lean forward and slap both hands to the ground.

It shakes.

I only realize my eyes are open when I see the pattern growing, a web of silver, radiating out from my hands. Shouts of alarm come, but they are paltry human things, beneath notice. I am broad of shoulder, long of limb, my ribs black caves, my spine the ridge of hills that marches into the sea. It only requires the merest of shrugs to rend the ground apart. I force it up with a roar, humped and high, before driving it left and right until it circles Dunbriga and meets the cliff edge – I leave only one gap before the gates.

I am dimly aware of screams, but the voice of the earth drowns them. There is an urge to follow the pattern further, into sea and sediment and on towards the underground realms only the dwarf king has seen.

A presence intrudes, firm but familiar, and I remember who I am and why I'm here. My sigh is regretful as the silver web fades. It takes my strength with it – Myrdhin has to help me stand. 'This would have taken men months to build,' he says, nodding at the massive earthwork.

'I feel as if I've worked for months,' I grumble, rubbing my neck. But inside I am tingling with the after-effects of the magic, with the wonder of being able to shape stone. If Mori hadn't revealed it that night in the nemeton, would this power have been lost to me?

We make our way through the gap in the mounded earth, heading for the gates. It's deathly quiet after the rumble and grate of rock. When I look up, faces line the wall. Dozens of men stare down at us, no, at *me*. Some stand open-mouthed. Others are frowning or looking between Myrdhin and me. They wear shock and awe. They wear fear. I can almost smell it on the earthy wind. I wonder how many are remembering Father and the power he could call up from the land. How many have once used that power themselves to sharpen a blade or light a fire? Do any of them mourn its loss?

They open the gates for us. Still no one says a word. The silence is beginning to unsettle me. 'Why are they staring?' I mutter to Myrdhin.

He looks at me sidelong. 'Because the last person to raise the earth as you did was Cador. The king and the land are one.'

Something buried in his words unnerves me; something I fear I already know. I gaze straight ahead, refusing to meet any of the eyes I can feel.

'You danced with the fire, wielded blade in battle, shed blood for your kinsmen,' Myrdhin says. 'You brought Herla and his deadly crew into your father's hall. You shaped fire and earth in defence of your home. In short, you have proven beyond a shadow of doubt that *you* are the land's heir.'

I swallow. Clouds are rolling in from the west, drowning the sunset in grey. The last beams gild the roof of the king's hall. Spattered head to toe in mud with the almost-real ache of a thousand tons of earth upon my shoulders, I feel suddenly small in its shadow.

'You are the heir to Dunbriga, to all Dumnonia.'

Heart pounding now, I look into Myrdhin's blue eyes. His voice echoes in my head. *War is coming and Dumnonia needs a king.*

My mind and belly are still churning with his words by the time I reach our quarters.

Dumnonia needs a king.

Well, it has a king, I tell myself. It has Father. Then I picture him as I saw him last, pallid as a ghost, seeming only half present.

The memory of the man who wore the light, who drank from the skulls of his enemies, who called upon the beasts of the forest, is all washed out – and I fear I know why Father isn't recovering. His is more than a physical wound. It is a wound of the spirit, and it's been bleeding for far longer than any of us realized.

War is coming.

I remember Herla and his curse. I'd held so many threads the evening I told his story – inflection, sound, silence, movement. I'd juggled the flare of firelight, the wind's wailing, the scrape of benches, the odd cough or creak. All had to be taken up and woven into my tale. Father's hall had to become Herla's and the dwarven king's, lit with eldritch flame. It had to become the far-future land of an invading people. My illusions were of air and darkness, not as solid as Myrdhin's, but the best I could conjure. I remember the moment it all unravelled. I remember the glimpse of something terrible, something inevitable, like a storm on the horizon. It galloped towards me on hooves shod with iron, it roared from men's throats and glared from black-painted eyes.

War is coming.

I shake off the memory. It's suppertime – what little supper there is to be had – and I'm hoping to find the quarters empty so I can wash in peace. But Sinne sits on a bench beside the hearth, prodding the fire desultorily with a stick. Her shoulders are pulled up around her ears. Bent over like that, she seems an old woman. 'Why aren't you at supper?' I ask.

'Why aren't *you*?' she retorts, but it lacks bite.

I pluck at my clothes. 'I was training. I can hardly eat splattered in mud.'

My sister's eyes move to the weapons at my waist. Since Moriduno, I've worn Mori's scabbard and dagger openly. 'I always knew you were different,' Sinne says.

I freeze as I inevitably do whenever I am discussed, braced for confusion, dismay or outright anger. But I think of Mori and

Myrdhin and I allow myself to relax. I have no wish to hide any longer. I should not have to. 'And how does that make *you* feel?' I ask bluntly.

'I don't quite know yet,' she says, returning her gaze to the fire. 'But I'm getting used to the idea.'

At least she's honest, I tell myself, a spark of hope growing inside me. My sisters are what my parents, Dunbriga and our world have made them. I ought to understand that better than most. I fight it every day.

So I sit beside her and take her hand – and am surprised at myself. 'Is it so hard to see me as a brother, instead of a sister?'

She lifts her eyes to my face. It's disconcerting to remain still and be studied, but I don't move. Finally, she says, 'No, it isn't.' A pause. 'Your hands are warm.'

Hers are cold, I realize, winter-river-cold. I take her other hand and hold them both between my own and that's how we sit for a time until Sinne pulls away. 'I need to talk to you about Tristan,' she says.

The strange peace that's stolen over me, sitting beside my silent sister, is shattered. And for Sinne to *be* silent . . . that's almost more concerning than her words. I watch her take a breath, as if to steel herself for some great duty. 'This might sound stupid. But I don't think he is who he claims to be.'

The words shiver in the air between us. 'I know,' I say and Sinne's eyes snap to mine again. 'Gildas sent a man to Vortipor. Dyfed's king claims ignorance of him.'

Her face pales. '*What?*'

'I said the same. But then if Tristan and Os *were* sent to spy for Vortipor, he would be the last to admit it – wouldn't he?'

'Why would King Vortipor want to spy on us? He's our ally.' Sinne stands. 'We must tell Father.'

I catch her arm. 'Gildas has tried already. Father didn't listen. He thinks Tristan only lied about being a noble – which would be serious, if Tristan hadn't saved Father's life.' Even as I say it, I remember Tristan's eyes meeting mine across the battlefield, that knife-edge moment. 'Father's not going to want to believe ill of him. When it comes down to it, it's our word against Tristan's. We don't have enough to go on yet.'

Sinne's brow furrows, but a moment later, she exclaims, 'Yes, we do! Tristan showed me a missive Os brought him. I didn't recognize the writing, but perhaps Gildas or Father might. If we can get hold of it . . .' The light in her face fades a little. 'He put it in his tunic. How are we supposed to snatch it from there?'

We are equally silent, me staring at the dark rafters, Sinne at her hands. Then, struck by the same thought, we both say together, 'Riva.'

38

RIVA

I won't be able to hide it much longer. I've tried hard not to think of it, as if not thinking will make it not so. Others can be fooled by layers of cloth, layers we all wear to keep out the chill. But I cannot fool myself. And I have only myself to blame.

I'm not alone in the women's quarters when Samhain morning dawns. Instead of preparing offerings of food which we can't spare, Mother's ladies sit with piles of old tunics, ripping them up to create new, thicker ones to wear under armour. Surreptitiously, I spread the fingers of my good hand across my belly; a slight swell that can still be hidden. *For how long?* I force myself to ask. *What will they say when they see?* I shudder, imagining Mother's face, the hold's condemnation. And for what? I don't want this child. At least not now, while our people starve, while Father lies sick and war glowers like lightning on the horizon. How can I have been so stupid?

Tristan . . . I can't tell him. I'm not sure what stops me, save for the fact he hasn't spoken any further of marriage. Perhaps a child will persuade him, or perhaps it will cause him to run. He told me he wasn't ready to settle yet. It will be simple for him to leave me behind.

A sob escapes, which I am forced to turn into a cough. A

moment later, I feel ashamed of it. What happened to the girl who returned from death? What happened to the woman who carried the banner of the old ways? *I lost her that day in the forest*, I think. *I lost her the day I met Tristan.*

My hand goes to the acorn strung on a cord around my neck. It amplifies my magic, I am sure, but seems a poor trade for the life of the wisp. Still, I feel better holding it and swallow my self-pity. Tristan is equally responsible for this child, and I have no intention of bearing it outside wedlock. He will *have to* offer for my hand.

A gust stirs my hair. Two figures, a man and a woman, stand in the doorway. They are just outlines against the morning light. A moment later, when they step inside, I realize it's Keyne and Sinne. Their eyes range across the room, settling on me. Then Keyne claps and says loudly, 'Out. Leave us.'

So strong is the command that several women are halfway to their feet before they know it. Then Locinna says, 'Lady Keyne, really. There is no need to take such a tone with us.'

'I wish to speak to my sisters alone,' Keyne replies coldly and I find myself frowning. Sinne meets my eyes and I don't like what I see there. I almost place my hand on my belly again without thinking.

'Lady Keyne, surely there is no need to send us all away. Where are we to go?'

'I don't care.' Keyne's tone softens a little at their shocked faces. 'I only wish a few moments.'

With a good deal of grumbling, the women leave – but I note that they obey despite their protests. Locinna gives Keyne a dark look as she passes and mutters something about bullying old nurses.

Soon the room contains just us three. 'What do you want then?' I say more harshly than intended. They come to sit by me. Keyne's already-dark eyes are ringed with sleepless nights.

'It's about Tristan,' Sinne says and I have to suppress a ground-swell of resentment. I don't like hearing his name in her mouth, not when I carry his child. When I say nothing, she adds, 'We need you to find a letter.'

'What letter?'

'Os gave Tristan a sealed missive from their king,' Keyne says. 'It was written in a strange language.'

'Or a code,' Sinne puts in. 'We think Tristan is hiding some-thing and we want to know what.'

'If it was sealed,' I say coolly, 'then it was private. You have no right to go through a man's private possessions.'

They exchange looks as if they anticipated this reaction and dread it. It only makes me angrier. 'I know where this is going. You want *me* to find the letter.'

'Yes,' Keyne says.

'I won't do it. King Vortipor's orders are none of our business.' When they exchange another look, I snap, 'What?'

'It isn't *from* Vortipor,' Sinne says. 'That's the point. Gildas sent word to him and Vortipor claims he doesn't know Tristan.'

'He might be lying.' Keyne readjusts that long dagger in its sheath. 'But we can't be sure. We need to see the letter.'

I feel a lurch in my belly and wonder whether it's too early for the child to be moving. Perhaps I imagined it; maybe it's just hunger. I lick dry lips. 'What are you implying?'

'Nothing,' Keyne says. 'At least, not yet. Tristan has proven himself a . . . friend to Father, so Father won't order him to give up the letter. Besides, the king is not in a fit state. I'd rather not bother him if we can solve this mystery ourselves.'

'There is no mystery,' I snarl with a new surge of anger. 'You've said it already. Tristan has proven himself a friend. I'm not going to break his trust.'

'You're the only person he'll let close,' Sinne says with just a hint of bitterness. 'The letter will be on him. Or in the quarters Father gave him.'

'I don't wish to listen to this any more.' I rise, wincing at a stab of discomfort in my back. Their words have woken a bubbling ire and I'm not sure why – save that they are calling Tristan's integrity into question. 'All men have secrets.' I stride as straight as I can manage to the door. My foot hurts all the time now; it will only get worse over the coming months. I pause with my hand on the bolt. 'Don't speak to me of this again.'

'Riva—'

I slam the door on my name.

Curse them both for sowing doubt when I so little need it. That doubt is like a fly buzzing beneath a ceiling, always seeking an exit and never finding one. Their words stay with me too. *It isn't from Vortipor. Gildas sent word to him and he claims he doesn't know Tristan.* If Sinne came to me with such a tale, I'd dismiss it as a jealous trick. But Keyne would never make up something like that.

A wife is entitled to know some of her husband's secrets; she's entitled to hoard them as closely as her own. But I am not a wife. Tristan is under no obligation to tell me anything, especially not words written by a king.

Still I doubt him and it fills me with a sense of dread.

I am raw with scratches by the time I climb out of the gorse tunnel. The woolly hood of a sea fret hides me as I dart through the gap in the new wall. This will be our last meeting. Winter is coming and the new defences make it harder to escape notice. Forcing down hurt, I brush a hand across the solid earth that towers above my head. I've heard the whispers, but can hardly believe it Keyne's work. My healing pales beside this power. What does it mean?

Tristan and I decided to travel separately so as not to attract attention. I walk fast and further than I usually do, but keep to our agreed path through the wood. Eventually I hear roaring and follow it to the brink of the stream – or what used to be the stream. It's now a foaming torrent that would send men running for a ford. Water has spilled down from the hills, gnawed at its old banks and torn out a wider course on its route to the ocean. I stare into its white tumbling maw like one ensorcelled.

'Riva.'

My name precedes him as he emerges from the mist. Tristan's shoulders are damp with spray; mine are no better. For all my earlier intentions, I cling to him and let his lips thaw a little of the chill. When he pulls back, I see the same intensity in his eyes that caused my current predicament, but it's not desire now. This is different. Something flutters in my chest: a presentiment, a foreboding.

When he says, 'I will have to leave you soon,' I am not surprised.

'Why?'

He holds me at arm's length. 'Because it's time.'

Tears threaten and I blink them fiercely back. 'I don't understand.'

'I told you Os and I would stay a while. Only a while.'

'But I thought that we – us . . .'

Tristan lets me stumble into silence. 'Would you leave here, Riva?' he asks after a moment. 'Would you leave your family behind?'

'Yes, of course – if we were married.'

'No,' he says, unsmiling. 'Would you leave them behind *forever*?'

I feel my brow furrow. 'Forever? You mean . . . I wouldn't see them again? Do you live so far away then?'

'Far enough,' he says and the words disappear like pebbles into the torrent at our feet.

I think of them all: Keyne and Sinne, my parents and Locinna.

And Arlyn – poor Arlyn. I know I can never bring myself to care for him, despite realizing, deep down, how much he cares for me. I think of Dunbriga and its soft red cliffs that turn the waters ruddy with their grit in high weather. I think of my father's lush valleys and the trees whose roots drink the blood of the land.

And then I look at Tristan, imagine the scars beneath his clothes. There is a fire in his face which I shrink from, as I shrink from all fire. But I've tasted this one and now carry it within me – for better or for worse. So with a heavy heart I say, 'Yes. I would leave them.'

'Then I promise to come back for you.'

He lets go of me, but I seize his wrist. 'When? How long will you be gone?'

'Not so long,' he says, a little warmer this time. 'All I ask for is your trust.'

Keyne's voice and Sinne's come back to me then. Vortipor, Gildas. The doubt Tristan has kissed to sleep wakes and begins to buzz inside my head. I don't have the words to ask him about it. I've already given my words away – with my promise to leave my family. What purpose can doubt now serve? So I reach up and tug at the cord holding the acorn around my neck until it comes free. 'I want you to take this.'

Tristan frowns at the black seed dangling from my fist. 'What is it?'

'Just . . . something that led me to you. It has power, Tristan. It will keep you safe.'

'But . . .'

'You asked for my trust. Well, I ask for yours. Please wear it. For me.'

His eyes are on mine as he takes the acorn and ties it around his own neck. I feel relief at seeing it nestled there against his chest, though I don't know why. 'Thank you.'

'We will be missed,' Tristan says then. 'Let's not tarry.'

I open my mouth to tell him of the child; I have words enough for that, but he's already turned away. 'I will go first, to check the coast is clear. Be swift to follow, Riva. The night comes on.'

I watch his shoulders disappear into the grey, my lips still parted. 'I carry your child,' I tell the uncaring river. 'So you must come back. You must come back for us both.'

39

SINNE

'*What?*'

The word is out of my mouth before I can stop it. Riva whirls around, searching the mist for me and, numbly, I step from concealment. I am damp, skirts heavy and suffocating, but that's nothing to the blow Riva has dealt me. *Us*: Keyne and Mother too. And Father, who tires from merely sitting up. I heard her through the river's rumble; she's going to leave us all behind. She's going to choose Tristan. And her last words . . .

I hadn't misheard. She's standing with a hand on her middle. That truth is another blow and maybe it hurts even more than her disloyalty.

'Sinne. What are you doing here?'

Her voice trembles on my name. Mine does too when I answer, 'A child? It can't be true.'

Her hand contracts. 'It's no business of yours.'

'You . . . you . . .' I can't put it into words. 'With Tristan?'

Riva's face hardens. 'That is certainly no business of yours.'

Although I can't stop looking, there's nothing to see, not yet. I always knew they sneaked off together, but to have taken it this far . . . Everything is knotted up inside me: a great burdensome tangle I can't unpick. Disappointment, anger and – running through it all – jealousy. I want to deny it. Why should I be jealous? There are few fates worse than to be unmarried and with child. But my mind keeps showing me pictures of what might have been.

'What are you doing here?' she asks again.

I take a few steps closer. 'I followed you.'

'Why?'

I don't know. No, I do know. 'To make you see sense,' I say. 'You can't trust him, Riva.'

'You don't know him,' she flares. 'You're jealous – that's why you're saying this. You've made up a story to put me off, so you can step in and take what's *mine*.'

I stare at her, stunned. It's worse because there's a grain of truth in her words. 'I don't want your leftovers,' I say coldly. 'Keyne and I are trying to warn you.'

There – a flicker. Some of what we said must have reached her. 'Do you think I have a choice?' she suddenly cries. 'Your words only sow doubt where I need assurances.'

'You do have a choice,' I shout back, coming closer. 'Your family, Riva. We would look after you. *We* would never abandon *you*.'

She flinches at the inflection, but instead of conceding, straightens her shoulders. Mother's stubbornness runs through us all. 'Tristan is offering me a life, Sinne. What would I have by staying here? Locked up in the women's quarters or sent in shame to a convent to reflect on my sins? Is it a sin to love? Is it?'

She's hit a nerve. She knows how I dread a loveless marriage, how I spend my time dreaming of someone better, more exciting than a local lord. Someone like Tristan. All at once my resentment rears up again, a many-headed hydra. If Riva hadn't run away, hadn't thrown herself into Tristan's path, I could have found myself in a different story, one that wasn't full of suspicions and lies. 'You stole any chance I had at love,' I snarl.

Her good hand balls into a fist, mirroring the other. I can hear the river at my back, white with foam and tumbled rocks. I don't want Tristan. I don't. But I do want a story like Myrdhin tells. I want adventure. I want to be lost then found. I want to fall in love – and I want my lover to take me away.

I want Riva's story.

'I stole nothing, Sinne. He was never yours to claim. And you who have *everything* –' she gestures, a sweeping accusation that takes me in entirely – 'beautiful, graceful, whole. You begrudge me my chance of happiness? *Me*, the damaged daughter everyone pities?' Tears in her eyes. 'Who daily sees them flinch away from my hand as if it's a piece of rotten meat?'

'Not everyone,' I say. 'What about Arlyn? Could you not have been happy with him?'

It's my turn to hit a nerve. 'A smith's apprentice?' Riva swallows. 'A king's daughter cannot marry a commoner.'

'Even a commoner who loves her? Who could have made her happy?' Despite myself, I add, 'Because who else would have her – a king's *damaged* daughter? Certainly no lord.'

Maybe I've gone too far; she advances on me, a dangerous light in her eyes and I stumble back. But my anger has a will of its own, beating hot in my breast, through my limbs, making me reckless. I can feel heat on my skin and I don't care – let it come. 'I heard you forsake us. I heard you betray us. All for a man.'

Riva gasps at the crackle of flame. Her face is bloodless. 'Is that . . . wildfire?'

I didn't want to show her, but any control I might have had has burned away. I nod.

'How, Sinne?'

'I don't know,' I say. 'Myrdhin doesn't know. It only comes when I'm angry.'

'Myrdhin . . .' Her lips move without sound. I can almost hear her thoughts as she stares at the leaping flames that lick me. 'Myrdhin said . . . wounds caused by wildfire . . .'

I see it: the moment of understanding. It is like the little puzzle cube I had as a child, wooden pieces slotting into place against each other. I feel sick; the fire falters. On Riva's face, the truth is worse, so much worse than it was when I had remembered, horrified, at the edge of the sea.

She holds out her scarred hand. 'You. It was you.' The wildfire jerks, lashing its tongues, but for once Riva doesn't flinch away. It's me who flinches.

'I didn't mean it.'

'You did this to me.'

'It was an accident.'

'Accident?' Her voice is louder now, climbing in pitch, and my wildfire flares in response. 'I nearly *died*.'

'Riva—'

'How long have you known?'

The river leaps at my back. 'Only weeks—'

'Liar.' The word is like a blow. 'You're lying! You've always known. And you let me believe it was *my fault*.'

That light in her eyes seems brighter than the wildfire, hotter. Riva's good hand is at her throat, reaching for something that isn't there, clutching air. 'And he knows too, doesn't he? Myrdhin.' She spits the name like venom. 'He knew and he never told Mother or Father. He . . . covered it up.'

I don't have an answer to that because it's true. For the first time, I wonder what punishment my parents would have meted out to me. Something so terrible that Myrdhin couldn't let them learn the truth? 'I'm sorry, Riva. I'm so sorry.'

'You . . . you ruined me, Sinne. But that's not enough, is it? Now you want what's mine too.'

My heart is as dangerous as the fire. It steals my tongue, pouring poison into my mouth. 'I don't want anything you've touched,' I hear myself say.

She screams at me, an animal scream so fierce it knocks me

back. But I have run out of land. My foot meets air and for a moment I can't believe it, I can't believe I will fall. My other foot slips on the bank and I reach out to Riva in an agony of slowness.

Her hand twitches, her good hand, the only one that can help me. But it doesn't move. In the second it could, it doesn't move. She doesn't. Because of course I am alight with the fire that scarred her, the fire that started it all.

'*Riva!*' The name is torn from me as I see blood. It's all I see as I fall: red and foaming white, like Lir's curse.

40

KEYNE

I gasp myself awake. Urgency, like some dark geas, jerks me to my feet. I have fallen asleep on one of Mori's scrolls and torn a corner in my haste. I can't spare guilt. Thunder rumbles. I can taste lightning in the sky, a spiked, raw pattern like the shipwreck's broken spars. Abandoning the scroll, I flee from the little room where Father keeps his codices and treasures, startling two of his personal guards. 'Saxons?' one shouts despite the fact I've clearly come from a closed room. They are in everyone's minds; an invisible threat we can all still see.

I say nothing. What can I say? *Something snapped like an overstrained rope, a rope I didn't know I held until it was gone.* There is a difference in the hold. I have the sense of a piece missing, so I search for it, ignoring the ordinary smells of animal dung and hay, and the ordinary shouts of people afraid of their shadows. I open myself to instinct and let it guide me.

Someone yanks me to a halt. Winded, I look round. Os is a bulky figure against the dying afternoon, a mountain moved only by his breath. But his eyes betray panic. 'What is it?' I ask, knowing he can't answer.

Despite this, he tries. Sinne might understand him, but all I grasp is his fear. So I say, 'I feel the same. Something's wrong,' and he nods vigorously. We set off together, Os following my lead. It feels dreamlike, this dash – and I half expect my feet to slow, the earth rearing to drag me back as it does in dreams.

Before long, we're at the main gates. 'Let me through,' I rasp at the guards. The two of us must be a sight, appearing out of the storm-light like ghouls. Os's eyes are as wide and pale as a night bird's.

'We cannot let you out, La—' he trips over the word, 'Keyne. Your father's orders. None are to pass.'

'I don't have time for this.' I force myself to speak slowly, despite the roiling in my gut. 'I need to find my sisters.'

Confusion mars the guard's brow. It does sound mad – that Riva and Sinne would be outside on such a night. But they are. I know it. 'They will surely be in the women's quarters,' he says.

'Please.' I squint through the gloom, trying for his name. It comes to me after a moment. 'Roderc. They are not in the women's quarters. They are outside the hold.'

'That's impossible.' He emphasizes the word with the butt of his spear. 'They could not have passed the gates without being seen.'

I know perfectly well how they did so, but I don't have time to explain. 'Let me through.' I straighten my shoulders. 'That's an order.'

He scratches a bearded cheek, looking between Os and me. 'You have no authority to tell me to abandon my post.'

'Then accompany us,' I say. 'If I am wrong, I will make amends. But I am not wrong.'

'My orders—'

'My Father will not be king forever.' The words are out of my mouth before I can feel any horror that I spoke them. 'And I will remember this, Roderc. I will remember this day.'

His mouth opens and shuts like a live catch. His eyes flicker to the wall I raised, the towering ring of earth. Os rumbles – a menacing sound of impatience – and Roderc finally steps aside, signalling to another man to lift the bar on the gates. 'I will come with you,' he says stiffly.

'My thanks,' I toss over my shoulder; I am already moving, squeezing through the gap before the gates are fully open, Os at my heels.

I lead the three of us into the wood, casting about for signs of my sisters. I don't know what I'm looking for, but my every sense screams *Wrong*, driving me on until I'm haring through the undergrowth like a thing pursued. The other men struggle to keep up.

'Where are we going?' Roderc calls. I don't have an answer. A gurgling chuckle tells me we're near the river and I push forward, its laughter growing louder with every step. A flood from the high hills has turned it into a demon, its pattern warped and torrid, painful to touch. I should have brought a torch. No matter. I snatch up a fallen branch and it bursts into flame. Roderc yelps.

I spot her first: a huddled shape in the gloom. Riva is on her knees at the water's edge. When she raises her face to me, it's streaked with tears, bloody in places where her nails have scored her flesh. Her lips move, but I can't hear her.

'Lady Riva,' Roderc declares, clearly at a loss. He glances at me once before hurrying over to my sister. 'What are you doing out here? It isn't safe.'

Riva cries fresh tears. Instead of turning to Roderc, her eyes rest on Os and I see fear in them. Before I can stop him, the big man seizes Riva's shoulders and yanks her roughly to her feet. She cries out and Roderc grabs Os from behind, but it's like trying to drag a boat single-handed across sand – he can't move the big man even an inch.

Os's mouth is open and soundless as he shakes Riva. I can almost hear him crying, *Where is she?* 'Os, stop.' I pull at his hands and surprisingly he lets go.

Riva crumples again. 'She . . . fell,' she gasps. 'Sinne. She fell.'

There is silence save for the murderous water. The geas that compelled me here has lifted and I am stranded at the river's edge, my sister's words tolling in my head.

Only Roderc is brave enough to break that quiet. '*Lady Sinne*... no, it cannot be true. Are you sure? Did you see her?'

Riva's face is terrible. 'We were ... talking.'

I can see it now. Two figures on the brink, the icy water just a misstep away. My heart stops trying to beat an escape. It feels as if it stops entirely.

'Sinne fell,' Riva says again, as if she can't believe it. 'She slipped and fell.'

It's my turn to grab her shoulders. 'When?'

'I don't know. Maybe ... minutes.'

'Os, Roderc,' I snap, whirling to face them, trying to ignore that awful stillness in my chest. 'We need to find her. The river will have carried her downstream towards the hold. If we split up—'

'You didn't see,' Riva cries. 'You don't understand. She's ... she's gone.'

Gods. 'She can't swim.'

'No,' Riva moans. 'Not just that. She hit her head. There was blood, blood in the water ...'

A part of me wants to crumple as she has, to beat the ground senseless with my fists. But I can't, I can't give up. 'Os, Roderc,' I say again. 'Let's go.'

They don't need telling twice. Os grabs the torch and hurls himself downriver, Roderc is moving more slowly, checking each leafy inlet where Sinne might have clawed free of the water. As for me, I sink to the ground near Riva, her sobs in my ears. I need better eyes than mine.

This is foolish. Dangerous. I ignore the voice that chides me in Myrdhin's tones. If I am the land's heir, it will help me find my kin. I am more used to searching out elemental patterns: fire, earth, air, water. The patterns of living beings are smaller. But I remember Mori's words and know it's possible. *Magic lets me run with the deer, hunt with the eagle, even swim with the fish.*

I lean forward, both hands on the damp bank, and let the silver carry me away. Keeping to the air this time, I flow through the insides of trees, up into branches, searching. Eventually I find what I'm looking for: an owl, tawny-feathered and amber-eyed. Its pattern is built for hunting the night, to search the curve of the sleeping land. *Fly*, I whisper to it, and hope I can keep hold.

Wind in my feathers. Despite my fear for Sinne, the euphoria of flight fills my heart. I let out a cry, eerie between the branches, sending prey scurrying for cover. With my new eyes, I follow the river. I can pick out every rock in the twilight, every fern fringing the broken banks. A moving spot of light is Os, dangerously close to the water himself. I fly on.

It seems our search takes a life-age. The Samhain sky darkens to indigo, and once the thunder passes, the stars shine like the cold white eyes of a spider I once found above my pallet. I can't help but see the image as an omen. As soon as I think it, I spot something out of place. A glimmer of pale on dark. I swoop down with a screech, a call to Os, who is only yards from the place.

His answering howl could have been a wolf, a bear – or a great stag on the end of a hunter's spear. Gooseflesh erupts along my skin; my gut twists as if I've eaten bad berries and those sensations – human sensations – wrench the owl's pattern out of my grasp. I'm back in my body, retching at the speed of my return, at the sudden loss of wings. I rise, stiff-limbed, the inlet with its pale shape held close in my mind.

I stumble over my own feet, my hands hit the dew-laden earth, then I'm up and running again, following the sounds Os is making. I half expect to encounter a wight or a ghost freed from the veil; on Samhain night it's said they walk our world. In the end there is nothing but a huddled shape at the river's brink. It's a quiet inlet, a silted bank where the river turns sharply for the sea.

Driftwood litters it, along with other flotsam – wreckage the water no longer wants.

White glimmers. A swan, I think madly, its feathers matted and bruised. Its long neck is twisted back, legs folded and broken beneath it. Os cradles it, on his knees in the damp sand. His big hand lies across its breast, trying to smooth the feathers, to wake the dead heart. I blink and it is no swan. Os holds a limp girl, my sister, my little sister, clad in white and I cannot bear it. I fall beside him, crawling towards her, splinters of wood in my palms.

Blood on her temple, in her hair, her golden hair full of silt and river muck. Her eyes are open and they are bluer than the twilight and blanker – and slightly surprised too, as if all of this is a great and terrible jest. Os is moaning. The wights are amongst us after all; I see them at the edge of my vision, shimmers on the bank, a gathering of souls come to take another.

No. Perhaps I shout the word aloud. *No. You will not have her.*

Os glances at me, and sobs swell in my throat at the sight of his face. I throw back my head and look at the spider-eye stars and something leaves me: a concussion, a silent thunder. It roars out across the land.

Keyne?

I don't recognize the name, still crying, one hand on my sister's wet dress.

What has happened? Where are you?

It's Myrdhin. I hear his voice in my head, or in the reeds that fringe the shore. All I can say is *Sinne, Sinne.*

He's asking me questions, too many questions. I have no room for them. Sinne fills me completely or her absence does, or the memory of her.

Bring her to me, comes Mori's voice. *Bring her to my cottage, Keyne.*

It is an order. Uncurling, I say to Os, 'We must take her to Myrdhin.'

I have to repeat it three times before he seems to hear me. Carefully, as if she's a brideog held together by the thinnest of bindings, Os lifts Sinne and looks at me. Taking a deep, shaking breath, I turn for Mori's home, barely able to see save for the cursed stars. Numbness is spreading; it is there to help me, to protect me from the madness of grief, but I want to feel. *I want to feel.*

I can't think of anything. I can't picture my parents or comprehend the fact we will be missed. Behind me, Os's ragged breathing. In front of me, light – it's the cottage's lamps, finally, spilling into the night. A figure stands in the open doorway: Myrdhin, his face grave. But he raises an eyebrow when he sees Os.

'He knew,' I say, trembling. 'Os knew something was wrong.'

'Did he now?' Myrdhin says under his breath. Then Os steps into the light and the cruel illumination falls hard on my sister. 'Oh, lass,' Myrdhin whispers, 'little mistress.' He lays the back of his hand against one of Sinne's cold cheeks and grief hits me again, knocks me almost senseless, pulls a choke and a cry from my throat, and Os echoes it.

'Bring her inside.'

The softness has left Myrdhin's voice. When Sinne lies on the table where I broke my first fast with Mori, he asks, 'How did this happen?'

I have to force down sobs to speak. 'Riva. She says they were talking, that Sinne . . . that she slipped and fell.'

'She said that?' Myrdhin turns his head in the direction of the river, as if he can see my elder sister crumpled at its edge. 'And how did they come to be outside the hold, talking?'

'They went through the gorse passage,' I say in a low voice, suddenly swamped by guilt. If only I'd been more careful, Riva would never have known. She'd never have been able to meet Tristan in secret, Sinne would never have . . .

Myrdhin grabs me roughly by the upper arms, shakes me, as

if he can hear every word. 'Stop, lad. It's done. What would they have been talking about?'

'Tristan,' I say with a glance at Os, but the big man is still staring at my sister, caught in his misery. I hadn't realized he'd come to care so much for her. Another sob threatens and I swallow hard. 'After what Gildas said about Vortipor, we asked Riva to steal Tristan's letter. But she refused. Sinne must have seen her leave through the tunnel and followed. Perhaps she tried to convince her and . . . and they fought.'

'The truth will out,' Myrdhin says in a murmur. 'Samhain night. Perhaps it is not too late.'

Os looks up. We both do, staring hard at the magician. 'What do you mean?' I say. 'Sinne . . . Sinne's gone.'

'Yes,' he replies and that little word brings it home to me, the raw knowledge that I will never hear my sister's voice again, her laughter, her complaining. I will never see her dance, or lie on the rug in the women's quarters kicking her heels. I will never hear her sing.

I curl over, fighting sickness. How can this be real – any of it? How can Sinne be lying here, cold and still, when I spoke to her just hours ago? There's a rushing in my ears; it is Lir laughing, his sons become rivers, drowning the land in their grief.

Keyne. The name pierces froth and foam; like sunlight slanting through water. I seize it, blinking. Myrdhin's hand rests on my brow. 'Lad,' he speaks aloud this time. 'I said it's not too late. And I cannot do it without you.'

'Do what?' I choke out.

'Call Sinne's spirit back.'

'Is that *possible*?'

'Tonight, maybe.'

I stare at him, heart thudding, remembering the ghosts on the bank. 'You mean Samhain.'

He nods. 'If it can be done, it will be done tonight, when life and death and everything in between are as one.'

Os steps back, red-rimmed eyes moving between Sinne and Myrdhin. They brim with hope. Myrdhin raises a hand. 'Keep watch, man. Let nothing pass my threshold and I will do what I can for the lass.'

Os hesitates, gaze still torn between Sinne's face and Myrdhin. But he nods, once, and leaves the house. I watch him draw his sword and plant it blade first in the soft earth. Then he folds his arms and stills.

The moment he's gone and the windows and doors are shuttered tight, Myrdhin bursts into motion. 'There is a lot to do and little time, lad,' he throws over his shoulder while his hands reach for pouches and phials, pots of unguent and the same eerie instruments he used to treat Father. I stand silent until he picks up a serrated saw – not dissimilar to a woodsman's – and an icy shock goes through me.

'What – what's that for?'

When he looks at me, there is no humour in his face. And it's not him any more. It's Mori. I grasp the edge of her pattern and I want to draw back because there is a darkness to it, a deep river through rock, and it fills me with dread.

I take a breath, eyes flicking to the bone saw. 'What must I do?'

'I am hoping Sinne's spirit – her pattern – hasn't yet faded from the world. She may not be the land's heir, but she has ties to it, you all do.'

I swallow hard and look at my sister, gone away from me into a silent place. Outside, the wind howls about the eaves. 'And you can use these ties to bring her back?' I whisper.

'Yes,' Mori says. 'But we will have to make her a new body. This –' she gestures at it – 'is empty. Even I cannot revive dead flesh, or spark a stilled heart.'

'What do you mean?'

'She must be tethered to this world, tethered to her bones. With ties as strong as we can make them. And she needs a voice.'

I feel like a ship tossed on high seas, nothing to hold onto but the knowledge of the abyss beneath my feet. Death is a pattern I cannot master. It isn't a pattern, but the absence of one.

The bone saw gleams in the lamplight.

'I want you to call her,' Mori is saying. 'Or she might not choose to return.'

I lick dry lips. Although my heart aches at the thought, I say, 'If she doesn't want to come back, shouldn't we leave her to rest?'

'Sinne's was a sudden death. I don't believe she will be at peace until she shares the truth. Too much has been left unsaid. She deserves the chance to speak.'

I nod. It is something to hold onto, something to justify my own selfishness at wanting my sister back. But cold spins its web around me. No magic comes without cost.

I do not know how I survive Samhain night. I tell myself it is a dream, a nightmare, a waking madness, as Mori saws and sews, taking my sister apart. I spill the contents of my stomach when hers spills, the stench of bile turning the cottage into a slaughterhouse. The little table so awash with red that the wood disappears and it seems Sinne lies on a bier of blood, her exposed ribcage white, swan white. We split my sister like game, so we can get at the sinew that holds her together.

I am witness, participant, perpetrator. To a miracle or a misdeed so grave none might speak of it – save in brief, one day, skimming a stone over the truth. Mori takes the bones from Sinne's chest, paring back her flesh. She takes the bones from her delicate fingers and feet. It is I who shape them into pins, at Mori's instruction, and all I can imagine is my sister's voice and how I'll hear it again if only I have the courage to challenge death. This body, I tell myself, desperate to believe my own words, is nothing but meat that will eventually spoil.

I've always possessed nimble hands. I used them to weave brideogs, making a person from a few dry, gold strands. Sinne's golden hair is matted with blood, but I cut it, wash it, comb it out and I weave it into strings. They are good and taut and I am making Brigid, just Brigid, a wheat woman to guard us. I wind the ends around the pins, binding them tight with sinew.

At first the whispers are on the edge of hearing, but once I start to listen, they grow louder. They press against the shuttered windows and doors, working soft fleshless throats. They can sense our creation, ready to receive a soul, and they want it.

'Samhain is a night of power, and a night of thresholds,' Mori says, also looking up. 'Guard against them, Keyne. If they breach the door, all our work will be for naught.'

I realize what she means a moment later when bodiless lips caress my ear. I slap a hand to my head, but there's nothing there, only the whisper urging me – *up and open, open, open . . .*

I clench my teeth, trying to shut out the words. They are insistent; something will happen unless I reach the door. This house reeks of death and so do I. Blood runs down my nails, it's in my hair; a second skin. I am butcher, carrion-lover, shade. I have to get out. I have to get out.

I am halfway across the room before Mori's hand clamps bloody around my wrist. '*Guard against them*, I said.'

I shudder, thrusting aside the desire to flee, unsure how much of it is my own. 'Here,' she adds, passing me the pins I scattered in my haste. 'It's time we gave Sinne back her voice.'

'Who are they?' I cannot help but ask.

'Restless souls,' Mori says, 'forgotten things that usually sleep, uneasy. But Samhain has called them up and now they roam, seeking to return to life.'

I catch odd glimpses; the suggestion of hands or gaping mouths massed against the walls. 'What about Os?'

'Ach, they can't harm him. And he won't see them.'

When I turn towards the table, there is little of my sister left. We have hollowed her out, scraped her clean, a bloody harvest. In her place lies a breast-bone frame, its graceful structure waiting for my pins and strings. Mori shows me how to attach them, then tighten them so they will sing to the correct pitch. I'm aware of a muttering, murmuring swell – like waves at the foot of Dunbriga's cliff. 'She comes,' Mori says. 'Put your hands on her.'

I don't want to. The harp is beautiful, white and awful as winter. Sinne was a summer child.

'Call her.'

Gingerly I touch the frame, gasp at its heat. There's a pulse under my fingers, a growing swell, as of something coming closer, and suddenly I'm afraid. This is wrong. I should have let Sinne go, let her rest – however uneasily. But it's too late: we have carved her, changed her and she is coming back. She can't help it, called to her bones.

'*Sinne!*' I hear myself cry and beneath my hands the harp shudders. A shiver of sound cascades through the strings. Thwarted, shut out, the fleshless voices howl. 'Sinne,' I sob. 'I'm sorry. I'm sorry.'

More sound: discordant, furious: a minstrel's mad lament. She's here, but I can't understand her. Music is not a language I know. 'Please, Sinne.' My heart fills my chest, bruised and swollen. 'Stop, please. Speak to us in words.'

The harp trembles and grows hotter. I let go with a yelp, stagger back. Light streams through the shutters; someone pounds on the door. Mori cries a word and then it is over, that terrible saw of notes. My breath is loud in the sudden silence; it is the only thing I can hear.

And then Sinne starts to sing.

41

RIVA

I don't know how long I crouch beside the river. Long enough to grow stiff with dew-chill. Long enough for every limb to seize up and for the night wind to scour my face of tears. More come and they too are scoured clean. My cheeks feel like the salt-stained rocks of the beach bared at low tide.

In the end I remember that I am not alone. I carry another who will not care for the cold. My first attempt at rising fails, my knees too sore to support me, burned foot turning on the uneven ground. When I finally stand, a great shuddering seizes me and I can't stop. It makes it hard to walk and I often fall. But the sky is bright with stars, their sharp faces staring down on me as if they sit in judgement. I deserve it.

Sinne's face is always before me, her final cry in my ears as the river took her, quenching that awful fire. Blood in the water, her tumbled body like a doll's, swept downstream. Keyne's cries, Os's terror – I will have bruises on my arms from his grip. Now the night is silent; even the owls have ceased to hoot. Perhaps they cannot stand the sight of me.

The thought of going home is abhorrent, knowing Sinne will never follow. But where else can I go? And what about the child? I have to get warm or risk losing it.

Torches burn on the walls as I approach. The hold is a beehive, gates thrown wide, guards buzzing, organizing search parties, it seems. One cries out when he sees me. 'Lady.' He takes my arm and I let him guide me through the gates. 'Where have you been? Roderc has taken men down to the beach to search for Lady Sinne and sent out others to fetch you.'

Fresh tears spill down my cheeks and I feel myself passed swiftly into Locinna's care. We reach the women's quarters, where a good fire burns despite the hour. Locinna sits me in front of it, rubs my good hand and foot and begins pulling off my damp clothes until I remember myself enough to stop her.

'You're wet through, Riva,' she says, going back to chafing my hand. 'What in holy God's name were you doing outside? We must get you warm.'

'Bring water,' I say through chattering teeth and as soon as she leaves, I strip behind a screen, pulling a clean shift over my head. Cloth can still hide what nakedness cannot. As warmth returns, so does feeling, even sharper and brighter than the stiff grief of earlier. And it brings memories, clear as a summer sky: Sinne as a child, sticky with strawberries, her hair like sun. Her tiny feet fleeing through the meadow grass and me running after her, my own foot still whole, unburned, shouting for her to stop. The way she sometimes sang in the moonlight, an old song to Andraste that I'd taught her in my halting voice.

And this time I cannot cry; the tears are gone, given to the night and the river. All I can do is curl over my belly and the cursed child – and stare at the hand that had hung at my side, when it could have reached through flames to save my sister.

All that eve, Samhain eve, the hold is roused. No sacred fires are lit to plead a mild winter; no offerings of food are made to keep the spirits from our doors. Nothing can be spared this year. It isn't spirits we need to fear, but men of flesh and blood bent on taking our land for their own. This disregard of tradition would once have horrified me, but I have no strength for horror; grief has drained me dry.

Mother comes at dawn, her eyes raw. 'Oh, Riva,' she says and gathers me up as she has not done since my accident, years before. Her tears slide down my neck.

'What news?' I whisper. 'Have they found her?'

'Roderc took a search party to comb the riverbank from Cēd Hen to the sea and there was nothing.' She shudders and pulls away, looking into my face. 'What happened, Riva?'

'She slipped.' The words are like lumps of clay in my mouth. 'The bank was icy.'

'Why were you even out there? *How?*'

'I needed . . . space,' I hear myself say. 'I didn't know Sinne would follow.' My voice cracks on her name, breaks it in two, so it sounds like *sin*.

Mother grips me hard, in the same place Os did. I flinch as her fingers dig into the bruises and the memory of Os with his face like a howl. 'You told Roderc you talked. What about, Riva? What about?'

His name is on my lips, chapped and bitten as they are. His name and my vow: to leave my family, my home, for some unknown future. That was the vow Sinne overheard. A betrayal, she'd called it.

Perhaps that's what love really is, I think, the price it demands. But what of *her* betrayal? She burned me, accidentally or not, and lied about it ever since.

'Riva.' Mother shakes me, as Os shook me. And I find I am tired of being shaken.

'Tristan,' I say, breaking away. 'We talked about Tristan.'

Mother's mouth turns down in obvious disapproval. 'I have spoken to you already about this.'

'Oh and that's the end of the matter.' It is the same anger Sinne stirred in me earlier and I am both frightened and glad of it. Frightened because I know where it led. Glad because it makes a change from guilt. 'You've spoken, so all feelings are gone, promises are nothing, words become unsaid. Because. You. Have. Spoken.'

I spit the last, now on my feet, and that blinding rage – the rage which forced Sinne to the river's brink – forces my mother back too. She stumbles into the screen, sends it crashing, splintering, and I stand over her. I hear the pain in my voice – the years of being pitied and viewed askance, seen as damaged goods. My life has never been my own, even before the accident. I have little more importance in this world than a bale of wool, waiting to be sold off.

'My lady, you must come . . .' Locinna falters at the scene. 'Oh what goes here?' She hurries over, helping my mother to her feet, while I tremble with pent-up thunder. Mother's face is very pale, save for two bright spots on her cheeks. A splinter is lodged in her palm, oozing crimson. Locinna frowns at it, looking between the two of us. Then she says, 'You must attend the main hall at once. The king commands it.'

'Cador?' Mother murmurs. My father hasn't set foot in the hall since Moriduno. The rage is turning to dust inside me. Have they found her? Have they found Sinne? We leave without another word, all three of us: me bone-weary, my foot on fire as if it still burns all these years later; Mother with the imprint of my anger on her cheeks.

A peculiar silence hangs over the hold. The light is not quite right either; perhaps it has leaked from the otherworld. People stare as we pass and I feel like one condemned.

The hall doors are open. The first person I see is Father, slumped in his great chair, pillows failing to keep him upright. I mended his skin, but haven't been able to regrow the splintered bone beneath. His jaw is misshapen, as if part of it has melted like wax in the sun. His remaining lords stand around him and several other faces I know line the walls: prominent folk of the hold such as Arlyn and his master; Bradan, Cadfan, Drem and Dinuus. Mother goes immediately to Father's side and bends down to whisper to him. Locinna retires to a quiet corner and I am left standing alone in the centre of the hall. The fire crackles brightly, despite the dread sunlight coming in at either end of the roof.

I jump when the doors clang shut. Gildas stands there, one hand on the latch. When he turns to glare at something, I follow his gaze and see Myrdhin, Keyne and Os. The big man's face still bears traces of last night's bestial howl. But his expression is some-how worse this morning, as if his heart is being torn out in front of him. I survey the hall, staring into every dark corner, but cannot see Tristan. What is going on?

'I have done all I can,' Myrdhin says. He walks forward, places something cloth-covered on a table. Then he raises a hand. Cold takes me, despite the fire. All I know is that I don't want the cloth lifted, don't wish to see whatever lies beneath it. But my wish counts for nothing. The cloth falls away.

It's a harp. Just a harp.

About to let out a relieved breath, I realize how silent the hall has gone, how the instrument has caught everyone's eyes and won't let them go. Reluctantly, I turn back to it. The longer I stare, the stronger grows my unease. It is dangerously beautiful in the way that a sword is beautiful, or a storm, or a thorned rose. But a sword is *meant* for killing, a storm can sink the best-made ship, and a rose's thorns pierce unwary hands. The harp's strings are golden, a familiar gold, and its frame is white, its pins so delicate. It has a graceful neck and shoulder . . . and I fear it, with every fibre of my flesh.

Myrdhin's voice strikes the hall like hammer on anvil, freezing us all in place. 'Let her sing for you,' he says.

The Twa Sisters

A king lived on the westward shore,
Swift the river runs,
A kingdom on the grey seashore   **it was red sometimes**
And all about obeyed his law,
Deep the river runs.

His eldest girl had raven hair,   **Riva**
Swift the river runs,
His youngest sweet and golden fair   **it is coarse I must**
And both of them beyond compare,   **have a comb**
Deep the river runs.

A man he came with story wild,   **cannot be trusted**
Swift the river runs,
The elder girl he got with child,
The younger knew she'd been beguiled,   **yes, yes**
Deep the river runs.

In him the eldest placed her trust,   **I told her**
Swift the river runs,
Believing love would come from lust,
She closed her ears, she knew she must,   **what was in**
Deep the river runs.   **the letter**

One day the sisters walked alone,
Swift the river runs.
The youngest begged her to come home,   **she was going to**
She begged her sister to atone,   **leave us, she was**
Deep the river runs.   **going away**

337

Scream she did, the raven one,
Swift the river runs,
She screamed and then the deed was done,   I fell?
The girl was gone – the girl of sun,   no I could not fall
Deep the river runs.

She floated far afore she drowned,   no no no no no no no
Swift the river runs,
The greedy waters sucked and ground,   I can't get out,
A miracle that she was found,   I want to get out
Deep the river runs.

The best of men be mute and true,   Os
Swift the river runs,
He took her up and then he knew   please don't leave me
And wept and closed her eyes of blue,   I am here, I am here
Deep the river runs.

The wild one of the hills is he,
Swift the river runs,
He split her into two and three   my hands, my fingers
And more – he caught her spirit free,   my ... I can't
Deep the river runs.   feel them

Her hair was gold and gold he strung,   this hair can't be mine
Swift the river runs,
Her bones were white, he wasted none,   what am I
Though cold and dead, how well she sung,   what have you
Deep the river runs.   done to me

And now I sit, to you I sing,   I want to go home
Swift the river runs,
My father there – he is the king,   Father I am here

My mother wears his wedding ring,   **Mother I want mamma**
Deep the river runs.

My family, who you forsook,   **Sister**
Swift the river runs,
You murdered for a butcher's look, **I am not dead I cannot**
I curse you for the life you took,   **be dead I am screaming**
The endless river runs.   **why can't you hear me**

It is her voice, Sinne's voice, here in the hall. Nobody's fingers pluck those strings. They sing under their own magic. I am shaking. The song has travelled into every corner, every ear. Now every eye is fixed upon me.

Dizziness hits, but I do not fall. I cannot; held in place by stares. A susurrus stirs the watchers like a breeze. And then Gildas says, clearly and quietly, 'What is this sorcery?'

Os falls to his knees before the harp. The instrument is silent now, gleaming in the half-light. Bone, it's bone. What has Myrdhin done? It can't be *her*. It can't be Sinne. I clutch my belly, swallowing bile.

'She is here to tell you,' Myrdhin says.

'Tell us what?' Mother looks on the verge of fainting, so white are her cheeks, so wide her eyes.

'Her story. Riva's story. What happened on the riverbank . . .' He pauses and for the first time I see anguish in his face. 'So I gave her a voice.'

'This,' Gildas says, pointing a finger at the harp, 'is foulest blasphemy, the work of dark powers. If the child is dead, her spirit should be free to find its way to the kingdom of God, not bound to a witch's instrument.'

Myrdhin bows his head and Mother makes a tiny sound. The

rest of the hall is silent, bound too – though with shock and horror instead of magic.

And then Father, in his new and terrible voice, says into the quiet, 'Is it true, Riva? What . . . it sang?'

I feel Myrdhin's eyes upon me; they are blue and limpid as a yuletide sky. They make me cry, 'I *didn't* push her!'

The earlier susurrus becomes a roar. Everyone is talking at once and I try to shout over them. 'Sinne – it's lying. My sister *fell*. I couldn't save her.'

'But why did she fall?' Mother asks, her voice breaking on the question. 'You told me you just talked.'

'Yes, but . . .'

The harp is singing again, a background hum. And though it sings softly, I can hear it is singing the same song – again. It is singing my guilt over and over. My dry eyes betray me; these people cannot know I've given all my tears to Sinne already.

'You talked and . . . *she fell*?'

'It wasn't like that,' I shout. But I have no witnesses to confirm my story and I can feel her here, Sinne, in this very room . . . Myrdhin really has brought her back, *caught her spirit free* – just as the song says. She is in the harp. Oh goddess. She is in the harp.

'Riva.' It's Father. One of Mother's hands holds him upright; I can see a line of spittle on the side of his mouth. 'Is there a child?'

They are all staring at my belly, hidden beneath careful layers and cold sweat. *They can't harm me if I am with child.* My short sharp nod elicits gasps from the women, raised eyebrows from the men. But they all share a sense of disgust; I can smell it in the hot stale air of the hall. I try to avoid their stares and spot Arlyn. He's standing with clenched fists, eyes raking the crowd. Then he steps forward and cries, without looking at me, 'This is not Riva's doing alone. Where is Tristan?'

I just know he is gone. He's left Os, as he's left me. And despite his promise, he will not be coming back. I am too numb with the long night to feel betrayed. That will come later – with the child. Still, I cannot stop myself from looking, cannot dampen a slim hope that he is choosing his moment – that he'll somehow step from the crowd to defend my honour and my actions. But seconds pass, no one stirs and I cannot look at Arlyn.

'Where is your master?' someone cries at Os, whose eyes have not once left the awful harp.

'Os cannot answer you,' I say.

'But *you* can.' Gildas comes to stand close to me. 'Where is Tristan, Riva?'

'I don't know,' I answer truthfully. Then, in a burst of defiance, I add, 'And I would not tell you if I did.'

The priest considers me. I know why Sinne – *oh Sinne* – had called him a crow: his dark eyes study me as if I am a piece of fresh carrion. 'No matter,' he says eventually. 'He will show himself when you stand upon the scaffold.'

Sinne was well-loved. How could she not be beside her sister – a fire-eaten girl who takes no joy in song, prefers books to company and doesn't care to dance. At least, not before Tristan came. Ugly yells turn the hall into a theatre, where I suddenly feel my life is a mummers' play, a warning to other young girls: a tragedy more powerful than the truth.

A voice cuts through the tumult. Keyne strides forward to stand before our parents. 'You cannot execute her, Father. She is of royal blood and we do not know the full story.' Keyne glances back at me. 'Confine her instead until tempers calm, heads are clearer and Tristan can be found.'

'Merely confining her will not coerce Tristan to show himself,' Gildas declares. I breathe out, glad to escape the oppressive heat of his attention. 'A more serious gesture is needed.'

'And what if he doesn't show?' Keyne says, rounding on Gildas. 'Will you hang my sister regardless?'

'It is a murderer's punishment. So just.'

'Father . . .'

But Cador raises a trembling finger. It points beyond Keyne and Gildas to the back of the hall. It points to the harp. 'Bring it,' he says. At a nod from Myrdhin, Os meekly picks it up, cradling it in his large hands, and carries it to the king.

Father hesitates before his palms touch the alabaster surface. Then it is in his grasp, hideous and lovely, its golden strings bright in the smoky air. The hall quietens. My father lifts trembling fingers and the instrument sighs in answer. But Keyne stiffens and I think I hear something beneath that sweet ripple of notes: a voice crying in the dark, confused and alone.

Tears spill down Father's cheeks. Suddenly he thrusts the harp away, back into Os's arms and the big man holds it tenderly. I shiver. When Father looks at me, I see Sinne in his eyes. He gestures. My arms are yanked behind me and I cry out.

'Gently,' Keyne snaps. 'Father, Mother, please. She's with child.'

The word *child* seems to revive my mother. She nods and the guards loosen their hold a little. But her eyes are cold on me. In them I see her sprawling after our confrontation, shattering the cutwork screen. Dried blood still smears her palm. 'Take her out of here.'

'Wait.' It is Gildas. He comes before the king, an image of piety. 'I have tried my best to curb the heathen powers and practices that damn this hold.' He bows his head. 'I have failed. The Devil's influence is stronger than ever. We see it here today.' Gildas nods to the harp. 'This poor child, *your child*, has paid the price.'

No one speaks.

'There stands the one responsible.' Gildas's tone has changed. He raises an accusatory hand. 'He has thwarted my efforts ever since his arrival, fanned the flames of the heresy you so wisely rejected.'

'No, Father,' Keyne argues. 'Myrdhin is a friend, has only ever done us good.'

But Gildas's speech has hardened the king's face. He stares at Myrdhin without warmth. 'Stand down, Keyne. Magician, how do you answer?'

Myrdhin steps forward. 'Truthfully, Cador. If heresy is the term you use for magic, the priest's words are fair.'

Father stands with a grunt of effort. When he sways on his feet, Mother steadies him. 'You don't deny any of it?' His eyes drift to the harp. 'You don't deny what you did to . . . to my daughter?'

'I do not. I sought to heal the rift in this land, restore the protection you have so rashly thrown away.' His voice lowers. 'I sought to save what I could of Sinne.'

'You have betrayed my trust,' Cador says and for a moment he sounds like the king I remember from childhood. 'Betrayed my family and my hold.' Then he wavers and the illusion is shattered. 'You will leave my lands and never return.'

'*No!*' Keyne cries and rushes to stand in front of Myrdhin. 'Father, this is not Myrdhin's fault. He didn't act alone. I—'

'Quiet,' Myrdhin snaps, his eyes flashing. In a quieter voice – too quiet, I guess, for the king to hear – he adds, 'or all our time together will be for naught.'

Keyne's mouth opens, shuts.

'I will go,' the magician tells the king, 'if you insist upon it.'

'I do.' Cador gestures and four more guards surround Myrdhin. They seem reluctant to reach for him, though, and Myrdhin actually smiles.

'Really, Cador. Do you think you could remove me from this hall if I did not agree to it?'

The silence that follows is like one that comes before a storm. Father tenses. So do the guards. But all Myrdhin does is turn on his heel. 'We will not meet again in this life, Cador.' A blink, and he is gone. I half expect the doors to open of their own accord, but they stay shut.

As my own guards begin to pull me away, I dig up my dying

anger and shout, 'And what of *her* crime? The crime you have hidden all these years? She did it.' With both arms behind my back, I can't show them my scarred hand. 'Sinne burned me with wildfire.'

'Preposterous,' Mother says; the word is half sob. 'Sinne never had that kind of power.' She turns away from me, so all I can see is a tearstained cheek. 'To blame your own clumsiness on her when she's . . . when she's . . .' She cannot say the word.

'She's right there!' I cry, watching their eyes go to the harp. 'Ask her yourself.'

'*She screamed and then the deed was done, the girl was gone the girl of sun—*'

I scream now. I scream as I am dragged towards the doors. 'Mother, Father. It was an accident. I *didn't* push her. Mother!' And in my head, I hear an echo. I hear her voice and mine. In that moment, as they mingle, I cannot tell whose is whose.

You. It was you.

I didn't mean to.

You did this to me.

It was an accident.

They put me in a storeroom with a bare pallet, no windows and a cracked ewer and basin for washing. I am spared prison, or the building that serves as one, on account of my status. Perhaps Keyne interceded again. I lie on the lumpy straw that first day and night, my face turned to the wall, and don't speak a word when a guard brings food and water. The hard biscuits taste of sand. I force them down.

When I dream, I dream of the harp. Unseen fingers tune it and there is blood on the pins, marrow in the heart of the frame. Sometimes it cries in a child's thin voice. Other times it laughs: Sinne's laugh, wicked and low. It laughs as I am led naked to a hanging tree, my belly huge and round. Every person watching has Gildas's eyes.

And then I wake, drenched in sweat despite the cold, and vomit my meagre dinner into the basin. I try not to, for the child's sake, but it is hard not to retch at the imagined feel of the gag in my mouth.

The day Keyne first comes to see me, I say, 'How *could* you? Why did you let them condemn me?'

Now we are together, my little prison-room is even more full of Sinne's absence. We stare at each other and I notice the hollowness in my sibling's cheeks. 'Are you saying you're innocent?' Keyne asks.

'No,' I whisper, dry-mouthed. 'But I *didn't* push her. You have to know that.' I lean forward. 'If anyone is guilty, it's Myrdhin – for what he did to Sinne.' Gildas was right: it had taken a wicked power to change my sister, my human sister, into an object other hands could pluck. Anger shudders through me. 'Who is he to preside over life and death? Only gods have such power.'

'There are no gods, Riva.'

'What Myrdhin did was an abomination.' I stare at my hand, imagining it turning translucent with healing power. In my mind I see another hand, a smaller hand, wreathed in hungry flame as it reaches to burn me. 'Magic is an abomination.'

'Magic is a tool,' Keyne replies firmly, 'and a means of understanding. It can be used for good or ill.'

'You're defending him? He . . . he carved Sinne up, as if she were meat.' Keyne flinches, pale-faced all of a sudden and – 'You were there, weren't you?' I whisper with a dawning horror. 'You helped him.'

'I was there.'

I want to fly at my sibling, want to beat my fists against Keyne's chest. But it won't bring Sinne back. It won't absolve my own guilt. So all I say is, 'Get out. *Get out!*'

Keyne leaves without a fight and I know I am right. They'd both done it: pulled Sinne apart and put her back together, all wrong, just to condemn me.

Weeks pass. I scratch them off on the soft wood; a mark for every dinner. And I grow thinner except for my middle, until my wrists look as fragile as a sparrow's foot. Keyne comes again, but I refuse to answer any questions about Tristan, and eventually my only remaining sibling stops coming.

Arlyn comes instead.

I can hear his voice outside, talking heatedly to the guards that must be stationed there. After a few moments, the bar lifts and the smith's apprentice steps inside, squinting in the dimness. I am allowed only a single tallow candle. Probably one of those I'd dipped myself – a lifetime ago, at Imbolc.

'Riva.'

Arlyn looks down on me as if I am a rabbit not quite dead in a snare. The image pushes me roughly to my feet. I will not take his pity ever again. 'What do you want?' My neglected voice shudders out the words and I cough. 'Come to mock the disgraced daughter?'

'No,' he says simply and hesitates. 'I . . . I've come to offer to marry you.'

I stare at him. 'What?'

'The king is prepared to forgive you, Riva, on these conditions: you give up your name and any rights you might have in the hold, and take mine. We would marry, live together. I would –' his eyes drop – 'raise your child as my own. We could stay here, have a life here. We wouldn't have to leave.'

The room begins to spin. Arlyn moves to steady me, but I throw out my hand, my burned hand, warning him off. 'Is this plan your doing?'

'I couldn't bear it if . . . Oh, Riva. Gildas still demands your execution. And he's not alone. The people say—'

'I don't care what they say,' I snarl.

'You should.' Arlyn takes a steadying breath. 'It's only your child that keeps you alive. No one wants an innocent's blood on their hands. But after it's born . . .'

'After it's born, they will execute me,' I say and try to keep the terror out of my voice. 'They will orphan my child.'

Arlyn stumbles forward and seizes both of my hands before I can stop him, clutching tight. 'It doesn't have to be that way, Riva. Only marry me, please. Then you'll both be safe.'

'And when would this marriage take place?' I ask, though bile rises in my throat.

'Tomorrow, if you willed it, if you agree,' he says, and I do not care one bit for the eagerness in his face. 'And after it's consummated, you would be—'

'Wait.' I feel a chill. 'You would lie with me while I carry another man's child?'

He scratches his neck, looks uncomfortable. 'It wouldn't be a true marriage, else.'

'No,' I say, pulling away.

A flush rises in his cheeks. 'This is your only chance, Riva. Is it such a terrible thing?'

'Being forced into marriage—'

'Is no different from what your father had planned.'

He is right; this fate has always awaited me. But I hate him for saying it because – for a few brief months – I allowed myself to believe in something better.

'I love you,' he is saying through the ringing in my ears. 'We've known each other for years, Riva. I'm no ungentle stranger. I would never hurt you.'

'You hurt me just by standing there,' I say, though I can see the words hurt him far more. 'I thank you for your . . . offer, but my answer is no.'

His flush deepens. 'Your stubbornness will kill you.' It is almost a sob. 'Nothing will ever be good enough, Riva, will it? *I* will never be good enough.' He turns with tears in his eyes and beats his fist against the door until the guards open it for him.

I slump to the ground when he is gone. I weep at the thought of being executed and at the thought of being Arlyn's wife – living each day under the eyes of folk who despise me. They would never forget. I cry for my sister, who I have lost, and for my faith in the old ways, which had once been so secure. I cry for my nameless child who will grow up in the shadow of my disgrace.

And I weep for Tristan. Because, gods help me, I love him even now.

42

KEYNE

Yule – the festival of midwinter

Must the world fall apart before I'm permitted to change it? I walk whole, flesh and blood, through a realm of dust – that's what it feels like, every footfall stirring up the motes of brighter days. Days before Tristan came and unpicked the threads of my family's pattern.

The harp sits in the great hall, where it sings its awful song for any who come near. It can't seem to help itself – and no one dares to move it. This surely can't be Sinne. My light, dancing sister, who liked to keep the old songs alive. Did we really lash her spirit to the harp that night? Samhain is a fading dream, and the instrument's beauty helps to hide the horror of our butchery. I do not know if Mori and I did right. Perhaps we should have let Sinne rest, burned her story with her body. But we gave her voice back, let her speak, and now I will lose yet another sister.

The rigid lines of Riva's cheekbones haunt me. She is not eating enough and we cannot spare more for her, not when the people are starving and think her a murderer besides. 'Do you believe she did it?' Gwen asked me in a low voice, the day after Sinne sang. 'Do you think Riva pushed her?'

I recall the last conversation Sinne and I had with Riva, begging her to be wary of Tristan, to steal his letter. I remember her hard eyes and proud jaw. What if our words woke a terrible anger in her? Anger that led her to . . . to kill Sinne?

'No,' I murmur to Gwen, dismissing that fear. 'But I don't believe she is wholly innocent either.'

'Gildas won't be satisfied until she is executed. He's already made up his mind.'

'Then he'll have to go through me.' I will not let Father execute my sister, especially while she's with child. And afterwards –

A gust of cold brings me back to the present. The snowstorm hides the warriors that threaten us, but we've all seen fire in the hills, heard the snap of the golden dragon banner on the wind. Afterwards . . . there may not now be an afterwards for any of us. I shrug my fur cloak higher up my shoulders, force numb fingers to grip the ladder as I descend from the sentry post, fear in the pit of my empty stomach.

They have us penned in: Cynric and his Gewisse. I haven't seen the man himself, only his message: surrender or die on the over-morrow. Just a day remains to us. Even those lords who love war more than peace cannot believe the Saxons would countenance a winter campaign. *But why not?* I think. *We are crushed by famine, cold and heartbreak. What better time to strike?*

I swallow misery. Myrdhin's absence is like a tree ripped, roots and all, from the earth of my life. Only the hole remains, empty, awaiting something else. But I don't know what to plant instead. I've relied on him too much, relied on Mori too much. Her house is shut up now, cold and dark and looking as if no one ever lived there. When Father exiled Myrdhin, the land itself heard him. He might be weak, but he's still the king and I know in my bones that as long as Father lives, Myrdhin cannot return.

It's oddly quiet on the ground. Folk ought to be coming and going, preparing for the siege we all know awaits us. But I hear only the mournful wail of the wind. It blows from the frozen north, bringing snow. If I concentrate, I can see the pattern of cold spun around stones and eaves. It wraps infants and makes them cry. The sea is thick with it.

With a brief twist of effort, I step outside the pattern and draw on another – one of the strands that forms fire. Warmth envelops me and I sigh. It's as if I'm standing near a hearth, watching snow fall outside. Feeling stronger, I set out to find the reason for the quiet. As I cross into the middle terrace, a warrior catches my arm. Beneath his helm, his eyes are uneasy. 'You want to get up there,' he says gruffly and jerks his chin towards the church. 'The priest summoned everyone. I heard shouting.'

Gildas. Torn by sudden dread, I break into a run.

It isn't long before I hear it: the unmistakable rumble of a crowd. I skid around the last corner only to collide with a group of men. One turns with a snarl, which falters when he sees me. 'What's going on?' I demand.

'She's a murderer. She's getting what she deserves.'

I can feel the colour draining from my face. 'My father has not passed judgement on Riva. Who authorized this?'

'Only know that the priest called us here,' the man says, rubbing the shoulder I bumped in my mad dash. 'Said God will be her judge.'

Cursing, I start to elbow my way through the people, but they're packed too closely. Instead I bring my hands together and then spread them, palm down. The air ripples in response, solidifies on either side of me, forcing people back. I see fervour in their eyes as they turn, the same bright zeal as lives in Gildas. Heart pounding now, I speed up.

'Keyne, thank Brigid,' comes a shout; the crowd holds Arlyn captive too. I can see him trying to break through, to get to Riva. 'Do something! Everyone's gone mad.'

He's right. It's in their upraised fists, their ugly words. I'm nearly at the front now and as the last people are forced to part before me, I shudder to a stop.

The scaffold has been cobbled together from bits of wood, wood we cannot spare. It is more sinister for its lopsidedness. Riva stands with a rope around her neck. Her hands are tied, wrenched behind her back, and her dress is dirty and torn. But the worst sight is her belly, swollen with the child they mean to murder.

'Stop.'

My voice is the roar of the sea, the breaking of a thunderhead. It commands silence and silence falls. Riva's eyes meet mine, dark and desperate. Gildas is near her, severe in black. He smiles when he sees me. 'What is this?' I yell at him.

'Justice,' he says. 'A crime – the worst possible – has been committed here. Or are you content to let murderers walk free?'

I hear mutters of agreement at my back and my fists clench. 'You call her a murderer. But what of you, priest?' I turn to stare at the crowd. 'What of all of you? Today, you murder an innocent.'

More mutters and this time they sound uneasy. 'Heaven will receive the child,' Gildas declares, 'as Hell will receive the mother. A better fate than being born into disgrace.'

'This is evil,' I say. Riva trembles and so does my heart. If the stool she stands on were to slip – 'Enough, Gildas. I order you to free her.'

'Order me?' Gildas slowly shakes his head. 'But you are not the king, and even if you were, what authority do you have over a man of the Church?'

'While you're in my lands—'

'How persistent you are, Keyne.' He raises his voice. 'This is not your land.'

'You are wrong,' I say more calmly than I feel. 'It has always been mine.' Before I can think better of it, I thrust a hand skywards and the silver flares on my wrist. I know that the bands strengthen my connection with the magic of the land, just as I know that one day, I will not need them. 'Let me show you,' I say and I summon the wind.

I meant only to part the clouds, to stop the drifting snow – but a gale roars through the crowd, scattering people like fallen leaves. It doesn't touch me . . . or Gildas. The priest has a hand raised too, palm out. I can see what he's doing, bending the pattern of wind around him. I smile coldly at him. 'You think you can command the wind in my own home?'

Folk nearby have regained their feet. They stare at us both, shock-eyed. 'I command no such thing,' the priest says loudly. 'It is the Lord Himself who protects me against your heathen magics. And this interruption has gone on long enough.' Before I can stop him, he sends a gust of wind towards Riva. She screams as the stool is torn out from under her.

I scream too, an animal sound of rage, of pain. She is twisting on the rope, choking as it tightens around her neck, kicking fruitlessly. Before two seconds have passed, I point at the space beneath her feet and will the air solid.

Her bulging eyes widen further as the rope loosens its grip. To everyone watching, she stands on nothing. But to me it's a tangle of pattern, trapping air inside it. She's coughing now, and it is a miracle her neck did not snap. I breathe out, my heart pounding. I should have been faster. Oh goddesses. I should have been faster.

Before Gildas can retaliate, I feel out the pattern of the ropes holding Riva and snap them. Her arms spring apart, the noose disintegrates and she falls to her knees, racked with sobs.

'No,' Gildas snarls, a sound I've never heard from him. He starts forward, but I block his path to the scaffold.

'How *dare you* use magic to kill my sister?' I ask, trying to still my shaking.

My words travel back through the crowd as a whisper. *Magic, Keyne said. The priest used magic.*

'Lunacy,' Gildas barks, but he's paled. 'Magic is a heathen's tool. I am an agent of the Lord.'

'I don't know if you really believe that.' I take a slow walk towards him and am satisfied to see him edging back. 'If so, I pity you. The walls you have raised against the truth will crush you when they fall.'

'You speak in Myrdhin's riddles. I should not be surprised.'

In front of them all, I draw Mori's dagger. 'If I were to hurl this blade at your throat, priest, would your god step in to save you?'

Amidst exclamations from the crowd, Gildas hesitates. 'I am happy to die a martyr,' he says finally. 'If you wish to damn yourself by making me one.'

'I thought I was already damned,' I say and I hurl the dagger.

I know it's a good throw as it leaves my hand, just as I know I can't miss at this range. The watchers barely have time to gasp before it's over. Gildas's hands are spread before him, just as mine were. The blade is an inch from his throat, held fast in air.

'Don't fancy martyrdom, after all?' I ask him.

'You will burn for this,' he says through gritted teeth as I call the dagger back to my hand. Its tip nicks his throat. Petty, I suppose, but he deserves it and more. 'You and all your people will burn in the fires of the Saxon horde.'

'You lied to us!' comes a shout. It is Arlyn at Riva's side. He turns to the crowd. 'You all saw. None of his power comes from God. And he told us magic was evil.'

Thank you, I think at him and he nods at me, seeming only slightly surprised at hearing my voice in his head. I can almost see the shock, the bitter anger travelling back through the assembled folk. Though some – Gildas's faithful and the families he helped most – still seem unsure.

'You saw him put out the Beltane fires,' I cry, one finger levelled at Gildas. 'You saw Myrdhin relight them. What other "miracles" has he performed in secret, with the aid of the very power he condemns?'

Arlyn stands. Raised up by the scaffold, he shouts, 'Remember Siaun. Lady Riva tried to heal him, but the priest ensured she failed.'

'Aye,' a female voice calls and I squint through the snow. A young woman, very like Siaun in looks. 'That is true. My brother might have lived were it not for the priest.'

'Since he came, my magic has failed me,' cries another woman. A man touches her shoulder in warning, but she shrugs him off. 'He has slandered our gods, and they have abandoned us.'

I can feel the tide turning, as I never thought it would. The crowd that was ready to see my sister hanged like a common brigand now yells insults at Gildas. But I wonder how many would have shed a tear if Riva *had* been executed. Time to get her away.

'Guards,' I order the soldiers watching, leaving no room in my tone for refusal. 'Lock the priest up until my father has time to deal with him.'

'You cannot do this,' Gildas flings at me, as men move to flank him. 'The queen herself invited me here.'

'Unfortunately for you, my mother is not the King of Dumnonia,' I say and I turn my back.

'Keyne!' He screams the name, but he has no power over me any more.

I hurry to Riva. 'Let me take her.'

Arlyn moves to stop me. 'Not back to that storehouse. I won't let you.'

'Not to the storehouse. She and the child need hot food and rest. I will bring her to the women's quarters.'

The smith's apprentice eyes me sidelong. 'But the king . . .'

I stare at him until he drops his gaze. 'As you say.'

When I stoop to pick up Riva, I'm shocked at how light she is.

She says nothing, but cries silently against my shoulder as I carry her through the hold. I glare at anyone who looks as if they want to challenge me. The snow has thickened now, obscuring the prints I leave behind. Perhaps it's my fault for meddling with the wind.

By the time I reach the women's quarters, I'm exhausted. Riva seems to weigh more with every step and I've never used so much magic so quickly. 'Thank you,' she whispers as I shoulder open the door. Snow gusts in around us. 'You can put me down.'

I do so, but immediately have to catch her as her knees fold. 'Careful, you've had a shock,' I say and then wince at the inadequacy of my words. The noose has left a weal around her neck, livid purple.

'Keyne.' Mother appears from behind Locinna. 'What is going on? What is *she* doing here?'

'Look after her,' I say to the old nurse. 'Give her hot food and clean clothes. I will know if it isn't done.'

'Answer me.' Mother marches over, but stops short of reaching me. She has to look up to meet my eyes. 'The king hasn't changed his mind. She ought to be—'

'*She* is your daughter,' I say. 'And Gildas just tried to hang her.'

'*What?*'

'In front of the people. If I hadn't been there to stop it, she would be dead.' Curled by the fire pit, Riva hunches over her belly. Tears are still streaming down her face.

'I don't believe it.' Mother's hand flutters to her mouth. 'He wouldn't.'

'I don't think you know what Gildas would or wouldn't do. And it's irrelevant now. I've dealt with him.'

She stumbles away, her eyes going to my gloved hands. 'You killed him?'

I stare at her, a deeper weariness weighing on my heart. 'Do you so readily believe me a murderer, Mother?'

She opens her mouth, but no words come.

'You have never understood me, or wanted to understand. I accept that. But a murderer?' I swallow hard to keep the tears inside. 'If you can believe that of me, you've never known me at all.'

'Keyne—'

'I think we've said all we can to each other.' I nod at Riva. 'Look after your daughter, Mother. She's all you have left.'

I can see she wants to speak, to fill the room with denials, accusations or perhaps pleading. But the door latch clanks, revealing Gwen; she's more snow than woman. Clumps of white fall from her cloak to the wooden floor. 'Your father wants to see you, Keyne.'

Here we go. I square my shoulders, wishing I could sleep before having to face Cador. I should have known the story would reach him sooner rather than later. I did condemn Gildas in front of half the hold. 'Thank you, Gwen.' I brush some snow from her dark hair and she straightens the buckle of my cloak with a serious smile.

'Good luck.'

'I'll need it,' I mutter before heading out.

In an ideal world – a world in which a priest had not just tried to murder my sister – I would arrive comfortable and dry for an audience with my king. But I'm too exhausted to banish the cold and have to put up with the snow sneaking under my collar.

It isn't much warmer in the hall. Fuel is rationed: it's too dangerous for woodsmen to venture out and our stores of peat are low. The fire pit that once danced to my tale of Herla is banked, tame and dying. Apart from a few inconspicuous servants, the hall is empty save for Father's pale shadow spilling across the floor. It merges with the greater shadows that cling to every corner . . . except Sinne's. I spare a glance; her golden strings gleam with their own light. Perhaps she knows I'm looking, as a single trill fills the space and Father jerks awake.

He sleeps a lot, even when he doesn't mean to do so. His eyes slip shut during our councils of war, composed of me, Mother, Trachmyr and Paternus. We've been trying to plan a defence of the hold with the scanty forces we managed to gather before the snow set in. The lords always look at King Cador askance and I know what they're thinking: he will not last the winter.

'I'm here, Father.'

It is hard to believe he's the same man I shamed before the lords – the same man with whom I locked arms, the day he decided on that ill-fated mission to Moriduno. He is in every way shrunken, except that tonight his eyes are bright, feverish bright. I wonder whether he was dreaming of his youth and has brought some of its strength back with him.

'Keyne,' he gasps. My name seems to cause him pain. 'Sit by me.'

I do so and he lays a hand on my shoulder. It is claw-like with illness and hunger, and I force down a shudder. It's not the illness that's broken him, though, it's us. Sinne has sprinkled grey across his fair head and Riva's crimes are writ large in his wrinkles. As for me, who knows? I don't even feature in the harp's terrible song. Perhaps nothing rhymes with me.

'I heard what you did,' he says slowly. 'A boy brought the news.'

'I wasn't about to let Gildas hang Riva like a criminal,' I snap, newly outraged at the thought of what had almost happened. 'At least in a cell, he can't do any more damage.'

To my surprise, Father laughs. It's a strained sound, not the tumble and boom I'm used to hearing. 'I am sure we will pay for the insult he's suffered, but I cannot be too sorry.'

'He's caused enough harm,' I say soberly. *As have you.*

Perhaps he hears me, for his smile cracks. 'They say you called up the land against him.'

We look at each other. The fire pops and another precious log splits into embers. 'Do you remember?' I ask finally. 'Do you remember what it was like to be one with the land?'

Cador's eyes close. His frail chest rises, falls. 'Only in dreams.'

'*Why?*' I ask. Inside me is a well of anger. It's so strong, it frightens me and I can't keep it out of my voice. 'You had the power to stop all this. To keep the fields fertile, to guard us from invasion.' I pause. 'But you turned your back on the land. Why?'

His eyes open again, slowly blinking. 'I thought your mother spoke sense, Keyne. We had come to rely too heavily on magic. We were not growing, or changing. No new inventions, no new ideas. Because we had magic. It could do everything for us. And with fewer tribes following the old ways, I knew it was only a matter of time before we ran out of allies and trading partners.' It is the longest speech I've heard from him in months. 'Gildas's influence, however, I admit I underestimated.'

'But we were *strong*,' I say and my father flinches. 'We were thriving . . . Now look at us.' I gesture at the bolted doors, the failing fire. 'We are cowering behind walls and locks. Is that worth a trade deal?' I clench my fists. 'We are dying. And it is your fault.'

'I do not deny it,' he whispers.

Disgusted, I rise to my feet. 'I have a defence to plan. Issue whatever punishment you like against me, as long as you are swift about it.'

He straightens with a visible effort, thin hands gripping the arms of his chair. 'I did not ask you here to punish you, Keyne.'

I let out a breath. 'Then why?'

'Enica tells me of you,' he says without answering. 'The way you have taken up command.' He is sweating with the effort of speaking. 'I am proud of you, Keyne. Of what you did at Moriduno.'

I gaze at him, my mouth slightly open. Praise is the very last thing I expected. I've always been a shameful enigma to him, someone he would prefer not to deal with or understand. To hear him speak of pride . . . I shake my head. 'I have done nothing beyond my duty to my home.'

'It is not a . . . daughter's duty to take up arms,' Cador rasps and I stiffen, noticing how his eyes have strayed to the sword at my hip. 'Or lead men in battle and council.'

'The lords would agree with you,' I say bitterly. 'They already resent Mother's presence at their table.'

'You misunderstand.' He beckons weakly to the nearest servant. 'Summon lords Trachmyr and Paternus.'

The girl hurries away and I feel a furrow growing between my brows. Does he mean to strip me of what little authority I've gained amongst the lords, and the fighting men? My palms grow damp at the thought. I hadn't realized how deeply I'd come to care for the responsibility of command: of drilling the men, checking defences, drawing up battle plans. My fear of having that taken away is visceral, as if Father is threatening to cut off a limb – some part integral to *me*.

'Keyne.' His voice breaks into my tortured musing. 'I called you here . . . to make you my heir.'

Pure unfiltered shock roots me where I stand. But my father hasn't finished. 'The land hears you, as it once heard me. It would be folly to ignore it again. All I have goes to you. The kingship. The titles.' He pauses to cough. 'I only regret how poor your inheritance is, how you will have to defend it to the death. I am sorry to leave you such a burden.'

The word *heir* rings in my ears like the sentry bell when it calls us to fight. My mouth is scrubland-dry, but I force myself to say, 'The hold will never accept me.'

'Deeds and words make a leader,' Cador answers. 'Not trappings. Not convention.'

Anger boils back up. 'Why preach something you don't believe? All my life you have shunned me and stripped me of identity and voice, pretended I do not exist. But now trappings count for nothing? Convention is to be overturned?'

He doesn't flinch at the heat of my anger, only regards me sadly. 'I am sorry for it, Keyne. Sorrier . . . that I must be brought to the edge of ruin before I can see what matters.' His whole body rattles. 'And . . . what does not matter. Do you accept? It is not . . . too late?'

A part of me wants to tell him it is, to hurl back his apologies and his offer. But Mori's blade is strapped to my thigh, my hip feels the grim weight of the sword, and the shadows in the hall will overwhelm us all if I turn my back. *War is coming*, Myrdhin's voice whispers in my head. *Dumnonia needs a king.*

'My king,' comes a voice and I jump at the echo of the word. I hadn't even heard the door open. Paternus bows and Trachmyr follows suit. Then their eyes lift to me where I stand rigid before my father. 'Why have you called us here?'

'To bear witness,' Cador says shortly.

'To?'

'The succession.'

The lords make twin noises of surprise. 'Cador, it is hardly the moment,' Paternus says. 'Such matters would be best discussed when we do not have a crisis on our hands.'

'No.' Father's tone brooks no argument. He is struggling to sit up straighter in his chair and I steady him. Cador grunts thanks but doesn't let me go. Instead he looks up at me through pale, lucid eyes and says, 'Keyne, please kneel.'

The two lords are still nonplussed, even when I kneel before my father and he pulls a large ring from his finger. It is not until it's placed on mine, a curve of gold, that their incredulous spluttering fills the hall. My father lets out a sigh, as if the ring held the last of his failing life.

'What foolishness is this?' The question is almost a snarl and I twist to look at Paternus. He's always been the more hostile of the pair. His lips are white as he glares from me to Cador and back again, chest swelling with words one should not say to one's king.

'My decision is final,' Father tells him faintly, but firmly. 'Keyne is the only fit choice.'

Paternus's shock echoes my own; I stare at the signet ring, too big for the finger it rests on, and watch firelight dance in the gold. Then the lord says, coldly, 'For all her pretences, she is a woman. A woman cannot be king.'

Before the outrage boiling up in me forces an exit, Trachmyr interrupts. 'There is a precedent,' he says, and Paternus turns slowly to look at him. I do too. 'The woman heir,' Trachmyr continues, 'called banchomarba in Éire.'

'We are not in Éire,' Paternus growls at him and whirls back to the king. 'My lord, I must insist—'

'*Know your place.*' It is almost a bark and if I closed my eyes, I could half believe my father returned to full strength. But no illusions can survive this sickly firelight. Cador sinks back into his throne, spent. 'And Keyne is no banchomarba, but my true heir, entitled to every right due a royal son.'

Shockingly, my eyes prickle, anger arrested in its tracks. I look at my father through a haze of disbelief. So do the lords. A hush falls. Outside, the wind howls on, uncaring of humans and the dramas they act out. It will blow across this land long after all of us are dust. After Dunbriga is dust. And other lives call this place home.

'Leave me,' Father whispers. 'Spread the word . . . tell the hold my will.'

Because he is king, they do. They have to. Or they declare themselves traitors, here and now, on the eve of battle. 'Stay with me, Keyne,' Cador adds before I can move too.

So I sit with him, a shade in the long shadows, my ring the only point of light. Mother joins us sometime past midnight. She sees my hand and says not a word, but stays beside her husband and curls his own fragile fingers through hers. I do not build up the fire. The vanishing embers suit us more and, besides, we cannot spare the fuel.

I feel cocooned in darkness and silence, in suspended time. I am changing, waiting, though the change is not so great and the wait is not so long. I watch my father's pattern unravel and I see how its threads intertwine with the hold's. As each one fails and falls away, I weave my own there instead: a hundred points of golden light.

And then I am aware of them, of the fragile lives that call Dunbriga their home. Someone is dying nearby – a child, I think, too weak to battle illness. A man is weeping. Another on the gates stamps to ward off the chill. I feel a pressure below my feet now, as if the buildings had put down roots, and those roots had tangled with others left over from a more primitive age. Thousands have lived and died on this land.

It isn't like the time I lost myself in the great pattern, in the frenzy of life. Now I understand it, the delicate balance between leader and land. How blood ties us together, and power seals the bond. The magic sings to me, a welcome, a lament. Because outside my walls there is a darkness where the Saxons tread. A void or absence of magic – ready to overwhelm us as it has so many others.

'Enica,' Father says suddenly, near dawn.

Mother's eyes are wet. She leans closer. 'Cador?' But he has already left us.

Her sobs cover the pop of my joints as I stand, stiff from long vigil. I walk to the fire pit, and poke the embers to brief, flaring life. They brighten when I lay fresh kindling amongst them to call up the flames. The tips of my fingers tingle; as if all my will is pent therein. Slowly, I draw Mori's knife from its sheath.

I feel lighter a moment or so later, without the thick dark braid

I've long disguised as a warrior's. When I toss it onto the fire and run my hand over my new-shorn hair, a sigh leaves me.

The doors are opening. Trachmyr and Paternus – now with Cadfan and Dinuus in tow – enter in a billow of snow. Half a dozen figures trail them: my father's servants go wordless to the fire, adding more peat. I don't stop them. It is the time for light.

'God preserve us,' Dinuus says when he sees my father. 'The king is *dead*.' The others clamour around and Mother spares me a glance, but we both know she cannot help me. This is something I must do alone. The ring is heavy on my finger as I turn to face them.

Paternus glares at it. 'The impropriety—'

'There is no impropriety.' I match him stare for angry stare. 'We are on the brink of ruin, Paternus. Father knew it, just as he knew I would not flinch from this duty.'

'You –' his jaw clenches so that he can barely force words out – 'a woman . . . is not a man.'

Although it's one voice, it might as well be the whole of Dunbriga. The silence is charged, as if we stand at the peak of a storyteller's tale and no one knows how the story will end. They hope it will end the way they want it to. But this is *my* story. And here, in this hall that has witnessed the death of a king and the birth of another, *I* am the storyteller.

So I tell them, 'You are wrong. My name is Constantine ap Cador of Dumnonia. I am your lord by blood and by right – and you owe me allegiance.'

43

CONSTANTINE

If this really was a story, they'd have fallen to their knees, sworn themselves to my rule and pledged to stand beside me in defence of the realm. That's the way I'd have liked it to be told. In reality, there is a lot of shouting – and only the servants bend their knees, before making a hasty exit.

'We don't have time for this,' I say loudly. 'I am Cador's heir, whether you like it or not. And I am myself, whether you like it or not.' I turn on my heel and flick a hand at the doors, which crash open before I reach them. I hear exclamations behind me and smile. But it fades when I see what awaits me outside.

They gather, hundreds of bodies pushing into the space before the main hall. Heart hammering, I stand on the top step, looking from face to serious face. The servants must have run to spread word of Father. Spread word of me.

'I am not done with . . .' Paternus stutters to a halt as he catches sight of the crowd. 'What is this?'

No one answers him. It's so quiet I can hear the distant toss of the sea, the sweep of wind over wood. Clouds scud above us and the snow ebbs, revealing a bright patch of sky.

'King Cador is gone,' I tell the people, watching my words pass like a shadow across the sun. 'I am his heir. I did not ask for it. Who would willingly shoulder such a burden?' I steel myself. 'But I will *not* turn away,' I shout, so all can hear me. 'Not when the enemy waits beyond our walls. Not when I can make a difference.'

I draw a breath, realizing now is the time to claim my inheritance before the people. I look at the blur of faces, can pick a few out of the throng: Arlyn and Bradan, Locinna. Siaun's sister, link-armed with his widow. Os, strange and silent Os, the claws of grief sunk deep in his skin. Gwen. And I think of how I came to be here, the road that led me to these steps, this morning. Mori told me I'd abandoned the usual path. That I'd chosen to walk another. I'd chosen *this*.

Guards stand on either side of me. I look unflinching into the burnished shield of one and see a person: a young man armoured for war, with wild eyes and dark hair, and on his head . . . a crown of light. Constantine. And I find I can smile at him. He smiles back.

'My uncle is dead.'

Gwen's voice cuts through the sigh of the crowd. She steps forward. 'I am the last of my family. I speak for the people of Moriduno when I say we will follow you, King Constantine.' A shouted round of *ayes* come from men I recognize, who rode beside me on that fateful day. My heart is still hammering, but now it soars too. I meet Gwen's eyes; it is hard to tear myself away when another voice pipes up.

'I can speak for no one but myself, my lord,' a woman calls. She is dressed thinly, the bones of her face showing stark. 'But you have done what I thought impossible. You have brought the magic back. The favour of our gods.'

Others clamour to agree, or exclaim or delight – and it warms me to know that they can feel it too, the current flowing through overland and underland. Never mind that it isn't really god-given. Even now the ground beneath my feet thrums like a giant's heartbeat. I stamp on the earth and gold – not silver – bursts from it, a thousand tributaries rushing in all directions.

'We have no time to waste,' I call. 'Warriors – bring any unblessed weapons and armour to the smithy.'

Arlyn raises a hand. 'Aye, we'll make sure your sword aims true and your cuirass turns a blade.'

'And what of Cador?' Mother has come up silently behind me. Her eyes are dry, though red with weeping. 'Is he to be given a funeral befitting a king?'

'I will do my duty to him,' I say to her – and to everyone watching. 'I will do my duty to you all.'

That vow is still ringing in my head when I head alone to the gorse passage. It's been nagging at me, a fire too dangerous to leave unattended. If I had blocked it up on the day I raised the earthen wall, Riva and Sinne would never have been able to escape the fort. They would never have been together beside that river. Never –

I grit my teeth, swallow hard. *Stop it.* What good can regret do now? Only four people including me knew of the passage: one gone, another locked up, the third . . . I don't know where Tristan is or why he left, but I do know the value of information. An unguarded way into the Dumnonian capital? Plenty would pay gold for that.

Before me lies the tunnel, swamped as always in thorns. How many scars have they given me over the years? I stand and look, and I remember. Outside Dunbriga, I had felt free. Outside, I could be myself, unjudged. There was nobody who could strip, with a careless word, the layers I'd wrapped around myself – layers that had helped me survive in a world which pretended people like me did not exist.

When I pour earth into the passage, sealing it forever, I find myself whispering, 'Thank you.' It sounds like a goodbye to the person I was.

*

'We are out of time,' Trachmyr reports later as we stand looking over the walls. Unlike Paternus, he knows how foolish it is to squabble amongst ourselves right now. 'They are bringing up ram and tower.' He looks warily at me. 'Paternus advises riding out . . .?'

'This is not Moriduno and Paternus is not our general,' I argue, squinting through the grey. The snow-mist conceals Cynric's army so well that it's hard to believe it lies in wait. 'Our horsemen might take a few hundred lives that way, but Gewisse numbers would overwhelm us in the end. We're well defended here.'

'Well defended is a stretch . . . We are poorly provisioned, poorly manned and cannot outlast them if they dig in for a siege.'

'Perhaps it is a case of dying swiftly or slowly, then.' I can feel his surprise in the way he stiffens. Does he think me ignorant of the ways of war? 'But riding out in a blaze of glory benefits no one, least of all the people we leave behind. I doubt we could break the back of Cynric's army with one or two charges.'

Trachmyr eyes me with reluctant respect. 'Is there anything you can . . . do?'

'Perhaps,' I say. 'Though I don't know as much about magic as Myrdhin.' I can't mask my bitterness, remembering how Cador sent him away. 'And meddling with nature can have unpredictable effects.' I hesitate, knowing he'll likely shout me down. 'But maybe we're overlooking the simplest answer: words.'

Just as I feared, the other man's mouth creases. 'You would talk to Cynric? Talk to the butcher who said, "surrender or die"?'

Although I grimace at the truth of that, I'm remembering what the warrior from Lindinis had said: that the Gewisse claim to civility. But if he thinks he can win, Cynric's terms aren't likely to be to our taste. 'We must consider the people,' I say, sweeping my gaze over the suffering hold. 'If there is a chance to save lives . . .'

'And what kind of lives might our people have under Saxon rule?' Trachmyr demands. It is starting to snow again. I watch a few flakes melt on the oiled leather of his cuirass. 'They will strip us of power and possession. We will become little more than slaves.'

'I'm not going to hand over Dunbriga without a fight,' I assure him. 'I am simply voicing our options, as limited as they may be.'

'You are not your father.'

I take a deep breath, face him squarely. 'No, I am not. And I don't doubt he'd do things differently. But *I* am king now. It is a poor ruler who refuses to consider every approach.'

'Time will tell,' he replies darkly. 'If we survive this.'

It's the best I can hope for. 'Is everyone in position?' I ask instead.

He nods. 'We will keep them from breaching the walls as long as we can.'

Dawn and Cynric's threatened attack is still hours away, but I make my final preparations. Father's battle mail was a little big for me, but I had Arlyn alter it and now it fits well enough. Fear prickles down my arms and legs, leaving gooseflesh in its wake. I've been tested only once in battle and that was when I had Nimue to guard me. I don't know how I will cope amidst the blood and screaming, when the bodies of fallen comrades become obstacles to trip the unwary. I really hope I will not lose my nerve – I've heard that happens to some men, despite their best intentions. A king must stand until the last.

I look up at a knock on the door. 'Come in.' I have the royal rooms now, aired out after Father's long illness. Mother moved willingly into the women's quarters, into my old place. She's been quiet all day, quiet but steely, and she wears a knife at her hip. I fear what she plans to do with it.

Gwen slips in and closes the door behind her. And despite the looming conflict, I find myself smiling at her. She always manages to make me smile. My heart matches her quick steps as she crosses over to me. It's a large room, but it suddenly feels a lot smaller when she stands before me, only inches away. She's carrying something, a round pot. Her face is very serious. A moment later, I realize it's paint, warrior blue.

'Let me?' she says and, throat tight, I nod. Gwen bids me sit, awkward in my armour, and she kneels before me. She's wearing clothes similar to those she wore at Moriduno, has even found a leather cuirass to fit her. I watch her twirl a finger in the paint, lift it to my face. 'Close your eyes,' she whispers. I hesitate only a moment.

The paint is cold, but not cold enough to mask the heat of her fingertip. I shiver as she draws it gently down my forehead, over my brow, my eyelid. Three straight lines, for the people, for the land, for the king. My skin flushes beneath her touch; I can feel the slight tickle of her breath on my bare cheek.

'There,' she murmurs. Hardly daring to breathe, I open my eyes. The paint shifts and settles. Gwen sets the pot aside. 'You look handsome in your armour,' she says, trying for lightness, though her voice is tight with worry. She helps me to my feet. 'I . . . I wanted to wish you luck, my lord.'

I hold up a gauntleted hand. 'You don't need to call me that.'

'And,' she says, ignoring me, 'I wanted to tell you to be careful.' I swallow as she takes my upraised hand, sliding the gauntlet off. Then she brings my palm to her lips, kisses it slowly. Another shiver, more powerful, runs through me. '*Please* be careful,' she whispers. 'I could not bear it if—'

I take her into my arms, an impulsive embrace – I'm sure she'll break away. But she doesn't. She holds me as tightly as I hold her. The top of her head barely reaches my chin. I bury my face in her brown hair, which smells of sweet smoke, and lose myself for a few perfect moments.

I wish we could have stayed that way. But Gwen shyly kisses my cheek, draws back, and cold rushes in to replace her. I brush a thumb across her cheek, her strong jaw. 'I will be careful,' I promise her. 'As careful as I can afford to be.'

'That's all I ask, Constantine.' She pauses. 'It's a good choice for a king.'

I force a smile. 'Someone once told me that the only names that matter are the ones we take for ourselves.'

Hammering shatters the moment and a warrior bursts in without invitation. 'It's begun,' he shouts, red-faced and sweating. 'They're at the walls.'

'Go to the women's quarters,' I say to Gwen, as I stuff my hand back into the gauntlet. 'I've already posted men there with orders to follow your command.'

Gwen's eyes widen, but her nod is brisk. 'I understand. I will keep them safe.'

I throw her a last grateful look before following the warrior outside. As we dash through the upper, middle and then lower terraces, frightened faces peer at me from open doorways. 'Inside!' I order them. 'Fasten your doors.' I hope Mother and Riva have the sense to stay in the women's quarters, far from the gates.

'Why now?' I shout at Paternus when I reach the wall, ablaze with torches and braziers, buzzing with woad-painted men. It's a foolish question – it's not as if a pact exists between us and our enemies that demands we fight at dawn. An ominous creaking fills the snowy night. I cannot borrow aerial eyes – the winds are too strong for flying – so I must rely on my own.

Squinting between gusts, I see the bones of a siege tower edging closer. Of course. Assaulting the walls directly above the gates is their only option; my earthwork protects Dunbriga from raids on three sides, the sea on the fourth. I smile grimly. The gap in the earthworks is narrow. If they manage to storm the main gates, they won't be able to charge in force.

'Ready the fire pots!' Trachmyr yells and all along the wall men touch torches to the volatile weapons. Paternus's reply to my question is lost in their crack and roar, as a hundred warriors hurl them. They were my idea; I'd encountered them in one of Mori's manuscripts: a Roman tactic used to repel invaders from walls.

The Saxon siege tower is draped in damp skins to ward off flames and our pots do more damage to the men pushing it. Fires spring up amongst them and, as if these are a sign, other blazes flare into life, travelling back through the massed Saxon army. I realize they are lighting torches, all the better to terrify us. It works. I can feel the warriors around me standing stiff with horror.

How has Cynric raised so many men? My blood chills. There must be a hundred or more separate warbands here, thousands gathered under the Gewisse flag. The golden dragon snarls in the wind, well out of arrow range. I frown at the banner, seeing no sign of Cynric beneath it; no sign of any mounted commander, in fact. Where *is* he?

Our fire arrows scream overhead, a deadly wind cutting through the snowstorm, to *thunk* into the siege tower. The animal skins repel some, but a few fires take hold of the structure. By the light of the torches, I see Saxon bowmen nock their own arrows.

'Raise shields,' I shout, and hear others pass on the command, but not swiftly enough. My men are crying out around me. I watch as one topples from the wall, throat pierced clean through. I have to do *something*.

Before the Saxons have a chance to shoot again, I raise a hand, fingers spread wide. I remember that awful moment when Gildas ripped the stool out from under Riva's feet and, as I did then, I reach for air.

I needed only a small amount of power to save Riva, but seizing this much air, to form a barrier around us, sends me to my knees. Teeth gritted, I watch the Saxon arrow flight. Men huddle on either side of me, clinging to desperate shields. Ten feet above our heads, the arrows just stop. The sight of hundreds of them hanging in the still air is ghostly, like an omen. I stagger upright, one hand still raised. When I clench it, the air softens and the arrows tumble harmlessly to earth.

A great roar goes up behind me. *Constantine*, the men are chanting – and Trachmyr's look of joy is fierce. And despite the effort the shield cost me, my heart is full at the sound of my name.

My trick might have caused the Saxons to pause, but a burst of activity beyond the gates shows me they are quick to regroup. As I peer through storm and smoky torch-glow, my heart contracts. I see a battering ram, larger than the one used at Moriduno, and surrounded by fields of bristling spearmen.

Maintaining the air shield would block our arrows too. I let it go and reach out to the earth instead, to crack the ground beneath the heavy ram.

Or I try to. Although the pattern is deep and strong beneath *me*, it rips like rotten cloth beyond the gates. Where the Saxons tread, magic dies.

My elation evaporates. How am I to destroy the ram if I cannot reach it? Both lords are looking at me expectantly, as are the men lining the wall. There's no time to explain why I can't ask the ground to swallow our enemy, so I bring my hands together, summoning the storm.

The snow thickens, bathing everything in eerie light. I shudder at the power in the clouds. Patterns tangle there – wind, thunder, fire, water – it is a volatile mix that I'm not sure I can control. I crook the fingers of my left hand and a spiralling gust roars down to slam into the siege tower. The moment it passes above the Gewisse, its pattern unravels, but it retains enough force to shatter the top of the tower. Wood rains down on the men below.

Tensed against the screams, sweating with the effort, I curl my right hand into a fist. Beneath my helm, the roots of my hair tingle, the strands lifting away from my scalp. The pattern of fire changes when it's in the sky. It is part thunder and part air, spitting and bucking. I try to aim for the ram now, but the lightning strikes the ground instead, throwing dozens of men from their feet before its power withers.

My actions sow silence rather than jubilation amongst my men. Trachmyr wears a kind of muddled awe on his face, some of which I'm sure is fear. The whirling snow makes it hard to see below, but the Saxons seem slower to regroup this time. I can feel their eyes, as I stand brazen on the wall, only a bowshot away. Had they known what they would face here? Did they believe in magic? Did they *know* that their mere presence was enough to kill it?

As if in mysterious answer, a chant begins amongst the massed Saxons: a wordless sound. The front lines take it up and we defenders can only stand and listen as it travels through the ranks, like thunder trying to find its way back to the sky. Lightning snaps across the moorland beyond Dunbriga and in its split-second flash I see another siege tower and a third behind it. The Saxons beat their shields to the rhythm of the chant until the sound itself loses all meaning. My instincts prickle.

I touch the air again, a different strand of the pattern this time. And I dampen the roaring from thousands of throats until it seems no more than angry surf. It is only then that I hear another sound beneath the rumble . . . screaming.

Standing so close beside me, Trachmyr and Paternus hear it too. 'What . . .?' Paternus begins, but I hold up a hand to silence him, reaching out with my senses across Dunbriga. A part of me must have known what I'd find, had feared it – because the first place I look is the place I find my enemy. A black absence is flooding into the hold by the eastern wall. Our one weakness, the tunnel I made sure to *block*. How did they find it? And even if they did, it should have been impassable. Have I been so focused on the attack – the *diversion* I realize now – that I didn't feel them breaking through?

'They're inside the hold,' I say, sick at my own failure. It *is*

Moriduno over again. I should have remembered that nothing is as it seems where the Saxons are concerned. 'There's another way in.'

Trachmyr stiffens. 'What? Impossible.'

'It's well hidden, and I blocked it up completely, only hours ago.' I'm furious with myself. *How* did they get in? 'I don't know how they've broken through, but they've just been distracting us here, wasting our strength, while they *attack elsewhere*.' I gesture at the chanting hoard, at the too-bold torches lighting them up, drawing our eyes. 'Don't you remember Moriduno?'

'This is madness,' Paternus says. 'How could the Saxons know of such a place?'

There's only one person who could have told them. 'Tristan,' I say, the sweat chilling under my armour.

Trachmyr pales. 'But . . . but he aided us, fought alongside us.' I glimpse the reflection of Moriduno in his eyes. 'He saved the king.'

'Or he executed the man who failed to kill the king,' I finish, remembering that terrible moment our eyes locked as Tristan raised his sword over my father. 'As he also executed the Saxon captive, who might have given him away . . .' I can hardly breathe for chagrin; at my own failure to see the truth. Why did he spare my father? What elaborate game has he been playing? 'We have to go. Leave half the men here so the Saxons don't suspect. The gates must hold.'

44

RIVA

I can hear it outside: shouts, the clashing of metal and occasionally a woman's scream. So the Saxons are inside the walls. I put my hand on my belly, now too large to hide, as if I can somehow block the child's ears. I let it fall a moment later. Why shouldn't it hear? Why shouldn't it know what kind of world lies outside? Better to be prepared, to steel both heart and mind for pain. Every time I swallow, I feel the echo of the noose around my neck and have to force down panic. If not for . . . No, I will go mad if I dwell on it.

The shouting grows louder. At the far end of our quarters, Mother looks up. Our eyes meet. I am alone here by the doors, save for Gwen, the other women sitting as far from me as possible. Fighting erupts just outside. Two screams followed by the wet thump of flesh hitting wood. Locinna lets out a little cry. I can almost see it: the bloody form sliding down the door; the last of our guards.

And then it shakes. Someone is pounding on it, pounding until the hinges rattle and the wood begins to split. Gwen hisses, draws her blade, but I touch her arm. 'Don't give them an excuse to hurt you. Keyne would never forgive me.' She glowers, but lets me pull her back to the central fire pit. Breathless, terrified, I stare at the door which suddenly seems no barrier at all. Perhaps the Saxons think this a treasure room ripe for plundering. But they'll find no treasure here. Just a woman, despised by her people almost as much as they are.

A shuddering crack and then light pours in. Only a torch, but it's like a sun against our dying fire. When I dare to open my eyes, he is standing before me.

Snow dampens his auburn curls; a cut on his cheek seeps red. His mail is bloody with battle and he holds a sword in his hand. But all I can see is his face, the jaw I had cupped, the lips I had kissed, the grey eyes that had smiled at me. They smile at me now – through the black paint that streaks them.

For a long frozen moment I stare at him and then understanding tears through me. I am breathing too fast, backed against the fire pit, held there by a maelstrom of memory and horror. I pull my blankets around me, hiding my belly and the child sheltering within it.

'Forlæt mec – find þone cyning,' he throws over his shoulder, and the shadow of a man nods and leaves. 'Take the other women to the main hall,' he adds in our language and ten more Saxons enter, swords drawn.

I do not look as my mother and Locinna are rounded up with the others. I cannot face them. Gwen brandishes her weapon, standing bravely before us, but even a veteran warrior would quail at ten against one. The blade is knocked from her hand and she is dragged off with the rest, cursing her captors all the way.

We are alone then, on an island of quiet. Battle rages outside the walls, as his people fight mine – or slaughter them.

'Riva,' he says.

My name carries the power to free me, to unfreeze my lips. 'Gods,' I cry, my voice still hoarse from the rope. 'It cannot be true.'

'I said I would come back for you.' Tristan steps nearer and all I can see is the black claw across his eyes, the smudges it's left on his cheeks. How many times have I kissed them, clinging tightly to him as we moved together? I cough in the smoke of my burning home, taste embers.

'Who *are* you?' Though what does it matter beyond the evidence of my own eyes? He is the enemy of my people; that is enough.

'A man who keeps his promises,' he says.

The hard knot of fear, which has steadily tightened over the weeks of my imprisonment, abruptly flares and flashes to anger. 'Worthless promises when every word out of your mouth has been a lie.'

He begins to pace in front of me, restless as a caged beast. 'I could hardly reveal my true allegiance. My whole purpose depended on subterfuge.'

'And what purpose was that? Beyond breaking my family apart and destroying my home?'

'Yours is a powerful kingdom,' he replies steadily, 'which ruled itself for generations, despite being a vassal of the Roman Empire. It's made you fiercely independent, stronger than most, a difficult prize to win.' When he looks back at me, his eyes glitter. 'Assailing you blind would have been too costly. Dumnonia called for a subtler approach. We needed better information – your numbers, for example, the layout of this hold.'

And I'd given it all to him. 'No,' I croak, covering my mouth. I had answered his questions with eagerness, so foolishly pleased he was spending time with me, the daughter everyone pitied.

I am the one who has doomed us.

'You are the key to the west,' Tristan is saying. 'If Dunbriga falls, and with it one of the greatest tribes in Britain, we will hold more land than either Northumberland or Mercia.'

Through the terrible consuming guilt, I force myself to say, 'Land that is not yours.'

His fists curl. 'My father's mother was a Briton. We have as much right to settle here as you. Your own mother is of Roman descent, or so she claims.'

'Descent has nothing to do with it. You are butchers, slaughtering your way across this country.' I pause then, struck by a sickening thought. 'You killed that warrior, didn't you? The one that came with Bedeu, after Lindinis fell. Isberir.'

By the grim set of his lips, I know I am right. 'Goddess.' It is almost a moan.

'He would have recognized me,' Tristan says coldly, 'from when I took their city at Imbolc. And he was at death's door already. I only helped him along a little.'

'That captive too, the scout we apprehended . . . But he was one of your own!'

'And just another Saxon brute to you,' Tristan says, his face hard. 'Why should you care?'

I look away. That he's fooled us all so easily . . . Everyone believes the Saxons uncivilized: barbarian invaders, grunting in their guttural tongue, the blood of innocents on their blades. I think of Tristan's rich voice, that slight accent I'd never been able to place. His Brythonic is as fluent as mine. And I realize, with an awful sense of falling, that *fear* allowed him to deceive us. We had all believed the story – the one women still tell their children to ensure good behaviour – of blood and Saxon brutality. Like children, we had never questioned it. The enemy could *never* be someone like Tristan.

Against the grating melody of battle, he says, 'I hate to see you like this.'

I shake my head. 'You expect me to believe that? Where were you when they accused me of murder? Where were you when Gildas tried to hang me?' Despite myself, my hand goes to my throat.

Tristan follows my gaze and his eyes widen. 'I will kill him for it.'

'He's already locked away.'

A great crash outside, the ring of metal on metal. Tristan does not flinch. 'I gave a man my name,' he tells me, 'and asked him where you were. In the dark, he didn't see I was painted for battle. He gasped out a wild story.' He pauses to let me speak, but I say nothing. 'That you killed your sister. That the magician turned her into a harp?'

A great shudder racks me. It sounds so outlandish, like one of Myrdhin's tales. What will Tristan say if I tell him he played a part in Sinne's death?

'Is it *true*?' he demands.

'Why don't you ask Os,' I say bitterly. 'If you remember who he is.'

His face darkens. 'I will find that turncoat and it will not go well with him when I do. I can only conclude that your sister bewitched him, stripped him of sense.'

I remember Os's face as he shook me on the riverbank, stark and stricken. Whatever bond he'd shared with Sinne went beyond bewitchment or glamour. He might have loved her, but it wasn't the love a man felt for a woman. It was a deeper love: not so hard, not so brittle.

Another *boom* shakes the floorboards, raising dust. Automatically, my hand strays to my belly, the blanket sliding from my shoulders. Tristan's eyes follow, and finally make out the shape of me through the gloom. He takes another step closer. 'Riva . . . Is the child *mine*?' I think I hear a catch in his voice.

'Who else's?' I snap. 'Do you think I'd spread my legs for any man who asked?' My hand falls. 'Besides, who would touch a kinslayer and a traitor – even if they do not know the half of my treachery?'

Tristan moves to stand before me and I tense, looking up at him. 'I told you I would marry you,' he says. That surely can't be nervousness in his voice. 'Will you accept me?'

After years of nothing, *two* offers of marriage in a matter of weeks. I feel a mad desire to laugh. The wife of a blacksmith or the wife of a Saxon – what amusement the gods derive at my expense.

But perhaps there truly aren't any gods, or God, and I am alone with my choices. The thought is an unexpected comfort. If we really are alone in the world, my life is mine, wholly mine, and no judgement higher than my own matters.

'You have shown me great loyalty, given me a gift I hadn't any hope to expect.' He could be talking of the child. He could be talking of the secret passage I had shown him, an act that has surely doomed my people – for how else can he have entered the hold so quickly? Around his neck hangs my black acorn, mocking me, glinting in the gloom. 'Riva,' he says and he lays his hand on my belly. I shiver despite myself. 'Marry me. Please. Come back with me to Uintancæstir – as my queen.'

I look into his black-painted eyes and feel a tear roll down my cheek. I am already reviled by my people. What future do I have here, amongst those who remember Sinne? I think of Keyne, or Constantine as he is now – as I realize he's always been. I have no doubt he will make a good king, if the Saxons allow him to live.

I swallow the rest of my tears. There might be something I can do, after all.

The child moves beneath Tristan's hand and I close my eyes. 'I cannot marry you if I do not know your name. Your real name.'

When I open them, he is smiling. 'It's Cynric,' he says and he gives me that same flamboyant bow as on the day we first met. 'Son of Cerdic. Cynric of Wessex.'

45

CONSTANTINE

'Too late,' I cry, 'we're too late.' Leaving Paternus to oversee the defence, Trachmyr and I rush through the hold, gathering men as we go. Mist rises from the dirt streets, turning them into a labyrinth. It isn't natural. Rounding a corner, we find its cause, almost colliding with a group of women. They stand in a circle, hands linked. I recognize one of them – the woman who spoke of magic's return. Only this morning, though it seems a life-age ago.

Their lips move in unison: a prayer to Brigid. But it isn't a goddess who calls the mist to confuse the enemy. It is the land that answers them. A fierce pride lifts me, dispels a little of my despair. 'Thank you,' I call as we pass, and the woman spares me a nod.

I can hear the Saxons stumbling around in the murk as we scythe through it, our footing sure within our own hold, blades biting into unwary backs. Scattered throughout Dunbriga, a settlement steeped in ancient power, there aren't enough of them to rend the magic apart. I smile.

It fades when I catch sight of Arlyn, bloody hammer in hand. Some roofs are aflame; others smoke stubbornly, too damp to burn. 'Riva!' Arlyn shouts. 'Riva is missing. They've taken the other women to the main hall.'

A chill goes through me. When we reach the women's quarters, the door is bashed in, the snow churned up outside, littered with broken boards and the corpses of guards. *Gwen*, I think with a pang and despite knowing that the gods aren't real, I send up a prayer for her safety. Staring at the devastation, I hear myself snarl, '*Tristan.*'

Arlyn seizes my arm, his eyes ragged. 'What?'

'He's with the Saxons,' I say shortly. 'I know it. That's how they got in. Riva knew a secret passage, showed it to him. I blocked it up, but they must have found a way to clear it.' Guilt churns; it was *my* passage, and therefore my fault we're facing this danger. But I've no time to explain. I look into the faces that surround me. 'This is our home, our ground. The Saxons do not know it as we know it and that gives us the advantage.' Despite the words, doubt pierces me. Tristan knew the hold well. Hadn't I seen him, eyes bright, as Riva gave him an innocent tour of Dunbriga? He'd lived here for months.

Abruptly I am staggered by the magnitude of his deception. The enemy walked amongst us in plain sight and we never spotted him. Was his plan to gain intelligence or to shatter our family: weakening Father, ensnaring Riva, driving a wedge between her and Sinne? I think of Moriduno, our run for supplies, where Tristan had laid his trap so cleverly. That trap would have sprung if not for Gwen and me, riding out to warn our people. Father would have died and Tristan could have given up his pretence of friendship then. My sister, I am sure, has only ever been a means to an end.

Hatred spikes through me like black ice.

Arlyn yells as a blade scythes in from the dark. The man at the other end has a smear of black across his eyes and he snarls as I dodge. I draw Mori's dagger, a smooth flick of the wrist. My other hand tightens on my sword. I'm aware that fighting has erupted all around us, but I keep my eyes on my opponent, careful of his shield. He feints to the left. I almost go for it before the eager light in his eyes betrays him. Instead, I dart right, sweeping a leg out to trip him. He goes down with a startled yell and I plunge my sword into his throat before I can stop to think.

He jerks and gurgles: an awful sound, a sound I've caused. But I'm forced to pull the sword free, its silver turned dark, and counter another strike. Both my blades are red before long, stained with lifeblood and the stink of gore. Father's warriors always seemed eager for battle. They talked of glory, of honour. But there is nothing glorious about this. There is no honour to be found in a man's spilled guts.

I steel my heart as I cut and hack, fighting my way through the frozen streets, Trachmyr, Arlyn and a couple of other men forming a defensive circle around me. Our skirmish is drawing more Saxons, giving away our position in the mist, but slowly, slowly, we gain ground, forcing a path to the main hall. Men begin scrambling to get out of our way, because we do not pause and we do not give quarter.

My sword clangs, grates against another. I'm at the bottom of the hall steps. For the first time, I falter and disengage, the battle trance lifting. It's hidden myriad injuries, nicks and scratches that sting in the pause. I grit my teeth as my opponent nods at me. Then he smiles. It is the same smile he wore in the barn when he told me I wasn't like my sisters.

'It seems I came too late for Cador,' he says. 'Fate has done my work for me.'

'Cynric,' I answer and I know I've named him truly at the slight crinkle of his eyes.

'And Constantine, I hear. Another strong name. Very Roman. A shame you won't have a chance to make it yours.' In his own language he shouts, '*Wíf árærdon on cyninges stede! Héo híe sylfe cyning nemneð!*' and guffaws break out amongst his men, as they stare at me. I can guess their meaning. 'But I am impressed,' he adds, turning back to me. 'It must have taken cunning to convince your father.' He tilts his head. 'Or to get him out of the way.'

There is muttering. He was wise to speak in Brythonic so my people could understand. Doubt is already a stitch in their sides. I clench my fists. 'I do not need to prove myself to you, of all people,' I say loudly. 'I am my father's heir and I will *die* before I let Dunbriga fall.'

This time my words raise ragged yells. Tristan – Cynric – stills. 'I would expect nothing less of you.' All trace of mockery is gone. Now his eyes are narrow and calculating through the paint. I can feel them on my wounds, trying to guess how much of the blood that soaks me is mine. I examine him in turn with a bellyful of dread, noticing how fresh he seems, how few swords have marked him. I am weary from wielding wind, thunder and blade. How can I best him in a duel – me with my scanty months of knife-work? Battle is still a foreign word, one I never thought I'd learn. And though I'm beginning to understand, Cynric has had a lifetime of practice.

But Dunbriga looks on. The Saxons look on. I am locked into my story now and only blood can free me.

Cynric moves before I'm ready, his sword biting into the meat of my arm. Just a teasing blow to test my mettle and my skill. He must think I lack both: his next strike near takes my head, but I dodge and parry weakly. He slaps my blade aside. There is no pattern to make one a better fighter and Cynric doesn't give me an instant to call on the land. I have only myself and my training. However, our duel demands an uneasy truce from our warriors. Out of the corner of my eye, I see stilled blades, ready to swing again at a moment's notice, but for now, the men of Dumnonia stand almost shoulder to shoulder with the Gewisse. The sight sears itself into my mind like a promise.

I stumble and Cynric's blade sends warmth sheeting down the side of my face. Angry, I drag my arm across my cheek, spit blood and dive into a roll. He's not expecting it. I come out, dagger in my right hand, and I slash it across the back of his calf.

He cries out, staggers, but straightens. His armour must have stopped my knife before it reached the tendon. It's his turn to roll, lithe despite the injury, opening the distance between us again.

Blood runs into my eyes. My hands slip on the hilts of my weapons. I can smell it: like iron cooling in a forge. A distant rumble tells me the battle for the gates rages on, the sky above a cloudy orange, as dawn starts to break. I have to finish this quickly, cut off the head of the serpent by any means. Perhaps then we'll have a chance to rout them.

My muscles are like water, sword arm trembling with exhaustion. But sweat now smudges Cynric's black paint, draws it down his face like talons. Summoning a last scrap of strength, I leap at him, feinting low, going high, seeing my opening: a gap in his armour, a glimpse of skin at his neck.

It happens so fast I still think I've won. I still think I've won when the point of his sword presses into my side, a mere thrust away from death. I can't imagine how he did it. There's no room for anything in me but terror. We stare into each other's eyes and I think, wildly, *Death is intimate*. Dealing it and being dealt it, iron binding us together at the last. Almost a pattern –

'Stop!'

We both jerk and turn our heads. Ash in her dark hair, Riva stands at the top of the hall's steps, looking down at us. She holds a knife to her own throat, right over the livid mark of the noose. 'Don't move,' she cries and her hand trembles and nicks her skin. Cynric flinches – it travels along the blade to me. No one is near enough to stop her.

'Let my brother live,' she tells Cynric. 'Or I will die beside him.'

Tears come and they are so bittersweet. To hear her say the words openly, to acknowledge me as a man – it is all I've ever wanted from my family. Why must I stand upon the brink of death before I'm granted this one small right?

Cynric mistakes my tears for horror at her threats. 'Don't, Riva,' he says. 'Keyne doesn't want this. Gods, *I* don't want this. Put the knife down.'

'Only if you let him live. Then you will leave here . . . and I with you.'

This close to him, I notice Cynric wears an amulet on a cord around his neck: an acorn, oddly black and gleaming. Focusing on it, I'm forced to swallow a gasp. It's magic. I can sense the land in it, a piece captured and held like a promise. Where did he get it? Could it be how he breached the passage? He's looking at Riva and I follow his gaze. The snow has turned to sleet now, each drop hurled by a vengeful Lir, and her wet dress makes her pregnancy all the more obvious. A murmur travels through the Gewisse. They are staring at their future king, looking between him and my sister, putting it together. 'I can't do that,' Cynric says. 'You know I can't.'

Riva presses the blade harder; more blood trickles down her neck. 'Then your child and I will die here. And you will go to your grave knowing you could have stopped it.'

Cynric thrusts me away. I don't know who is more shocked – me, him or the watching men. I splash into a sleety puddle, pick myself up. The sudden lifting of danger makes me giddy. Riva looks at me; her face tells me she gambled and I cannot believe her nerve. She had no idea whether Cynric loved her enough to abandon his conquest. He's looking at her now, tense until the knife falls into the mud at her feet. Then something leaves him in a great sigh.

Thank you, I tell Riva silently. His back is facing me, unprotected. Over his shoulder, I see her mouth open to shape his name, a howl in her eyes as she realizes what I'm about to do.

I raise my sword.

46

SINNE . . .?

I can see his heart.

It is all laid bare to me, as bare as his hands on my skin. I've always had smooth skin, bone pale and unblemished, the envy of my sister. I'm not sure what I think of his hands on it now, but he is gentle and he holds me against his chest, so I don't mind. When he strokes my golden hair, I sigh, and the sigh is like music, like a wind in the trees. I've always had a lovely voice, the envy of my sister. He carries me in his arms, my slim frame an easy burden. My feet are tucked up beneath me, my dancing feet, dainty and whole, the envy of my sister.

I can see his heart. He doesn't know and I don't tell him. In it are memories of black paint and blood, a dragging guilt. *Shhh*, I murmur, wanting to soothe it. *I am here now.*

Sinne? he says and his heart swells dangerously. *Oh, Sinne.*

Be careful, I tell him. *Your heart is not as strong as you think.*

I know. Know that now. Sinne. Sinne. You can hear me.

I've always been able to hear you, Osred.

Tried to tell you, Sinne. Couldn't bear the thought of their coming here. But it wasn't them, wasn't us, you had to fear in the end.

An ugly chord sounds and I close my ears. That music is madness. I don't want to hear it. I am the daughter of a king.

I'm sorry, he says. *I won't speak of it. Oh, Sinne.*

I don't want to sing, I tell him, shuddering. When I try, only one song comes out, despite the fact I know a hundred. It is always the same one too, a dreadful song, and once I start, I can't stop until it's done. It won't let me stop. I have to close my eyes until my lips close too, shut and silent. Silence is better than singing the only song I'm allowed to voice. It's the story of two sisters, I know that much. And it isn't the whole story, it isn't.

You don't have to sing, Os whispers. *Not to me.*

Contented, I curl up against him, though my arms are oddly stiff. After a while, I realize he is crying. I can feel his tears on the back of my neck. The back of my neck is hard. Perhaps I slept badly.

Os's grip tightens. It rouses me. *They are here*, he says. *He is here. We are not safe.*

Then we must go elsewhere, I tell him. *Somewhere we* will *be safe.* I feel his nod and am glad. I always wanted to run away. Wanted to run away with . . . there is a memory, a memory of a man. I do not like memories. They are broken glass, shining and deadly, and I am not wearing shoes. But I know the man. I had hopes of him once.

Cold my skin, cold my bones. Shoes are not the only things missing. Why am I naked in winter? Os cannot carry a naked woman around. People will talk. The air is not only cold; it is thick with burning. I can hear screams.

Os is the only one who doesn't make me sing. But the others: there are a great many others outside and I can feel the song building in me, an implacable rhythm that will sweep me away into darkness. I don't want to go; it always takes me a long time to return. The song is stronger than me, though. It shoulders me aside, replaces my words with rhyme. My mouth stretches, my hair hums, as if the sound is hidden in the strands.

Then other hands take me. Brown hands, cool hands that also

quench the imminent song. A woman's hands . . . or are they a man's hands? I am relieved until I recognize them. And then I am terrified because these are the last hands that touched me before the song came. I think they meant to save me back then, but they did something else instead. Or I did something else. Perhaps the jealousy and the hurt were too strong. Perhaps I am not capable of truth.

'Yes, you are, Sinne,' a voice says – the voice that belongs to those hands. It's a voice I know. Though now it's laced with another tone, softer, as if I'd only ever heard it imperfectly. And I remember that those hands also picked me up and swung me round as a laughing child. Those hands were gentle. 'Look, Sinne,' the voice says. 'Look around.'

I look. And I see them: the people from my song. There is my sister, bloody-throated as a robin. A boy child sleeps under her skin. There *he* is too – the man from the east. He is a liar, but his lies are shaping a country.

Someone stands behind him, someone who has no part in the terrible song. A king, a brother, a storyteller, a collector of names. I sense his intent to kill, though it shakes him. He believes his story must end in blood, as mine has. I do not wish such an ending on anyone.

So I sing to him and – as long as those cooling hands hold me – I find the words for another song. Not *that* song, which doesn't tell the whole story. That is a song of sisters, its notes drawn from the only life the world allowed me. This new song is for Constantine and the world he is trying to build. I alter the notes; the melody is unusual, but underneath beats the same metre as that other song. Because we are not so very different, he and Riva and I, and our bonds are as strong as the land.

The last notes fade. I know I will never sing them again. After we part this night, the only song people will remember is the other song, the sistersong, with its easy rhyme and grisly story that ends in blood. That is what the world understands. Unless one day it understands more.

I have held them all spellbound, defender and invader alike. It is my gift and my curse. Tears flow freely down the king's cheeks. His sword point dips to the ground and he reaches out to me. 'Sinne.' But that name hurts, my strength is spent and those slim cool hands that hold me are stroking me to sleep.

47

RIVA

I know he doesn't want to do it, just as I know he *will*. To save Dunbriga, to save our people. The sword trembles in his hand. I can see it all: Cynric turning, just too late, the blade stabbing into his heart. The snow has started to fall as rain.

I blink. Someone is singing.

A short woman, familiar, stands on the steps of the great hall just behind me. In her hands, she holds the harp. But it isn't a harp, or not only a harp. A golden-haired girl lingers nearby, barefoot in the melting snow. She wears the dress she died in. I swallow, unable to tear my eyes away. Her hair lifts; its ends are the harp's strings that thrum without being touched. Her skin is *its* skin, white as bone. A stillness like death takes me, takes us all. Together – ally and enemy – we watch the ghost of my sister. When she opens her mouth, I hear them both: girl and instrument in one pure harmony.

I cannot tell if there are words; all I see are pictures. Three children playing in the sand, screaming at a wave; three faces tipped star-ward, in love with wonder; three hands poised above a steaming honey cake; three pairs of feet sunk in snow. Laughter, tears and living. I am weeping now, for sorrow and joy – and for the years we had and the years we have lost.

When I can see again, all I see is the older woman and the harp she holds, its glow dimmed, its strings silent. 'Sinne . . .' comes a voice: my brother reaching out a hand. That lethal sword-tip now rests against the earth. Men stir and shake their heads. Some touch their cheeks and frown to find tears there. Cynric – that name still so shocking, so strange – meets my eyes across the intervening distance, and all unwillingly I think of how warm his arms were, how sweet his kiss.

An arrow erupts from his chest.

He is still looking at me, I at him. Brief confusion knits his brows before he collapses at the same moment I scream. Constantine catches him as he falls and in the clear space behind, I see Arlyn lower the bow to his side. Even from here, I sense the power that hums in its wood, enough to drive the arrow right through Cynric's body.

'No!' In the next instant I tear down the steps, slipping on sleet and blood. It has happened so fast, everyone still frozen in place, but they are beginning to awaken around me. I hear yelling, the ring of swords, but I keep my eyes on Cynric's crumpled form. My breath sears my throat as I gasp for air.

'I'm sorry, Riva,' my brother says to me as I fall to my knees beside him. 'I didn't want this.'

'Why weep for a murderer?' comes a voice and I raise my tear-streaked face. 'I did it for you, Riva,' Arlyn tells me, a frightening bleakness in his eyes. 'Now you don't have to leave.'

'Get him away from me,' I rasp at Constantine. 'Get him away.'

I don't look to see what he does, but all at once I am alone with Cynric, his head in my lap. Everything else fades around me. He coughs, blood leaking from the corner of his mouth. He still wears my acorn, stained red. 'The boy is right,' he whispers. 'Why weep for . . . a murderer?'

'You could have killed my brother,' I say. 'You didn't.'

He presses a bloody hand against my dress. 'I wanted to meet my son.'

Fresh tears, hot tears, spill down my cheeks. 'It might be a daughter. And you will.'

He smiles weakly. 'I don't think so.'

'None of that,' I say and I draw a breath. 'All I ask is your trust.'

'You have it,' he murmurs, closing his eyes. 'You will always have it.'

Panic rises, but I force it down. I have only moments. The future king of the Gewisse lies dying in my lap. If he survives, war will too. Conquest is in his blood, as healing is in mine. What I do today will change the future in ways I cannot foresee. But I have to try. I touch the token around his neck – its magic brought us together for a reason.

I lay my good hand on his chest, sticky and hot with blood. But blood has never worried me. As I did on that day in the nemeton, I shut my eyes, searching for the flickering silver thread. I can't find it. From far away, my body tenses. No, it has to be here. I reach outwards, upwards, almost to the limits of consciousness, as my pulse races. Beneath my hand, Cynric lies still. Is it his Saxon blood which blocks my powers? But I healed him before. And he wears my acorn, a gift of the land.

And then, without warning, another hand covers mine. I almost open my eyes. It feels cool and somehow familiar. *Look*, a voice says and the landscape in my mind changes.

I haven't found the thread because its power is *everywhere*. The land hums with magic, golden now, not silver. I feel it in my bones, under my feet. A huge web, strung between rock, tree and water, spanning time itself. I sense the power of ages, hidden in life, in death.

Lightly, the voice says and I understand. How tempting it is to lose myself in the ebb and flow of this magic, the great circle that has no end and no beginning. But I hold lives in my hands.

Though they might be small against this vastness of being, I want them. I draw only what I need and, oh – the body before me is so simple in its structure compared to what lies all around me. I see the tear and I mend it, no harder than stitching cloth.

I hear the arrow clatter to the ground and open my eyes. Resting on Cynric's chest, my hand glows bright gold. Each vein pulses, as if gilded. Even my burned hand seems lit from within and as I look, I realize how it might be healed too. How it and my foot might be whole again.

I let go and the magic rushes out of me, back into the land. I will not take more than I need. It seems like madness, not to want it, when it's within my grasp. Not to want to mend the damage my sister has done me. But in a way the hurt *is* mended, I think, weari-ly, strangely, at peace. It is part of our history – Sinne's and mine. And it has long been a part of me. I will not renounce myself now.

Cynric groans, raises a trembling hand to his chest. Beneath the blood, his skin is whole and ever so slightly golden. I help him sit up and a sigh spills from many throats. We are the centre of a crowd of watching Saxons, anxious for their captain. Some wear wonder, others fear. Still more stand empty-handed, weapons fallen at their feet.

The old woman who had held the harp kneels opposite, eyes blue as lapis. 'Myrdhin?' I whisper.

She smiles. 'You can call me Mori.'

Cynric raises a bloody hand to my face. 'This land saved you,' I tell him, taking it. 'I hope you will remember.'

'Will you honour your word?' The moment between us shatters at that question. Cynric and I help each other to stand and I see Constantine. It has taken me a long time to truly see him, but I see him now. How can I not, dressed in blood and battle as he is? But more than that: it is in his eyes, in the way he holds himself. It is in the strength that fairly shimmers around him. The magic of the land hums beneath his feet.

'I will,' Cynric says beside me and a whisper travels through the surviving Gewisse. He turns to look at me. 'If Lady Riva still desires it.'

'I do,' I say, though I feel a sinking in my chest. Magic does not live in Saxon lands. There would be no more miracles.

'You will be needing this then,' Mori says as if she can read my thoughts, and she hands me my healer's bag. I don't ask how she has it, but curl my fingers about its leather handle. It's good to hold it again, a comforting weight.

'Are you certain, Riva?' my brother asks, coming forward. He takes my burned hand in both of his. 'It is a long way.'

I sense something in his words, an ending of sorts, but a beginning too. 'Yes,' I whisper, because if I speak aloud, he will hear tears. 'It is where I am supposed to be.'

'Then I wish you happiness,' he says, a catch in his voice. 'And health to you and your children.'

I can't hold them in any more. I drop the bag and throw both arms around his neck, holding him tightly. Because in my heart, I know I will never see him again.

The Saxons pull back from the gates, leaving the dead in their shadow. But Cynric insists on collecting the bodies, then building a great pyre in sight of the sea. After that, there is nothing to keep us here. With blood spilled on both sides, the truce is still too new, too raw, to withstand a longer stay in Dumnonian lands.

I ride in front of him on Nihthelm, his hand curled protectively around us both, the child and I, and the horse doesn't seem to mind. 'You saved my life,' he murmurs into my hair when I can no longer see Dunbriga in the distance. 'A heavy debt.'

'There is no debt,' I say, my voice ringing. 'Without you, I would have died at the forest's edge.'

'So we're even,' he replies.

'For now.'

The further we ride from Dunbriga, the fainter grows the magic. Yet I cannot mourn its loss. I have long put my trust in other aspects of the land: in the herbs and plants that spring from its soil. How will it feel to practise my art on the people we have fought? Knowing blood stains the ground between us? I swallow a surge of apprehension at the thought of Uintancæstir, the Gewisse capital, of what I will find there. It is Cynric's home and will soon be mine too.

'Riva,' he says after a few minutes. 'Will you ever forgive me?'

I am silent. So much has happened. My father gone, my sister . . . When I close my eyes, I still see her reaching out to me, aflame. But I also hear an echo of her last song and its lilting strains sound a little like forgiveness.

I turn my head. He's washed the paint from his grey eyes and looks as he did on the day we first met, though a few new lines mark him. We stare at each other. 'I think I can,' I say.

When I face forward again, I feel his heartbeat against my back. His words are a whisper. 'I love you, Riva.'

I draw a breath, my own heart thumping. 'How do you say it in your language?'

He hesitates a second. '*Ic lufie þē.*'

'*Ic lufie þē,*' I repeat. 'Cynric.'

As his arms tighten around me, my spirits lift. Because weaving through everything that has happened between us, I hear the echo of another song, a long and lasting song we have only just begun to sing.

48

CONSTANTINE

Looking back, it seems like a dream. As real as the story of Lir, or Herla. For a few spellbound minutes, Dunbriga's people trembled with the princes and drank sweet wine beneath the dwarf king's mountain. Then the final words were spoken, the final chord was plucked, and they returned to their lives, blinking in the light.

That's what it feels like now – the night after Sinne sang and helped to end a battle. Tears prick my eyes at the memory. She sang of our childhood, before the rules of home and people had taken us, dressed us up and driven us apart. She sang of the little joys we managed to find all the same, of our squabbles, games and laughter at being caught by a rogue wave in the surf. She didn't speak of Saxons, or the man we'd known as Tristan. She didn't mention Mother, or Father's illness. And she didn't remind us of jealousy, anger, or fear. Because we knew that song already; its words went round and around our heads to the point where we forgot there was ever another song to sing.

And it freed me. My story didn't have to end in blood.

She disappeared afterwards. Only I saw Os wrap her in lambs-wool and steal her away across the battlefield our home had become. I didn't stop him. I don't think anyone could have done. And Sinne had always wanted to see the world.

So neither of my sisters are here, several days later, to watch our father burn. Mother touches torch to pyre on the grey headland behind the great hall and, after looking long at Cador's sunken face, I urge the flames through the wet logs. Should I weep? I find I cannot, the battle having washed me clean of tears. I am painfully aware, however, of the empty spaces on either side of me, where my sisters ought to stand. At that, I do cry again. Because fate pulled us apart in the cruellest of ways. But was it fate, really? Maybe it was simply the choices we made.

Hundreds of eyes witness the king's last journey. Rather magnanimously, I even permitted Gildas to attend, despite the pagan burial. He worked so hard to charm the people, and my revealing that he used magic in front of them has soured our relationship even further – if that were possible. I have no idea what I'm going to do with him.

So when he says, 'I will depart on the morrow,' I am secretly relieved. He is seemingly oblivious of his guards, waiting to lock him up again on my command. And I know I can't keep a man of his influence in a cell forever, no matter my feelings. 'We are not finished, *Constantine*,' he fair hisses at me, as Cador's pyre crumbles to embers. A stray spark skims his cheek. 'I won't rest until all of Britain knows of your heresies.'

'Please don't tire yourself on my account,' I say, as airily as I can manage. 'Besides –' and now I look him dead in the eye – 'I could do without having to explain how a magician managed to masquerade as a priest for so long.'

Gildas flinches, but his sneer stays in place. 'No one would take your word over *mine*.'

'Perhaps I would need to throw another knife at you, in that case. Would your god step in to "save" you a second time?'

Despite Mother's weak protestations, the priest is gone before sundown.

'Cynric and Gildas have left,' I say to Mori the next morning, as we stand on the steps of the great hall – in the very place I sat nearly a year ago to weave my brideog. 'But I doubt I've seen the last of either.' Although the sunshine has broken through, it's still bitterly cold and will be for months. A difficult spring lies ahead.

'I am sure you haven't,' she agrees and for a few moments we watch in silence as roofs are patched, walls are mended – my people trying to bury the signs that Dunbriga ever felt the enemy's sword. The gorse passage was the first to be repaired. Again. The acorn I'd seen around Cynric's neck had parted the earth for him. Given to him by a child of Dumnonia, and that made all the difference. I could have felt anger at Riva, but I haven't room for it now. She did as her heart bid her, and maybe it was meant to be. Perhaps it was even her way of saving us all, ultimately. Her alliance with Cynric should keep us safe, for a generation or two at least.

I glance at Mori. The hair that frames her dark face is grey, but her eyes are as sharp as ever. 'Trust you to turn up when the battle was almost over,' I say.

She looks at me in the same way she did when I was a child, lost in a witch's forest. 'I am no hero from the old tales, Constantine, to break the back of an army with a word. Besides, Cador banished me, if you recall.'

'My father is dead,' I say with a frown. 'Is that why you're here now?'

Her eyes crinkle. 'I'm here because the land listens to a new king.'

After a moment, I say, 'I don't know how to be king.'

'Then don't be.' Mori straightens her cloak. 'Or be king for a little while, until you've learned all you can. Then be something else.'

I smile drily, gesturing at her patchwork cloak. 'A wandering storyteller, perhaps.'

'There are worse things to be.'

'Or a magician?'

Her smile matches mine. 'A magician, a meddler, a pattern-chaser, someone who sees things as they really are and helps others to see them too.' Mori hoists a pack onto her shoulder. The cloak made by improbable worms in Sinae flutters a farewell. 'Remember. This is *your* story, no matter what history will claim or what songs people sing. And it's no one's place to stop you from telling it.'

I don't try to swallow my tears, but press my wet cheek to hers. 'Maybe we'll see each other again,' I say.

Mori holds me a long moment before drawing back to smile. 'I think we will,' she says.

Cynric keeps his promise and doesn't press us. We are his wife's people, after all, though I don't know if that means much to him beyond Riva's happiness. I don't know whether she is even happy shut up in Uintancæstir, surrounded by those she once called enemy. But now that Cerdic is dead, she is the Lady of Wessex. It's a great realm, greater than mine. And Cynric has responsibilities to occupy him beyond its expansion. I wager he won't forget us, though, or our kingdom in the west. Neither will his son, Ceawlin, who, I hear, is the image of Riva. Young as he is, they already call him the Bear. We are living on borrowed time, time Riva won for us. But she won't be around forever. Someday her children or their children's children will look at their grandmother's home with hungry eyes and they will come for it. I hope they follow her example and come with words, not swords.

As for me . . . well. The tale of my sisters lives on, but my part in it is lost. They tell different tales about me now: wild peerless flags of tales, with trappings fit for a king. I am a man. I am a woman. I am neither and wear a sorcerer's skin. I am the uncle of a Saxon legend. I murder children. I married Brittany's daughter. I am a creature of vice, as Gildas was fond of saying. And I am also a saint, who abandoned my people for a life of faith and was martyred for it.

Gwen says it doesn't matter who they think I am. But I know better than most that songs have power. They have immortality, whereas I of a certainty do not. All I can do is follow Myrdhin's example and sing the song that I want the years to remember.

epilogue

This is the story I sing.

In a hot country, beneath stars that have not yet been named, an old man lifts an awning on a market stall to peer beneath. There . . . is that the gleam of swan's feathers, virgin snow or the new-risen moon? It is none of these. Rather he finds a slender spine, bone pale, bound with taut strings of woven gold. A harp, more beautiful than any other. More terrible, too.

Those strings quiver, beginning to hum, but they still at the touch of his hand. 'No need, lass,' the old man says. 'No need for that.'

Wrapping the harp in a cloak whose ribbons snap in the desert wind, he whispers as he walks across the bazaar, dust whirling round his feet. 'Have you seen the world?' he asks and nods a moment later, as if he received an answer. 'Would you like to go home?'

He must have received another, for he turns his face northwards, sniffs the breeze. 'Yes, a long journey. I will tell you stories to pass the time.'

And that's how they come, finally, to shores of green, a land where the old magic slumbers too deeply to be roused – at least by those who call it home now. The harp trembles when the air of that land touches its frame. 'You know these hills,' the old man says, pointing to the gentle forested slopes. 'And this coast.' He walks to its edge. The cliffs have retreated in the long centuries, their red skirts cracked and rugged. But the sea sings with the same voice as ever. And the gulls, just waking to greet the dawn, hunger for the same scraps.

'I am sorry, Sinne,' Myrdhin says, as they navigate a steep path down the cliffs. Time has worn away the buildings that once stood here, unmoored the boats that once docked below. The people live in the more fertile valley now, no longer fearful of war. 'I hope you can forgive me.'

'Forgive us both,' says a new voice and a shadow comes to stand at Myrdhin's shoulder.

The old man smiles. 'I didn't mean to wake you.'

'I was hoping you would.' A pause. 'May I?'

Myrdhin nods and the shadowed figure takes the harp in his not-quite-solid hands. 'You brought her home,' he whispers.

'She wanted to come.'

Both are silent, waiting for the dawn. 'Myrdhin,' the shadow says. Golden threads trail from the bottom of his robe to merge with the sand of the seashore. 'Did we do wrong?'

'Ask her yourself, Constantine.'

So the robed figure holds the harp close, listens. After a while, he smiles and sheds a single tear that disappears as soon as it falls.

I cannot tell you what she said. Only that, as the sun breaks over the water, the ancient king kneels spectral at its edge, his oldest friend beside him. When they give the harp to the sighing sea, watching as it gently comes apart, they think they see a girl. Her soaring song lifts skyward, at last.

acknowledgements

This book has travelled a long way to reach the world and I am profoundly grateful to those who helped it arrive, not just intact, but better for the journey. Earliest thanks go to my friend and fellow author, Dr Victoria James, for championing the book from day one, recommending research materials and taking me along to an actual Beltane Fire Festival. I loved every minute.

My agent, Veronique Baxter, worked hard to find *Sistersong* a home, and my editor, Bella Pagan, helped hone the book into the best version of itself. Thank you both so much for your guidance and support.

To the teams at Pan Macmillan in editorial, art, rights, sales and marketing: thank you for giving *Sistersong* such a warm home. I deeply appreciate everything you've done to bring the book to readers. Thank you too to Jamie-Lee Nardone for her work in publicizing it.

To Cheryl Morgan for sharing her exceptional knowledge of transgender history, and to Alex Boon for reading an early draft and giving me vital encouragement. Thank you both so much for your insights.

2020 was a difficult year for everyone. A big shout-out to my friends and colleagues at Waterstones Exeter who are just endlessly fun and upbeat to work with – even during a pandemic. Special thanks to Paul Rowley, who played me the album featuring 'The Twa Sisters' ballad on it in the first place. Hearing that track inspired me to write *Sistersong*.

An ongoing thank you to my *Breaking the Glass Slipper* co-hosts, Megan Leigh and Charlotte Bond, who have become wonderful friends too. Our work on the podcast has broadened my horizons and I'm so grateful to be part of the team.

There are many friends I haven't been able to see in recent months, but knowing you're out there has meant so much to me. To the university crew: Reda Haq, Josi Palm and James Southwood, and my salty ladies who know who they are. Thanks to all of you for being excellent people.

To Becky Pepperdine, crafting god, for collaborating with me on the bone harp project. Thank you for all the incredible ideas, enthusiasm and hard work. It's been a lot of creepy fun.

My sister, Laura Madeleine, to whom this book is dedicated: thank you for rescuing me from my – usually plot-related – tangles. And, obviously, for being an epic sister. I promise never to make you into a harp. I'm lucky to have such a great family around me, to support me in innumerable ways. As always, deep love and gratitude, especially to my parents, Dee and Terry.

Last but not in any way least to *you*, reader, who invited Keyne, Riva and Sinne into your life and allowed me to tell their stories. I hope you will allow me to tell you many more.